ALSO AVAILABLE FROM BLOOM BOOKS

CANE BROTHERS

A Not So Meet Cute
So Not Meant to Be
A Long Time Coming

BRIDESMAID FOR HIRE

Bridesmaid for Hire
Bridesmaid Undercover

HOW MY NEIGHBOR STOLE CHRISTMAS

MEGHAN QUINN

Bloom books

Published by Bloom Books, an imprint of Sourcebooks
P.O. Box 4410, Naperville, Illinois 60567-4410
(630) 961-3900
sourcebooks.com

Cataloging-in-Publication data is on file with the Library of Congress.

Printed and bound in the United States of America.
LSC 10 9 8 7 6 5 4 3 2

PROLOGUE

Every Kringle in Kringletown
celebrated Christmas a lot.
But Cole Black on Whistler Lane,
unfortunately, did not.

Cole became a recluse during the
Kringle Christmas season.
No one knew why; no one could quite give a reason.

Martha said it was because he was
alone and very single.
Mae said it was because he was never
named the Town Kringle.

But to me, the true reason is a story far too sad.
For at the age of eighteen, he
lost both Mom and Dad.

Whatever the reason, his loss or
his status of being single,
he spent Christmas in the dark, hating
the cheery people of Kringle.

From his window, he would stare
with a crinkle of a frown,
at the lights and the wreaths spread
all throughout town.

They would sing, they would smile,
they would offer him a wave.
All the while he would scowl from
atop his dim, dreary cave.

For him no decorations, no cookies,
no little boy drumming.
For December 1st was tomorrow, and
he knew what was coming.

The town would awake, the snow
lightly packed in rows.
The baubles would shine; there'd
be tying of the bows.

Because just around the corner, the
bells would soon jingle,
announcing the start of who's
named the Town Kringle.

Cole Black had no interest, not a lick nor a care.
Why would he take part in such an asinine affair?

"Who cares who celebrates Christmas
more?" he would grumpily say,
his motto until a shift of the wind on one blustery day.

From his window he peered at the
commotion over the fence.
The sight of a familiar redhead made
his soulless heart grow tense.

"What is she doing here? There has to be a reason.
She can't possibly be here for the
entire Christmas season."

But her bags stacked high, in the
middle of the driveway,
were a red flag waving, announcing a very long vacay.

But why? It's been years, exactly ten, to be fair,
since she strutted around with her deep red hair.

No, he must find out; he must stop her visit right now.
She can't stay here, not for Christmas;
he must stop it…but how?

CHAPTER ONE
STOREE

"YOU KNOW, YOU NEVER TRULY get over the first pucker of your nips when that mountain air hits you," I say as I stuff my mittened hands into my jacket pockets while I survey the backdrop of freshly powdered mountains.

Taran, my sister, looks at me from over her shoulder and dramatically rolls her eyes. "It's thirty-seven degrees—pretty nice for being at an elevation of over ten thousand feet at the beginning of December."

"Pretty nice?" Good God, this is not pretty nice; this is frigid. "Guess I need to be grateful for global warming then, or else I think my breasts would be two pucks of ice on the ground right now."

Taran stands tall with two duffel bags in hand. "Global warming is never something to joke about." With that, she walks up the snow-cleared sidewalk to Aunt Cindy's pink Victorian house.

In case you didn't catch it from her tone, Taran is the uptight one of the two of us. Being the older sister has led her to adopt a starchy, prickly, slightly severe personality. She's always dealing with a crisis, there's always something to complain about, and nothing ever goes our way in the Taylor family.

Hence the five bags of luggage and trip to Kringletown, Colorado, for the unforeseeable future at the beginning of December.

No, this is not our hometown.

No, this is not the place I'd choose to visit in the wintertime thanks to my body's affinity for the California climate.

And no, I would not jump at the chance to spend Christmas with my cranky, well-mannered, loves-a-good-lecture sister.

I love her, but she sure knows how to take the J-O-Y out of jolly.

Unfortunately for yours truly, Aunt Cindy had a recent fall—the tell-tale occurrence of many an octogenarian.

Once a spry sprite, known throughout her small town as the jolliest of them all, Aunt Cindy was on her way to remove a fresh batch of gingerbread cookies out of her oven when she, as she put it, felt a squeeze in her hip, then a seize in her left butt cheek, which in turn caused her to spin, wobble, and then fall to the ground. And because she's a frail old coot, she had nothing to cushion the blow to the hip, and well… she broke it.

From there, you can imagine what happened. A broken hip to an elderly human is considered a death sentence—according to Aunt Cindy.

So of course, all hell broke loose.

Siren emojis went off in the family group text.

An emergency family meeting was called.

And before I knew it, I was staring at my computer screen, a shot of my father's nostrils clouded in hair as the main image while he attempted to figure out "this Zoom thing."

Mom sobbed in a sarong decorated with birds of paradise from her timeshare balcony in Cancún.

Dad consoled her while he wore a straw hat with a sunblock-painted nose.

Taran rapidly jotted down her issues on a notepad, like the good nurse she is.

And I sat back in my oversized, single-lady recliner, braless and snacking on a canister of chocolate-covered raisins I purchased from Costco that day, watching it all unfold.

"Something has to be done. Someone has to take care of her," Mom squealed about her only living relative.

Did I mention, to me and my sister, she's *Great-Aunt* Cindy? But what a freaking mouthful, so we just say Aunt Cindy.

But she means the world to our mom.

She's the matriarch of a very small family on my mom's side.

And despite the adoration my mom has for this woman who has taken seriously the role of dedicated parent in her life, the Horbachs and the Lindons were just coming into town, and my mother couldn't possibly leave her tropical paradise, because that would mean missing the pinochle tournament that was about to begin—she and Dad have been practicing and they were going to win it this year.

Which meant...I was brought into the picture.

You know, because even though I have a remote job editing Lovemark Channel movies, I have all the time in the world to tend to an elderly woman who broke her hip.

Now, just between you and me, I do have the time because I'm not currently editing anything—currently on a break with editing, putting me more in watch mode right now, leaning into the Lovemark holiday movie schedule—but *they* didn't need to know that.

But it was decided that I, Storee Taylor, was nominated to take care of Aunt Cindy.

And frankly, I have no clue how to take care of an old woman with a bum hip—so probably not a bright move on the family's part.

"Are you just going to stand there or are you going to help with the bags?" Taran asks, snapping me out of my thoughts.

"Just getting used to the thin air," I say and press my hand to my chest. "Oof, hard to breathe. You know, I think I might be experiencing altitude sickness, not sure this is the place for me to be. Perhaps we airlift Aunt Cindy to California."

Taran whips the pillow I couldn't live without into my chest and says, "You're fine," before picking up the bag of snacks I made her stop to get before driving into the mountains and heading back into the house.

She never truly mastered the art of good bedside manner.

Grumbling under my breath—breath that I swear I can see as I huff along the sidewalk—I make my way up the porch of the familiar Victorian house that we used to visit every Christmas before Mom and Dad purchased their Cancún timeshare—Bosom Bungalow. My mom's "bosom" buddy owns part of the timeshare as well, and they think it's a funny name. Ahhh, parents, aren't they fun?

As I get close to the door, I can practically smell the warm gingerbread and freshly harvested pine—a combination of scents that I associate with one person and one person alone—Aunt Cindy.

Hate to admit it, but even though I'd rather be wrapped up in the comfort of my childhood twin-sized Barbie comforter while talking to my ficus, Alexander, about Lovemark's lineup for the season, being here—the scents, the scenery, the snow—it's making me a little—and I mean a little, just the tiniest, minute, so-small-you-can-barely-even-recognize-it bit—warm and fuzzy inside.

And I mean that, because this town and I...we have history.

Sordid history.

Embarrassing history.

The kind of history that has kept me away for ten years.

But my mortifying history doesn't negate the fact that Aunt Cindy's house has always provided a sense of comfort during the holiday season.

I'm just about to cross the threshold of the house when Taran buzzes out, a mission to accomplish. This girl is a workhorse, and when her mind is set on something, she doesn't stop until it's accomplished.

"If you're going to stand still, mouth agape, please do it off to the side." Her shoulder bumps into mine as she moves past me and heads to the car.

Sheesh!

"My mouth wasn't agape," I mutter before heading into the foyer of the old, creaky house that I know has been home to Aunt Cindy for longer than I've been alive.

This place *is* Christmas. It's the pine garland-wrapped staircase and the battery-operated lights in the window. The delicately executed velvet bows strategically placed in every greenery-swathed doorframe. The single piece of mistletoe hanging in the living room leading you to the expertly decorated tree full of matching baubles and bulbs, ribbons, and the golden angel at the top. It's the hand-crafted green-and-red quilts hanging like tapestries on the walls, the crystal stemware used as candy dishes full of pillow mints that melt on your tongue the moment they enter your mouth. And it's the exquisitely wrapped presents under the tree decorated in matching paper, bows, and gift tags. Together, it's a snapshot of my childhood, where Christmas made me believe in miracles, made me believe in magic, and gave me all the warm feelings about the holiday season.

But as I scan the house from the nonexistent entry rug where I'm supposed to dust off my shoes, my eyes fixate on the bare banister, the naked doorframes, the missing stemware—not a pillow mint to be found.

What the hell?

"Seriously, Storee, can you please make yourself helpful?" Taran says as she plops another bag of food on the floor.

"Where're...where're the decorations?" I ask.

"What?" Taran asks as she wipes the back of her hand over her brow.

She can't possibly be sweating. I know she lives in Denver, but these are arctic temperatures we're dealing with here.

I gesture to the empty space. "There aren't any Christmas decorations."

Taran looks over her shoulder and then back at me. "Correct."

"Um...why not?"

"Oh, I don't know," Taran says sarcastically. "Maybe because Aunt Cindy broke her hip, and the last thing she can manage right now is decorating her house so you can feel the Christmas magic the moment you walk in." *Ah, excuse me, Miss Rude.*

She blows past me again, back to the clown car to unload God knows what at this point.

"A simple answer of 'she hasn't had time' would have sufficed," I call after her.

Yikes, she's ripe.

I tuck my pillow under my arm, take off my shoes, and then head into the living room, the bare and very odd-looking living room.

I've never seen it like this before. Normally where the tree would go, there's a pink Victorian chair in impeccable shape for what I assume is its age. The *Happy Days* nativity scene, which Aunt Cindy pays homage to every year, is *not* perched on the fireplace. No stockings hung, no logs by the fire, no cranberry garland draping along with her green damask curtains.

It's just…plain.

And frankly, it's scaring me.

I know I joked about a broken hip being a death sentence, but this decidedly barren room is making me feel like I'm visiting a mortuary rather than a place full of the Christmas spirit.

Also, color me confused because I didn't think she ever took her decorations down. Naïve, perhaps, but this *is* Kringletown—well, just Kringle if you're local—the most highly elevated Christmas town in the country. Year-round, instrumental Christmas music plays from speakers strategically placed along the main streets. Light post decorations are only switched out for a different style every month but never stray from the classic red, green, and gold hues of the jolly holiday. Twinkle lights are never taken down, hot chocolate never stops being pumped into visitors, and you can't walk down the street without being told at least twice that Santa is always watching.

So pardon my confusion in thinking that Christmas decorations remain a fixed aesthetic in the homes as well.

Guess I was wrong.

The front door shuts, and Taran stands in the entryway, hands on her hips.

I turn toward her. "Why is it so quiet in here? Where's Aunt Cindy?"

"With Martha and Mae at their house."

"The Bawhovier twins?" I ask, referring to the center of gossip in Kringletown. If you want to know anything—and I mean anything—about the town, Martha and Mae Bawhovier are the people to ask.

They keep notes; I've seen them. Stacks and stacks of town gossip disguised as leather-bound books on their bookshelves. One day, when they both die, I have no doubt Kringletown will archive said gossip books in the town library, revealing all of the innermost secrets of those who have lived through a lifetime of holiday festivities.

"Yes, they've been watching over Aunt Cindy for us. Were you not paying attention to the emergency family meeting?" Taran asked.

"Kind of blacked out after I was forced to be a caretaker for my foreseeable future."

"You're being dramatic."

"Says the one who gets to go back to the comfort of their home while I have to sponge bathe an elderly woman who I've only seen wear a turtleneck and slacks my entire life," I reply.

"It should be an honor for you."

My eyebrows shoot up as I lean forward and whisper, "An honor to see Aunt Cindy naked? What's wrong with you?"

Taran's jaw clenches. "An honor to take care of a relative who has provided you with many wonderful memories throughout your young years. This is the circle of life, Storee. They take care of us while we navigate life at a young age, and when they become old and feeble, it's our turn to repay them."

God, she's so... annoyingly right.

"Doesn't mean I need to be honored to see her naked," I say with a lift of my chin.

Taran shakes her head and then pushes a large black suitcase forward. It's not mine.

"What's that?" I point to the suitcase.

"That's mine."

Hope springs forward.

"Wait, are you staying?"

"I don't think I have a choice in the matter," she says. "I was going to see how this plays out, but from the few short minutes we've been here, I can confidently state that I can't trust you to take care of Aunt Cindy on your own."

I clasp my hands together in excitement. "Great, then should I just take off?" I thumb behind me toward the door. "I mean, weird that you brought me all the way here just to tell me that you're going to take care of everything, but you have demonstrated a flair for the dramatic every now and then."

"You're not leaving—we're doing this together." She starts carting her large black suitcase up the stairs.

"Um, care to repeat that?" I say while moving toward the stairs to watch my sister manhandle her suitcase, which is three-quarters her size, up the wooden steps.

When she reaches the top, she stares down at me. "Depending on what the hospital says about my request for time off, there might be days that I have to drive back into Denver for a day or two of work. I need you to stay here with Aunt Cindy, but I refuse to let you do this alone, given your inexperience in taking care of anything."

"Pardon me," I say with a stomp of my foot. "But do you not recall how I've raised Alexander? He's flourishing. And because Harriot, my neighbor, is taking care of him while I'm here, he will continue to flourish."

"Comparing our Aunt Cindy to a ficus is not even close to the same thing, Storee."

I cross my arms over my chest in defiance. "Says the person who bought Alexander a birthday present this year."

"You asked me to grab some fertilizer when I came out to visit you. I highly disagree with calling that a birthday gift."

"It was his birthday, and you brought it to him. I see it differently."

With another roll of her eyes, she pushes her suitcase toward the red room.

"Uh, what are you doing?" I ask, heading up the stairs as quickly as my frozen legs will take me.

"Being productive…unlike you," she says.

With my pillow still tucked under my arm, I reach the top of the stairs. "You know the red room is mine."

Taran stands in front of the doorway, her five-foot-seven frame just an inch taller than me, but from the straight set in her spine and staunch attitude, she seems almost like she's seven feet tall, staring down at me, the oblivious peon.

"The red room is bigger."

"Well aware, as that's why I always stayed in it." I thumb behind me again and add, "That nightmare of a room is yours."

"Nope, not this time," she says.

I take a hesitant step forward. "Taran, you know I can't sleep in there."

"You're older now—you'll be fine."

"I won't be," I say in a panic. "They…they come alive."

"Oh my God, Storee, seriously, you need to grow up." She pushes through the door of the red room with her bag while I chase after her, heat enveloping my ears and cheeks.

"I am grown up, and I'm even more hyper aware of what that room has to offer. The nightmares…the exorcism it needs to cleanse the air."

Taran opens her suitcase and starts unpacking, loading up the provided dresser with her clothes. The red room is a familiar comfort with its red walls, red carpet, red curtains, and red bedding. Every Christmas, Taran and I would share this room, the trundle under the bed an easy pull out for her to sleep on. Originally, the nightmare room was Taran's, and she was fine with it. Mom and Dad would sleep in the room next to the red room, but once Aunt Cindy turned that into her own personal gym,

Taran started sleeping on the trundle in the red room with me while Mom and Dad took...the other room.

"Fine, I'll just sleep on the trundle," I say, finding my way around it.

"No, you won't," Taran says. "I'm going to be away from Guy for a while, and I promised him I would...keep in touch."

My nose crinkles in disgust.

Guy is Taran's boyfriend.

I don't know much about him, but I can tell you this—I don't like the way she said "keep in touch" like there was a sexual innuendo attached to it.

"Ew," I say. "Please tell me you're not going to be doing dirty things in Aunt Cindy's house."

"What I do in my room is my business."

"Do it in the other room, then. I'm sure you'd appreciate the audience."

Her eyes snap up to mine. "The Wi-Fi is better in this room, you know that, and given that you're single and can't be relied on to take care of our aunt by yourself, therefore uprooting me from my life, I'll take the comfort I need to make it through the next few weeks."

"What about my comfort?" I say, pointing to my chest. "Do I not matter?"

She gestures to where I clutch my pillow. "You have your special pillow, so you have all the comfort you need." With that, she pushes me out of the room and shuts the door on me.

"You're rude!" I shout, and then turn on my heel like a chastised child. I stare at the door to the other bedroom, my skin already itching from the thought of it.

Perhaps...just perhaps, she redecorated and has turned what was once a hell-on-earth room into a peaceful sanctuary. With scent diffusers on a white oak dresser, sage bedding draped over a cloud-like mattress, and a Hatch alarm clock on the nightstand peacefully setting the tone for every night...and gracefully waking me up in the morning.

One can only hope.

I close the space between me and the room and then, on a hope and a prayer, open the door, eyes closed.

Please be redecorated.

Please be redecorated.

I peek one eye open only for my hopes and prayers to come to a crashing halt as I go eye to eye with Josefina.

And Felicity.

And Molly.

And Addy.

And Kirsten.

And that perfect bitch, Samantha.

There are multiples of them, all set up in different dioramas. The six "queens" of the American Girl dolls, as Aunt Cindy would say, are all in their original outfits and posed in cases overlooking the floral canopy bed, but the duplicates are spread around strategically, offering a taste of historic opulence from the good ol' days…and not-so-good ol' days.

Molly in her velvet Christmas dress, rocking in the corner.

Felicity in her "saves the day" white gown, with a basket of fresh-cut flowers.

Addy acting as the puppet master of her puppy puppet show.

Josefina with her turtle and her piano, playing a ditty for the other girls.

And Samantha…oh, Samantha with the perfect hair, crimson bow, and batting eyelashes. The absolute worst, propped up next to her white fluffy bed and red trunk, looking through her clothes like the princess of the Progressive Era that she is. Sure, she's an "orphan," but she lives with her rich grandmother in upstate New York—compare that to freaking Addy, who had to pick her own birthday date because she didn't know when it was. Samantha had it good.

But I digress. This room was made for torture.

It was decorated with horror in mind.

It's a room shrouded in American Girl dolls, accessories, scenes…and they're all staring at me.

All begging to be touched.

To be rotated.

To have their arms and legs lubricated with innocent child play. But instead of fulfilling their fates as toys, they've been set up for a life of boredom as decorations. And I can see the anger in their eyes. They were destined for so much more when they were manufactured, only to be brought to a home where they were to be looked at, not touched.

Treated just the same as a wall sconce, stared at for its beauty but never truly, properly used, these dolls have pent-up energy, deep-rooted depression, and I know for a fact they come alive at night.

And don't come at me and say I'm being dramatic, because I'm not. I will stand here right now and swear on my left nostril that when I was eleven, one of the dolls winked at me.

Actually winked.

One guess as to which doll it was.

It startled me so badly that I screamed bloody murder, ran down the stairs, and tripped over the *Santa Claus is Comin' to Town* rug that's usually in front of the door, causing me to slide right into the wall and break my wrist.

I still have the pain during cold, wet nights to prove it.

So pardon me for not wanting to sleep in a room that has caused me to nearly lose a wrist.

"Your clothes aren't going to unpack themselves," Taran calls from her open door across the hall. "And we need to get this place settled—Martha and Mae are bringing Aunt Cindy back to the house in about an hour."

I turn toward Taran. "You know, we should really play rock, paper, scissors to see who gets the red room. It would only be fair." I hold my hand out in position, ready to play. "Best of three?" I ask with hope.

"It's adorable how delusional you are," Taran says and then powers down the stairs, picks up the food bags, and heads to the kitchen.

Well, that's one way to squash the tidings of joy.

CHAPTER TWO
COLE

Snow from the night before glistens
across the bitter ground,
while news of the sisters' arrival
spreads all throughout town.

The gossip is crisp, the excitement oh so thick,
while Cole stomps around as a very unhappy dick.

"DID YOU KNOW THEY WERE coming?" I say to my best friend Max.

Max pauses from where he's sharpening his axe and quirks a brow in my direction.

"Did I know who was coming?" he asks.

I sit on one of the old farm chairs that's one large man away from its wood crushing into sawdust—I like to take risks—and lean my forearms on my thighs. "The Taylor sisters."

"Who are the Taylor sisters?" he asks before wiping down his axe and inspecting it.

A chilly wind blows through the open gap of the barn door, reminding me once again that fall has ended and winter is here. The cold has never bothered me. I'm accustomed to the blistering Colorado mountain winters, hence why I'm only wearing a pair of jeans and a long-sleeved flannel shirt. That's what happens when you spend your entire life in a mountain town. You adapt to the weather conditions, expecting the unpredictable, but confident the sun will shine at least once during the day.

"You know who the Taylor sisters are," I say. "Cindy Louis's great-grandnieces Taran and Storee."

"Ohhh," Max says with a nod and a wink. "Storee Taylor."

"Can you not?" I say, shaking my head, seeing exactly where he wants to take this.

"She's back in town, huh? Are you going to try to ask her out again?"

"I didn't ask her out in the first place," I say, hating that I brought up the topic.

"That's right, you didn't—you didn't get the chance to before she blew you off."

"She didn't blow me off," I say, irritated. "She changed the subject and then had to leave, simple as that." There's so much more to the story, but it's not something I want to relive.

"Weren't you seventeen and she was fifteen?"

I drag my hand over my face. "Uh, no, we were both eighteen." I shake my head because he's not getting it. "Never mind," I say as bells jingle nearby, sounding off that another ride through the evergreens is about to start.

Evergreen Farm is Kringletown's pride and joy. Well…one of them. Known as the highest incorporated town in the country, sitting at 10,522 feet, Kringle is a year-round Christmas town.

Yup, we celebrate Christmas…year…round.

The holly jolly music never ceases.

The twinkle lights never turn off.

And Santa—aka Bob Krampus—never stops ho-ho-hoing from his house at the top of Ornament Park—also known as the town park, which is in the shape of a bulb ornament.

The Bavarian-style buildings that line Ornament Avenue, Krampus

Court, and Route 25 are continuously adorned with wreaths, lights, and freshly fluffed garland. The Christmas stalls behind the Myrrh-cantile are always open, offering the latest in homemade crafts for those looking for that unique gift for the holiday season.

And Evergreen Farm, owned by the Maxheimers—Max's family—is always running. During the summer, there's tree planting, paintball, live bands, and an animal farm that teaches respect for all animals. During the holiday season, there's tree cutting, ice skating, sleigh rides—powered by electric snowmobiles—s'mores around the many campfires, gingerbread baking classes, and every vendor this side of the Rocky Mountains looking to grow their business.

As for me, I hide out in here, the reindeer barn, where I take care of the Maxheimers' precious and very famous reindeer. I don't mind the smell. I don't mind the snorts or the shaking of antlers or even the wet snouts looking for snacks in my pockets. I like the solitude, I like the hard labor of shoveling reindeer shit into a wheelbarrow, and if I'm going to be truly honest, I like the sound of their clomping hooves.

No one bothers me—besides Max—and no one dares try to take my job, because between the three Maxheimer siblings, none of them want to do what I do. And since I'm an honorary Maxheimer, I take on the tasks with pride.

Max lifts his axe over his shoulder and rests his hand on his hip as he stares down at me. Standing at six foot four, one inch taller than me, Max—or Atlas, his real name—has been my best friend since we were babies. Otto and Ida, Max's parents, were best friends with my parents. When my parents passed away ten years ago, they took me under their wing. Which means Max treats me like a brother. In other words, he pulls no punches and takes no shit.

"You really think I'm going to drop the fact that the girl you used to dream about all the time is back in town after how many years and act like it doesn't mean anything to you?" he asks.

"First of all, I didn't dream about her. Jesus, I'm not a pathetic, love-sick asshole. I just thought she was hot." I shrug nonchalantly. "That's it. Secondly, we don't need that kind of disturbance at the start of December."

"Why not?" he asks.

"Because you know how this town is. They're already starting to talk about it. I overheard Sherry Conrad talking to Thachary down by the Polar Freeze about the Taylor sisters coming into town and what kind of shenanigans they might get up to."

"Shenanigans?" Max raises a brow. "What kind of shenanigans did they ever get up to?"

I study him for a prolonged moment, blinking a few times to see if he was kidding. "Max, we grew up in the same town. You were here for the year of Bob Krampus's Santa reveal, the hot cocoa shortage of 2012, and the year the signature tree in Baubles and Wrappings tipped over. *They* caused all those misfortunes."

He scratches the side of his cheek. "Huh. I guess I never thought about it, but hey, they're older now. They're probably here to take care of Cindy. Martha and Mae can only play nurse for so long before they start erupting from the inside out. You know better than me that the twins are a nuclear bomb waiting to explode."

Martha and Mae Bawhovier are twin sisters. They've lived together ever since I've known them, and they are very hot-headed, a source of strife in the town with their constant jabbering. They also stick their noses in everyone's business. Luckily for me, or rather unluckily, they live on my cul-de-sac.

"I think you're internally freaking out because you like Storee," Max adds.

"I don't like her, and I'm not internally freaking out," I say. "Trust me, she's the last person I want to fucking see…especially now."

"Why especially now?"

I didn't mean to say that last part out loud.

Normally I tell Max everything. Like I said, he's basically a brother, but there's one conversation I never shared with him because, well, it hurt just a bit too much.

"Because we're so busy," I say.

"Says the guy sitting on a chair from the 1800s, gossiping about out-of-towners settling into the house next to his."

"Am I not allowed to have a conversation with my best friend while he sharpens his axe? According to your dad, I'm required to take breaks."

Max shakes his head. "Whatever makes you feel better, man." He heads toward the barn door and then turns to me. "So, what are you going to do about the Taylor sisters being in town? Knock on Cindy's door and see if they need help? Offer to shovel snow? Perhaps show them a few ways to warm themselves up?"

"I'm not going to do anything," I say with a stern expression. "I have no intention of even speaking to them."

"So then why bring it up?" Max asks, seeing right through me.

I have no idea why I brought it up, except that ever since I saw them unloading their car, I haven't been able to free my mind from the image of Storee's deep red hair blowing in the breeze.

"To warn you," I say.

"Warn me of what?" he asks. "I'm not scared of the Taylor sisters. I've never even met them, since they always stuck close to their aunt. I only know them through what you've told me."

"Not warning you about them," I reply. "I'm warning you about me, because now that they're in town I'm going to be unpleasant to be around until they leave."

"How is that any different from how you are regularly?"

My expression flattens, unamused.

He chuckles. "You know, your self-reflection and emotional intelligence have truly grown over the years."

That's better.

"Thank you. And don't worry, I know you're shivering over there from the thought of having to deal with me in my rawest and rarest form of grumpiness—"

"Dude, you say that as if it's not an everyday occurrence."

I'm not a grump all the time...there are moments when one of the reindeer makes me smile. They're few and far between, but they're there.

"Either way, I have no intention of going near either of the Taylor sisters. It's going to be a Storee-free Christmas. Mark my words."

"Hold the door," a female voice says as I step into Kringle Krampus, the local deli and meat shop owned by the one and only Bob Krampus.

I prop the door open, the wind whooshing around outside, upturning some of the powdery snow that hasn't packed itself in for the long haul of the season just yet.

"Oh my God, it's cold," says the woman as she steps in behind me, her long black parka jacket falling past her knees, the hood encased in faux fur nearly covering her entire head.

"Yeah, that's the elevation for you," I say as she lowers her hood—

Motherfucker.

Lo and behold, a cloud of red hair floats around her face and shoulders. When she looks up, I'm nearly shocked by her stunningly beautiful gray eyes, just as I was all those years ago.

Storee Taylor.

I knew it was wishful thinking that I wasn't going to have an interaction with her given the size of this town, but on the first fucking day? What kind of universe would create such chaos?

If it were me controlling this scenario, I would have given it at least a week of built-up tension and anticipation. Seems like the person in charge doesn't know what the hell they're doing.

When her eyes meet mine, she smiles softly, and then, for a brief moment, she tilts her head to the side, recognition crossing her features.

Now, it's been about ten years, and I've matured...to put it modestly. No longer am I the idiot with the long, flipped-out hair that would cover my eyes if I didn't flick it to the side just right. I've grown into my own skin, I've filled out in the proper places, and I now have a thick coat of facial hair that can't be defined as a hefty beard. Nor can it be described as just scruff, so it's a healthy in-between that keeps my face warm without becoming itchy.

And yet she recognizes me. Hate to admit it, but I'm kind of impress—

"Conner, right?" she says. "It's so good to see you."

Never mind, scratch that last thought.

"Cole," I say.

"Coal?" she asks with a crinkle in her nose.

"Yes, Cole."

"Coal what?" she says, looking around, confusion deep on her brow.

"Uh, Cole Black."

She glances to the side, to the person behind me, and then back to me. "Umm...yes, coal is black." She nervously laughs. "Are you okay, Connor?"

"Cole," I repeat, my hands turning into fists at my sides.

I can see the polite smile cross her face, her expression morphing into a veil of fakeness, ready to put on a show to not hurt my feelings. "That's... that's nice." She points to the menu above the counter. "You know, I'm just going to figure out what to get everyone, if you'll excuse me."

I should leave it at that, just let her think that I've hit my head over the years and now mutter things like "coal black," but the prideful ass inside of me can't let it go.

"My name," I say, "is Cole Black."

She brings her attention back to me and tilts her head again, this time to the right as she studies me, tapping her chin with her finger. "Are you sure?"

"Am I sure if my name is Cole Black?"

"Yes, I mean...I could have sworn it was Connor." She wags her finger at me. "Is this a Kringle thing? Mess with the newbies?"

"No. Why would I do that?"

"I don't know, Connor, why does this town play 'Grandma Got Run Over by a Reindeer' year-round?"

Classic Storee. Sweet persona. Charismatic. Beautiful smile that masks the person she is on the inside.

She questions.

She challenges.

She drives me fucking mad.

"Because they like the song," I answer. "There's nothing wrong with that."

"It is when poor grandma is getting massacred every day of the year. Maybe we could give her a break."

I cross my arms over my chest, turning fully toward her now while we wait in line to be called up. *It feels like we're eighteen all over again.* "Maybe Grandma is into it, ever think about that?"

"I'm no newbie when it comes to kink, but getting run over by a reindeer is by no means a kink anyone wants to entertain. Because that's called death."

"Maybe she wandered out into the snow because she wanted to be run over. Grandpa didn't even mourn for a second. He went back to watching football and playing cards with Cousin Belle, so it seems a bit suspicious if you ask me."

"Are you saying an elderly lady *wanted* to be hoofed in the forehead?" she asks, crossing her arms as well.

"The evidence is there."

"Okay, so if this octogenarian wandered into the snowstorm looking for her medication because she wanted to get away from her useless counterpart in exchange for death, then why does the song continue to play over and over in this town, celebrating her demise?"

She lifts her chin, almost as if she believes she's pinned me. A *gotcha* look spreads across her face, the smallest of smirks pulling at the corner of her lips.

I work my jaw from side to side, attempting to come up with a valid reason why we play it, but nothing comes to mind, which only makes her grin grow.

This is exactly what I'm talking about.

She gets under my skin, and she knows exactly how to do it.

It's been like that ever since I met her during her first visit to Kringle. We were both eight at the time. Cindy thought it would be nice for us to build a snowman together since we were the same age. Storee wanted to do it her way because she thought she knew best—the girl from *California*—and I wanted to do it the correct way based on my experience *living* in snow, and we bickered.

We fought.

And it's never stopped.

Sure…there were moments when we didn't bicker and fight. Moments when we'd talk on my front porch about everything and nothing. Quiet, subdued, real moments when I got to know her on a deeper level, but whenever we got back together, the fighting always started again.

Without fail.

"That's what I thought, Connor." She turns back to the menu.

"It's Cole," I say through clenched teeth.

"Oh right, Cole." She offers me a grin. Then with her wandering eyes, she gives me a sparse once-over, taking in my muddy work boots, worn jeans, and black-and-navy flannel shirt before meeting my eyes again. "Cole…the neighbor, right?"

"You know exactly who I am—don't play with me, Storee."

"Grumpy as usual, I see," she says with a smirk. And that smirk says it all. She's fucking with me. She knew damn well who I was the whole time. "Although you are taller now."

Trying not to show my frustration, I say, "That's what happens when you grow."

"You have...broader shoulders." She motions to my chest. "More muscles." Okay, so she's just going to say whatever's on her mind?

"Yup, when you work on a farm, you tend to gain muscles."

She leans in an inch, studying my face. "And facial hair."

"A given, since I'm in my late twenties and live in a colder climate," I reply.

She slowly nods. "Well, congratulations on growing up."

"Thanks. Congratulations on maintaining your habit of being massively annoying."

Her mouth parts in shock. "Well, that was rude. I complimented you on your muscles that were not there five years ago—"

"Ten," I correct her.

"Whatever, ten. And then you say I'm annoying. How is that being welcoming?"

"Wasn't trying to be welcoming," I say.

"What about neighborly?" she asks as we take a step forward in line.

"Wasn't trying to be neighborly either."

"Well, you should," she replies. "I'm going to be here for a while, and I think it would be best if we could live harmoniously—don't you?"

"We're not living in the same house, so I have no need to interact with you."

"Sheesh," she says, her hand landing on her hip. "I know I pretended to get your name wrong, but there's no need to be so rude. Remember...I complimented your muscles."

I roll my eyes. "Do you really think I'm that vain?"

"No," she says. "But I thought it would butter you up after I called you Connor." She winks.

"Not interested in being buttered up."

"What *are* you interested in?" she asks.

I'm getting sucked in again. This is what she does, pulls me in with conversation, challenges, and questions, and before I know it, I'm ready to fly off the deep end with irritation.

"I think it's best for the both of us if we just…don't talk to each other."

She shrugs. "I'm fine with that." She turns toward the menu again, and I do the same.

There. Silence.

As long as we ignore each other, everything will be fine.

"For the record, I wasn't trying to be rude or condescending. I really thought we could joke around with each other. That's why I called you Connor."

"For the record," I mimic, "I couldn't care less."

"Well…kind of seems like you cared a little."

I glance at her. "We're not talking to each other, remember?"

"Yup, I get that, but I felt like I needed to clear the air. Didn't want you to think I came into town to disrupt your grumpy peace."

"You didn't need to put *grumpy* in front of *peace*," I shoot back.

"It felt fitting."

"It's not." Even though it is. "Let's just get back to not talking to each other."

"Couldn't have said it better myself," she replies and sticks her hands in her pockets, tuning me out. Just the way I like it.

Silence falls between us once again as we move forward in line.

The Krampus family—comprised of at least twenty members with different occupations all throughout town—works behind the counter, filling orders, shouting at each other because it's the only way they know how to communicate, and then slapping orders on the counter to pick up.

"What to get, what to get?" Storee mumbles to herself.

I ignore her and focus on the one thing on the menu that I care about…the chicken parm sandwich. Out of this world.

The breading is crisp.

The sauce is remarkable.

And the bread is toasted just perfectly with cheese oozing over it.

Fucking chef's kiss.

And exactly what I need after a hard day.

"Italian sub...no, Aunt Cindy will want soup. Do I want soup? It will probably warm me up."

I clench my jaw, irritated with her verbal processing. It feels like she's trying to goad me into conversation. Not falling for it.

"Taran is not partial to soup, so do I get her tuna? Eh, I hate the smell, so maybe I'll get her a grilled cheese..."

Sort of wish Taran would get the tuna.

"But she's also partial to ham and cheese." I feel her body move closer to mine. "What are you getting?"

I sigh heavily. "Chicken parm."

"Huh, would have pegged you for an 'all the meat' kind of guy."

I don't bother commenting because I'm not interested in opening up the conversation. So instead, I rock on my heels, hating this time of year with the crowds that flock to the town, holding up my ability to partake in a sandwich after a long day of taking care of reindeer.

"You know, since you grew so well."

"Huh?" I say.

"The meat. The muscles. They correspond. More protein means more muscles, unless you supplement. Are you supplementing, Connor?"

"Cole," I remind her, my patience wearing thin.

"Oh shit, sorry." She chuckles. "Just got Connor stuck in my head now. Anywho, are you supplementing?"

"I'm trying not to have a conversation with you, remember?"

"Sure...right. Wasn't sure if the awkward silence was making your skin crawl like it is mine. But I'm going to take that as a no, so I'll just stand here and wait."

"Thanks," I say, feeling settled finally.

Christ, what does it take to get Storee to understand? The best thing we can do is just avoid each other. Nothing good comes from us being near each other.

Thankful for some peace, I focus on my evening, how I plan on eating my sandwich in front of the TV and catching up on the latest—

"So what have you been up to the six years since I saw you?" Storee asks, breaking the silence again. When I turn to look at her, she adds, "Eh, was it six years? Can't quite remember. Wait, I think you said ten. That's right, ten years."

"Storee, stop talking to me."

"I can't." She shrugs.

"Yes, you can. You're choosing not to," I reply, my irritation ramping up.

"No, I actually have a really hard time dealing with awkward silence, and it propels me to want to fill in that silence with gibberish, hence what's happening right now. So, uh…what have you been up to?"

"Nothing," I say, turning away from her and stuffing my hands in my pockets.

I feel her move up beside me and catch her peeking around my shoulder from the corner of my eye. "For ten years you've been up to nothing? Seems like a giant waste of time."

"Leave me alone," I say.

"Hard to."

"Try harder."

"I am. Believe me, I've held back on at least twenty questions already."

"Should I be thankful?"

"Very," she replies. "So, anyway, want to tell me what about the chicken parm gets your taste buds ready to do a happy dance?"

"No."

"Is it the cheese?"

"Leave me alone."

"The sauce?"

"Storee…"

"The chicken?"

"For fuck's sake," I say, turning on her.

She smiles up at me. "Sorry, but like I said, it's really hard for me to be quiet."

"Well, let me make it easy for you," I say as I step out of line, ignoring my craving for a chicken parm sandwich and settling for the leftovers in my fridge. "I'll leave."

"But your sandwich!"

"Not worth it," I reply.

"Okay, but if you change your mind, I'm not letting you back in line. You leave now, you lose your spot."

"Well aware," I say as I walk away and push the door open, freeing myself from her irritating presence.

It's going to be a long fucking holiday if this is how it's going to go.

CHAPTER THREE
STOREE

Cole tried, he truly did; he attempted
to keep his poise.
But how could he with her? All that noise, noise, noise.

She was very unpleasant; he couldn't
stand her in the least.
Especially after she took away his chicken parm feast.

"SHE'S HEADED OVER RIGHT NOW," Taran says. "Can you stop fumbling with that soup?"

"I'm not fumbling, I'm eating," I say after a gulp of tomato bisque. "I'm starving."

"It's rude to eat before everyone is present for dinner."

"It's rude to hold off on showing up until *Jeopardy!* is over. You and I both know she's terrible and doesn't know a single question," I say.

Not to mention the Kringle Krampus was soooooo slow. By the time I got up to the register to order, I was gnawing a part of my arm off. Didn't help that I ran into Cole. Totally misjudged the dynamic. Man, the look he gave me—pure murder.

He's sort of always been like that—a touch on the grumpy side—but this time? It was like he took on a whole persona of "look at me and die."

But the brief look that I did take, umm...let's just say the boy grew into a man. I've always thought Cole was cute. How could I not with that brown hair that he liked to flip to the side and those penetrating blue eyes that always had a heavy set of brows over them? Not to mention I've always tended to flock toward the grumpier sort. But wow, I wasn't expecting to be bowled over by just how handsome he is now. How sharp his jawline is, peppered in a thick scruff, how tall…how broad. The deep tone of his voice and the even surlier disposition. Talk about the kind of hero you look for in a Lovemark movie.

In a huff, Taran turns toward me. "Can you please, please try not to be difficult?"

"How am I being difficult? I wasn't aware we needed to stand in a single file, waiting for our aunt to greet us as if we're the house staff." I take another slurp of my soup. "When she *finally* shows up, I'll be there to greet her—"

The front door opens, startling me, and I jump, my spoon clattering into the bowl in front of me. Anxiety zings through me as I bolt over to Taran and stand at her side, our arms pressing together as the door swings open, revealing Aunt Cindy with a walker, Martha and Mae standing on either side.

And it's a sight to behold.

Martha and Mae both sport their signature high-rise hair—that's what I like to call it. They like to say the higher the hair, the closer to the North Pole. But it's the matching cerulean-blue, velour track suits that send me, because Aunt Cindy is wearing one as well.

"My girls," Aunt Cindy coos with more enthusiasm than I expected. I might have been totally wrong to assume, but I just thought that we'd be coming here to care for an elderly woman in her bed, her shaky arm lifting up to point to her ice water for a palate cleanse. Sure, Mom said she'd had some recovery time in an assisted living facility where they focused on getting her up and walking. But this…this vibrant, smiling, velour-track-suit-wearing woman in her tinted blue glasses is not the human I was expecting.

"Aren't they magnificent?" Aunt Cindy says, gesturing to me and Taran.

"Positively radiant," Martha says.

"And how wonderful that they grew into their noses," Mae adds.

Brow creased, I touch my nose and look toward Taran, who seems unfazed.

"Good to see you, Aunt Cindy," Taran says, stepping up and hugging her. "You look so well."

"We spent the morning watching YouTube videos of some naughty Thunder from Down Under men dressed in Santa costumes, thrusting their way around Santa's workshop. Had no idea it was a Bawhovier tradition, but it sure did put some color in my cheeks."

Ew.

Gross.

"Niall was her favorite," Mae says with a nudging elbow to Aunt Cindy. Niall?

And look at that, I'm witness to more color in Aunt Cindy's cheeks. Not how I envisioned starting off the visit.

"Hi, Aunt Cindy," I say, moving in and giving her a hug. "Glad you, uh, found Niall."

Not sure why I said that. I say stupid things when I'm uncomfortable.

"Thank you, dear. He was quite charming."

Charming is a nice way to describe a thrusting man in a G-string.

"Here, let me help you in," Taran says. "We have dinner ready on the table."

"How lovely." She looks between us, a shaky smile on her lips. "I'm so lucky to have you two in my life, dropping everything to help me out."

Ugh, when she says things like that, it makes me feel guilty for being annoyed by the horrendously cold weather, grumpy neighbor, and winking doll room.

She then turns to Martha and Mae. "Thank you, ladies, for your hospitality. Once I'm better, I'll be bringing over brownies."

"Not if you put those black beans in them," Martha says with a point of her finger. "I know you're a health nut, but black beans shouldn't be in the same sentence as the word brownie."

Mae nods with a snort. "I second that."

And then together they take off toward their house, the yellow one diagonally across from Aunt Cindy's.

The entire cul-de-sac is like a pastel Christmas palette: pink, green, light green, red, and yellow. It somehow all goes together. And with poinsettias adorning each porch and entryway, the houses have a brand of cohesiveness that says *hey, we celebrate Christmas, but it's like we've been designed by a single girl who decorates her house for the holidays in her own magical Barbie way.*

I shut the door as Taran helps Aunt Cindy to the table.

For someone who broke her hip, she's moving around pretty well. I know she's had time to heal in the hospital, but it makes me wonder if she brought us here for any other reason. I wouldn't put it past her, as Aunt Cindy has been known to pull some fast ones on people.

Once we're all settled, she removes her cloth napkin from under her silverware—Aunt Cindy always appreciates a well-dressed table—and places it on her lap. "My, this looks delicious."

She smiles at us and then digs her spoon into her soup, indicating that we're allowed to do the same.

Thank God, because my body is starting to fail me from lack of nourishment.

Sure, I might have eaten an entire bag of pretzels on the way up here, along with two clementines, a box of Raisinets, and three applesauce-to-go pouches, but it clearly wasn't enough.

"How was the drive in? Good thing you were able to make it on a nice day when the sun was out and the roads were clear."

"It was a great drive," Taran says.

"So sunny I had to put on my sunglasses," I add.

"See, I told you it's the same here as in California," Aunt Cindy says.

Yeah, not even close.

Don't get me wrong, it's beautiful here. With the Rocky Mountains as the backdrop, it almost feels like Kringletown is inside a movie set, but California doesn't quite reach the kinds of temperatures that would freeze my nipples off.

"So," I say, wanting to change the subject and not talk about how much Aunt Cindy wishes I'd give up my bikini for a pair of snow boots, "how is the hip feeling?"

"Okay," she says. "I can get around at a slow pace, but everyday activities are difficult, which is why I'm glad you're here. Why I'm glad you're both here." She sets down her spoon, pats her face with her napkin, and says, "I actually have something to speak to you two about. It's quite important."

Mom warned us about this.

It's the death talk; I can feel it. Mom said Aunt Cindy was in her feels about her broken hip and how that ultimately leads to death for old people, so I'm mentally prepared to assure Aunt Cindy she's not dying and I know Taran is as well.

"What do you need to talk to us about?" Taran asks in a calm, almost sweet voice. It's nice that at least one of us gets to hear it.

"As you know, Kringletown means a lot to me."

"Yes," Taran says. "We're very aware."

"And for the last few years, I've taken part in the Christmas Kringle contest. A contest the town puts on every year where we name who is the most Christmas-y of them all." Hmm, is this where she says she's going to keel over before she can enter? "And for the last few years, I've come in second, meaning I haven't earned the title of Christmas Kringle."

"Second place is better than last," I say with a lift of my spoon.

Aunt Cindy flashes her weary eyes at me. "Second place is still a loss." Should have seen that coming, given her competitive spirit. "And last year, after I took second again, I decided that I was going to step up my game."

"Oof, such a shame you broke your hip," I say. "At least there's next year."

"There will be no next year," Aunt Cindy says with a hint of sass in her voice.

I set my spoon down as well, looking toward Taran, who seems to prefer observing rather than joining the conversation. She does that a lot, stays quiet while I do all the talking. She's been like that my entire life.

"We love you, Aunt Cindy, and I say this with the utmost respect, but you thinking you're going to die at any minute from a broken hip has to stop."

"What are you gabbing on about?" she asks. "I don't think I'm going to croak this very second."

"Well, I mean, I wasn't saying that, but—"

"If you'd let me finish, you'd know that I don't plan on participating this year...but you are."

Umm...say that again? I think candy canes were stuffed in my ears because it almost sounded like she said I would be the one entering the Christmas Kringle contest.

I glance at Taran and when I'm greeted with a grin that tends to eat... something, if you catch my drift, I realize I heard correctly.

Holding one finger up in question, eyes squinted, I clear my throat. "Funny, I thought I heard you say one of us would be participating."

"That's exactly what I said."

I nod and lean back in my chair. Looking at my sister, I say, "Well, Taran, good luck with that. If anyone can do it for the family, it would be you with your boundless determination and need for perfection."

Taran slowly shakes her head. "Afraid it can't be me."

"Why? You said you were staying."

"I am, to take care of our dear aunt Cindy."

"Oh"—I wave her off—"I've got that covered."

"You do? So you don't mind giving her sponge baths?"

Dear God in heaven.

Hold back the dry heave.

I glance over at Aunt Cindy, hiding the shiver that races up my spine, making the hairs on the back of my neck stand straight into the air.

"As, uh, as tempting as it is to have such a deep-rooted bonding moment with someone so important in my life, I just don't know how good I'd be at getting…all the crevices. But, hey, how about you take care of the bathing." I point to my sister. "And then I will take care of the rest while you work tirelessly on becoming the Kringleton."

"Christmas Kringle," Aunt Cindy corrects me.

"Right, the Christmas Kringle." I take my spoon and dip it into my soup. "Glad we settled that."

"I'm afraid that can't be the case," Aunt Cindy says as I have my spoon halfway to my mouth. She leans over, pats my hand, and looks me in the eyes. "I love you, sweetheart, but unfortunately, I don't trust you with my life."

Wow!

Okay, that stings.

Uh, can we say *a bit harsh*?

Taran snorts but is smart enough not to make eye contact with me.

Keeping my expression controlled, I say, "As nice a compliment as that is to Taran, may I ask why?"

"Oh Storee, you've never been the caring kind."

Now, there's shocking someone with an opinion, and then there's straight up insulting someone to their face.

Seems like Aunt Cindy chose violence today.

"I do too care. I'm here, aren't I?" I ask. Ha! Got her there.

"Yes, and I appreciate that, but as you know, your sister is a nurse and just…more equipped for taking care of me in a way that I need to survive this horrible tragedy."

My God, she broke a hip while retrieving gingerbread cookies. It's not like she got mauled by a bear and her body is being held together by stitches and glue.

"And I'll be sure to give you the best of care," Taran says.

Does that care include sticking your nose up Aunt Cindy's ass? Because if so, show me the way to the Kringle award—I will not stoop to such levels.

"I know you will, dear," Aunt Cindy says and then turns to me. "Which means you, my Storeebook, will be my protégée."

Yup, don't like the sound of that.

I check my nonexistent watch on my wrist. "Oof, as great as that sounds, I just remembered I need to—"

"You will do this for me," Aunt Cindy says, using her stern, don't-mess-with-me voice. The only other time I ever heard her use such a tone was when Taran and I accidentally chopped down her most prized potted poinsettia in her front yard. It took her a whole year to forgive us.

I let out a nervous laugh. "Um, okay, but you know, you will make it through this hip thing, and there's always next year. Also, ever think about the sympathy you can garner from participating with a broken hip? It's practically a fast-track right to first place."

"I refuse to wait another year with the bias floating through this town—no one will believe I'm up for it next year if I don't already have a representative on the throne. I need someone young, a whippersnapper who can lead the charge, impress the judges, flirt with them, pull out all the tricks to secure the title." From the drop of spittle that flew out of her mouth onto the fine lace tablecloth, I'm getting the impression that this award means a lot more to her than I thought.

"I first want to say thank you for calling me young. Coming up on thirty has made me feel like I have one foot in the grave. So, bless you. But unfortunately, I don't know anything about this Kringle thing."

"That's why you'll be my protégée. While your sister cleans my crevices, you shall perfect the act of becoming the Town Kringle."

The image of all of that is just too disturbing.

I offer my aunt a gentle smile, trying to ease her into accepting that I won't be participating. "It really sounds like a great time, but I must admit, I'm not sure—"

"I had your application dropped off today. Bob Krampus is excited to see what you can bring to the competition."

My expression falls. "You already gave my application to Santa? A *forged* application?"

She nods. "Yup. Quite thrilled you're giving your performative spirit another try."

And there it is...a mention of the past that still likes to haunt me in my dreams.

"Aunt Cindy—"

"It's a done deal," Taran chimes in. "You're going to participate in the Christmas Kringle, and I'm going to take care of Aunt Cindy."

"But—"

"You know, I'm feeling a little weak," Aunt Cindy says, bringing her hand up to her cheek. "I think...I think I should lie down." Oh my God, a few seconds ago she was frothing at the mouth, excited about the Christmas Kringle, and now she's feeling weak. Someone has been attending acting school.

"Let me help you to your room," Taran says as she assists Aunt Cindy to a standing position with her walker.

I sit back in my chair and watch as my great-aunt hunches over, pretending to be feeble and incapable when minutes ago she was blushing from the thought of Niall, the G-string-thrusting Santa.

I knew I was going to get played. I just didn't realize it was going to be like this.

———————

"That should do it," I mutter to myself as I finish turning all the dolls in the room around so I don't have to look at their faces.

I take a step back, observing my work, making sure I didn't miss any, when there's a knock at my door.

Taran appears, leaning against the doorframe with her arms crossed. "You really think that's going to help?" she asks.

"It will," I say and then look her in the eyes. "And I swear to God, Taran, if you come in here and turn one of them around, I will be a fixture on that trundle bed, offering you zero privacy with Guy."

She smirks, as she probably already had the thought to mess with me. But at least the threat is out there. I will not tolerate any sort of funny business when it comes to me and these dolls.

"Did Aunt Cindy go to bed?"

"Yes," Taran says while I take a seat on the bed.

"Now, about this Christmas Kringle thing. Do we think that she is possibly mistaken, that maybe she turned in an application for herself? You know, I think I saw an article somewhere that linked dementia with broken hips. Maybe dinner tonight was a dementia moment for her."

"First of all, dementia is not something to joke about."

"I wasn't joking. I'm serious about the article," I say.

"And secondly," she continues, completely ignoring me, "she was very serious. While I was helping her into her nightgown, she made me promise her that I'd make sure to keep you in the competition."

"And you said no, I'd never do that to my sister, right? After everything she's been through, I wouldn't torture her like that?"

"I told her you'd do it."

I flop back on the floral bedspread and stare up at the canopy. "Taran, why? You know I can't...I can't do anything that requires performing."

"You don't even know what the Christmas Kringle thing is," Taran says.

I sit back up, propped up by my hands behind me, and say, "Uh, yeah, I do. While you were combing Aunt Cindy's hair, I was looking it up online. There are several competitions required to become the Christmas Kringle, and they all play out in front of the town. I'm not doing it."

Taran sighs and walks over to the bed, where she takes a seat. "Storee, don't you think it's time that you get over your fears?"

"Get over my fears?" I say, exasperated. "Taran, I was humiliated in front of this town. The last thing I want to do is relive that."

"You were eighteen."

"Which was a very impactful year for me. A fresh adult with possibilities in front of her. And then for *that* to happen…" I shake my head. "I won't relive it."

Taran takes my hand in hers. "You tripped over your elf shoe and knocked over a cutout wooden present. It wasn't that big of a deal."

"Uh, are you forgetting the fact that the wooden present knocked into Mrs. Fiskers, who lost her balance and tumbled down the hill and into the river, where there was a rescue effort full of fireman, police officers, and medics to pull her out?"

Yeah, that happened.

I sent a lady in her fifties tumbling down a hill and into a freezing cold river.

"It was humiliating, Taran. I didn't want to do the stupid Santa reveal in the first place, but I needed the volunteer hours for school, so I was forced to parade around in an elf costume. I should have known it wasn't going to go well."

"Didn't you forget a line you had to say too?" she asks, just sticking the knife further into the back of my memories.

"Thanks for bringing it up." I lean against the headboard and draw my knees into my chest. "Ever since then, I've made it my mission to always be the person behind the screen, editing out the embarrassment, rather than the girl in front of the camera."

"And you're very good at your job," Taran says, a rare compliment from her. "But this is going to be different. You're older now. Less…clumsy."

"I'm still clumsy, and the town knows it—they don't ever forget any-thing. They didn't forget about the hot chocolate shortage of 2012. They didn't let me live down the signature tree-tipping over in Baubles and Wrappings. And they most definitely will never forget about Mrs. Fiskers being knocked into the river." Whispering, I add, "They had to treat her for hypothermia. The river was mostly frozen, but her elbow hit the ice, cracked it just enough for a rush of water to wash over her.

"I think she was being dramatic. It wasn't *that* cold out that day."

"Doesn't mean the water wasn't cold."

Taran sighs and then places her hand on my knee. "Storee, I under-stand that you're nervous, and rightfully so. You haven't had the best of luck in this town, but this is for Aunt Cindy. She's the one who created all of the magical Christmas moments we've had in our lives. It wasn't Mom and Dad; it was her. And she's asking for help, so I think we owe it to her."

I groan because I know that she's right.

Aunt Cindy was the one who welcomed us into her house during Christmas, wrapped us in the deepest and warmest hugs, included us in decorating the tree, made cookies with us, and allowed us to use her dining room table as Santa's sleigh and her chairs as the reindeer.

She was the one who created the magic.

I lean my head back. "Taran…I'm going to humiliate myself again."

"You won't," she says. "You're older, wiser, and you have Aunt Cindy mentoring you. If anything, you're going to succeed. Promise."

Why do I feel like this is a disaster waiting to happen?

CHAPTER FOUR
COLE

Christmas Kringle? No, thank you.
She was still very scared.
"I don't think I can do this," she constantly declared.

Her hat was in the ring, for it was a Kringletown honor.
And guess who totally noticed?
The grumpy Cole/Connor.

"OKAY, IF I'M GOING TO sit back and watch this story unfold, the least I can do is set you straight. It's just Cole…no Connor involved."

Narrator: Yes, but Connor rhymed with honor, so it worked better.

"You're giving readers the wrong impression."

Narrator: Would you have preferred if I found a way to rhyme Cole with A-hole?

"Never mind."

Narrator: That's what I thought. You focus on your part, and I'll handle the narrating. Now, back to the story.

"Did you see the names that were put in for the Christmas Kringle?" Max asks as he walks up to me from a shift out in the forest. It's about noon and he just got done setting up tree plots with families investing in the ever-growing forest so we can keep the farm constantly thriving.

I open the reindeer feed bin and pour a sack of food inside, letting the new food go in first and then topping it off with the old food I already pulled out.

"Does it look like I stand around Ornament Park waiting to see who's entering the asinine competition?"

"Oooh, you're extra grumpy today. Any reason why? Maybe because there's a certain sister now in town?" When I glance at him and catch him waggling his eyebrows, it takes everything in me not to grip the back of his head and dip it into the reindeer feed.

"I'm regularly like this," I remind him on a huff.

"I would agree that this attitude is a normal occurrence for you, but I also feel there's a bit of snap to it. Some might even say spicy."

I roll up the empty burlap bag of feed and store it away for when I go to the feed farm to restock. "Is there a point to you coming in here? Or is it just to annoy me?"

"Yes, I already said it, but I shall repeat myself. I came to see if you saw who entered the Kringle contest."

And here it is, the most annoying thing about this town where I live. December hits, and all they start talking about is who is going to be named Town Kringle for the year.

Confused?

Let me lay it out for you.

A few years back, the proprietors in the town gathered with their Christmas cups full of mulled cider, called in the honorary mayor, Bob Krampus, and came up with the idea to start the Kringle competition as a way to draw in even more people from out of town. Throughout the month of December, those who enter the competition have certain tasks and mini tests they're graded on, and then all those scores are accumulated to see who is the merriest of them all. That's the person named Town Kringle—a totally pointless title they get to lord over the rest of us yearlong. When it was introduced, everyone was beside themselves to the point that they limited it to one entry per household. And each competition goes hand in hand with one of the town's proprietors acting as the judge.

For example, handmade candy canes are judged by Old Man Chadwick, who owns the candy shop in town. He gets to cut people down on their candy cane making abilities and gather some advertising for his own store as he boasts about his products being better, and points are awarded to the participants.

This way, the businesses in town are offered some sponsorship and advertisement while keeping the competitive spirit alive.

The whole thing is stupid. I've never entered, and I have zero plans to ever enter.

But the people of Kringle, they think differently. To them, it's the greatest honor of all time. To them, this is what the year has built up to. For the entire month of December, it's all they ever talk about.

And I thought Max was better than them, but I guess not.

"Like I said, I don't care who enters."

"You don't?" Max replies with a frown. "Huh. I guess I was wrong then."

He's baiting me, and unfortunately, I take the bait.

"Fine. Who the hell is it?"

He smirks. "Your new neighbor."

"New neighbor?" I ask, confused. "I don't have a new—" I pause, my mind short-circuiting as I start to clue in. "Wait…" I meet Max's gaze and he slowly nods. "Storee entered the contest?"

"Yup. Saw her name up on the board today. It's all anyone is talking about. They're drawing conclusions about why. Some think it's because Cindy can't compete this year, so Storee is taking her place. Others think it's because she's trying to make up for what happened to Mrs. Fiskers by taking part in celebrating the town tradition."

Storee's going to need more than participation in a Christmas competition to redeem herself after pushing a fifty-year-old woman down a hill and into a frozen river.

"And there is a small batch of townies who think she's out to ruin Christmas and possibly take out the signature tree again—but that's mainly coming from the Dankworths. I personally think she's trying to irritate you."

"Why would that irritate me?" I ask, even though I can feel my blood pressure start to rise.

"I don't know." Max leans against a wooden pillar in the barn. "You tell me."

"I don't care what she does," I say as I spin away and move over to the hose to fill up the reindeers' water.

"And yet you said that like you *do* care."

I pause, gripping the hose tightly, because…the fucking audacity.

After everything she said about this town, she's going to try to be the Christmas Kringle? She's going to act like the goddamn belle of the ball and try to show her Christmas spirit? Like I said, I don't give a shit who wins or about anything in the competition, but to see her try to snatch up a top honor in a town she hates?

Yeah, hates.

From her lips to my ears. *Hate.*

I don't fucking think so.

"You know, people think she has a good chance at winning too," Max presses. "Given that Cindy has come in second the last few years, they think that with her guidance, Storee can pull the win."

That's great…I don't care.

I really shouldn't care.

Sure, it's annoying that someone like her would even attempt the competition, but I don't care.

I turn on the hose and direct the water into the trough, trying to ignore the irritating feelings pulsing through me.

"In all honestly, I could see it happening. New girl in town, embracing Kringle for everything it has to offer, and being the merriest of them all. She has what it takes."

No, she doesn't.

Not that I know what it takes, because like I said, I don't pay attention, but she most definitely does not have what it takes.

"And honestly, I think I might be rooting for her."

That makes me snap because *the fuck he is.*

I turn off the water, set the hose down, and face my friend. "You will not be rooting for her. And no, she doesn't have what it takes. Not even close."

"Oh?" he asks, lifting one eyebrow. "I'm surprised you have an opinion."

"It's not an opinion; it's a fact. And she doesn't deserve to win. She shouldn't even be in the competition. She's not part of the town; she doesn't live here. She doesn't even like it here. Yeah, she told me that to my face. She said she hates this town, called it stupid."

Max's face goes from playful to hurt. All joking is aside now.

"She said that?"

I nod.

"When?"

"Doesn't matter," I practically huff as I turn to pick up the hose, but Max stops me.

"No, it clearly does because you're angry about it. When did she say that to you?"

I twist my lips to the side, hating that I even brought it up, because I've bottled up this interaction for a long fucking time. But then one mention of her just pushes me over the edge, and I spill everything.

"It was…uh, it was the night my parents passed."

"What?" he asks, his face growing even more serious. "You never told me that. What did she say?"

Looks like I'm unloading.

I lean against a wooden beam. "I had just found out about the accident but didn't know any details. I was sitting on my porch, waiting for more news, when she was walking down the street. This was after Mrs. Fiskers was dumped in the river. Anyway, Storee spotted me and joined me on the porch. It was a common place for us to gather and just talk. At that point, we knew each other well enough for me to realize she was upset, so I asked her what was wrong, trying to get my mind off what had happened to my parents. Well, that was a huge goddamn mistake because she went on a tirade about the town. How the Christmas year-round thing was stupid, the stores were annoyingly cheesy, and that she hated coming here to visit. Just basically shit on everything about Kringle. No holding back—she just went for it."

"Jesus. What did you say?"

"Nothing." I cross my arms over my chest and toe the ground. "I said nothing, because how could I? I was just so...lost. Thinking, how could my parents have been in an accident together? How was I going to live without them if they died? She didn't know about the accident, so a part of me can forgive what she said because of that. But in that moment, when I was simply gutted...well, you know. She left, on fucking Christmas of all days, and she didn't see how the town rallied behind me when it was confirmed that my parents hadn't survived." And then, all I could do was drown in grief. "This town has its annoyances and can be tough to live in at times, but the things she said about it weren't true. They angered me, and my grief is wrapped up in that too. I'm still *here* because of how this town picked me up when I was at my lowest. How it looks after its own."

"Yeah, I get that. I know your loyalty." He scratches the back of his head. "Man, I wonder what changed her mind. Do you think she likes this town now?"

"No," I answer. I'm honestly not sure, but given that I can't seem to let go of a grudge, I refuse to paint her in a good light.

"Well, everyone thinks she has a good chance at winning."

"She doesn't deserve to win."

She doesn't deserve the glory of the title. Pointless though it may be.

She doesn't even deserve to be part of the competition at all.

It's not fair.

I glance out at the reindeer, my mind whirling…

His brain spun with thoughts,
some big and some small.
And then an idea came to him, the
greatest idea of them all…

"Oh shit, I have a thought," I say, a grin tugging on my lips. "A wonderfully horrible thought."

"I'm listening," Max says, leaning in.

"What if I enter the contest?"

"You?" Max scoffs on a laugh. "Dude, come on, be serious."

"I am serious," I say. "What if I enter? It would easily become the talk of the town, eclipsing any conversation about Storee. No one would expect it, and given the standing I have here as the person who takes care of Santa's reindeer, I could take the win. Steal Christmas, some might say."

Max stares at me, blinking a few times.

When he doesn't answer, I press, "What do you think?"

"I think you've lost your mind."

I shake my head. "No, I'm starting to see it all clearly. This is the perfect way to fix the problem."

"Um, okay, first of all, there really isn't a true problem here. Sure, Storee said some shit things, but maybe she's really trying here. Secondly, dude, you know what the competition is like; you know they accept applications and choose the contestants they want, and you are not that kind of person." Whispering, he continues, "They judge you on jolliness. I don't think you have a jolly bone in your body."

Oh really?

Not a jolly bone in my body...wait until he gets a load of this.

Shoulders back, chest puffed, I smile widely, flashing all of my teeth, my eyes crinkling in the corners.

Max takes a step back, shielding his eyes. "What the hell are you doing?"

"Showing you my jolliness."

"Well, fuck, stop. It's terrifying."

My smile droops and my eyes narrow. "It was a nice smile."

"How would you know? You didn't look in a mirror." Max shakes his head. "That was uncomfortable to witness."

"Oh, fuck off. Like you could do better."

"Is that a challenge?"

I cross my arms over my chest. "Yeah...it is."

"Fine." He sticks his hands in his pockets, leans a little to the left, and pops an eyebrow and a smirk at the same time, flashing me some sort of movie star smile.

I try to look away, act disgusted, attempt to shield my eyes, but hell, it's a great smile. Nice to look at.

Some might say a jolly fucking experience.

"I can see from your stare that you're mesmerized."

"Oh fuck off," I scoff.

He chuckles for a few seconds and then rubs his palms together. "In all seriousness, man, this is a bad idea. You're going to scare people more than inject them with holiday spirit. Hate to say it, but you're not the jolliest. The...the town proprietors might ask you to leave the competition, and that will be more humiliating than anything."

I shake my head. "No, you're wrong. This feels right. This feels like it's meant to be," I say, feeling the high of this wonderful, yet terrible, idea.

"Okay, I can see that you've reached a manic state, so I'm going to let you live in it for a moment as I remind you exactly what's involved in the competition." He uses his fingers to tick off the different tasks. "The Eggnog Wars. Not sure you've ever made eggnog in your life."

"I've drunk it."

"Not a qualification, but okay. Then there's Upcycle Christmas, the human diorama in front of the whole town, and you don't do public scenes."

"Nothing like getting out of my comfort zone to get the blood pumping."

"The Fruitcake Festivus," he says. "You hate fruitcake."

"And this gives me the perfect opportunity to make it better," I counter.

Max's face shows he's annoyed. "The light display...the candy cane making."

I wave my hand at him in dismissal. "I was born to hang lights. Who do you think hangs them for the cul-de-sac? And candy cane making... well, that I'll have to work around."

"Okay," Max says with a grin, looking like he has me on his next point. "The Christmas caroling. You really going to sing at the Caroling Café, put on a public performance? You don't sing in front of other people, dickhead, unless it's family."

"I haven't yet. But you've heard my voice—some might say it sounds like angels are whispering to you."

"You are so full of shit," Max scoffs. "Dude, this is not for you. You know it, I know it. This is going to end in tragedy."

"It won't." I shake my head. "Do you know why?" I stare at my best friend, arms crossed, a Grinch-sized smile on my face.

"Why do I feel like I'm not going to like what you say next?"

"It's not going to be a tragedy, because you're going to enter the competition with me as my holly jolly sidekick."

"No fucking way," Max says. "No. Not happening. History has shown us that the holly jolly sidekick is the one who's humiliated the most. That's why there aren't many in the competition."

"How could I possibly humiliate you?" I ask. "You're my lifeline in all of this—I'd never humiliate you."

"I don't believe you. You have that look in your eyes, the one that says you will win at all costs."

"That's right, I will win at all costs, which means I have no issue standing on a table at the Caroling Café and belting out 'Rudolph the Red-Nosed Fucking Reindeer' while you shower me with fake snow."

"Pretty sure *fucking* isn't in the title."

"And while you shower me with fake snow," I continue, ignoring him completely, "I'll hop around, arms tucked in, flashing my hoof hands and making a scene of it all. You will look positively serious in comparison."

"Do you hear what you're saying?"

"I do." I nod. "And I've never been surer of anything in my entire life. If Storee wants to pretend like she's a part of this town, like this town means something to her, then she's going to have to go up against me." I point to my chest. "If anything, this town means more to me than to anyone else living here. I might bitch about it during this time of year, and I might have some dark history concerning this month in particular, but maybe... maybe this is something I need," I say, my voice growing soft.

The high starts to taper off and the realization begins to set in.

The realization of how alone this season makes me feel.

My family's traditions, once shared every year, are now faded into distant memories. The Maxheimers made sure I was never alone at Christmas. That I received gifts. Ate copious amounts of food. Felt included.

But I never had a Christmas with my parents again. That all stopped nearly a decade ago.

The spirit of Christmas—no longer a warm, familiar embrace, now just a mere afterthought. That's what it *had* to become.

And a season that should be full of the happy smiles of my family gathering around a tree is now empty, bleak, and just another day to scratch off the calendar.

Sensing the shift in mood, Max places his hand on my shoulder. "Cole, man…"

"They would have loved seeing me do this," I say solemnly. "Fuck, my dad would have cackled his ass off while my mom would have been my holly jolly sidekick." I look him in the eyes. "I hate this time of year. And don't get me wrong, I'm grateful to your family for adopting me as one of theirs, but that night my parents passed, they took away all of the magic with them."

"I understand, man," he says and then grimaces. "Fuck, fine, I'll do it."

"Max, I didn't say that—"

"I know." He nods. "But you're my best friend, and I know you'd do the same for me. Reluctantly, but you'd do the same."

I smile softly at him. "I'd bitch about it the entire time, but I would."

Max chuckles. "Yeah, I know." He clasps his hands together and blows out a heavy breath. "Okay, if we're going to do this, then we're going to do it right. There will be no cutting corners, no scoffing at ideas. We gotta be all in." He quirks a brow at me. "You all in?"

He holds his hand out to me, and I take it, offering him a strong shake. "I'm all in."

CHAPTER FIVE
STOREE

They chuckled and high-fived. Oh
what an unexpected trick!
Cole Black as the Kringle, with
Max his holly jolly sidekick.

"She won't know what's coming,"
they said with a cheerful gloat.
Never has a Kringle competition
been so holly jolly cutthroat.

"YOU NEED A NOTEBOOK AND a pen," Aunt Cindy says as she props herself up in her bed.

Yesterday she was walking around, watching videos of Niall the G-string man, and today she's feeble, pointing around with a shaking hand, asking for ice chips. When I say that she knows how to work the room, I'm not lying, because she has my sister practically eating out of her hand.

"Here are those ice chips for you, Aunt Cindy," Taran says as she enters the room.

"You are such a dear," Aunt Cindy says as she pats Taran on the cheek. Slowly, she lifts one to her mouth and rolls it around, letting the cold hit every inch of her tongue and cheeks.

Meanwhile, I sit in the corner of her first-floor bedroom, trying not to get dizzy from the array of varying floral prints, ranging from curtains to wallpaper to bedding to, yes, you guessed it, flooring. Well, more like an area rug, but it's floral. I've been in her room a number of times, but it's generally been a quick in and out. This extended period is giving me all sorts of confusion with a headache developing at the base of my skull.

Sure, the headache could also be from the worrying I've been doing all night, but we don't need to get into that.

"Now that my mouth is moistened," Aunt Cindy says as I try not to flinch from the use of *moist*, "we should get started on our chat."

"If you don't need anything else, I'll work on taking those Christmas boxes downstairs so we can decorate later," Taran says…a little brown on her nose.

"You are so helpful, thank you, dear."

Oh my God.

Yes, Taran is perfect.

She gave Aunt Cindy a sponge bath this morning, helped her into her clothes, and has been at her beck and call, but I was the one who brought home pastries from Warm Your Spirit, the local coffee shop, and made everyone a protein smoothie to go with it. Not sure Taran would have the strength to scrub the crevices if it weren't for my nourishment.

Not that I'm looking for praise, but I braved the frigid temperatures this morning as I hiked into town.

Aunt Cindy thought it would be best if I showed my face around more, especially since I entered the Kringle competition.

Entered being a loose term…more like forced into slapping down my name.

But I chose to be cooperative this morning as I strutted into town, bundled up so as to prevent wind burn. People were lucky to see my face through the gaiter I pulled on and the ski goggles I wore because of how windy it was. Snow in the eyes is not my idea of fun.

When Taran leaves the room, Aunt Cindy focuses her attention back on me. "Do you have that notepad and pen?"

I hold up my phone. "I take all my notes in here."

Aunt Cindy's brow creases. "A phone? How can you possibly take proper notes on that device?"

"In the notes app," I say. "It's where I make all of my notes when I'm editing or on a Zoom chat. Between my phone and my tablet, I'm set."

She studies me for a moment, clearly not thrilled with my choice. But after a few awkward seconds of silence and a subtle stare down, Aunt Cindy accepts my note-taking device.

"As you know, I had you entered into the competition, so the town is very much aware of your desire to become the Christmas Kringle."

"Well, *your* desire for me to become the Christmas Kringle, technically," I add with a smile. "I'd be very happy staying out of the limelight and watching the events unfold from a healthy distance where no one can be pushed into rivers and children won't scream because the signature tree in Baubles and Wrappings tips over..."

Aunt Cindy waves her hand in dismissal. "That's in the past, Storee. We're looking toward the future now. You're older, wiser, and you've grown into your nose."

I grip my nose again, taking in the backhanded compliment for the second time since I've been here. I make a mental note to talk to Taran about this, because I think we're missing something here.

"This is your time to shine, but it's only going to work if you commit to it," Aunt Cindy continues. "Which means you need to stop being shy about the task in front of you and jump in feet first." She makes a shaky fist with her hand, pumping it with encouragement.

I don't think she realizes pep talks aren't my thing.

"I don't know, Aunt Cindy. I really came here to help you, not to go around town taking part in a silly Christmas competition."

"Silly?" She gasps at the insult. "There is nothing silly about wanting to become the Christmas Kringle. It's the highest honor, Storee. People around town beg and plead to even be welcomed into the competition. And if you were to enter on your own, there's no way you would get in, but with you representing me...well, we have a surefire way to slip you in. Just five are selected every year, and then there is only one winner. Out of all the people in town, only one person prevails. There's nothing silly about it—it's a time-honored tradition that dates back a few years."

Well, some might not call that time-honored if it only dates back a few years, but I'm not going to be the one who sets her straight. I've already tipped the scale of annoying her.

"Sorry," I say, realizing *silly* was a very stupid adjective to use.

"I appreciate the apology." She clears her throat. "I would like for you to look at the situation with a different perspective." She struggles to sit up and I attempt to help her, but she waves me off. When she's finally settled, she looks me in the eyes. "I've always felt like we share a kindred spirit." She glances toward the door and then back at me. "I love your sister dearly, but she's more...how do I put this...robotic?" I hold back my snort, because she couldn't have described Taran better.

"She can be a bit tense at times," I say.

"Yes, tense, stiff, sometimes unwelcoming, but with you, it's always felt...easy. We share the same interests and we have the same thirst for life, even if that means you tend to find joy in taking care of a ficus rather than a Christmas tree."

I press my hand to my chest. "Alexander and I have a special bond."

"Precisely." Aunt Cindy's smile grows wide. "Your sister would never bond with a tree."

"She refuses to claim Alexander as a nephew, and I know it hurts him."

"And I doubt she ever will, because that's her personality. She will not be the one who gives an inanimate object feelings. She'd be a terrible choice as someone to enter into the Kringle competition, because she wouldn't add flair. She'd go by the book and never stray to add her own personality to it. Whereas you, my dear...you have that creative spirit. And I know in the past you've been burned by happenings in this town, but you can do this; I know you can. And better yet, you and I can do this together."

Hell, when she puts it like that, she actually makes me believe I have the ability to set aside my fears and take this head-on.

"Tell me," she continues, "how has life been?"

"What do you mean?" I ask as I cross one leg over the other.

"Any excitement? Anything taking you out of your comfort zone? Anything that removes you from whatever film you're editing, lets you experience the sun shining, the birds chirping, the world turning around you, the stars twinkling above you at night, and the crisp winter air breathing life back into your lungs?"

"Uh..." I pick a piece of lint off my joggers. "Well, it's been pretty busy lately with all the work I've been given"—a total lie, but she doesn't need to know that—"so I haven't really had a chance to look up. I think this is the first time in months that I don't have my computer in front of me."

She slowly nods. "Well, let me tell you something, Storee. There comes a time when you realize that there aren't many years left on your life card, and you start thinking back to everything you accomplished. And you start wondering...did I do it right? I don't want you to look back on your life one day from a hospital bed and regret never taking full advantage of all the opportunities presented to you."

"I know," I say softly as I bite down on the corner of my mouth.

"Your sister, she's programmed to find happiness within her confines of functionality. She finds her greatest comfort in being the robotic human that she is. She likes taking care of people, helping them, making them better; she always has. I don't worry about her because I know that she's found a kind of solace in her life. But you…you're the one I worry about. I'm not sure you've found that inner peace. It took me a while to find it. Actually, it wasn't until I moved into this house that I knew…this is where my peace is. I'd like you to find the same thing."

"I love visiting you, Aunt Cindy, but I don't think the tundra is where I'm going to find my peace."

She chuckles. "I'm not talking about moving here, but I am talking about you finding that peace. That's so important. And stepping out of your comfort zone and doing things that open your eyes to the world around you are the first steps."

I sigh and lean back in my chair. "So what you're saying to me is that if I jump into this Kringle competition feet first, not holding back, embracing the challenge, then it will set me up for so much more in life, possibly finding a sense of calm you don't think I possess?"

"You tell me…do you feel calm?"

I shift my legs, switching which one is crossed over the other. "I mean, I was very comfortable in my chair, in my home, ready to watch Lovemark Christmas movies."

"But were you experiencing life?"

"No," I answer honestly.

"Did you have plans to celebrate Christmas?"

"No," I reply, feeling a touch of shame.

She looks out the window of her room, toward the backyard that's shrouded in tall pines dusted in fluffy white snow. "That makes me sad, Storee. When your parents would bring you here for Christmas, it was… well." She clears her throat and turns to look at me again. "Those days hold my most cherished memories. Watching you girls run up and down the stairwell when you smelled fresh cookies. How we would sit in front of the fireplace, cross-stitching silly Christmas sayings to hang in the bathroom. Those late nights we would hunker under blanket forts, discussing when we thought Santa was going to arrive. I will leave this earth with those memories close to my heart. I don't want those memories to die with me."

"They won't," I say, my throat growing tight. I thought I was prepared for such a conversation, but if I'm honest, I can't imagine my life without her in it. Even we weren't visiting, she would continue to send us emails and letters, and we stayed in touch—just not in person. We've always been closer to Aunt Cindy than we were to our actual grandparents. She's so warm and full of love...and sass. She gave us amazing Christmases, and I'm sad that I've let that go. Let the magic go. In some sense, to not celebrate here, to not celebrate in Kringletown is to not celebrate Aunt Cindy. And that's not okay.

"What good are memories if you don't replicate them, if you don't repeat them...if you don't share them?"

She's right. I know she is.

I think over the last few years...and I know I've grown complacent in my life.

In my job.

In everything I do.

My friends asked me if I wanted to go out on Friday nights, and instead I stayed home and I worked. To the point that now...they don't even ask anymore.

My love life is nonexistent. I haven't even attempted to go out on a date, just sat at home, in my blanket hoodie, watching cooking videos but never cooking for myself.

I've found a certain comfort in not doing anything, but Aunt Cindy is right: That's not really living; that's skating by. If I've learned anything from Aunt Cindy throughout all these years of being around her, observing her, it's that she lives a spirited, free life with no shame.

Meanwhile, I've closed in on myself.

And maybe...just maybe...it's time to change that.

A smile crosses Aunt Cindy's lips when I look up at her.

"You're going to jump in feet first, aren't you?"

Chin held high, I fold my hands in my lap. "Well, if we're going to do this, we really should do it right."

CHAPTER SIX
COLE

So the people of Kringle all gathered around.
The twinkling lights shimmered;
snow fell to the ground.

Bob Krampus in the center with a smile and a list.
A list of all contestants, held tightly in his fist.

What a wonderful time, the start
of a very joyful season!
But Cole and Max were there for one specific reason...

"THANK YOU FOR JOINING US," Bob Krampus bellows from his Santa house at the very top of Ornament Park. It's a picturesque storybook house, as if it were plucked straight from the minds of Disney animators, with its fake thatched roof, Bavarian-style moldings, stained-glass windows in green and red, and the quintessential limestone that wraps the bottom perimeter of the cottage.

The people around us cheer, their breaths turning into mist as mittens are pressed together, winter hats cover ears, and the town band, which is off to the right, gets ready to start the Christmas season with the Kringletown favorite, "Santa Claus is Comin' to Town."

"I should have worn a jacket," Max mutters next to me. "Fuck, it's chillier than I expected it to be. I told you we should have stood closer to one of the firepits."

"And risk the chance of not being able to hear all of the rules because the kids around us are high off s'mores? No, we're here for a reason, and I will not let anyone distract us from the win."

"Okay, settle down, Michael Jordan."

"Huh?"

Max rolls his eyes. "Never mind."

"I'm happy to announce that all applications for this year's Christmas Kringle have been reviewed and we are ready to announce the competitors." Bob Krampus pauses, letting the crowd cheer again.

Not me. I stand there stiffly, mentally ready to take all the notes, not letting one thing distract me from—

A flash of red.

I look in that direction, wondering if it's Storee Taylor, only to see that it's someone tossing a red scarf around their neck.

Christ.

As I was saying, I'm not letting one thing distract me from what I have planned, and that's winning the Christmas Kringle.

"And this year, we have quite the competitors," Bob Krampus says as he pats his belly, shaking it like it's a bowl of fucking jelly. "I'm going to call out their names, and I'd like them to join me up on the stage."

"What?" I hiss. "That wasn't part of the plan—did you know about that?" I ask Max.

He shudders next to me. "Dude, I can't feel my nipples right now. I have no idea what's going on."

"When do you ever feel your nipples?" I ask.

He pauses for a second. "Good point. How about I can't feel my toes?"

"Better. Should have led with that."

"Nipples felt more dramatic."

I roll my eyes. "Well, you're coming up there with me, whether you can feel your nipples or not."

"You wound me, you know that?" he says.

"Jimmy Short, representing the Short family, please come up here." The crowd cheers as Jimmy Short makes his way to the stage. "Ursula Kronk, representing our first responders and our incumbent Kringle from last year, please join us." The crowd goes wild. She's going to be stiff competition. How can you not root for a first responder? "Dr. Beatrice Pedigree, representing our furry animals, please join us." I swear I hear a dog bark in the distance.

"And..." Bob Krampus pauses for a long moment. I know why... because he sees my name and he's probably just as shocked as the rest of the town will be since we slipped my application in at the last minute. I have a good idea as to why I was probably selected: Martha and Mae. They, along with the other proprietors, select the applicants, and they've always been advocates for me. Gripping the mic tightly, Bob says, "A new entry this year, Cole Black." The crowd's enthusiasm dies down, confusion written all over their faces. *I could really do without the dramatics.* "Representing Santa's reindeer. Please...please come join us."

I turn to Max, who turned in the application. "Representing Santa's reindeer?"

Max smirks. "I thought it was a nice touch."

I tug on his arm, and as we head up toward the stage—reluctantly—Bob Krampus says, "I promise I won't show favoritism just because Cole will be representing my reindeer."

The crowd laughs while I roll my eyes.

When we reach the stage, Max and I stand shoulder to shoulder, and I attempt to look as happy and pleased as can be, because that's part of the competition, embodying the spirit of Christmas, despite the urge I feel to kick over the plastic candy cane that's a few feet away.

"And lastly," Bob Krampus says, just as I see movement off to the left.

Cindy Louis, and two women pushing her in a wheelchair across the lawn. From the red hair peeking out from under a winter hat, I spot Storee heading right toward us. "We have Storee Taylor, representing Cindy Louis." Bob Krampus looks up from his notes. With a jolly grin, he says, "Now, I *might* be playing favorites when it comes to our beloved Cindy Louis. Storee, please join us up on the stage. Don't worry, no one is near the river for you to knock them in."

I nearly snort out loud but keep it together as Storee climbs the steps and stops...unfortunately right next to me.

Immediately I'm hit with her perfume, which smells more like an ocean breeze than the familiar scent of gingerbread and pine that I associate with living here.

Next, I feel her warmth as she sidles up close, her arm brushing against mine, sending a shiver all the way up my spine and then back down to my toes.

"Freezing," she says. "Isn't it?"

"I don't think the contestants are allowed to talk to each other," I mumble.

"Really?" Max says, leaning forward to look at me. "Where did it say that in the rule book?"

"It didn't," Storee says, leaning forward as well. "He just tends to not want to hear my voice whenever we're around each other."

"Ah, well, if it makes you feel better, I don't like hearing his voice when he's around me," Max says.

Storee laughs as I scowl at my best friend.

He reaches his hand out and says, "I'm Atlas, but this big lug calls me Max. I'm his best friend and his holly jolly sidekick. Don't think we ever officially met."

"Atlas, it's so nice to meet you." Storee shakes his hand. "I'm Storee Taylor, and apparently a thorn in the big lug's side. Not sure how that happened, but it seems over time he developed a strong distaste for little ol' me."

"A strong distaste?" Max asks as Bob Krampus drones on about the tradition of the Christmas Kringle, acting as though it dates back to the 1800s for the people who have gathered around, when in reality we haven't even reached a decade yet. "How could he have developed a strong distaste? I didn't even know he tasted you, unless... Dude, did you forget to tell me something?"

"I never once tasted her," I say, the words feeling really stupid as they fly out of my mouth.

"What a loss," Storee says. "He could have had a real feast."

"Jesus," I mutter. "We are in public."

"And if you were in private, would this conversation be different?" Max asks with a little waggle of his brows.

This was a bad idea. I knew it might backfire on me, having Max by my side, but I didn't think it would be this quickly.

"Can you please be quiet? I'm trying to listen to Bob Krampus," I say, gesturing to the town Santa who has built his life around becoming the epitome of a ho-ho-hoing head elf.

"Oh, I forgot," Max says and then whispers to Storee, though I'm between them and can hear everything. "He was always a Goody Two-shoes in school."

"Really?" Storee asks. I can feel her eyes scanning me. "A Goody Two-shoes? I don't buy it."

"And then we come to this year's competition," Bob Krampus says with force in his voice, clearly annoyed with the chattering behind him. It shuts us all up as we stand in a row, directing our attention to the head of the show. "We'll be testing these brave souls on their Christmas prowess. Can they rival the eggnog of Prancer's Libations? Can they cut a candy cane as well as Jefferson Chadwick? Are they able to dazzle Tanya over at Warm Your Spirits with their take on fruitcake? Will they blind us with their brilliant light display, or tap right into our hearts with their rendition of a favorite Christmas song?" Bob Krampus gestures to us.

"Only time will tell, but over the course of the next few weeks, leading up to Christmas Eve, these brave souls will be taking part in a series of competitions that will determine if they really have what it takes to be the Christmas Kringle."

The crowd cheers, and I can already feel my competitive spirit kick up a notch.

Did I ever see myself being so involved in the town that I'd learn how to make fruitcake to earn points toward a Christmas competition? Never.

But now that I'm in it, I'm *in it*. There is no pulling out.

Looking at the competition up here, I can tell that Ursula will be a challenge. Jimmy is a joke, and Dr. Pedigree will peter out toward the end like she did last year. It's really between me, Ursula, and Storee, and I'll be damned if I'll see *her* up here on December 25th, receiving the robe, crown, and scepter that are awarded to the Christmas Kringle.

Over my dead fucking body.

"We'll be keeping track of their progress up on the leaderboard next to my house, and this goes further than just the competitions. It's up to you, our friends and family, to report back to us if you can feel the Christmas spirit from our contestants. For instance, if one of the Kringle-ees is walking down the street wearing antlers and a festive sweater." Max elbows me, and I know immediately what he's thinking. "Or if they wish you a merry Christmas. Or if they somehow sprinkle a little bit of that holiday magic on your day."

Christ.

This is going to be a full-time job.

"Because this honor is deep-rooted in the tradition of this town."

Okay, Bob Krampus, bring it down a notch. There are just few out-of-towners here, so remember the audience—we all know how deep-rooted it is. Not.

"So good luck to our contestants and may the best Kringle-ee win!"

The crowd cheers again, and then Bob turns around and levels a serious look at us. "Meet me in my house to go over the rules."

Okay.

We all head off the stage while Bob finishes up and follow Mrs. Claus, aka Sylvia Krampus, into their storybook house that's just off to the right of the stage.

Looking like it was plucked right out of *Snow White and the Seven Dwarves*, the house has a thatched roof, Bavarian-style siding, and lights sprinkled on every surface of the outside.

I've been in the cottage a few times to help Bob with some chores, like painting the living room and changing out the kitchen sink, so the dwelling is nothing new to me. The house is picturesque on the outside and like a holiday card come to life on the inside, with its green-and-red plaid wallpaper, red carpet, and white doilies on every surface. If anyone lives with the theme of Christmas for their entire life, it's Bob and Sylvia Krampus.

"Right this way," Sylvia coos. "Let me get you some hot chocolate—it was quite chilly out there." Dressed in a red dress with a white frilly apron and bonnet, Sylvia has also committed to the part, allowing us to live in her world where Santa isn't just magic, but real, in the flesh, with the wife to prove it.

We all file into the living room where Bob's green recliner is angled toward the age-old TV, a wooden magazine holder next to the chair full of crossword puzzle books that seem like they're ruffled through on the daily. A pair of spectacles rests on an end table, along with a giant remote control the size of a laptop. What are the spectacles for if the remote is big enough to require two hands?

"Wow, I've never been in here before," Storee says. "It's so...real."

"Did you think it was like a movie set?" I ask. "Real on the outside, plywood on the inside? They actually live here."

She gives me a death look and then says, "I meant that this is what I'd expect Santa's house to look like."

"That's because he *is* Santa," I whisper to her.

"You know, you were much nicer when we were younger."

"Funny how people change," I say, crossing my arms over my chest.

"I guess so. And here I thought we could be friendly and help each other out in this competition."

"Ha!" I guffaw loud enough for Jimmy, Beatrice, and Ursula to glance in our direction.

Our groups have split up, so it's the older Kringle-ees—*hate that term*—and the younger Kringle-ees standing in circles talking to each other.

"Help you? No chance." I shake my head.

"I think he said earlier that he's taking you down," Max says, leaning toward Storee.

"I did not say 'take her down.'"

"I think you did," Max argues.

"I don't think so."

"Ehh, I think so."

I open my mouth to disagree once again when Storee steps in. "What's the hate for? Last I remember, we were pleasant to each other back…oh wait." Storee rolls her eyes dramatically. "Oh my God, is this because I called you Connor at the Kringle Krampus?"

"She called you Connor?" Max says with such a large smile on his face that it grates on my nerves. "You didn't tell me that, man."

"Probably because he was too embarrassed," Storee says.

"I was not embarrassed," I say.

"Um, you seemed embarrassed."

"Oh really?" I ask, folding my arms. "Please tell me what that looks like."

"Okay," she says and then shakes out her body. Then, on a deep breath, she puckers her entire face, clasps her hands in front of her—shoulders inward—and then shifts side to side, making a fucking show of it.

It's ridiculous.

Absurd.

And has Max bending over—actually bending over—in laughter.

Jesus.

Christ.

"That's not what I looked like," I scoff.

Storee pauses. "I mean, maybe your face was a little sourer looking, but it's hard to mimic."

Max is still laughing, his hands on his knees as he gasps for air. I nudge his shin, reminding him whose holly jolly sidekick he is—because at the moment, it seems like he's forgetting.

"Oh, that's amazing." Max nods. "Yup, I've seen that face before."

"Bullshit," I shout just as Bob Krampus walks into the house, his overwhelming presence sucking the air right out of the room.

"Now, is that part of the Christmas spirit?" he booms in the small space.

"It's not," Storee says, shaking her head. "Very much the opposite."

"You are correct, Storee."

Jesus, suck up much?

"This is a gentle reminder that you are now my special elves. Not everyone is picked out of the applicants to be a Kringle-ee. We have room for five contestants, and because of that, you must hold up your end of the bargain, which includes not shouting 'bullshit' in Santa's house."

I swallow, feeling a hard lump rise in my throat. You never want to be told off by Bob Krampus. The baritone of his voice alone will make your nerves shiver. "Sorry," I mutter.

He offers me a curt nod. "Now, where is my wife?"

"Getting us hot chocolate," Max says and then elbows me.

"Yes," I say. "And I was just about to go help."

Now look who's the suck up.

Points at self.

"You're a good lad," Bob says as he makes his way toward his chair. He lets out a huff, a gruff, undoes the belt buckle that cinches his waist, and then flops back into his chair, the footrest following with a lift to his legs. "That's the good stuff," he says.

Looks like Santa is taking a break, so I head back to the kitchen, where Sylvia is starting to pick up a tray full of mugs.

"Here, let me get that for you," I say before she breaks one of her brittle bones trying to lift it.

"Why, thank you so much, dear." She pats my cheek. "You know, I'm rooting for you, Cole. When I saw your name appear in the applications, it truly warmed my heart. After everything you've been through with your parents, seeing that Christmas spirit reawaken within you, it just...well, it brings a tear to my eye."

I smile kindly at Sylvia. "Thank you. That means a lot to me." And I mean that, even though her compliment makes me feel like shit. Because little does she know the real reason I'm doing all of this.

She presses her hand to my back and together we head back to the living room, where we hand out hot chocolate to everyone, the biggest cup going to Bob.

He sits up in his chair, takes a large sip, and then sighs as the chocolate sticks to the hairs of his mustache. With the back of his beefy hand, he wipes it away and then addresses us.

"Mrs. Claus will hand you all folders. Ursula, Jimmy, and Beatrice, you're familiar with the folder, but for you newbies, it will have everything you need to know about the contest. The dates of each competition, how the competition will be judged, and who it will be judged by. These will be your bibles moving forward, so don't lose them, because they won't be replaced." He pauses as Sylvia makes the rounds with the sacred folders. "Please open them up to page one."

Fumbling with our hot chocolate and the folders, we all manage to get them open.

"By turning in your application, you've accepted the responsibility of holding this tradition and this town in the best of lights. Meaning you are a representative now of Kringle, of the businesses, the people, and of Mrs. Claus and me. Under no circumstances will we tolerate anything less. This is your code of conduct. Moving forward, we expect you to stand out among all of the holiday tidings. We want people walking around town knowing you're a Kringle-ee, which is why we've decided to make you wear sashes this year."

Sashes?

What kind of sashes...?

Sylvia opens a trunk in the middle of the room and pulls out hand-made, freshly stitched sashes in a vibrant gold that have bold lettering down the length, designating us as the Kringle-ees.

And fringe is at the end of each...with dangling pom-poms.

Yikes.

"If you appear in public, these must be worn. Get used to them, because they're your new adornment. Consider yourself a tree and this your tree topper. You can't go anywhere without it. If you are caught not wearing your sash, then points will be marked from your grand total, so keep that in mind. We have increased the number of spies this year as well, who will keep an eye on what you're doing, what you're saying, and how you're acting around town. So always think to yourself: Someone is watching me."

Perfect, just what I want as the man who likes to hide out in the rein-deer barn, away from humans.

What did I get myself into?

"And if you have any questions, feel free to come visit me and Mrs. Claus during off hours. And if you do come to visit, we're no strangers to cookies as a gift."

He's really not. I learned that the hard way.

Bob takes a sip of his drink and then leans back in his chair. "Any questions now?"

If we ask, do we need to bring you cookies later?

Jimmy raises his hand, and Bob calls on him. "Yes?"

"Um, will the Eggnog Wars be alcoholic again this year?"

Bob shakes his head. "No. After nearly poisoning our judges last year, the competition has now switched to nonalcoholic."

"The judges were almost poisoned last year?" Storee asks.

"Yes, if you lived here, you would know that," I mutter to her, which grants me a serious side-eye.

"Will Sherry be judging the Upcycle Christmas event again?" Beatrice asks.

"Yes," Bob says. "And before you say anything, we've already talked to her about you being an applicant, and she said she will judge you fairly."

Max leans into Storee and mutters, "Beatrice is now dating Sherry's ex-husband."

Storee nods in understanding and then sips her hot cocoa.

"Will there be a secondary judge to help her stay neutral?" Beatrice continues. "I appreciate her willingness to be fair, but I don't trust her bias."

"I'll bring it up with the council and see what we can do."

Beatrice nods. "Thank you.

"What about the candy cane making?" Jimmy says, not raising his hand this time, taking a cue from Beatrice. "Will Jefferson be offering classes this year?"

Bob shakes his head. "No. After the debacle from two years ago, he's told us he refuses to give away his secrets, so if you want firsthand lessons, take them from his competitor an hour away. That information is in the packet."

"Theodore Garvey took lessons from him and opened up his own candy shop over in Clayton," Max says to Storee. Not sure why he's giving her the lowdown.

"That's messed up. Why would people go to him for lessons?" Storee asks.

"Because Jefferson likes to see just how well his lessons can transfer over, like a game of telephone. If the contestant does well, he takes credit for it. If they don't, he blames Theodore and his inability to understand sugar."

"Any other questions?" Bob asks.

"Um, are we going to be judged on past indiscretions?" Storee asks.

The room falls silent as Bob straightens up in his chair, the squeaking of the hinges filling the silence as his eyes land on Storee.

"This is a clean slate, my dear." He smiles softly at her. "Anything that might have happened in the past involving Mrs. Fiskers or the signature tree…or the hot chocolate stash, they've all been expunged from your record. We're just happy that Cindy has family back in town. She's been… well, she's not been herself."

From the corner of my eye, I catch the frown that tugs on Storee's lips. It's brief, but I see it.

"We're glad we can be here for her," Storee says demurely.

"Yes, and hopefully this isn't just a one-time thing, because we love having you and your sister here," Sylvia says.

Who is we?

Sure as hell isn't me.

"Thank you," Storee says.

I can see the twinkle in her eyes.

The appreciation in her gaze.

And this is exactly what I was afraid of.

She's putting on a show for the people of this town who don't know the truth.

She's going to walk around Kringle with her gold fucking sash draped over her shoulder, announcing her bid for the town's most sought-after Christmas honor, and people are going to be so thrilled, so pleased, so over-fucking-joyed that she's here to help Cindy that they won't even see what's truly going on.

She doesn't care about them. She made that clear ten years ago. She's just a con artist.

Yup, I said it.

A con artist.

"Are there any other questions?" Bob asks, looking like he's one hot chocolate sip away from passing out in his recliner.

When no one answers, he nods, his eyes drifting shut. "Then best of luck to you all. May the cheeriest and most skilled win."

With that, we all leave our mugs on Sylvia's tray and head out of the house, to an empty park.

"So," Max says to Storee, "looks like your family went back home."

Storee sticks her hands in her coat pockets as she glances around. "Looks like it."

"Don't worry." He clasps my shoulder. "My good friend, Cole, will walk you back to your house since you're both headed in the same direction."

"Oh, I wasn't going back home," I say, wondering what the hell my soon-to-be-ex-best friend is up to.

"No?" He quirks one brow. "Then what were you planning on doing?"

"Uh…" I drag out, nothing coming to mind.

"That's what I thought. Now be the gentleman you are, wear your sash with pride, and escort this lovely lady so she doesn't have to walk alone on a dark, wintry night."

I really shouldn't have named him my holly jolly sidekick.

I should have known this is what he was going to do.

When I spoke of him being my sidekick, I meant in the pursuit of the Christmas Kringle title—not a wingman trying to set me up with the girl next door.

"It's really okay. I can see from the pain on his face that he doesn't want to walk me home," Storee says. "I have no problem walking alone."

"Nonsense," Max announces in a cheery voice. "He'd be more than happy to."

I would not, actually.

I would rather army-crawl my way home across broken glass ornaments.

He shoves my shoulder, encouraging me to take the lead.

I let out a heavy sigh. "Come on, let's get this over with."

"Wow, you can really feel the Christmas spirit pouring off him," Storee says.

Max beams with pride as he looks me up and down. "Yes, he's one of a kind." He then salutes us and adds, "See you tomorrow, bright and early—we have some planning to do. And don't forget your sash." He pats my face. "Love you, pal." Then he takes off.

A part of me feels that he's going to get way more joy out of this than I am.

Now alone with Storee, I nod toward Whistler Lane, the street I live on and the street she's visiting. "Let's go."

I take off at a brisk pace, forcing her to catch up to me. "You really don't have to do this," she says.

"It's fine. I'm walking back home anyway."

And then we fall into silence as we make our way across Ornament Park, where the turf grass is heated from below, keeping it in a constant state of Christmas green. The town took their time deciding if they wanted to put in the heated turf with drains, given the massive expense it would incur, but after some serious debates and consideration, Bob Krampus made the executive decision that it would be great for the town and the events they hold year-round to have the lawn open all the time rather than having it covered in snow. There was pushback, there was celebration, but all in all...I was on the team of *I don't give a crap*.

"So," Storee says. "You know I have a hard time being quiet when I'm next to someone I'm familiar with."

"Yes, learned that when you drove me away from my sandwich."

"Drove you away from your sandwich? Uh, I remember it differently. Leaving was your choice," she says.

"You were insufferable."

She pauses in her steps, and I can feel her eyes on me. "Insufferable? That's a pretty strong word for such a small interaction. You know, the word *insufferable* almost seems like it stems from you harboring some sort of distaste for me."

I glance in her direction and nod toward the street to keep her moving. Thankfully, she follows.

"Harboring distaste? What makes you think that?" I ask, even though she just called me out.

"Uh, the fact that you're being so rude."

"I'm always rude. Ask Max."

"You weren't rude when we were younger," she counters.

"Age will do that to you."

"I grew older too. You don't see me flaring my nostrils like a bull ready to charge."

I grimace as I glance in her direction again. "A bull ready to charge? You've got me all wrong."

"No, I think I've pegged you pretty well," she says as we both walk across the near-empty streets of Kringle, only a few people milling about on the sidewalks, doing some window-shopping before the stores open back up tomorrow.

Since it's past eight o'clock, there are very few places still open. Prancer's Libations, a bar, is one of them. And Poinsettia Pizza is always open until the early morning because of the people who funnel out of Prancer's and right into the pizza shop to score a slice.

"I can practically hear the snorting now," she adds.

"I think you're hearing yourself."

"I do not snort," she says in defiance.

"Says the person breathing heavily as we casually walk down the street."

"Hey," she snaps. "Not all of us are used to this altitude."

"The Myrrh-cantile has oxygen canisters if you need a shot, although they won't open until tomorrow."

"I don't need a canister shot," she says, sounding cranky about it.

"No shame in it," I say.

"I just need a moment to adjust. While you grew cranky as we got older, I adapted to sea level."

"That's all you think has changed?" I ask. "Don't recall you being as insufferable."

"Oh my God," she says, her voice carrying through the cool night air. "What the hell is wrong with you?"

"Nothing's wrong with me," I say as our houses come into view.

"Uh, yes, something is wrong with you, because you were never this rude before. And don't blame it on age. So tell me what's happening. What did I do that you don't approve of?"

"Nothing," I say.

"You're a liar," she says as we reach my house and I start to turn down the path that leads to my porch steps. She grabs my shoulder, halting me. "I know we were friendly as kids, and we tried being pen pals that one year and I failed at replying...wait...is that it? You're mad that I wasn't a good pen pal?"

"Jesus, no," I say. "Do you really think I'm that petty?"

"I don't know—you tell me."

"I'm not," I say, folding my arms.

"Okay, then what's your problem?"

"You really want to know?" I say, since she seems to be so insistent.

"Yeah, I really want to know."

"Okay, fine. You don't deserve to be in the Kringle competition," I say.

Her brow creases, her shock clear at my statement. Not sure why. It's clear as day—anyone would be able to understand my reasoning.

"I don't deserve to be in it?" Now her face morphs into humor as she mimics my stance, arms crossed over her chest, her puffy coat nearly swallowing her whole. "And who are you to decide who deserves to be in the Kringle competition?"

"Uh, someone who has lived here their entire life."

"Eh, barely a qualification."

"Well, I'm more qualified than you."

She slowly nods. "Uh-huh. You know, Aunt Cindy was telling me that she was very surprised to see that you were even at the event, let alone that you were called up on stage as a Kringle-ee. One might say it's very unlike you."

"It is," I say, not denying it.

"So this unexpected entrance, does it have anything to do with me?"

"Yup," I say, spitting out the truth, which seems to surprise her.

"Really?" she asks, standing taller.

"Yes," I reply. "You don't deserve to win. You aren't a part of this town, and with all the buzz you're getting by taking part in the competition, I decided that I will do everything I can to make sure you lose."

Her jaw falls open for a moment before she closes it.

"Well, I'm doing this for Aunt Cindy," she says.

"And I'm doing this for everyone in town who believes in the spirit of Christmas."

"I believe in the spirit of Christmas," she says.

"Says the girl who hasn't been here in years."

"Uh, it's called going to college and getting a job."

"Still could have visited."

"What I did on my vacation time is none of your business," she snaps.

"Clearly it wasn't spending time with your aunt Cindy."

Her brows form a V on her forehead while her eyes grow angrier by the second. "How dare you."

"How dare I?" I say, pointing to my chest. "How dare *you!*"

"Oh, great comeback." She rolls her eyes.

"It wasn't a comeback—it was a statement. How dare you."

"No...how dare *you.*" She pokes my chest.

Flustered, I poke her shoulder. "How dare *you*."

"Stop repeating what I'm saying or else this will go nowhere."

"Yeah, just like your chances at becoming Christmas Kringle."

"Oh, and you think you'll be able to shed the grumpiness and become a holly jolly asshole?"

"Pardon me?" I blink a few times. "If anyone is an asshole, it's you for not coming around the last ten years."

The gasp that falls past her lips could wake the entire neighborhood. None too pleased, she takes a step forward so we're toe to toe, her eyes burning with anger, her fists clenched at her sides. "You know what? You just made this personal...*Connor*."

Oh...that...troll.

Nostrils flaring, I stare down at her, meeting her gaze. "You know damn well it's Cole."

"Oops," she says, not even sorry, "my mistake."

And then we stand there staring at each other, animosity sizzling between us, building into a dark cloud that I'm sure will stay until she decides to part ways with the town she hates so much.

She pulls her sash out of her pocket and drapes it over her head. When it's fitting her properly, she says, "You, Cole, are about to see an exhibition on what true Christmas spirit is all about."

Meeting her intensity, because I'm never one to back down from a challenge, I slip my sash over my head as well. "You have *no* idea the kind of Christmas spirit I possess. I cough up tinsel on the daily."

Her nose crinkles. "Yeah, well, I drink eggnog like it's water."

"I bench Santa's sleigh...with Bob Krampus ho-ho-hoing in the driver's seat."

Her body grows more tense. "I dream of sugar plum fairies every night."

"I can pull candy canes out of my ears," I say, realizing this makes zero sense but finding it more important to drive home the point.

"My sweat smells like freshly iced cookies."

"My hair is as coarse as the straw the reindeers eat."

"My...my..." She glances around, clearly trying to think of anything that could compete. "My nipples shine just as bright as the lights on every single house in this town."

Silence falls between us because...straw hair and twinkling nipples, is that really what this has come down to?

Yes.

Yes, it has.

"Party tricks aren't going to win you the Christmas Kringle." I motion to her chest with my finger. "So you might want to cover those neon nips."

"Yeah, well, feeding the reindeer your hair isn't going to win it either," she replies.

"We'll just have to see then, won't we?"

"I guess we shall." She takes a step back. "I would say good luck, but I hope you fall flat on your face."

"And push someone into the river?" I ask, causing her entire expression to morph into shock.

She points a shaking finger at me. "It is on, Connor. It is so on. Watch your back, because I'm coming for the title."

"It's Cole," I virtually bark. "And if anyone needs to watch their back, it's you."

"Oooh, awesome comeback." She rolls her eyes. "See you around... Connor."

And then she takes off toward Cindy's house.

"I never should have walked you home," I call out.

"Trust me, it was more unpleasant for me. By the way, you have hot chocolate on your upper lip."

Then she slips into her house while I quickly wipe at my mouth, most likely falling for her trick.

Well…it's official; she is enemy number one. This only makes me more determined to do everything in my power to make sure she doesn't earn the Christmas Kringle crown.

CHAPTER SEVEN
STOREE

Shots have been fired; the tension is thick.
Bob Krampus is oblivious, just our charming St. Nick.

For preparations begin! The Eggnog Wars are up.
Who will make the best eggy drink in a cup?

Will it be Cole with his hazelnut rendition?
Or will it be Storee with her ginger addition?

Our judges Frank and Thachary will soon let us know,
on this beautiful, stormy day all covered in snow.

"I DON'T KNOW, AUNT CINDY, this seems like a lot of ginger to add to a drink."

"Are you questioning me?" she asks as she sits at the bistro table in her kitchen, watching me like a hawk.

"I am, actually," I say on a wince, knowing damn well I *shouldn't* be questioning her and her recipe since it came in second last year—as she has told me several times since we woke up this morning.

But second is second, and we're not gunning for second; we're gunning for first. First in every category.

After the other night when Cole said I didn't deserve to win, something lit within me. How dare he decide that for himself. I might not live here, but I love my aunt Cindy. I love the magic she created for us growing up, and I will do just about anything to prove someone wrong—Cole being that someone.

He thought he was shaming me, but he has no idea what he did. He poked the beast, and my chompers are ready to take him down.

"Perhaps we add some sugar, something to counteract the balance in the flavor," I say.

Aunt Cindy shakes her head as Taran enters the room, pine garland hanging around her neck. "Where are the scissors?"

"In the drawer under the telephone," Aunt Cindy says.

"Thanks." Taran finds the scissors and then takes off.

Taran, when not "cleaning the crevices," has been decorating the house. And given her determination to make everything perfect, she has spent a great deal of time measuring out the lengths of the garlands, making sure each drape matches the one next to it. Her bows are perfectly centered, the length of each ribbon precisely the same. And don't get me started on the lights she hung up around the living room windows. They're all facing inward, which took her a ludicrous amount of time. Hence why only the living room and now the hallway are decorated.

"Now, back to the ginger," Aunt Cindy says from her perch. "Just listen to me, because I know what I'm doing."

"Okay," I say on a sigh before dumping a tablespoon of ginger into the cup of eggnog.

"Now, give it a good stir and take a taste."

"You want me to drink this?"

"How else are you supposed to perfect your eggnog without tasting it?" Maybe with a touch less ginger, that's how.

"Uh, well, I didn't really think about it." I start stirring the eggnog with one of Aunt Cindy's glass stir sticks, the seasoning having a tough time blending with the thick concoction.

"These are things you need to think about, dear. Now go ahead, drink up."

I'd rather not.

It's all…clumpy, and the smell is unpleasant.

I know for a fact that this will singe my taste buds. There's no way this is going to taste anything like, as Aunt Cindy said, *Christmas in a cup.*

"We don't have all day," she says. "Competition is tonight, so we need to make sure this is right. Go on, drink."

Talk about pressure.

And from my aunt, of all people.

Knowing she's not going to drop it, I set the stir stick on the folded towel on the rose-pink marble counter, and I bring the hobnail glass up to my lips.

Oh fuck, that smells.

"You know, I think I can already tell this won't be good."

"Storee Taylor, we're never going to win with that kind of attitude—now, drink!"

This freaking old lady…

I smile at her, then bring the rim of the glass to my lips, tip my head back and sip.

Oh.

My.

Fuck.

Immediately I can feel hairs sprout from under my nose, my armpits…and my chest. The potency of ginger has instantly yeti-fied me. This drink embodies that term *hair of the dog.*

I set the glass down, brace both hands on the counter, and then cough.

And cough.

And cough.

Until I feel my stomach revolt.

I quickly run to the sink, turn on the water, and then point the faucet directly into my mouth as I try to wash the burning sensation of the ginger off my taste buds.

"Dear heavens," Aunt Cindy says from her table.

I turn off the water and stare down into the stainless-steel sink as I try to catch my breath.

"Was it…was it bad?" she asks.

How could you tell?

I swallow, praying that I didn't just lose all my ability to taste as I look over at my aunt, her expression innocent and genuinely concerned.

"It was horrific."

She leans back in her chair, her hand going to her chin, rubbing it a few times. "Hmm, maybe that's the amount I use for making actual gingerbread, not a drink. I tend to forget in my older years."

Oh.

My.

God.

"Maybe we should use that recipe card that you suggested," Aunt Cindy continues.

What a novel idea!

Trying not to grow irritated, I say, "Yes, I think that would be great."

"It's above the fridge, dear. Grab my recipe box."

Gladly.

I reach above the fridge, feel around for a box, and when I find it, I pull it down and then bring it over to Aunt Cindy. I take a seat next to her as she thumbs through the cards.

While she searches for her recipe, I look around the familiar kitchen with its dark mahogany wood, pink-and-white damask wallpaper, and her rose-and-gray marbled counters that I thought were a bold choice when I was young but can appreciate now for their timeless charm.

The kitchen was always one of my favorite places that she decorated because she matched the aesthetic to a gingerbread theme with her tea towels, cookie jars, and miniature winter village. It was playful and not as fussy with tradition as the front of her house. More whimsical, more *her*.

"Ah-ha, here we are." She lowers her reading glasses from the top of her head and places them over her eyes as she scans the recipe. "Goodness, yes, we were wrong with the one tablespoon of ginger."

Funny how she uses the term "we" so loosely.

"Ah, and we do need allspice too." She lifts her glasses. "You're going to have to run to the Myrrh-cantile to grab some more eggnog and allspice."

I saw that coming.

The wonderful thing about the Eggnog Wars is that we don't have to make the eggnog ourselves, which I was worried about. They give a basic nog mixture to all the contestants, and it's up to us to flavor it properly and give the judges a reason to choose ours based on the additions we make.

Which is great, because I have zero idea how to even begin the process of making eggnog—and I'm also not interested in learning it. I like the thick drink, but I'm not sure I want to know how it's made.

I stand up from the table. "Do you need anything else while I'm out?"

"No, dear, I think that will be it."

"Okay," I say.

"Don't be long—we have work to do."

COLE

So she's off to the store, looking
for eggnog and allspice.
Perhaps she might run into someone
who is not so nice.

"I'm nice."

Narrator: Sir, I have the receipts to prove otherwise.

"You're telling the story. If you're not happy with my attitude, then change it."

Narrator: Fine… How about this, then: Golly gee, what a glorious day it is. Do you hear those birds chirping, see the vibrant colors under their wings as they puff their feathery chests? It's so beautiful, it makes me want to cry… That better?

"Don't fucking do that again."

Narrator: Then mind your own business and carry on.

"Do you really think the traditional route is the way to go?" Max asks as he leans against the spice rack in the Myrrh-cantile.

"Yes," I say. "Everyone likes tradition."

"Yes, but this is Frank and Thachary we're talking about," Max says. "You've seen the cocktails they've created at Prancer's. They're not traditional in the slightest."

I pause as I reach for the cinnamon. "They're traditional," I say.

Max blinks a few times. "Uh, if you don't recall, they have a drink labeled Santa's Balls."

"I thought Krampus forced them to take that off the menu."

"It's on the secret menu," Max says.

"There's a secret menu?" I turn toward Max, who slowly nods.

"If you ever came out of your cave during the Christmas season, then you'd know that there's a secret menu during the month of December. All the banned drinks come back. Santa's Balls is on there, as well as Antler Sex, Tinsel Tits, and the very problematic Reindeer Hole."

I wince. "I still have nightmares about that drink."

"Exactly. But do you see what I'm saying?" Max says in a low voice as someone walks by us.

If there's one thing I learned during the Christmas Kringle orientation, it's that I'm going to have to step out of my comfort zone and be the jolliest dickhead I can muster.

So I straighten up, put on a large smile, and announce, "Merry Christmas! May your season be full of glad tidings."

The shopper nervously glances at me and walks away—clearly a tourist. Damn it, wasted some mustered-up cheer on the wrong person.

"May your season be full of glad tidings?" Max questions me. "What the hell was that?"

"I don't know," I say. "I'm new at this."

"New at what?"

"Uh, well, to name a few...talking to people I don't know, smiling, acting like I'm pleased to see another human walk by me, and offering a Christmas-y hello. All out of my wheelhouse, man."

"Huh, you're right." He scratches his chin. "Making a mental note to come up with some seasonal greetings for you. Now, back to Frank and—"

"Merry Christmas," someone says as they walk past us.

I curtsy, pulling at the hem of my jacket—for God knows what reason—and say, "Merry Christmas, dear sir. And top of the morning."

He smiles and walks around the corner while I feel Max's questioning eyes trained on me.

"Dude...the curtsy?"

"Shut up," I mutter. "I told you I'm not good at this shit. I feel like a goddamn robot out here trying to humanize myself."

"Well, saying *top of the morning* is not the way to do it. It's Christmas, not St. Patrick's Day."

"It just slipped out when I was mid-curtsy."

"Well, get it together. We can't have you—"

"Merry Christmas," an elderly woman says as she shuffles by.

Jesus Christ!

"By George, it is a merry Christmas," I say with a pump of my arm. "Can't get enough of those baubles, am I right?"

She smiles. "Oh yes. So beautiful."

"The most beautiful," I say, flashing my teeth because at this point, I don't even know what a genuine smile feels like.

When she's out of earshot, Max mutters, "Do I even need to say anything?"

"Nope." I shake my head in shame.

"It's actually sickening to watch you pretend to be in such a cheery mood. When was the last time you smiled this much?"

"Probably this past summer when you accidentally chopped into the water line at the farm and ran around like a lunatic, screaming for someone to turn off the water."

Max's face falls flat. "That was not funny."

"I thought it was." I smirk just as another person approaches. Gearing up, I say, "Season's greetings and good—" My words fall flat as I catch a glimmer of a gold sash and the flash of red hair.

When Storee's gray eyes meet mine, the smirk that tugs on the corner of her lips is unmistakable. "Why, season's greetings to you as well. What a fine morning to see such a cheery turd in the middle of the Myrrh-cantile."

The smile freezes on my face. "I was thinking the same thing—how it's so wonderful to come face to face with someone who has seen rock bottom on so many occasions. Truly gives one perspective."

Her lip twitches, but her fake smile doesn't fade. "And on such a bright and cheery Saturday morning, it's shocking and yet a pleasure to know that someone who truly smells worse than a rancid dumpster is still able to live their best life in the herbs and spices aisle."

Max snorts next to me but covers his mouth with his hand to suppress his obvious delight.

"Ah ha ha ha." I fake laugh, Storee joining in with me. "Yes, quite a season of giving, don't you think? And I see that you're giving away your ability to care about your appearance. Truly remarkable how comfortable you are looking so...how do I say it...ahh, like an aroused middle toe."

She playfully pushes at my chest and laughs as someone walks by. "Merry Christmas," we say in unison.

When the person is gone, she says, "An aroused middle toe, huh? Seems to me like someone might have a foot fetish."

"Ah, but that would mean I'd be into you, and as you know for a fact, that couldn't be further from the truth. So please take your toe head, have a blessed Christmas, and begone."

"I would love nothing more than to transport myself away from the putrid scent pouring out of your mouth, but unfortunately for me, you're standing in front of the spices, and I need to purchase some."

"Ah, I see." I don't move to the side though. "Unfortunately, ogres can't purchase these spices. You're going to have to go to Clayton for that."

"I heard of such a thing," she says as she nods to someone who walks by. "Which makes me wonder how on earth you were allowed into the store."

"If you're trying to piggyback off my insult by claiming I'm an ogre, I'm here to tell you you're going to have to do better than that." When I look up, I see Sylvia turn down our aisle, so I straighten up and offer her a demure wave. "Mrs. Claus, you look stunning this fine morning. How is the mister?"

At the appearance of Mrs. Claus, Storee straightens up too and turns toward her.

"Oh, he's gearing up for a day of boisterous laughter."

"I can only imagine," I say. "And I must say, you need to hand out that hot chocolate recipe. I haven't had any in years and now I'm craving it like a little schoolboy." I catch Storee's smirk out of the corner of my eye.

"Oh, you are such a dear. But you know I can't give that recipe away, Cole. Although I'm more than happy to make you some any time you come over."

"Don't tempt me—I'll be there every night."

She chuckles and then squeezes Storee's arm as she walks by. "Always lovely to see you. You have quite the blush in your cheeks this morning."

"Oh, do I?" she asks.

"You do. Maybe it's present company that's giving you such a stain."

Storee glances at me and then back at Mrs. Claus. I steady myself for the insult, for the denial, but then she says, "Oh, you know, you very well might be right."

Sylvia laughs. "Well, you three have a wonderful day. Can't wait for the Eggnog Wars tonight."

"Me either," I call out. "It's going to be the grandest of occasions."

Once Sylvia is down the aisle—after picking up some flour—Max turns to me. "Dude, I don't even know who you are anymore."

I press my hand to my forehead. "I don't either, man."

"Well, as fun as this has been, I must be going. I have a competition to win tonight," Storee says as she nudges me out of the way and grabs some allspice and nutmeg. What kind of drink does she have planned? I glance in her basket as well and notice a box of gingerbread cookies. When she catches my gaze, she gasps and moves her basket behind her. "My God, are you trying to scope out the competition?"

"Yes," I say, looking around. "Have you seen Ursula? Because she's the only one I'm worried about."

Storee's face flattens. "Cute." She waves to Max. "Always nice seeing you, Atlas."

"You as well, Storee. Good luck tonight."

"Thank you."

And she takes off, stopping to grab some sugar, and then she's down the aisle.

"You know, I think she's pretty nice, don't—*oof*." Max buckles over and grips his stomach where I've just tapped him in anger. Yes...tapped in anger. Not a punch, but not a playful slap, either. An anger tap. "Dude, what the fuck was that for?"

"I don't need you being nice to her and wishing her good luck. Whose team are you on?"

"The abusive one, clearly," he says.

"As my holly jolly sidekick, your allegiance is to me, so no wishing her good luck or thinking she's nice. She is enemy number one. We hate her. Repeat that to yourself. We. Hate. Her."

"Seems pretty harsh to hate someone, don't you think? Can't we say something like...we disagree with her heavily?"

"That doesn't sound good when you say it over and over again."

"We disagree with her heavily, we disagree with her heavily...you know, I think I disagree with *you* heavily."

I drag my hand over my face. "Listen, we don't have time to disagree with each other heavily. Did you see what was in her basket?"

Max outlandishly gasps and presses his hand to his chest. "You did scope out the competition. How dare you." He smirks. *I really can't stand him right now.*

"I glanced in her basket because my eyes didn't want to see her stupid face."

Max chuckles. "Nice save, man."

"Thank you." I lean in closer. "Did you happen to see what she grabbed?"

"No."

"Allspice, nutmeg, and she had gingerbread cookies in her basket. I think...I think she's going out of the box."

"See?" Max pushes at my shoulder. "Told you we had to be creative."

"No, *I'm thinking...*we *must* be creative."

"Jesus." Max rolls his eyes as I start to imagine all the different eggnog concoctions we could come up with.

"Come on, we have a job to do."

CHAPTER EIGHT
STOREE

Through the hush of the wind on a crisp winter night,
they're about to find out if their eggnog is just right.

They loaded up thermoses and some tasty additions,
and headed down Krampus Court,
dead set on a mission.

"DON'T FORGET TO SMILE," AUNT Cindy says as she jabs me with her finger when we step out onto the porch. I'm holding a thermos of our concoction while Taran is helping her down the steps and into a wheelchair.

"Hey, neighbors," Martha Bawhovier says from across the street.

Decked out in matching one-piece ski outfits, both Martha and Mae look like they've come straight from a time machine dating back to 1986 where teal-and-purple was the preferred color combination, seen in every Taco Bell and splashed across paper cups. A stirring mix, especially with their winter…earmuffs? Eh, I wouldn't call either contraption an earmuff, more like a fluffy winter headband that runs from forehead to ears to the back of the head. Both have their hair pulled into high, curly ponytails, the bottled blond a fantastic addition to the whole ensemble.

If there was a contest for best dressed, my vote would go to them.

It's time to turn on the charm—because I know how important

Martha and Mae are to the competition. According to Aunt Cindy, they're both secret spies, always keeping an eye on the Kringle-ees. I call out, "Hey, neighbors. How are you this evening?" It's shocking that my jaw works given it feels like it's frozen shut from the chill in the air. How do people live here? It's like being trapped in a freezer every day of your life with no respite.

They join us on the sidewalk right in front of Aunt Cindy's house. "We're great," Mae says, giving me a quick once-over.

Since I didn't bring any Christmas clothes with me and just packed for warmth—turtlenecks, thermals, multiple pairs of flannel leggings—Aunt Cindy had me invade her closet, which means I'm wearing what I can only describe as the kitchen sink of all Christmas sweaters.

I thought it might be too flashy for the first competition—aka I didn't want to wear it—but Aunt Cindy said I had to start out with a bang, so here I am in a red knit sweater adorned with numerous bells.

Countless bells.

So many bells that the sweater sags in the front.

There are bells on the collar.

On the chest.

On the...nipples.

In the armpits!

I have to walk around with my arms slightly propped up because of all the bells.

And boy, do they jingle jangle. I'm a walking sound machine with no exact tune, just noise.

And as if that's not enough, Aunt Cindy had me pull my hair up into a bun so she could direct Taran in fastening a velvet bow with ribbons so long that they tickle my ears.

I paired the entire ensemble with my winter boots that are encased in fur—did you just think "boots with the fur" in your head? Because I do, every time I wear them.

I feel like a genuine idiot though, with the sash and all, but this is what we do for our loved ones. This is what we do to prove to the grumpy next-door neighbor that we're not to be messed with. He wants to play games? He wants to challenge me? Well, come beat the old jingle jangle with the velvet bow in her hair.

I dare you.

"You look rather festive," Martha says to me.

"Why, thank you," I say and then shimmy at her, making her laugh.

That look on her face? That's Christmas joy.

I just brought her Christmas joy with a shake of my breasts.

I bet Cole can't do that.

"Can't get enough of this sweater."

"It looks spectacular on you," Mae says. "Very becoming."

"Thank you. And look at you two, my goodness; these outfits are everything. I'm obsessed."

Martha's smile grows wider. "Some of the youth might say we're vibing."

I smile. "Yes, you're right. You two are totally vibing—"

"Merry Christmas!" a deep voice bellows off to the right.

Goddamnit.

I know that obnoxiously fake voice.

I glance to the side just in time to see Cole step off his porch with a thermos as well. And instead of looking like a jingle bell factory exploded on him, he's wearing a very fetching red flannel shirt with a green Henley underneath. His sash is draped over his expansive chest, his jeans are rolled to just above his boots, and his hair is tucked under a Santa hat, giving him this whole lumberjack Santa look that's working very well on him.

And I'm not the only one to notice.

"Oh Cole, don't you look handsome," Martha says, beaming.

Christ.

Sure, he's a good-looking man.

He has a bone structure that was made with precise angles, so the light bounces off it in a magical way.

And yeah, he has light blue eyes that are framed by very dark and long—*the prick*—eyelashes.

And when he was being made, whoever was in charge decided to grace him with height, and thick dark hair, and…glutes.

High, tight glutes.

Frankly, it's kind of rude and offensive if you ask me.

No one should be that good-looking. There must be a fatal flaw somewhere in his appearance. Perhaps a mole on the tip of his penis. One of those raised ones that throws off the symmetry of his rod, making it difficult to pump with a steady, precise thrust.

One could only hope.

"I look handsome?" he asks with a large grin while pointing to himself. "Martha and Mae, you two never cease to amaze me. Another year in the ski outfits—you two truly are timeless."

Oh.

My.

God.

Gag me.

But of course, Martha and Mae fall for his phony-baloney behavior as they coo at him, thanking him for the compliments.

Then his gaze turns on Taran, Aunt Cindy, and me.

"Ladies, I can't tell you how great it is to see you together again after all these years."

Yup, that was a jab at me and a subtle reminder to Martha and Mae that we have been gone for a while. I'm not dumb—I see what he's doing.

"I'm so happy my girls are with me," Aunt Cindy says. "They're such a joy to have in the house, and the way they've been taking care of me, leaning into the spirit of Christmas that comes from being around family; it's just wonderful."

"I could not agree more," Martha says.

I glance at Cole, who's staring at the sidewalk, a hint of insecurity in the droop of his shoulders. If I wasn't watching at that moment, I never would have seen it, because when he looks back up, he smiles.

"Well, you look great, Storee, and I'm sure you came up with a delicious eggnog, especially if Cindy was by your side the whole time."

Ew. I don't like him saying cordial things to me like that. Even though I know he doesn't mean a word of it, I still don't like it.

But going along with the show, I say, "Thank you. And you look nice yourself."

He smirks and then holds his arms out to Martha and Mae. "May I have the pleasure of escorting you two beautiful ladies to Prancer's Libations?"

"We'd love that," Martha says as both she and Mae loop their arms through his.

"See you there," Cole tells us, and then together they all walk down the sidewalk toward town.

"Hold on a second," Aunt Cindy says as we start walking, pushing her along with us.

Taran and I both pause.

"Did you forget something?" Taran asks.

Aunt Cindy shakes her head and then looks up at me. "What did you do?"

"What did I do?" I ask, my brow crinkled. "What do you mean what did I do? I didn't do anything."

"You did something, because that interaction right there, it was tense. What's going on between you and Cole?"

"There's something going on between you two?" Taran asks.

"No," I say. "I mean, like...nothing except that he's my competition."

Aunt Cindy doesn't buy it, because she wiggles her finger at me, telling me to come closer. I don't want to, but I do.

When our faces are only a few inches apart, she says, "What…did… you…do?"

I swallow the lump forming in my throat as anxiety creeps up my back.

I wet my dry lips. "Um, nothing that I really know of, but, uh, he did have some words with me, and I'm not sure where they came from, but there were words."

"What kinds of words?" Taran asks.

"The kinds of words that weren't nice," I reply.

"Why?" Aunt Cindy asks.

"Uh, I don't know. He just said I didn't deserve to be the Christmas Kringle and that it was going to be his particular mission to make sure I didn't win."

"What?" Aunt Cindy snaps, and then leans back in her chair, looking defeated. "He said that to you?"

"Yes, was that…uh, was that not a Christmas-y thing to say? Maybe we should tell the council. Warn them of his Grinch-y behavior."

"No," Aunt Cindy says with a stern tone. "We're not going to say anything about it." She stares off at their retreating backs. "This is not good."

"Why not?" I ask. "I can beat Cole. I don't see him as a threat."

"You should," Aunt Cindy says. "He's a very large threat."

"Why? He's not very personable. That display right there was all fake, and sure, Martha and Mae might have bought it, but not everyone will."

"It's not that." Aunt Cindy folds her hands on her lap. "He'll be a large threat because this will be the first Christmas he's participated in since his parents passed away."

"His parents…passed away?" I ask. *How did I not know about that? It must have been recent.*

Aunt Cindy nods. "A terrible car accident a decade ago. He inherited their house and has worked over at Evergreen Farm with the Maxheimers ever since. He's kept to himself but has relied on the town to get him through the tragedy. Not everyone likes him, but everyone has been rooting for him. Which means..."

"They're going to favor him in the competition," I say, feeling dumbfounded and confused.

His parents passed away and he never said anything? *Why?*

"Wait." Taran steps in. "I don't understand—if he isn't a Christmas kind of guy, why is he suddenly joining the competition?"

"That's what I wondered the other night when his name was announced," Aunt Cindy said. "I thought it might be a bet between him and Atlas, and Cole lost. But after seeing you two interact, I'm thinking you're the reason he's doing it, not Atlas."

I nervously laugh, feeling the anger in Aunt Cindy's severe stare—she apparently wants this win a lot more than I suspected.

"So what did you do to him that would bring him out of hiding and into this competition?"

"Uh...nothing," I say. "I didn't do anything. Ever since I showed up, he's been irritated with me."

"Did you do something when you were younger?" Aunt Cindy asks.

"No," I say. "Nothing like that. I...I have no idea." I think back to our last interaction when we were teenagers, but nothing springs to mind. He was quiet that day, but it's not as though he was a loud, raucous boy. And I haven't seen him since. It's why I was so surprised that he seemed so...angry with me when we first saw each other a few days ago. I thought it was funny to pretend I didn't recognize him, but he certainly didn't appreciate my humor. So weird. "Look, all I know is that he said I don't deserve to win and he's going to make sure I don't."

"Well." Aunt Cindy sighs and stares toward town for a moment. "How do we handle this? The town will favor Cole, no matter what shenanigans he pulls. That was clear from watching Martha and Mae fawn over him just now. You might win some points for representing me, but you won't be favored because you're an out-of-towner."

"Maybe... What if Taran switches with me? I doubt Cole has any beef with her since they've never interacted. Taran can take over the Kringle duties and I can suck it up and wash the crevices."

Aunt Cindy gives me the stink eye, which makes me shiver on the spot. "The only one washing my crevices is Taran—not to mention, once the Kringle-ees are named, they can't change. Did you not read that in your folder? You're in this for the long run."

"Which means you need to get it together," Taran says, not adding any value to the conversation.

"I am getting it together. Look at me, for Christ's sake," I say, holding my arms out as I jingle. "I'm wearing an old-lady sweater and a velvet bow in my hair, standing in the arctic weather and trying to win a competition for my dying aunt."

"I'm not dying yet, but I like the angle you just took," Aunt Cindy says with a nod of approval. "Maybe we run with that. I could look weaker and feebler. You can play up how you just want to win this for me so my legacy of loving Christmas and this town can live on."

"I mean, that's a touch manipulative," I say.

"You don't think Cole is going to take advantage of his own tragedy and work the crowd with his charming smile that people have missed for so long?" Aunt Cindy asks.

"She has a point," Taran says. "It *is* a charming smile."

"Ugh!" I groan. "I don't want to tell people you're dying."

"You don't have to, but letting them know I'm weak? That hints toward a possible death. Besides, I'm old, so meeting my maker is right around the corner any day for me."

"Jesus, Aunt Cindy," Taran says.

"It's the truth. A ninety-one-year-old woman like me is grateful for every day she wakes up to. So we play off that. We work the town with our family bond, the fact that my great-grand niblings are here to take care of me."

"Great-grand niblings?" I ask.

"Yes, niblings. Now, go grab the powder in my room—I have some touch-ups to make. Then we need to get going. We don't want to be late to the first competition, but remember, we need to appear as a cohesive unit. When we walk into that bar, I need you holding my hand, Storee. The more sympathy we can garner, the better. This win is ours, and I'll be damned if we let anyone take it away."

Yikes.

COLE

"Did you put on a new cologne?" Max asks as he stands next to me.

Prancer's Libations may be our small town's bar, but it has big-city vibes. Frank and Thachary are transplants from New York City, where they grew up. Opting for a slower pace, they decided to move their life into the mountains, where they took ownership of two businesses in town, the bar and the candle store.

With Frank's background in window displays and Thachary's bartending experience, they've transformed Prancer's Libations from a run-of-the-mill small-town bar into a showstopping, must-see establishment that has been featured in many magazines and blogs. They tore out all the old booths that suffered from cracked leather and scuffed wood and installed a seating layout that is more in line with what you'd see in a New York City bar. Rather than booths, along the sprawling wall are benches covered with red plaid cushions, while the tables and chairs are in front. The bar made of rich wood is off to the right when you walk in, with green permanent bar stools that twirl. Antique liquor bottles line the back wall, bringing an elevated air to the space. And then the ceiling, the showstopper, is covered in hanging baubles, mistletoe, pine garland, and twinkle lights, all set at different heights, not a single inch of the ceiling showing. It's been featured in many social media posts and is one of the biggest attractions in the town.

The drinkware are all hobnail glasses.

The shakers are all gold.

The staff is in white button-down shirts with red-and-green plaid ties.

And classic Christmas music is constantly played through speakers placed throughout the space, not too loud but just loud enough to drown out the conversations around you so you feel like you're alone with your company.

"Uh, I asked you a question," Max says, nudging me with his shoulder. "Huh?"

"Your cologne? Is it new? Kind of sweet, and I like it. I think it will pair well with our drink." He leans in closer and smells my neck.

I swat at his face. "Can you not fucking do that? Jesus fuck, man. You gave me chills."

He smiles. "Didn't know I had that kind of effect on you."

I eye him. "It was your hot breath on my neck that gave me chills, not your. . .whatever you want to call yourself in those reindeer antlers."

"You know exactly what I'm called." He leans in close again. "Your holly jolly sidekick. And I thought the reindeer antlers added some whimsy to our team. You might be wearing the sash, but I'm bringing the sass."

"I hate you," I mutter. "I really hate you."

"Thank you, Ursula," Frank says as she steps away from the judging table.

Thachary flashes a smile at the crowd. "Storee Taylor, please bring your drink to the table and tell us what you've made."

Storee—in the most ridiculous sweater I've ever seen—jingles her way up to the judging table with her drinks on a tray. She smiles sweetly, which nearly makes me gag on the spot, but I'm sure to hold true to my alter ego—*Snow Daddy*, name provided by Max.

I wasn't on board with Snow Daddy, but after grumbling for a solid hour while trying to come up with a concoction that would blow the socks off Thachary and Frank, Max got sick of me and lectured me on the importance of staying positive and cheery, hence the new nickname.

"What do you have for us?" Frank asks.

Storee clasps her hand together in front of her. "I'm presenting you with my dear aunt Cindy's favorite way to drink her eggnog." *Insert eye roll.* Way to add Aunt Cindy in there, and I can tell it worked because Frank and Thachary glance over at Cindy, who—*dear God!* She's slumped in her chair, one shaky hand raised in the air as she attempts a crooked smile.

Uh, that's not the woman I just saw outside of her house.

That woman was lively.

She had some pink in her cheeks.

She...

"Holy shit," I mutter.

"What?" Max says.

"She's playing dead."

"Who's playing dead?"

"Cindy Louis," I say from the side of my mouth. "Look, they washed her face out with powder—she practically looks like a corpse in the wheelchair."

Max leans forward for a look and then leans back. "Yikes, that is some grim reaper-type shit over there."

Storee's voice rings through the bar. "The rims are coated in crushed gingerbread cookies, and the spices we used are allspice, nutmeg, cinnamon, and a dash of cardamom. I hope you enjoy." Then she shimmies toward the judges, earning a laugh with her jingling breasts.

Damn it.

Frank and Thachary love a good shimmy.

They sometimes hold dance classes in their bar before they open. I've walked by before and have seen a lot of shimmying. Cindy must have let Storee know.

This might be harder than I thought, especially with the nearly rotting corpse over there in the wheelchair.

The room falls silent, the only noise the music playing overhead. We watch as Frank and Thachary both take a sip and start marking away on their judging cards. I try to catch any sort of tell that they might like it...or, preferably, hate it.

Like a snarl to the lip.

A hiccup from a swallow.

Possibly some singeing of the tongue from too many spices.

But I see nothing.

"Presentation is beautiful," Frank says. "Thank you, Storee."

"Of course." She grabs her drinks and then walks back to her spot. We're next.

The judges cleanse their palates with sips of water as Max leans in close again. "Unbutton your Henley; show some chest hair."

"What? No."

"Dude, you have to do something—they're using Aunt Cindy for sympathy. Be Snow Daddy."

"I'm not going to—"

"Cole Black, we're ready for you," Frank says.

"Unbutton," Max whispers, but I shake him off and bring our drinks forward.

Two brown mugs have reindeer antlers for handles, and I've decorated the tray with fresh pine needles from the farm, some dark chocolate bars, and a few hazelnuts. I'm really attempting to add to the ambiance.

I set the tray in front of them and watch them examine it for a second before I say, "I have for you today my rendition of a dark chocolate hazelnut eggnog drink."

There's some chatter behind me, a small *oooh* with a matching *ahhh*.

"With some fresh-cut pine from Evergreen Farm, two handmade mugs from Baubles and Wrappings, and local dark chocolate from Chadwick's, I wanted to incorporate the town into this drink as much as I could."

I see the appreciation on their faces as they take their first sips, and I'll be honest, I'm slightly nervous. I mean, I want to win. I want to beat Storee, but I didn't think that I was going to be this anxious going into the competition.

After a few deathly silent seconds and some more sips, they jot away on their cards and then smile up at me.

"Wonderful. Thank you, Cole."

"You're welcome," I say as I reach for the tray.

Behind me, I hear Max cough into his hand while he says, "Shimmy." But I ignore him as I rejoin the crowd. We're going to let the drink speak for itself. We're not going to use cringeworthy tricks like making a lady with a broken hip look like she's on her deathbed.

No, we're going to win this on merit.

We're going to win this with dignity.

We're going to win this the right way.

Bob Krampus steps up to the table now, in his complete Santa costume. "Boys, have we reached a verdict?"

Frank offers a curt nod and then slips a sealed envelope into Bob's hands.

The room falls silent again, and tension rises.

I glance over at Storee. She's holding Cindy's hand, and Cindy is… good God, is her tongue dangling out of her mouth?

Taran is holding Cindy's shoulders, and both sisters are brimming with excitement.

Ursula is standing proudly, chin held high, already accepting the win in her mind.

Beatrice is holding a rose, part of her rose-flavored eggnog—I can tell you who'll be placed last.

And Jimmy is...God, he's disgusting. He's wiping his nose on the back of his hand and examining the result.

Max grips my shoulder and whispers, "No matter what happens, you're still Snow Daddy to me."

Christ.

Bob swipes his hand over his beard and speaks deeply, his voice booming through the bar. "Thank you all for coming. The Eggnog Wars always kick off the start of our Christmas Kringle search. We'd like to thank Frank and Thachary for hosting us this evening. They're offering ten percent off all drinks tonight and fifteen percent off your entire purchase at Frank 'n' Scents. For a valid coupon, please see Renee at the bar and she will hand you one. Now, for the winner. As in years past, Frank and Thachary will add the winning eggnog concoction to their menu for next year—a true Kringletown honor."

The crowd claps, and once the chatter dies down, Bob opens the envelope and pulls out the card with the names of the winners on it.

Here we go...here we go. First place goes to me!

He studies the list. His mustache twitches, and then he slowly looks up to the crowd. Having fun with everyone's impatience, he scans the restless contestants and then glances down at his card again. In a booming voice, he announces, "In last place..." He pauses. "We have our very own...Dr. Beatrice Pedigree."

Beatrice hangs her head but claps for herself along with the crowd.

Sorry, lady, but I called it. Rose and eggnog are not a combination anyone wants in their mouth.

When the crowd dies down, Bob once again scans the room and then, in a very William Shatner from *Miss Congeniality* voice—don't ask how I know—says, "In fourth place...Jimmy Short."

A round of soft applause rings through the room as Jimmy bows and then wipes his nose with the back of his hand again.

Dude, that's one nasty habit—grab a napkin.

Once again, the room falls silent and I move from side to side, gearing up for what's next. *Come on, we've made it this far already. Please not third. Please not third.*

"And in third place…"

Say Storee.

Say Storee.

He looks in my direction and my stomach bottoms out just before he says, "We have Ursula Kronk."

Jesus Christ. Why did he have to look at me?

Bob Krampus with the old fake-out.

The town collectively gasps while I exhale sharply at how the reigning champion has been upstaged by two newbies.

I was hoping Storee would take third, but it's fine—it's fine.

I'm going to take this win home. I know it. I can feel it in my bones. I made one hell of an eggnog, and I didn't make my aunt look sickly while doing it.

Dignity and merit. We're winning the right way.

"And our first winner of the Christmas Kringle season is…"

Max squeezes my shoulder.

My breath stills in my chest.

My hands turn incredibly clammy.

"No matter what happens, don't forget to smile," Max says through clenched teeth.

And…

"Storee Taylor!" Bob yells.

Mother…

Fucker!

An eruption of cheers rings through the room as I glance over at

Storee, who stands there blinking in shock and…are you fucking kidding me? Cindy is standing from her wheelchair, Taran holding on to her, whooping it up like she just won the two-hundred-meter freestyle against Michael Fucking Phelps.

Is anyone else seeing this?

She was clearly faking it.

Frank, Thachary, they played you!

The once-gray corpse in the wheelchair has resurrected herself into cheering so vivaciously that…yes, in fact, she is performing minute hip thrusts, to the crowd's delight.

Cheaters!

They're freaking cheaters.

What lowlifes, using an old woman's infirmity to win a competition.

Even if the old woman was certainly in on it the whole time.

"Clap, man. You have to clap," Max mutters.

Even though I hate it, I reluctantly put a smile on my face and clap.

But I don't just clap. I clap loud.

Loud enough that I feel Max wince next to me.

And then, in a boisterous voice, my alter ego, Snow Daddy, appears. "Well deserved, so well deserved. What a great competition and start to a lively holiday season."

Bob Krampus nods at me in approval.

Frank and Thachary congratulate Storee.

And I take it all in, revising my plan for total domination.

We're not going to lose like this. Nope. If they're going to pull out all of their tricks…

So are we!

CHAPTER NINE
STOREE

They thought they were so smart;
they thought they were slick.
But Cole thought up a reply, and
he thought it up real quick.

Dignity and merit were tossed out the window.
He's a man seeking revenge, our dear Daddy Snow.

THIS IS WHAT A HIGH feels like.

This effervescent, light, practically airless feeling pulsing through my veins as I levitate out of bed, toe on my slippers, mock-curtsy to that bitch doll Samantha, and then head down the creaky stairs, the smell of coffee leading the way.

Wow.

Just wow.

I can't believe we won last night.

I mean, I can.

Between the drink, the presentation, and Aunt Cindy's superb acting, it was hard to say we didn't have it in the bag.

And the look on Cole's face.

Chef's kiss.

Priceless.

I truly have never felt better. I've never felt more into anything in my entire life, and now, the bar has been set. I'm in game-plan mode now. We have a launch point, and we have to keep climbing.

I head toward the dining room, where coffee has been poured and oatmeal has been served.

"What's this?" I ask Aunt Cindy and Taran, who are both sitting at the table.

"I wanted to make you my famous oatmeal for a job well done last night," Aunt Cindy says.

I take a seat next to Taran and grab the milk for my coffee. "Aunt Cindy, I don't think you should be cooking in your condition."

"That's what I told her," Taran says. "It's why I'm the one who made it while she snapped at me—"

"Excuse me?" Aunt Cindy says.

"I mean *told*," Taran says with a cheeky grin. "Told me what to do."

"Well, it looks delicious, thank you." I pick up my spoon and stir my coffee when I notice that they're both staring at me. I look between the two of them. "What?"

"You seem…different," Taran says.

"She does, doesn't she?" Aunt Cindy says with a grin.

"Yes, quite different."

"I don't know what you're talking about," I say as I place my napkin on my lap.

"You know, Aunt Cindy, I think…yeah, I think she liked winning last night."

Aunt Cindy rests her chin in her hand as she gazes at me. "I think she did."

"Well, who doesn't like winning?" I ask as I drop a teaspoon of brown sugar in my oatmeal and give it a stir.

Raisins, chopped apples, and cinnamon. It's creamy, it's soft, it's delicious.

"But I think you liked it *a lot*," Taran says.

"It seems that way," Aunt Cindy continues. "I think she liked it so much that she cried."

"I did not cry," I say with an annoyed roll of my eyes.

"It felt like she was going to cry," Taran says.

"I could sense the emotions," Aunt Cindy replies.

"The only thing I sensed was a victorious swift kick to the air in celebration as Cole stared at us, dumbfounded." I bring my coffee to my lips and take a sip.

"Ah-ha!" Taran shouts, scaring the shit out of me and making me spill my coffee into my oatmeal.

"Jesus, Taran," I say as I try to clean up the mess with my cloth napkin. I fail miserably, because cloth napkins provide zero absorption. "Why did you yell like that?"

"I didn't yell," she says. "I'm pointing out the obvious."

"And what would that be?" I ask while I continue to clean up the mess.

"That you're overjoyed about beating Cole last night, so much so that there's color in your cheeks."

"There's color in my cheeks because it's freezing here and my body is attempting to self-regulate," I say.

"But also...because we beat Cole, right?" Aunt Cindy asks.

I look between Aunt Cindy and Taran, their expressions hinting at celebration. They clearly want me to say it's because of Cole and, well... damn it...it is!

I smile. "Yeah, because we beat Cole."

And then as one, we cheer.

We clasp our hands together, shake them in the air, and celebrate this one solid win.

We celebrate the concoction we made. And it *was* delicious, especially if you dipped one of those cookies into it. Yum.

We celebrate the dreary and sad expression on Cole's face when he saw our win.

We celebrate it all.

Once we're settled, I sit back and clear my throat. "Just because we won the first challenge doesn't mean we can get cocky, though." I dip my spoon into my mostly coffee-less oatmeal. "This is a great starting point. From here, we need to keep pushing forward, which means we need to go over the next competition."

"I could not agree more," Aunt Cindy says. "Taran, the board, please."

"The board?" I ask.

Aunt Cindy nods while Taran walks over to the buffet table, which she's decorated with one of Aunt Cindy's many Christmas villages, and from behind, slides out a piece of cardboard with a towel draped over it and props it on top of the buffet and against the wall.

"Shall I unveil it?" Taran asks Aunt Cindy.

"You shall."

What the...

Taran flips the towel over the cardboard, revealing an intricate display of the competitors and the competitions, strings stretched all over like a spider's web, connecting people to illustrated Christmas staples such as a tree, a candy cane, and the dreaded fruitcake.

"What is this?" I ask. "And when did you make it?"

"It's my board that I adjust every year," Aunt Cindy says. "It helps me keep track of who's involved, what competition we're gearing up for, who the judges are, and who is in the lead." She gestures to Taran. "Can you grab the binder as well?"

"It's right here," Taran says as she grabs a binder from the buffet and brings it over to Aunt Cindy. When on earth have they talked about this without me? Because I haven't really left their sides.

Well, I guess there was that nap I took the other day.

And that other nap before dinner because shivering all day takes it out of me.

Oh…and I can't forget about the two hours I spent sitting in front of the fire where I…happened to fall asleep as well.

So, yeah, I guess they've had some time to plan without me.

"Ah, yes," Aunt Cindy says as she refers to her binder and then back to the board. "Next we have the recycling—well, *upcycling*—portion of the competition."

"And what is that, exactly?" I ask her. "Are we supposed to see who can gather the most products and recycle them?"

"No." Aunt Cindy chuckles. "This is a competition put on by Sherry Conrad."

"Who's she?" I ask.

"Sherry is the owner of Antlers Antiques."

"Oh, okay. So what does she have to do with the competition?"

"Sherry's our local environmentalist. She's the one who holds all the proprietors to a high standard of sustainability. When our neighboring town, Vail, came out with their Mountain IDEAL—their sustainability standard—Sherry brought the idea to Bob Krampus to adopt, and he welcomed it with open arms, as long as she was the one who headed it up. So, she helped all the proprietors turn over a green leaf, if you will. We've done away with single-use plastic as much as we can—especially at our restaurants—we've installed solar panels, and we've opened up a section of our town parking to allow electric vehicle charging, which in return has made us a larger destination because travelers will charge and shop here in Kringle. She's done amazing things for our town, so Bob Krampus thought it would only be right to have a competition in honor of the work she's done."

"That's actually kind of amazing. I had no idea, but it explains why plant-based cutlery is offered for all takeout," I say.

"Exactly, so when they were coming up with a competition, they wanted to make it into an upcycling challenge. Contestants are supposed to create a live-action scene from one of their favorite Christmas movies and do it by using things that can be recycled, or by upcycling old items to give them a different purpose. The person who depicts the best scene and uses the materials in the best way wins."

"Okay. A bit more of a challenge. We're going to have to be creative, which I'm very good at," I say. "And Taran can help execute, with her anal retentiveness to make it perfect."

"That's what I'm here for," Taran says as she scoops a spoonful of oatmeal into her mouth.

"What scene did you do last year?"

"I'm glad you asked," Aunt Cindy says. "Because I won this competition last year."

"Really?"

Aunt Cindy nods, and a large grin spreads across her lips. "I recreated the scene from *Meet Me in St. Louis*, where Judy Garland is singing 'Have Yourself a Merry Little Christmas.' I styled my hair to look like hers, found some clothes from Antlers Antiques that represented the era, shoes and all, and then took a cardboard box, made it look like a window, and sat down, looking through the window like Judy in the movie and lip-synching the song. There wasn't a dry eye in the place."

I press my hand to my heart. "Aunt Cindy, that's...that's beautiful."

"Thank you." She smiles. "Now, I think we can achieve the same visceral reaction with you, but I think I should be involved. I say we reenact the same scene as last year, recycle the window, the outfit—showing Sherry that I didn't just dispose of the scene from the year before. This way, we're demonstrating the highest of all recycling by reusing what we've already created—but this time, you sing to me through the window while I slouch in my wheelchair like I'm knocking on death's door."

I hold my arm out and point to the goose bumps there. "Chills. Literal chills."

"I can make your cheeks look gaunt too," Taran says. "We can work the makeup in our favor."

Aunt Cindy smirks. "And this is why I love you two."

Proud of ourselves, we all dig into the oatmeal, knowing full well this competition is ours to take. And for the first time in a long time, I feel like our family is coming together again after a hiatus. A hiatus from me.

A stupid hiatus that I already regret, because this…this cohesiveness, this is what Christmas is all about.

That and winning!

COLE

"You know, unless you have binoculars, I don't think you're going to see anything," Max says as he comes up behind me.

I snap the blinds shut and move away from my window, trying to put the woman next door out of my mind. "Last night was bullshit. We should have won."

"Well, maybe if you'd listened to me about the chest hair, we could have won, but you were too much of a prude to puff it out."

"First of all, my chest hair is trimmed. Even if I wanted to 'puff it out' as you like to say, I wouldn't have been able to. And secondly, we were going to win on dignity and merit."

"Yes, and look how far that got you. You saw them last night, Cole. They came to play. Cindy put on the performance of her life. I genuinely thought she was taking her final breaths last night, and so did Thachary and Frank."

"Yeah, and did you see her pop out of her wheelchair like a freaking spring flower? The woman broke her hip and yet was able to awaken from a near-catatonic state in seconds."

"It was startling. I gasped when I witnessed her rise, like an erection sprung right from a pair of tighty-whities." I grimace at my friend, not liking that analogy. He continues, "But you know Frank and Thachary. They love their grandmas, and, well, the girls played toward their weakness, which got me thinking..." Max moves around my living room and takes a seat on the couch, pulling the suitcase he brought with him over to the coffee table. "I think we need to be more strategic about our approach."

I fold my arms across my chest. "And what exactly do you mean by that?"

"We need to start focusing on not just the competition, but the judges." Max opens his suitcase, flops open the top, and lifts out a large, folded piece of poster board, revealing a picture of every judge with a list of what seem to be personality traits underneath. "This is a comprehensive guide to every judge, what they're judging, and what they like and dislike. I scoured their social media profiles last night, stole their most unflattering pictures, printed them, and wrote down everything I know about them."

"Why the most unflattering picture?"

He looks at me as if I'm an idiot. "Uh, so you're not intimidated, obviously."

"Oh, yeah...that checks out." I take a seat next to him and settle into the lumpy couch from my childhood that I've never replaced.

Actually, not a single thing in this house has been moved or shifted since I lost my parents. My childhood bedroom remains mine, the holly berry dishes my mom would pull out on Christmas Eve have accumulated dust on the shelves, and not a square inch of this house has seen any sort of Christmas spirit in a decade. I rarely sit in this room, so I haven't really noticed how bereft it is, the way it seems to long for...what used to be.

Max smoothes his hand over the couch's wrinkles. "The key to winning this competition is not how many ways you can say *Season's Greetings* in the Myrrh-cantile, but how you can edge out the competition with your knowledge of the judges." He takes out a pointer from his suitcase and slaps it down on a picture of Sherry Conrad getting licked in the face by her dog. Her face is crinkled, one of her fake eyelashes is dangling off her eyelid, and her lipstick is smeared across her cheek. Yeah, not the most flattering. "Now, this is our judge for the Upcycle Christmas competition."

"This is the live-action one, right?" I ask.

He nods. "Yes, meaning you're going to have to pose in some sort of Christmas scene while we attack the town with a strategic, perfectly constructed sight to behold."

Don't like the sound of that.

He takes out a piece of folded paper and turns away from me, keeping it hidden from view. "Now, Cindy Louis won this round last year, and she killed it. She dressed up as Judy Garland and lip-synched 'Have Yourself a Merry Little Christmas.' Everyone cried—it was an ordeal."

"I think I remember hearing about it," I say.

"So, they're going to attack hard since Cindy is the reigning champion."

"Yeah, I could see them working the crowd with the old lady cadaver again."

"We need to keep in mind that they're going to use Cindy in every competition. My mom was even telling me that she overheard Nina Dirk talking to Martha about the status of Cindy's hip and how they're worried it might be her last Christmas."

"Damn it," I mutter as I drag my hand over my face. "But from the celebration last night, I assume she has a lot more Christmases left in her."

"Agreed, which means we have to remain educated about our judges, stay on our toes, and be sneaky about this. If they're going to use Cadaver Cindy, then we have to use our intelligence and inside information. I have my mom working the town. She's been putting in some good words for you, and so is her secret friend, Kathleen, who works over at stall twelve."

Stall twelve is one of fifteen craft stalls that surround the Tinsel Twirl just left of Ornament Park. They're open year-round and are usually occupied by craft vendors who sell their homemade goods to those traveling through town. Bob and Sylvia Krampus are very particular as to what is sold in the stalls because they don't want vendors competing with proprietors.

"Secret friend? Wait, is Kathleen the one who came in selling jellies and jams?" I ask.

Max nods. "The very one."

"I thought your mom was feuding with her because she was selling the same jam that your mom has at Evergreen?"

"They've kept up the farce but have secretly formed an alliance. This is top secret, man, and you can't say anything, but..." He glances over his shoulder, as if we're not alone in my house. "In order to drive up sales between the two locations, they've created a rivalry to see whose jam is better, when in reality they don't really care. So, out-of-towners will buy both jams and decide for themselves when they get home. Kind of like those competing cheesesteak places in Philly. The rivalry just drives up their sales as people try to form an opinion for themselves."

"Oh shit." I chuckle, impressed. "I had no idea."

"No one does besides me, my dad, and my mom, and of course Kathleen, and the only reason I know is because I walked in on my mom and dad talking about it. But I've been sworn to secrecy. Last night after we lost, I told her I needed her help and, well, we devised a plan. She'll have Kathleen talk about you around town, and people won't suspect a thing because you're aligned with my mom's side of the jam schism."

"That's good." I nod. "That's very good."

"You can thank my mom for that one. So, we have people buzzing about you around town, which is step number one. Step two, you have to continue showing yourself out in public and wishing people seasonal greetings, but I made you a list of different ways of saying it."

He pulls a list out of his pocket and hands it to me.

I stare down and read each entry in my head.

I hope you have a delightful holiday season—yeah, that works.

Warm wishes to you and your family—that's a good one.

Best wishes for a festive season—also another classic spin.

Sending holiday cheer to you and yours—a bit of a tongue-twister sentence for me.

May your holidays shine bright—not saying that.

Joyous Festivus...

I quirk my eyebrow and look up at Max. "Joyous Festivus?"

He smirks. "That was my favorite."

"I'm not saying that."

"I'm sure people would appreciate it if you did."

"That's great, but I'm not saying it. People will know I'm faking it."

"You know...it's okay for men to fake it every once in a while." He nudges me with his elbow and waggles his brows.

I swat at him. "Enough with that shit."

He chuckles. "Well, keep it in your back pocket if you ever need to gain a leg up. You can drop it like a holiday bomb. Joyous Festivus! People will fawn at your feet, and you might be crowned Christmas Kringle right there on the spot."

I stare at my best friend. "You know, I think you're getting way too into this."

"I'm the proper amount of into this. Now stop distracting me—we have to talk about the Upcycle Christmas challenge."

I lean back on the couch, knowing that even if I put up a fight, he's not going to let me win, so I give in to this insanity. I will store away Joyous Festivus and only use it when absolutely necessary.

"Since we want to attack on all senses, I was thinking we act out a scene from *The Grinch*."

I run my tongue over my teeth. "Let me guess, I'm the Grinch."

"Unless you want to be Cindy-Lou Who. Up to you." He grins.

"I think you know the answer to that."

Chuckling, he continues, "Now, back to my research about Sherry. She's a fan of dogs, one of her favorite movies is *The Grinch*, and most importantly, she's a secret fan of Thunder from Down Under."

Silence falls between us as I contemplate whether or not I need a new best friend, because I can see exactly where this is going.

"No," I say.

He removes tissue paper from his suitcase, revealing a set of lederhosen, the same style that the Grinch wore in the Jim Carrey version. "Oh yes," Max says.

"No," I repeat.

He takes it out of the suitcase and stands up. "Oh, fuck yes."

I look him up and down and uncross my arms. "No, Max. And that's fucking final."

CHAPTER TEN
STOREE

The warm lit houses shine all through the town,
while Cole walks around with a very grumpy frown.

For he knows every Kringle will think he's lost a screw,
as he traipses around whistling yodel-ay-hee-who.

But he is bound to win, and win it well,
even if that means a day in reality hell.

"HAVE YOU SEEN COLE?" I ask Taran as I adjust the red velvet dress Aunt Cindy made me try on this morning. It barely fits me. I'm wearing a cardigan to cover up the unzipped part of the dress.

"I haven't," Taran says, glancing around Ornament Park. "I'm not sure anyone has seen him. I'm worried he might try to shock the crowd."

"Nothing's going to shock the crowd more than Jimmy Short dressed in his version of Cousin Eddie's robe while handling an RV hose and telling everyone the shitter's full."

Taran shivers in disgust. "He didn't need to add the smell to it. Unnecessary touch."

"I know. I saw Sherry crinkle her nose."

"The guys from the hardware store loved it, though—really got into the *Christmas Vacation* spirit," Taran says. "And from what Aunt Cindy told me, she thinks Sherry might be privately involved with someone from the hardware store."

"What does *privately involved* mean? And I thought she was with Beatrice's ex?" I ask as Taran adjusts my hair. It took a while to get the bouffant right, but I'd say we got pretty close. It helps that my hair is red and so was Judy Garland's in the movie.

"I don't know. I didn't ask."

Because Antlers Antiques is so cluttered, with little space to host a competition, we're having the live-action Upcycle Christmas in Ornament Park on the stage. There's a tent for contestants to get ready in, but we haven't seen Cole or Max, which makes me think…did they drop out?

Wouldn't that be the best news? Given the competition we've seen so far, Ursula seems to be the only threat, especially when Dr. Beatrice Pedigree lay on the stage, dressed as a bloody Bruce Willis, and shouted "yippee ki-yay, mother-fudger" before tossing a felt flame at a fake toy plane that popped confetti, imitating an explosion.

Although a thoughtful rendition of a cinematic moment, *Die Hard* is not exactly a Christmas movie, and even worse, the scene she reenacted was from *Die Hard 2: Die Harder*, which is not even close to being considered a Christmas movie, so I think we all know who's getting last place—even if Jimmy's robe was short enough for us to see his hairy man thighs.

"You look nervous. Are you nervous?" Taran asks.

"I mean, yeah. Last time I had to do something onstage, I tossed a lady into the river behind us."

"First of all, you didn't toss her. Second of all, that was a long time ago, and we've taken out all opportunities for you to trip. It's why I'm going to wheel out Aunt Cindy from the crowd myself, bringing her onstage. And I'll even set up your window for you. You just have to walk on and sit. I think you can manage that, especially with how the dress hits above your ankles so you have nothing to trip over. And I checked with Bob about the stage—it's flat. Nothing will trip you, no obstacles; you are good."

"I know." I blow out a heavy breath. "But I'm still worried. I don't think I'll ever not worry about being in front of people."

"I get it, but we will be right there with you. You can do this." Taran adjusts the silver sparkly scarf that's fixed on my head. "Show me your teeth."

I bare my teeth to her, and she nods.

"No lipstick?" I ask.

"Nope, you're good."

"Okay." I shake out my hands. "God, I felt so confident this morning. I was envisioning success while taking a shower, remembering the look on Cole's face when he lost the other night, letting that propel me to this moment, but now...God, now I feel so shaky and scared."

"Don't be scared. Look around—Cole's not even here," Taran says. "He probably realized what stiff competition you are and didn't want to show up anymore."

"You think?" I ask.

"Yeah, I think so," she replies as Ursula wraps up her Upcycle Christmas scene as Kevin McCallister, BB gun and all, setting up her version of a booby-trapped house by using all upcycled products from Antlers Antiques. We heard whispers that she's transferring the scene over to her light display as well, which will earn her extra points.

The crowd cheers—loudly—and Ursula comes off the stage, wearing a red sweater, khakis, and a blond wig that looks more like Ellen DeGeneres circa 2000 than that eight-year-old snotty protagonist who gets away with stealing a toothbrush without an adult present.

"Great job," I tell Ursula. "Really loved the addition of the tarantula. It looked so real."

"Can you believe I found it at Antlers Antiques? Sherry and I were laughing so hard about how it was such kismet."

Insert eye roll here.

"What a gas," I say with a smile and chuckle.

Ursula moves along, and Taran whispers, "What a gas?"

"I don't know, this old-lady garb has brought me back to 1904, when the roads were dirt and horse-drawn carriages were the mode of transportation."

"Clearly," Taran says. "Okay, you're up next. You can do this. Just think—"

The tent flaps part and Cole and Atlas shuffle in, both wearing long coats, but Cole's face is painted green while Atlas is wearing dog ears and has a dog nose painted on his face.

What the hell are they up to?

"What's up?" Atlas says to me with a nod. He scans me up and down. "Recreating the magical scene from last year?"

"Yes, we thought it would be a nice ode to Aunt Cindy...given her condition."

Atlas slowly nods. "No doubt there won't be a dry eye in the park. Can't wait to see it."

"Thank you," I say as Cole shifts uncomfortably next to Atlas. "You're looking rather green, Cole. Nauseated maybe?"

"Funny," he says, not smiling. "Don't trip while you're up there."

My eyes narrow at him.

"Don't listen to him," Taran says into my ear. "He's trying to get under your skin."

"No, I'm not," Cole says. "Just wishing her good luck. I want nothing more than for her to sprinkle everyone with Christmas spirit."

"Which is exactly what she's going to do," Taran says. "Just watch how my sister makes everyone weep."

"Weep with embarrassment for performing a used set," Cole mutters.

"What was that?" I ask, stepping up to him.

"You heard me, Taylor."

"*Taylor?*" I ask. "Oh, are we going by last names now?"

"Does it matter?"

"I guess not, especially when I blow right by you in this competition."

"What a lame comeback."

From the side of the stage, Bob Krampus says, "Storee, you're next."

"Break a leg…please," Cole says with a grin.

"Lose a testicle…please," I say as I reach up and drag my finger over his cheek, wiping a large smear of green off his face.

Atlas gasps next to us. "Ah, she ruined your makeup. It took me ten minutes to get that right."

"Looks like you have a minute to fix it," I say, feeling all the confidence in the world now.

I wait to make my entrance, and I can hear them shuffling around trying to fix Cole's face as Bob introduces me. Head held high, I pose myself with shoulders tilted back, hands clasped in front of me, and while Taran rolls out the window, I walk onstage with elegance, not tripping once. The crowd cheers.

And as Ornament Park quiets down, the music starts playing and I position myself at the window, looking slightly up to the sky. Judy Garland's beautiful voice rings through the speakers while I mouth the words. I can feel the sentiment in the air as everyone's attention is on me. Chills break out over my arms as the lightest of snow showers starts falling across the park, adding perfectly to the moment, and as Aunt Cindy is rolled up onstage, tucked into a pile of blankets, she holds out her hand to me and I take it through the window, singing to her now.

From the corner of my eye, I catch a few people dabbing at their eyes, and when the song is over, the crowd erupts into the loudest cheer of the day. *We've won this competition as well.*

For the final cherry on top of the already first-place cake, I lean in and press a soft kiss to Aunt Cindy's cheek before standing up and waving to everyone. With a final flourish, I hurry offstage, wanting to get into the warm tent as quickly as possible while Taran takes care of Aunt Cindy.

Nailed it.

I absolutely nailed it, and I've never been prouder of myself than in this moment.

Nothing, and I mean nothing, will be able to take this away from me.

I got over my fears.

I performed.

I made Aunt Cindy proud and—

I come to a halt right at the entrance of the warm tent as I take in the scene unfolding.

Both Atlas and Cole are standing in front of me, sans coats...and shirtless.

Atlas is in a tiny pair of brown shorts, shoeless, his ripped chest and hard nipples on full display along with his dog ears dangling over the sides of his face.

And then Cole...

Oh.

My.

God.

Cole.

He...he looks unreal.

Wearing a pair of brown lederhosen with red stitching—which I saw the other day in Antlers Antiques—his ripped, yet green, chest is on full display. Thick, muscular pecs, trimmed chest hair, bulky shoulders, and carved arms...my God. And I have no idea what kind of makeup work Atlas did, if any, but Cole's stomach looks like it was carved out of clay, the definition of each ab so prominent that he's going to have every human in the crowd wanting to reach out and see if he's real.

Not to mention, the lederhosen are short, showing off his impressive thighs and calves.

But it's the green all over his body that's sending me because somehow, it's highlighting every ripple of muscle he possesses, every curve, every contour. And I hate to admit it, truly...truly hate it, but holy shit, he's *hot*.

The two of them together look like Christmas Chippendales, ready to strip down and give everyone a show. And I'm in the crowd, ready to watch.

"Cole, you're up," Bob shouts.

Cole steps forward, but then stops right next to me. "Get a good look?" he asks, shocking me right out of my green-muscle trance.

"Yes," I say, chin held high, not wanting him to see one ounce of my appreciation for the view. "And it's confirmed—you look like a jackass."

He lightly nods. "That's not what the drool from the corner of your mouth is telling me."

And with that, he steps around me and then up the steps, where he waits for Bob to announce him.

"I wasn't drooling," I say to myself, even though his back's toward me and he's not giving me the time of day.

Huff.

I was not drooling...at least not physically.

Maybe in my head I was.

Most definitely in my head.

COLE

"If this doesn't win us first place, I'm firing you," I say from the side of my mouth to Max.

"Trust me, this is going to get us first place. Sherry is going to lose her mind when she gets a load of these bodacious bods."

"Can you not say dumb shit like that?"

"It's true, though. Farm chores have done us a lot of good. Get ready to be ogled."

He's not wrong about the farm work.

"Okay, but I'm standing my ground on the hip thrusting. There will be no hip thrusting."

"Dude," he groans. "We talked about this. You have to hip thrust at the end. You'll make her wet."

"Ew, Jesus fuck, man. I don't want to make a seventy-year-old woman wet. Show some respect."

"I am," he counters. "Seventy-year-olds deserve to be wet too."

"Can we stop saying wet?" I shout-whisper.

"You're the one who brought it up."

"No, you did," I counter.

"Yeah, but you're the one who brought up the pelvic thrust."

"Because I don't want to do it."

"You're doing it!" Max says just as our music starts and Bob introduces us.

Max's plan is simple—put a spin on a Christmas classic. He mixed some audio on his computer to create the perfect soundtrack. How he learned to do that, I have no idea, but he did, and now we're recreating a scene from *The Grinch*.

I start over by the stairs, out of view while Max struts like a dog down the stage where he's going to sit, letting his "package," as he put it, hang for the crowd to gawk at.

Then, as audio from *The Grinch* plays—the scene where the Grinch is trying to find something to wear to the Whos' party—I'm going to toss clothes from Antlers Antiques on the stage until it's time for me to flash a leg. That's when I make my appearance, and the sound is mixed with some Thunder from Down Under-type jam—something not only Sherry will love but also Martha and Mae, which will bode well for us in the long run.

It's stupid.

It's ridiculous.

There is zero dignity and not an ounce of merit.

But it will cater to Sherry's wild side—we hope. Or else we're going to look like a couple of dumbasses.

The sound starts, and just as planned, Max "gets on his hind legs" and pants like a goddamn moron while I toss out the clothes. The crowd laughs, but it does nothing to boost my confidence because I know what I look like.

Painted all in green, sporting these fucking green hairy sideburns Max said were necessary, and wearing goddamn lederhosen, I feel like a dick.

Especially since Max said there was no way he was going to allow me to wear a mask. "They need to see your handsome face," he said.

Well…they're going to see it all right, and a whole lot more.

With the crowd roaring and Max panting like an asshole out on the stage, I wish I at least had a bag covering my face so no one knew my real identity.

The sound halts, and just as Max planned, "I Am the Grinch" by Fletcher Jones starts playing—my cue to join Max onstage. I glance behind me and catch Storee staring at me, arms crossed, looking none too pleased with the setup. It's the last bit of courage I need to walk out on that stage, because I'll be damned if Storee wins this.

So I flash my leg to the crowd, teasing them with the green lederhosen, wool socks, and hiking boots, and when it's time, I walk out in front of what looks to be the entire town, way out of my goddamn element.

But the hoots and the hollers that ring out over the crowd…they do something to me.

And I'm not proud of this, okay? But fuck…it gives me a pep to my step, a boost in the britches…a lift in the lederhosen. And before I know it, I'm going for it. The music plays in the background, the cardboard

backdrop we made last night adds flair to the scene, and Max pants next to me, hands held up to his chest like the good little dog that he is.

It just…

It…makes me think…

> *And up on the stage, Cole thought of*
> *something he'd never thought before:*
> *Perhaps he's been missing out, perhaps…*
> *these cheers, he wants more.*

> *And then what happened next? Some*
> *in Kringletown might say*
> *that Cole's repressed ego grew three sizes that day.*

I spin around—the catcalls resound through the park.

I flash my jazz hands—the squeals feed my brimming mood.

And when I smooth my hands over my backside and give it a wiggle, I feel a pulse of adrenaline shoot right through me. I turn toward the crowd, their hands raised joyfully in the air, smiles stretching across faces, mouths agape…

I am killing it!

I am entertaining.

I am owning this fucking audience!

And as the music builds and builds, I know what's next.

I spin again, point to Max, and with a wink from him, I turn back to the crowd and end the show with a solid pelvic thrust, right into the air.

The crowd goes wild.

Mae Bawhovier faints into Martha.

And Sherry leans on the edge of her judging chair, licking her lips.

She wants this.

They want this.

Everyone wants this!

Max stands from his squat, takes my hand in his, and we both raise our arms and take a bow as we soak in the chants, the cheers, the praise for a job well done.

And I know for a fact that we're winning this.

Storee might have pulled at the crowd's heartstrings, but as Max put it, we pulled at the judge's weakness. Sherry Conrad, a closet perv, can't resist a shirtless man, and we took advantage.

If they're going to use Cadaver Cindy, then we will use our bodies.

All's fair in love and jingle jangling, right?

And let me tell you…my jangle was jingling. It was jingling all over that stage.

We walk off the stage together, Bob Krampus giving us both a raised brow as we pass, but we just smile at him and head into the tent, where Storee's standing, hands on her hips. She looks pissed. An angry Storee I can enjoy.

I walk right up to her, lean forward, and whisper in her ear, "You're playing with fire, so you're going to get burned."

She stiffens next to me. "That wasn't even remotely close to a scene from a movie. At no time does the Grinch pelvic thrust at the crowd."

"Hmm, I guess we're watching two different versions then." I pat her shoulder and head toward the back, where Max is holding a bottle of water for me.

"Dude," he whispers. "You thrusted."

I nod. "I thrusted."

"That one thrust, man, it was like a cosmic boom that shook the whole town. I saw trees faint."

Usually, I'd tell Max he was stupid for saying such an idiotic thing, but I'm high on adrenaline and the glory of a job well done. So I say, "I saw it too, man. I saw those trees faint too. It was magical."

Max grips my shoulder.

"It sure was."

CHAPTER ELEVEN
STOREE

Cole hated Christmas; he hated the whole season.
And like I said before, the town debated the reason.

But last night his mood changed, and
now in the season he trusts,
all thanks to green body paint and
one flamboyant pelvic thrust.

The town is split. Some think it was
Cole's lederhosen that took it all.
But Martha says it was because Max's
shorts were two sizes too small.

"I STILL CAN'T BELIEVE HE won last night," I say as I grumpily sit on the couch in the living room, unable to get over the fact that Sherry Conrad chose Cole's joke of a show over mine.

Whereas mine was heartfelt and featured a beautiful moment with my aunt on the stage, Cole and Atlas made a mockery of the entire competition.

Shirtless.

Green.

Lederhosen!

Who does that?

It was absurd, it was stupid, and it was…I mean…sure, the green chest hair was interesting to look at, and his pecs were bigger than I expected them to be, and the abs, well, we won't go there, but the pelvic thrust…

The pelvic thrust!

That was not necessary.

That was a cheap shot, and he took it.

And I know that rolling Aunt Cindy out onstage was a cheap shot as well, but Christmas is about family. We were playing into the theme. Whereas Cole was sexualizing Christmas with that thrust.

And don't even get me started on Atlas's seated position. Let's just say the crowd got a good look at his holly stick and berries.

"You have to let it go," Aunt Cindy says. "We got second place."

"Yes, which means we're tied with Cole. I don't want to be tied with him. I want to beat him."

"We have five more competitions," Aunt Cindy says as Taran walks into the living room holding a Tupperware bin with tape all over it, stating the contents are fragile.

The coveted Happy Days *nativity set.*

It's always the last thing to be put out. Taran has taken her time decorating the house for Aunt Cindy, and she's done a fantastic job, measuring out every garland to the last centimeter. She's dusted every surface, polished, and carefully placed each decoration where Aunt Cindy has directed her.

And I can honestly say that now that everything is up—the tree brimming with ornaments, every window adorned with velvet ribbons and a battery-lit candle, the pine garland intricately wrapped around the banister, and the gingerbread-themed decor in the kitchen—it *feels* like Christmas.

The Christmas from my childhood, back when I felt excitement for the season all the way down to my toes. When I'd play board games with Taran by the fire. When we'd spend countless hours at the dining room table icing cookies. When we would stare out the window, looking up at the gray clouds, hoping that we'd wake up to freshly fallen snow the next morning.

The smell of it all.

The sight of the familiar decorations...

It's making me wonder why I pushed this side of my childhood out of my life for so long. Why I've neglected to live in this feeling. *For years.*

Why I told myself that I don't need to curl up on Aunt Cindy's couch next to the fire and listen to classic Christmas instrumentals, insisting that a Christmas in my apartment...alone...was a much better choice.

Being here again, it's made me realize it was not a better choice.

"Will you help me?" Taran asks as she opens the top of the container and starts carefully pulling out tissue paper.

I kneel in front of the bin and begin unwrapping the figurines. I have no idea where Aunt Cindy got this nativity set, but I will say, for being a novelty item, they did an excellent job on the figurines—very lifelike.

Naturally, Marion and Howard are Mary and Joseph. The three wise men are Richie, Potsie, and Ralph. Chachi is the shepherd, Joanie is the angel, and who else could be baby Jesus other than the Fonz, sideburns and all.

"I was speaking to Martha this morning," Aunt Cindy says, "when Taran helped me outside for my daily sun intake, and she was telling me that Sherry was enamored with Cole and Atlas."

"It was obvious," I say as I set Joanie on the coffee table. "I think I saw her drooling. And that pelvic thrust. Was that really necessary?"

"The pelvic thrust was shocking," Taran says.

"Just as shocking as Atlas was in those booty shorts," Aunt Cindy says, tugging her collar.

Um, pardon me? Is she sweating over there?

"The whole thing was ridiculous and uncalled for. They took a sacred tradition and turned it into a mockery," I say as I unwrap Richie, his still-vibrant red hair peeking past the tissue paper. "I mean, what we did up there, Aunt Cindy, was touching. I even teared up a bit. And then they came in with their sexually charged booty shorts and lederhosen and just ruined it all." I snort for good measure, making it clear how displeased I am.

"It was quite the scene," Taran says.

"Yes, who knew two farm boys could be so...entertaining," Aunt Cindy says, staring up at the ceiling as if she's reminiscing on what she saw.

What is going on with her?

First Niall the stripper and now this...

"Aunt Cindy?"

"Yes, dear?" she says, her sleepy eyes meeting mine.

"Were you...and pardon my language, but were you *cock shocked* last night?"

"Storee," Taran chastises. "Do not ask our great-aunt that."

"What?" I ask with a lift of my shoulders. "It's a fair question. She seems to be in some far-off land, and I feel like it's our right to know if she was just as mesmerized as the rest of the town last night."

"It's quite all right," Aunt Cindy says, pacifying Taran. "I will admit I was not expecting Cole—the recluse who chooses to stay in his house during the Christmas season rather than be involved—to be up there on the stage, dressed up as a sexy Grinch, thrusting away. It was a bit shocking and, well...yes, he's extremely attractive, and it reminded me of, well, you don't need to know what it reminded me of, but yes, I might have been a touch mesmerized. But no need to worry; I'm still very much in the game."

"Okay, because we still have a long way to go, and I can't lose you on this next competition since I have no idea what we're doing."

"The light display," she says. "They give us points in two parts. First for your initial setup and idea, and then on Christmas Eve, they give you points for how you improved the display throughout the season, because as Christmas decorators, we're always tinkering with our masterpieces. So they want to see how well we can add to the theme. This will be our most challenging competition. Cole has helped me in the past—"

"He has?" I ask.

Aunt Cindy nods. "Nothing too extravagant, but I believe it's why I've always come last in this category. Not because Cole wasn't good at hanging lights, but because I never wanted to use him too much. It's the category we need to improve on the most."

"And he probably knows that…damn it," I say, swatting at the coffee table and causing Joanie the angel to shake. Aunt Cindy gives me a warning glare.

"I can help with the lights," Taran says.

"That's right," Aunt Cindy says. "Look how well you did with the decorations in the house."

"She did do a wonderful job," I say, looking around. "Only problem is, we have three days to get the light display done and we have no plan, no lights, and no idea what we're going to do. And no offense, Taran, but hanging these decorations took you a week. We don't have that kind of time."

Aunt Cindy taps her chin as I unwrap the Fonz. His large head with sideburns on a baby-sized body always kills me. "That's true, you are slow," she says. "You take a long time cleaning my crevices too."

I shiver while Taran stands tall. "Do you want an infection?"

"I just want to be cleaned, not ogled."

"Good God," Taran says in disgust. "Trust me, if I could wash you with my eyes closed, I would."

"Well, that's rude," Aunt Cindy huffs.

"Well, it's rude to assume that I enjoy washing my great-aunt's crevices."

"Okay, okay…everyone, calm down," I say, using my hands to urge them down. "We can't be infighting—that's what Cole would want. We need to stay cohesive. A solid unit moving into this light display. Even though it pains me, we have to take note that right now we're not losing, we're just tied, and going into the light display knowing we took last place in previous years is not ideal. But I think…I think we can take this, or at least score higher points."

"And how do you think we do that?" Aunt Cindy asks. "Do you have an idea?"

I shake my head as I help Taran remove the manger—aka the diner—from the bin. "No, but I think I can do some snooping today." I pause and then ask, "Peach and Paula, they own the hardware store, right? They're the ones judging the light display?"

"Correct," Aunt Cindy says.

"Do you think we could take a page out of Cole's book and see if they're interested in a little…flirting?"

Aunt Cindy eyes me and slowly shakes her head. "No, not recommended. They're smart and not easily wooed by the human form in booty shorts like Sherry Conrad. If anything, I think they'd hold it against you because they'd see right through your tactics."

"Damn it." I lean against the coffee table as Taran gently places the "manger" on the mantel. "Then that brings me back to the snooping."

"What kind of snooping are you going to do?" Taran asks.

"Don't worry about it, but while I'm out, I need you two to look through the outside decorations we already have and start formulating ideas. We need something with pizzazz, something flashy—"

"I don't do flashy," Aunt Cindy says.

I point at her. "That's the problem. We need to garner attention, not be subtle. If we're going to beat the naked man twins, then we need to be smart about this. Flashy is the way to go, trust me."

———————

Winter hat on, scarf secured around my neck, and mittens on, I peer through the knotty fence, trying to see if Cole and Atlas have set anything up in Cole's backyard. Perhaps a layout of their plan, the untangling of lights, or even the suggestion of a blow-up character, but as I scan around, I find nothing.

Not a fake Santa.

Not a reindeer to be stuck on the roof.

Not even a piece of furniture.

Sheesh.

I move toward the front of the two houses and slip my sunglasses on. Given the amount of sun this town gets despite the winter season, sunglasses are a must—so you don't burn your retinas from the light rays bouncing off the white snow.

I face Aunt Cindy's house, pretending to observe it, when in reality, I have my eyes trained to the left, taking in Cole's house.

It's similar to Aunt Cindy's with the intricate architecture, a wrap-around porch, and an angled roof that's covered in snow from the night before—it never ends. Thankfully, Aunt Cindy has a shoveling service that does all the clearing of her sidewalk and driveway for her, or else we'd be out here almost every day.

The chill starts to seep through my jacket and into my bones as I survey his house and think about what he could possibly do.

Lights around the porch rails?

Playful window lights that aren't just candles like Aunt Cindy likes to do? A lit-up tunnel that runs from the sidewalk and down the path to his house?

Oooh, we should do that. Beat him to it.

I make a mental note.

Each house has black streetlights that resemble old gas lampposts.

We could wrap Aunt Cindy's with some garland and strings of lights as well, and change the color of the bulb…but theme, what kind of theme?

I stare at Cole's house some more, curious as to what he could be doing—

"Trying to get some ideas?" his deep voice asks from behind me, startling me nearly out of my winter boots.

I adjust my sunglasses, which have shifted down my nose as a result of being scared, and turn around to see him grinning at me, clearly pleased with himself.

"Don't you have to be at work?" I look him up and down, taking in his worn jeans and simple flannel over a Henley shirt—seems to be the grumpy uniform he wears so very often.

He sticks his hands in his pockets. "I have the day off. Why do you care?"

"I don't care."

"Clearly you do, since you asked."

"Because you startled me, and I didn't know what else to say," I counter.

"And why did I startle you? Maybe because you were snooping?"

"I was not snooping," I say. "I truly have better things to do with my life."

"Uh-huh, so then why did I see you over by the fence, looking through it and into my backyard?" He grins, knowing damn well he's caught me.

God, he's so irritating.

I fold my arms over my chest. "For your information, I saw a bunny and I was invested in seeing if he could escape the hellhole that is your side of the fence."

"Hellhole?" he asks with a lift of his brow. "That seems a bit harsh, don't you think?"

"Have you looked in your backyard? There isn't even a piece of furniture for someone to sit on to observe a bunny's journey if they wanted to."

"Maybe because the bunnies should be left alone and not preyed on by eager city folks."

"I was not preying on it."

"That's right." He nods and points at me. "Because there really wasn't a bunny at all, and you were snooping because you're scared about the light competition after losing last night."

"Oh please," I scoff, even though sweat starts to prickle at my scalp—despite the chilly weather. "I'm not worried in the slightest. The only reason you won last night was because Atlas was ridiculously panting like a dog."

His eyes narrow, and I can see that stung him, since *he* was supposed to be the main event. So I go with it.

"Yeah, I heard Martha and Mae discussing it, actually. It's all everyone can talk about—Atlas this, Atlas that. Word on the street is he stole the show."

"He did not steal the show," Cole says, clearly enraged, which is exactly what I wanted.

"Aww, are your man feelings hurt because they're not talking about you?" I rub my hand over his arm in a comforting way. However, I'm greeted by rock-hard skin with divots and curves, and damn it, it just reminds me of what he looked like last night...shirtless...and in those lederhosen that, I'll be honest, were more flattering than I would have assumed.

"I see what you're doing," he says.

"And what is that?"

"You're trying to get under my skin, but it's not going to work. I actually just came from Martha and Mae's house, and guess what, they told me *I* was all everyone could talk about."

I wince. "Oof, how do I explain this to you?" I steeple my hands together and place them under my chin. "You see, there is this thing called *lying*. People do it to spare others' feelings."

He rolls his eyes. "Nice try, but this tactic's not going to work. If you want to win, then you're going to have to try harder." He turns away from me and starts walking toward town.

Because I'm headed in the same direction, I walk after him. "I don't need to try harder." I struggle to keep up with his large steps.

"After last night, it seems like you might have to."

"Oh my God, you act like you're a million points ahead of me. You won one competition, I won the other, and we're tied right now."

"Yes, but I have the momentum," he counters.

I jog next to him to fully catch up. "Momentum means nothing."

"For you, clearly, since it didn't carry over to the next competition where you're concerned."

Ooooo, he's infuriating. It's like fighting with someone who never lets you win and always needs to have the last word.

"Let's be honest about it, Cole. The only reason you won last night was because you showed nipple."

That stops him and forces him to turn toward me. "Actually, my lederhosen covered my nipples—I know this because the fabric rubbed against them and made them tingle."

I crinkle my nose. "Ew."

"Just stating the facts."

"Fine, the only reason you won was because you showed off your stacked abs."

His brow quirks nearly into his hairline. "*Stacked* abs?" He smirks and sticks his hands in his pockets. "Like what you saw, Taylor?"

"What?" I say, my voice cracking and my cheeks flaming. "No. I was repulsed."

"Uh-huh. You know, someone who was repulsed wouldn't have said 'stacked abs;' they'd have just said 'stomach.'"

Like I said...infuriating.

"Why are you like this?"

"Like what?" he asks. "A man so attractive that you can't seem to stop thinking about his appearance last night?"

I toss my arms in the air and turn away from him to head toward the hardware store. "I give up. You clearly can't communicate like an adult."

"I'm communicating just fine. I think you're the one getting tongue-tied," he says and then leans close to me. "Maybe because of my *stacked* abs."

Irritated, I pick up my pace, walking faster so I don't need to be near him.

Sure, was that the wrong choice of words? Absolutely. But I'm not... I'm not good under high-pressure situations. I tend to say things I don't want people to hear. Hence the last few minutes.

"Where are you headed?" he says, barely breaking a sweat as he keeps up with my pace.

Damn him.

"None of your business."

"Is it the hardware store to see what kind of light display you should be creating?"

"Uh...no," I say, even though that's exactly where I'm headed.

"You know, I was the one who helped your aunt Cindy with her light display the last few years. So if you need help, I'd be more than happy to dress in my lederhosen again and hang lights for you, give you another good show."

My nostrils flare.

My fists clench at my sides.

And then I stop on the sidewalk and turn toward him and say, "Why on earth would I want your help with something you failed at? Aunt Cindy said the last few light displays put her in last place, so clearly you have no idea what you're doing. Keep your mediocre work to yourself while I work out a plan to annihilate you."

"Is that your trash talk?" he asks.

"Wouldn't you like to know," I say very immaturely, continuing my trek toward the hardware store.

"I wouldn't, actually," he says as he continues walking at my side.

Looks like we're going to the hardware store together. Great.

CHAPTER TWELVE
COLE

A blush crept up her cheeks; she
worried she'd be caught.
Surely she didn't think him attractive!
Surely she did not.

He was mean, conniving, the
absolute worst of them all.
His ears were too big for his head,
his lips entirely too small.

But of course, those were lies told
to make her feel better.
The truth was his pelvic thrust made
her wetter and wetter.

"YOU KNOW, IT'S NOT THAT cold out," I say as I walk next to a very disgruntled Storee Taylor.

Fuck, do I love seeing her like this.

Her cheeks pink with anger.

Her upper lip snarled with irritation.

Her fists clenching at her sides, ready to pounce with revenge.

I'm under her skin. There's fear there...and that's exactly what I want to see.

I'm not normally this arrogant or rude. Grumpy? Yes. Provoking? Not really. My interactions with women are generally limited to the realm of the very tame. I go out and find the occasional hookup because I have "needs," but no one's ever really excited me like Storee Taylor. Not that I want to hook up with her...of course I don't. But this is fun. And I haven't enjoyed myself like this for many years.

"I'm invoking the not-talking rule," she says, holding up her hand to me. "You invoked it in the Kringle Krampus, and I'm invoking it now."

"Oof." I wince. "Sorry, but that's not how it works."

"What do you mean that's not how it works? It's a tit for tat kind of thing."

I shake my head. "Unfortunately, it's not."

"Says who?"

"Says me." I rock on my heels, lips sealed together in an apologetic grimace.

"Who made you the authority?"

"Well, since you're in my town and I'm the one who has lived here longer, that gives me all the authority."

"Uh, but you're forgetting one thing," she says, looking like she's about to stun me with a comeback. "I belong to Aunt Cindy, so her years transfer over to me."

"Yeah, that's not how that works either," I say, ignoring the empty feeling in my stomach as I consider the years my parents missed out on. It frustrates me, how many more thoughts of my parents I have during this time of year. Not wanting her to see the change in my expression, I move past her toward the hardware store.

Paula is standing at the register when I walk in. She lifts a hand and grins. "Cole, heard about your pelvic thrusting last night. I didn't believe it until Martha showed me a video on her phone."

The door rings behind me, announcing Storee's arrival as well.

"Rude," she mutters. "You didn't have to shut the door on me."

Didn't realize I had, but that's a positive.

"I didn't know you had those kinds of moves," Paula says to me.

I smile at her. "Only pull them out for special occasions."

"Yes, well, Peach was saying at the breakfast table how you served last night, and Martha's sent the video to almost the entire town."

Great.

Just what I need. The entire town watching that display over and over.

Sure, I was proud of Max and myself, but I know a few months from now when the adrenaline has calmed down, I'm going to regret ever painting my body green and smoothing my hands over my ass, showing the town my Grinch-like figure.

"The more I can help people celebrate the Christmas season, the better," I say, and I suddenly remember my sash. *Fuck.* I pull it out of my back pocket and drape it over my chest. "Speaking of which, didn't want to get this wet when I was fixing Martha and Mae's kitchen sink."

"Leaking again?" Paula asks as Storee moves past me, acting like she's interested in some dowels. I know she's eavesdropping. She's not sneaky in the slightest—probably the worst sleuth I've ever seen.

"Yup. I told them after this round of adjustments, they might have to call a real plumber because I don't think I'm actually doing anything to fix it."

Paula chuckles. "Did they ask you to come over in your lederhosen?"

I chuckle as well. "As a matter of fact…they did."

Paula shakes her head. "You know they made it leak on purpose."

I wink at Paula. "Hence why I plan on telling them to call a real plumber."

"They never will."

I sigh heavily. "I know."

"Well, let me know if you need help finding anything, and hey, have you thought about your light display?"

"I have." I catch Storee leaning in to hear. Wanting to mess with her, I say, "I was thinking about going simple this year, understated. I know how much you love a classic Christmas."

Paula opens her mouth to protest, but I quickly press my finger to my lips and then nod toward Storee, who's feigning interest in the plunger in her hand. Paula glances in that direction and then offers me a conspiratorial smile. And this is why being known in the town is going to work to my advantage.

"Oh yes," she says robotically. "Classic Christmas. Subtle, understated. That's what we're looking for this year."

"And with a heavy focus on blow-up decorations, right?" I add. "Because I have that fifty-foot Santa that I'm chomping at the bit to use." Blow-up Christmas decorations are prohibited in the competition, which is spelled out in the rules. Not sure if Storee's read the rules or not, but if she's snooping around for ideas, I'm thinking that she doesn't have any idea what's going on.

"Fifty-foot, interesting. Where did you find a fifty-foot blowup?" Paula asks.

"Online. Shipping was a bitch, but he's ready to be inflated." I glance over at Storee, who knocks on the plunger, testing out the rubber. She nods in appreciation and then carries it against her shoulder as she heads down one of the aisles.

"Not going to work," Paula whispers. "She's smarter than you think."

"You're giving her too much credit," I say.

Paula shakes her head, mirth in her eyes. "If she puts a *sixty*-foot blowup in the front yard, you're the one who's going to have to face Krampus."

I hold up my hands. "Not my problem."

Chuckling, she nods toward the back. "You know the drill. If you need more of anything we have, I can pull from storage."

"Got it." I knock on her counter. "Thanks." Then with my eyes on a wandering Storee, I head to the back of the hardware store, where Paula and Peach keep all of their Christmas decorations. It's probably the most comprehensive collection of lights and adornments in the world thanks to where we live. The store opens up in the back, elevating the space into two stories of decorations, all sorted by need.

Strands of lights are divided up by type of bulb, color, and size.

Extension cords and hanging devices—the accessories, if you will—are all in one area.

And then there are the prelit garlands, the unlit garlands, and the tinsel garlands. The lit-up nets for bushes, the projectors, and the balled-up lights. Not to mention the lawn ornaments, which are displayed by pictures in a binder to sift through and stored in the back.

Everything you could ever want.

Not sure what Max has planned, since he's the one captaining the ship after last night. I pull out my phone and send him a text.

Cole: At the hardware store, anything you want me to grab for the light display?

While I wait for his response, I head upstairs, where I know they keep the string lights. I grab a basket while I'm at it, and from the corner of my eye I catch a glimpse of Storee sneaking behind a shelf down below, her stealthy moves not stealthy at all.

My phone beeps in my hand, so I glance at the text from Max.

Max: Green. We need all the green.
Cole: I'm going to call you. Storee is following me around, so just go with whatever I say, okay?
Max: Ha! Okay.

I call Max, and he answers on the second ring just as Storee creeps up the stairs, the creak of the old wood giving away her approach, but I act like I can't hear it.

"So Storee is trying to get the scoop on what you're doing?" Max answers.

"Hey man, yeah, I'm here at the hardware store," I say. "Yup, that's right."

"Ahh, okay. So we're roleplaying here," Max says. He clears his throat. "So glad you called, Cole. We need to figure out what we're doing with the decorations. I'm so scared, so worried, I actually threw up this morning from the nerves."

"Too much, man."

He chuckles. "Hey, I'm trying to play a role here, can you not disturb me?"

Ignoring him, I thumb through the storage catalog that Peach has put together and say, "Talked to Paula, and she said they were looking for understated this year. Classic Christmas."

"Oh shit, she said that out loud? I don't think Storee's going to believe it."

"Yeah, understated, but she also said she liked the fifty-foot Santa. I know, I know, a clash of ideas," I say. "But I got the feeling she was looking for an impressive blowup to be the centerpiece of the whole design, and then with understated lights around it."

"She's going to kill you, man," Max says on a laugh.

"Do you think fifty feet is big enough?"

"Is that even a thing?" Max asks. "That seems really big, man. You should have gone with twenty."

"Yeah, you're probably right," I say. "So, we do the Santa and a snow globe that blows up, the kind that makes all the noise."

"Are you talking about the one that George Whitmeyer had out on his front lawn that Bob Krampus popped in the middle of the night?"

"Yeah, that one," I say, still thumbing through the catalog as I catch

Storee move from one shelf to the other, picking up a candy cane lawn ornament and giving it a good examination from top to bottom.

"Krampus still denies popping that, you know. Even though they have him on camera. Said he'd never do something to destroy the Christmas spirit in town and that someone framed him."

"Really?" I ask.

"Oh yeah, I heard some people talking about it at Warm Your Spirit, but then Krampus walked in and they all got quiet before saying merry Christmas to him and walking away. I think he knew they were talking about him because his nose got red."

"Not the nose," I say, forgetting that I'm supposed to be acting.

"Yup, the nose. It was terrifying, or at least that's what I heard. Anyway, is she still following you?"

"Yes. Okay, so you want me to get that?" I say as Storee moves toward the stairs again, carefully walking down them.

"The green lights? Yeah, man. Grab them. I have plans."

"Want to tell me what they are?"

"Let's just say your house is going to be wrapped up like a bow. I was working on a design with my dad last night. We got this one in the bag."

"Who won last year? Do you remember?"

"Jimmy Short," he answers. "He's the one you need to be concerned about the most. Quite sure he enters the Kringle competition just to get credit for his displays. They're always phenomenal."

I grip the back of my neck. "Never seen them."

"Because you don't leave your cave during Christmas. Interesting that a girl has you changing your tune."

"That's not the reason," I grumble.

"Uh-huh, you keep telling yourself that."

Rolling my eyes, I say, "Okay, I'm hanging up now."

"Get all the green," he says right before I hang up.

STOREE

I fly into the house, slam the door shut, and then move into the living room, where I draw the curtains, shutting out the light from the outside world.

"What on earth are you doing?" Aunt Cindy says as I cast us into darkness.

I spin around toward Aunt Cindy and Taran, who are both looking at me as if I've lost my mind.

Since I practically sprinted back here, I'm sweating and need to free myself from my winter gear, so I tear off my coat, unravel my scarf, and then toss my mittens and winter hat into a pile on the floor before kneeling in front of the coffee table, staring at my sister and great-aunt.

"I know what he's doing."

"You know what *who* is doing?" Aunt Cindy asks, adjusting her glasses on her nose.

"Cole. I know what he's planning on doing for his light display. I overheard him talking to Paula in the hardware store."

"You did?" Aunt Cindy asks, looking hopeful.

I slowly nod. "Oh yes. He had no idea that I was listening in—I pretended to be invested in the curves and structure of a plunger, so much so that now all I can smell is the rubber of it all over me. Want to smell?" I lean toward my sister and aunt, but they both hold up their hands.

"No thanks, we don't want to smell the plunger on you," Taran says.

"Okay, well, it's there. I'm smelling very rubbery right now."

"You say that as if we should be proud."

"You should be," I say. "I did all the sleuthing, and now we have the upper hand because I know exactly what he's doing."

"Well, tell us, dear," Aunt Cindy says. "Don't keep us in suspense."

I run my hand over the surface of the coffee table. "Okay, get this…he has a fifty-foot blow-up Santa that he plans on centering his entire display around. Paula's looking for understated, classic Christmas, so I think he's going to have a few lights, but yeah, it's all about the Santa, so I think if we take that information and try to figure out…a…way…why are you looking at me like that?"

Aunt Cindy and Taran are both shaking their heads at me.

"What? What's wrong?"

Taran crosses one leg over the other. "Storee, are you being serious right now?"

"Uh, yeah." I thumb behind me. "I heard him—he said it several times. He even called Atlas and talked about it with him on the phone."

Aunt Cindy pinches the bridge of her nose while Taran keeps shaking her head.

"What?" I say, growing annoyed.

"Did it ever occur to you that maybe Cole was playing you?" Taran asks.

"What do you mean, playing me?"

"Trying to throw you off with misinformation so you try to beat him at, oh I don't know, a nice game of 'who has the biggest blowup in their front yard?'"

"I mean…no," I say. "He didn't know I was listening."

"He knew," Aunt Cindy says. "Trust me, he knew. He's a smart boy."

"He didn't. I was very stealthy about it. He probably thinks I went home with that plunger."

"Storee, he was playing with you," Taran says.

"He wasn't," I insist, standing my ground.

"He was," Aunt Cindy repeats.

"No. I swear, I was—"

"Storee," Taran interrupts. "Blowups are not allowed in town, let alone in the competition. Bob Krampus did away with them a few years ago."

I look between the two of them. "Are you sure? Because there were some in the store."

"Probably for out-of-towners," Taran says.

I bite on my lip. "I don't know about that. He was really enthusiastic about this fifty-foot Santa. I mean, I was impressed to hear about it. That seems pretty tall, but then I thought, *How big is a house? Who knows, maybe it's one of those house-sized blowups,* and I considered getting an even bigger one. I was so busy running back here to tell you the news that I didn't see if there was one that was bigger than—"

Taran tosses the Kringle competition folder on the coffee table. "It's in the rules, if you read them. No blowups. All light-up displays must be comprised of mostly lights and garland. Lawn ornaments can only make up about ten percent of the display, so you could have a light-up Santa on your roof and some reindeer, but the challenge is really about how well you can hang and maneuver the lights."

I stare down at the folder and then back up at them. "Are you sure?"

"Positive," Taran says.

I glance over at Aunt Cindy, and she slowly nods, bursting my sleuthing bubble.

I rock back on my heels and feel my entire body sag in defeat.

"That motherfucker," I whisper.

"Oh dear," Aunt Cindy says, pressing her hand to her chest.

"Seriously, Storee, did you really think he was going to give away his idea for his light display right in front of you?"

"I don't know...maybe?" I reply. "I was being sneaky."

"I've seen you try to be sneaky," Aunt Cindy says. "Trying to scope out your presents over the years. I love you, Storeebook, but you are anything but sneaky."

I lean back and lie flat on the carpet, staring up at the ceiling. "And here

I thought I had the scoop. Damn it." I clench my fists at my sides. "Well then, what are we going to do? Do you think Paula and Peach really want understated and classic like he said?"

"No," Taran says. "He was tricking you. Honestly, Storee, are you that gullible?"

"No, I just really believed I'm that good at going undetected. I guess I'm not." Huffing, I sit up and slam my fist on the coffee table. "We need to seek revenge."

"Careful on the wood, dear," Aunt Cindy says. "Taran just polished that for me."

"Sorry," I say. "But seriously, what's the plan?"

Taran pulls out a notebook and opens it up. "Here's what we have to do..."

"I'm freezing my ass off," I mutter to Taran as I shiver in my boots, holding on to rows and rows of string lights while she pulls out her tape measure once again.

"It's not even that cold out," Taran says as she marks a spot on the house with a piece of chalk.

"Aunt Cindy has a portable heater in front of her," I counter.

"Because she's supposed to be on her deathbed, remember? She told me she was getting toasty, so I had to pull her out of the sun and put her in the shade. It's all about appearances," Taran says, getting more into this than I expected.

"Why can't I have a portable heater?" I shiver, the cold tracing all the way down my spine, causing my body to convulse unattractively. "I can't feel my toes, Taran."

"We've been out here for ten minutes," Taran says on a huff. "How are we going to get this done if you keep complaining?"

"Um, how are we going to get this done if all you've done is measure?

We need to start hanging things up," I say. "Look at Cole and Max—they already have half of the house done."

"And in a sloppy manner," Taran says. "Trust me, precision is key when it comes to lights."

"How do you know?" I ask. "You've never hung lights in your life."

"I hung some on my apartment balcony," Taran counters. "And people appreciated them."

"Dear God," I mutter just as Cole walks up to us...wearing a T-shirt and jeans. What kind of thick-as-shit skin does that man have if he can walk around in a T-shirt in this weather?

"Hey, neighbors." He waves. That stupid sash we have to wear—which I'm not currently wearing—is draped across his chest. "How's it going?" He stands right at the base of our porch, smiling and looking far too pleased.

My eyes narrow at him as I attempt to give him my most menacing glare. "Excuse me. Please remove yourself from the premises, as we don't want our enemy scoping out the competition."

He looks around, making a real show of it. "What competition?"

What an inflated ass.

"I will have you know we're well on our way to executing a brilliant light display that will make your retinas burn with its brightness."

He nods. "Really looks like it. I can't wait to see how these twenty boxes of lights will look on this little side of the porch."

I glance down at the lights and then back at him. Will this not be enough? Twenty boxes seemed like a lot, and Taran did the calculations, right? "Well, that's...uh...that's not all we have. We have a lot more."

"Twenty's all we will need," Taran says from where she's still measuring, her tongue sticking out of her mouth as she concentrates.

"Twenty, huh?" Cole rocks on his heels. "Really going to burn those retinas then. I'll be sure to wear my sunglasses whenever I walk by."

Growing very frustrated, I drop the lights, stomp off the porch, and walk right up to him. "You've got a real bad attitude, you know that?" I point at his chest.

He grins. He towers over me as I attempt intimidation, but it doesn't seem to work on him. "Bad attitude? Oh no, I'm truly excited to see this light display you guys have planned. I can already tell it's going to be something magical."

"I know sarcasm when I hear it," I say, just as a family walks down the sidewalk toward us. Morphing my face into the epitome of Christmas joy, I smile at them and wave. "Good afternoon. Merry Christmas."

The family ignores me, crosses the street, and heads up the sidewalk to what I'm going to assume is their house.

"Well, that was rude," I say.

"No, seemed on par," Cole says.

"What do you mean?"

"That was the Dankworths. They own Baubles and Wrappings, and last I heard"—he snidely smirks—"they're still mad at you for tipping over their signature tree."

"Oh my God," I say. "That was an accident. Over ten years ago. I didn't do it on purpose. I'd never tip over a tree on purpose or even know how to tip over a tree." Why do people in this town hold grudges for so damn long, anyway?

"Running into it at full speed got the job done."

My expression falls flat as I quietly say, "You weren't even there; how would you know?"

"I live in this town, Storee. I know everything."

"Oh yeah?" I cross my arms over my chest. "Then did you know I despise you?"

"Was clued in from the spittle bubble on your lower lip."

I quickly wipe at my lips and then lift my chin, which of course makes him laugh. "You know, when I first saw you, I thought it might be nice to reconnect since I'd be here for a few weeks, but boy oh boy, was I wrong."

"You were incredibly wrong," he says.

"Clearly." I look him up and down. "Also, using your body as a weapon to win a competition...don't you think that's a little beneath you?"

"Not as *beneath you* as using your aunt's injury to convince the town she's on her deathbed."

I let out a strangled gasp. "How dare you imply—"

"Cut the shit, Storee. We know what you're doing, and it might work on some, but it won't work on everyone."

"Yeah, well, your sad attempt to try to throw me off at the hardware store didn't work either." He doesn't need to know the truth. We'll keep that just between us.

"Your sleuthing was pathetic."

"You're pathetic," I shoot back as I catch movement from the corner of my eye, spotting Martha and Mae in matching track suits, headed in our direction. I turn toward them, and with my cheeriest smile, I say, "Merry Christmas."

Blond hair bouncing up and down as they power-walk toward us, they wave as well. "Merry Christmas, Storee. What are you two up to?" Martha asks as she waggles her eyebrows.

Oh, please do not waggle your brows at us. There is absolutely nothing to waggle about—

Before I can finish my thought, Cole wraps his arm around my shoulders and pulls me into his side.

Immediately, the smell of his...is that deodorant? Cologne? Whatever it is, it smells annoyingly good. Really good. Too good for someone who is so...so...sour.

"We're just hanging out, chatting it up about our light displays," Cole says in a charming voice, which I think shocks Martha, Mae, and me at the same time.

"Oh, how nice," Mae says. "It's so great seeing you two back together.

I remember watching you from a distance, back when you'd sit on Cole's porch, chatting about the holidays and sharing hot cocoa."

"Eh, I don't think we ever shared hot cocoa," I say.

"Not from lack of me trying," Cole replies with a squeeze to my shoulder.

The twins laugh.

"Oh Cole, always charming. Maybe now that Storee's back in town, she'll give you the chance to share a drink this time."

"That's what I'm hoping," Cole says, and I feel his eyes on me.

What the hell is he up to?

"Oh please, give him a chance," Martha says, clasping her hands. "Cole is such a good man."

Uhh...

Please, someone, tell me what's happening.

"Not only is he handsome, but like Martha said, he's a very good man. He takes care of all of us around town. And you two would be so cute together."

"That's what I keep telling her," Cole says, nearly making my head explode. "I still have some time—maybe I'll impress her with my light display."

"I believe you will," Martha says with a wink. "Well, enjoy, and don't hurt yourselves up on the roof."

Martha and Mae both say their goodbyes, and once their backs are turned toward us, I push away from Cole. "What the hell was that?" I ask through clenched teeth.

"Those are called neighbors," Cole says. "They tend to say hi to you when they see you out and about on the cul-de-sac. Kind of the nice thing to do."

"I know what neighbors are, you nitwit. I'm talking about the hot-cocoa-sharing thing."

"Oh, that." He shrugs. "I don't know, spur-of-the-moment decision.

Kind of liked it, though, as they love a good romance, and that gave them the impression that you were the one holding out while I was over here trying to get your attention."

"Uh, yeah, I know. You just made me look bad."

He shrugs again. "Yeah, but it made me look like the ultimate hopeless romantic, so a win for me." He pats my shoulder. "Anyway, good luck with the lights, pal."

"I'm not your pal, and I'm not your...your hot-cocoa-sharing buddy."

"I know. Martha and Mae are pulling for me, though, so maybe I'll prevail by the end of this competition. Who knows? Crazier things have happened." He winks and then turns to take off, but not before I grab his hand and tug him back.

"Do not play with me, Cole Black. You might not like what happens."

"It's cute that you're trying to threaten me."

"I'm being serious."

"Yeah?" he asks. "What are you going to do, Storee?"

"I'm going to...well..." Nothing comes to mind, so I cross my arms and huff, "You're just going to have to wait and see."

He grins. "The anticipation is already eating me alive. Merry Christmas, Storee. May your days be not so merry and bright."

And with that, he heads toward his house, where Max steps out holding another bin of lights.

Crap.

I rush up to the porch, where Taran is still measuring and Aunt Cindy is nodding off in her chair.

"We need more lights," I say in a hushed tone, careful not to wake Aunt Cindy.

"I told you, twenty boxes are all we need," Taran says.

"No, we need more. Trust me, Taran. If we're going to win this...we need so much more."

CHAPTER THIRTEEN
STOREE

Green and red, all wrapped in a bow—
Cole's house was lit; it was entirely aglow.

While next door, the display was not so bright,
because twenty boxes of strands
were far too little light.

Did that stop Storee? No way. She simply said,
"If I can't win this one, I'll get revenge instead..."

"I TOLD YOU, TARAN. I freaking told you twenty boxes aren't enough," I say as I pace the living room, the evening just a few hours away, meaning that the competition will soon be judged.

"Twenty boxes are enough. They'll appreciate the straight lines and well-manicured display."

"No, they'll think, *Wow, they should have purchased more lights.*" I press my hand to my forehead. "I knew I shouldn't have listened to you. Twenty isn't enough!"

"Twenty is perfect," she shoots back. "Look how beautiful they are." She points to the window, where we can see the bright white of the lights beaming. I've gotta hand it to her—the new LED lights with their large bulbs really do burn the retinas, but I wish we had five times as many. We could have lit up the entire town of Kringle from Aunt Cindy's house.

"You just have them on the rain gutters. You didn't do anything special."

"We didn't need to," Taran says. "We're letting the lights speak for themselves."

"And they're screaming *we're boring*," I yell and then flop onto the couch.

"What's all this ruckus?" Aunt Cindy says as she slowly makes her way into the living room with her walker. Taran helps her the rest of the way and into her chair.

"Storee thinks the light display isn't good enough," Taran says.

"Because it's not," I say. "Did you see Cole's? They made a bow on the roof out of lights. His house looks like a freaking present. And here we are with a basic dad-light display."

"Basic dad-light display?" Taran asks with a crinkle to her nose. "What's that supposed to mean?"

"It means any dad looking to spend five hours out of the house and away from his family would do this display. There's nothing fancy about it."

"I beg to differ. There were many calculations that went into this display. Paula and Peach will appreciate it."

"Oh yeah?" I ask, challenging her. "You plan on giving them a report on your calculations? Showing them everything that went into it?"

"You know, that might not be a bad idea," Taran says. "I think I'm going to put that together." And then she heads up the stairs.

"Or you can spend your time putting up more lights!" I call after her.

The door to her room shuts, and I huff out my displeasure before leaning back on the couch.

"Ugh, Aunt Cindy, this is not good." I drag my hands over my face. "We're going to lose this competition."

"I don't think so," Aunt Cindy says. "We might not win, but we don't have to lose."

"What do you mean?" I ask as I glance her way.

She wiggles her finger at me, so I move in closer.

"As you mentioned the other day, Cole seems to be playing...dirty, correct?"

"Uh, yeah. Lederhosen aside, he's making it seem like he wants to date me but I'm the one holding out, breaking his heart or something. Of course, Martha and Mae ate it up, and I'm sure the news is all over town."

"Right...right..." She pauses and then adds, "Although I do think you two have more in common than you believe—"

"Aunt Cindy," I say, insulted, causing her to chuckle.

"I said *although*. You didn't let me finish. Although...you have some things in common, I don't think you're a match. You're not the type of girl who'd live in a Christmas town year-round. I don't think the spirit lives in you like I wish it did."

That makes my brow crinkle. "What do you mean by that? I think I have a lot of Christmas spirit."

Her eyes go sad as she takes my hand in hers. "My sweet Storeebook, if you had the spirit inside of you, nothing would have kept you from visiting me on Christmas."

Wow.

At least ten tons of guilt are immediately placed on my shoulders.

"And I don't say that to make you feel guilty," she adds. *Uh, too late.* "It's just the truth. But enough about you and Cole."

"There's...there's no 'you and Cole' to talk about," I say, wanting to reiterate that.

"I know, dear. But what I was going to say is if he's playing dirty, then you might as well play dirty too."

"Okay...should I find a blowup and put it in his front yard?"

Aunt Cindy smiles. "Though clever, I don't think we have the time for that. But if you're up for it, I think you can do a little more damage."

"Yeah?"

She nods. "We're going to need you to dress all in black."

———————

You are stealth.

You are quick.

You are practically invisible.

I repeat my affirmations as I make my way down the back porch of the house and into the backyard.

Stealth Storee.

Quick Storee.

Invisible Storee.

I must stay out of sight—my life depends on it!

Because I didn't have enough all-black items, I'm wearing Aunt Cindy's black winter fisherman's hat, her black scarf wrapped around my neck and forehead, and her gloves with the fur on the wrists. I tried sunglasses but realized it would be far too dark for me to see anything, so I took those off.

I tug on the scarf, tightening it to make sure it doesn't unravel, and then I head to the corner of the yard where the loose fence plank is located.

I'm on a mission, and it's to save Christmas!

Well, save Christmas from being stolen by a conniving, tricky man who's toying with the hearts of people in town to win him favor—and yes, I know, I was doing the same thing with Aunt Cindy, but this could be Aunt Cindy's last Christmas, we don't know…the broken hip could very well send her to an early grave—as she put it.

And sure, the doctor doesn't think that's the case, but we have to live this Christmas as if it's her last. So…if that means using her to our advantage when it comes to these competitions, then yes, we're going to make her look frail and wheel her around with a blanket over her lap.

"Okay, she said it was the third plank from the corner," I whisper to myself. Thankfully the glaring bulbs Taran hung on the house offer some light to the back corner of the yard—not enough to reveal myself, but enough that I can find the loose plank and easily pull it up. I glance at the slot I'm supposed to squeeze myself through and then down at my body.

Has Aunt Cindy lost her mind?

This is only about four inches wide. My thigh is not going to fit through this, let alone my ass.

Jesus.

I put the plank back down and then rest my hands on my hips. Looks like plan B is in order.

I tiptoe down toward the front of the fence to the gate, my feet crunching in the snow. This godforsaken white stuff, does it not ever melt?

I pause when I reach the gate and slow my breathing as I listen for anyone who might be outside. When all I hear is the wind whipping through the trees, I unlock the gate and attempt to pull it open, but because of the snow, it doesn't budge.

"For the love of God," I mutter and then bend down and start scooping snow away from the gate.

Immediately, my hands turn to ice since I'm wearing cotton gloves for better finger dexterity and not water-resistant ones. But I'm determined. There's no way I can let Cole take the W on this, not when our display looks so clinical.

Freaking Taran.

I continue to shovel and kick snow away until I can open the gate just wide enough to slip through. I stand next to the fence and adjust the tightness of my scarf as I glance around the neighborhood. Paula and

Peach should be making their way over here any time now, which means I need to move quickly and get the job done.

Back at the fence, I plaster my body against it and move around the corner, leading me right into Cole's yard and the magnificent display of lights he and Max created. Of course they did a good job. They're two hunky men who aren't afraid to fall off a snow-covered roof. Whereas Taran convinced me it would be more elegant to stay off the roof and really focus on the gutters. I think I was so tired of fighting with her that I just went with it.

Big mistake.

Now look what I have to do—schlep around in the freezing cold, my fingers about to fall off from frostbite, with a ridiculous scarf dangling over my line of sight, tempting me to make a fool of myself.

Not my ideal evening.

I eye the lights in front of me, hoping they are just dim enough they don't give me away as I look to my right, then to my left. The coast is clear. Light as a feather—well, in my head I tell myself that—I spring across the crunchy snow to a large, prickly bush that I bear-hug, attempting to camouflage myself against the dark leaves.

Oof. I can tell this bush does not want to bear-hug me back.

I have branches poking me in the nose, in the hip, and right in the chest. If it wasn't for my puffy coat, I would say this bush is trying to cop a feel.

Despite the handsy bush, I focus and assess my next move.

This mission will only be successful if I reach the lights at the front of the house, so I shimmy along the bush, taking a branch right to the old crotch, and I have to hold in my startled yelp while I jut my ass away.

The way I must look…

Please let no one be around. This would be humiliating.

Knowing time is ticking, I shimmy some more until I'm right up against the porch. I release the bush, thank it for its service, and then flip around so my back is against the porch. My arms are spread for balance, my eyes scanning the dark cul-de-sac.

Not a movement.

Not a sound.

Which means it's time to make my move.

Unraveling the scarf just enough so I can see better, I let it dangle in front of me as I glance over to Cole's front door. I still my breath, listening intently for any sort of movement, but when I don't hear anything, not even a creak, I eye the strand of lights in front of me and laser in on one single light bulb.

I inwardly cackle because *what a plan*.

What a way to take a nemesis down.

He'll have no idea.

Smirking against the wintry night air, I take the single bulb in hand and I...ugh, hold on a second...and I...grrr.

Damn it.

My fingers are not working.

They're...they're too frozen.

Panic ripples inside of me. Of course, this freaking snow! Ruining everything. Needing a quick solution, I bite one of the fingers of my glove, tear it off my hand, and then stick my frozen fingers right between my legs, where I clench down hard.

"Warm up, warm up," I mutter as I wiggle in place, looking like I'm having fun next to the handsy bush.

I glance down the road to see if Peach and Paula are coming...and then to my horror, I see a crowd gathering toward the end of Krampus Court.

No!

They're coming.

Crap.

Come on, come on. Warm up!

I wiggle some more, then bring my hand to my mouth and huff on it, trying anything and everything to get my fingers to work again.

After a few seconds, I make my second attempt to pull the bulb.

My fingers slip.

They slide.

They scream from the freezing weather.

"Come on, you dicks," I yell at my fingers. Then, with one last tug, my grip on the bulb is enough, and I pull it from its socket...causing the whole strand to go out.

Huzzah!

Uhh...hold on.

Why did only one strand of lights go out? Wasn't this supposed to make all of the lights go out? Is that not a thing anymore?

Damn it!

I take in the rest of the strands, knowing what a monumental task it would be to take them all out.

I don't have enough time for another, so this will have to do. I gently set the bulb back in its socket but don't connect it all the way, and then, out of sheer panic, I sprint toward the fence.

Unluckily for me, I trip over my scarf and fly headfirst into the fence, creating a loud bang that echoes through the night.

"Mother...Christmas," I groan as I blink a few times, questioning my consciousness and sanity.

I hear Cole's door open, and even though my brain is fuzzy and my head's throbbing with pain—*and I have snow in every orifice of my jacket now*—I get up on my elbows and slither through the snow toward the gate.

"Did you hear something?" I hear Cole say, which puts a little pep in my slither.

Pushing through the snow, I army-crawl through the thin opening, my face soaked, my jacket soaked, and my scarf nearly choking me to death.

But when I drag my body through the fence, surprisingly undetected, I carefully close the gate and then roll to my back, letting myself catch my breath as I listen in.

"It sounded like something fell," Max says.

More like something slammed, that something being my brain into a wooden plank.

I hear them move off the porch and then...

"Fuck, look, a strand of lights is out," Cole says.

"Shit, and Peach and Paula are headed our way," Max says.

"We're not supposed to be outside when they're judging," Cole replies in a panic.

And despite the brain damage I just suffered and my probably frost-bitten fingers, I inwardly cackle because *ah-ha*!

Don't mess with us if you can't take the heat—or something like that.

Either way... *muahahaha*.

COLE

"Quick, try to fix it," I say to Max as I glance toward the end of the street. "They're not here yet. Martha and Mae are talking to them."

Max moves to the end of the porch and crouches down to examine the offending lights. "Is it plugged in?" he asks.

"If it wasn't, the entire house wouldn't be shining right now."

"I mean into the other string of lights it's supposed to be attached to," Max says quickly.

"Oh, let me see." I get down on my knees beside the porch to find the plug. "It looks fine." But just to be safe, I unplug it and then plug it back in again. Nothing. "Is it one of the bulbs?" I ask.

"Possibly," Max says as he glances over his shoulder. "Shit, are they getting closer?"

"Looks like the convo is ending."

"Quick, hop over the railing—get to the other side of this bush and help me look at these lights."

Not even second-guessing, I hoist myself over the rail and land flat in the snow...the disturbed snow.

What the fuck? I look around, my eyes trailing across the tracks and then a giant flattening of the snow near the fence.

"Max," I shout-whisper.

"Did you find it?" he asks.

"No, but look." I point at the tracks in the snow.

He glances over the rail. "What?"

"Looks like someone paid our light display a visit."

"What are you talking about?"

"Look, footprints and then...what looks to be a major spill right next to the fence, and it looks like a body was dragged over to Cindy's fence gate."

It takes Max a second, but when his eyes adjust, he gasps. "No, you don't think *they* did this."

"They one hundred percent did this. They saw how nice our display was and they tampered with it. Maybe that's what the crashing sound was. Maybe they fell into the fence when they were trying to run away."

"But...do you really think they'd stoop that low?" Max asks as he checks the lights, but to no avail, and Peach and Paula start walking toward us.

"Fuck, we need to get inside." I hop up on the rail, and together we crawl back to the front door to let ourselves in undetected. Once the door is shut, we both lean against it. "They would stoop that low, yes," I say. "Did you see their house compared to ours? It's no contest. We easily have the better display."

"But to tamper with it? That just seems so...un-Christmas-y."

"I don't understand why you'd expect anything less from them."

He shrugs. "I don't know, I thought maybe the Christmas spirit was burying itself within them and that we'd all become friends at some point."

I turn to Max. *Has he lost his mind?* "Friends?" I ask. "What planet are you living on?"

"One where everyone gets along." He shuffles over to the window, where he attempts to look through the blinds. "It would have been nice to, you know, somehow find commonality with each other, and then somewhere along the way the feud turns to friendship...maybe love." He waggles his eyebrows at me.

"Jesus Christ, dude, have you been watching those Lovemark movies again?"

"You could learn a thing or two from them," he says and then gasps. "They're checking out the display. Fuck, they're pointing toward the corner with the unlit section. Nooooo, they're marking something on their clipboard."

"Fuck," I say as I grip my hair. "How bad do you think it is?"

"I don't know. But we're damn sure not going to come in first. One of the main rules is to check all lights and make sure they're working."

"We did," I growl. "We were just tampered with."

"Should we send an anonymous letter to Bob Krampus stating such?" Max asks. "You know, since apparently my dream of this feud turning into a friendship is not going to come true?"

"No," I say, my fists at my sides. "No, we're going to get even."

Max slowly turns toward me. "Umm, you said that in a scary voice."

"Because I'm pissed." I join Max at the window and stare out toward where Peach and Paula are talking. Paula is nodding while Peach points to the corner of the house again. "Damn it," I say as I take a seat. "Storee's going to regret this."

"You know, before we start an all-out war, maybe we should address the situation. See if she was the one who was crawling around. Could have been a coincidence."

"That was not a coincidence," I say. "That was Storee. She messed with our lights, and now we're going to mess with her."

"I hear you, man, I really do, but I think it would be best if we walk over there and just…talk to her. Maybe feel her out."

"Do you really think she's going to tell the truth?"

Max shrugs. "There's only one way to find out. Get your shoes on."

He stands, and I glance out the window and catch Paula and Peach walking back toward town. They took mere seconds grading Cindy's house. No surprise there. I could grade it with my eyes shut. Verdict is it sucks.

Might as well approach them now when they're at their lowest. I grab my brown boots and slip them on while Max does the same. I don't bother with a jacket because I barely use one anyway. And then together, we walk out the front door.

"Now, let me do the talking," Max says as we head down the sidewalk.

"Why would I let you do the talking?"

"Because you're snarling, and I don't think we want to put them on the defensive. We need to ease it out of them, you know? Get them to make the mistake of telling us. Catch them in the lie sort of thing."

"Fine," I say as we turn into their walkway and then head up to the porch.

When we reach the door, Max whispers, "Be cool," before knocking.

"I don't need the reminder."

"Oh, you definitely do," he says just as the door opens to reveal Taran standing on the other side. Storee and Taran share the same facial features, but what sets them apart is Taran's dark hair compared to Storee's deep red. That and Taran seems to have more of a snarl to her lip.

"Hello," Max says cordially. "You must be Taran. I don't think we've officially—"

"Where is she?" I ask, throwing "cool" out the window as I blow past Max and Taran and let myself in. I glance into the living room, where I spot Storee sitting on the couch, her feet in a bucket, multiple blankets wrapped around her, and an ice pack on her head held in place by a tightly wound scarf.

"Uh, Cole," Max calls out. "Remember what we talked about."

"What are you doing here?" Storee asks, her eyes narrowing on me.

"Oh, Cole," Cindy says as she walks into the living room with the aid of her walker. She's looking rather...alive! Imagine that! "How nice to see you."

"You," I say, pointing at Storee, who's clearly trying to warm herself up after attacking our lights. "You fucked with our light display."

"What?" she gasps. "I have no idea what you're talking about."

"There's something wrong with your display?" Cindy asks. "Oh, what a shame."

I'd expect Storee to stoop to such a low level, but Cindy...now this is a new rock bottom for her.

"You both know exactly what's going on. You know what you did."

"Are you accusing me of something?" Storee asks.

"No, no," Max says, stepping up. "We're not accusing anyone of anything. Actually, we came over here to have a nice—"

"I have camera footage," I say...even though I don't, but there's nothing like scaring them to get the truth out.

Storee's eyes widen. "You...you have camera footage of what?" She clutches the three blankets wrapped around her.

"Of you tampering with our lights and making a strand go dark."

"I have no idea what you're—"

"Cut the shit, Storee," I say, causing Cindy to gasp.

"Cole Black, is that how your mother taught you to speak to women?" Cindy asks. I ignore her, not wanting to talk about my mom at all. For the record, the answer is no, but I'm certain confronting a woman who sabotaged your light display warrants directness.

"I think what he's trying to say," Max says as he grips my shoulder, "is that he's disappointed in the conduct that has been going on between our two parties."

"The conduct?" Storee asks as she shifts, her ice pack slipping closer to her forehead. She props it back up and continues, "You're the one going around town telling people that I'm turning you down romantically."

"I said it once and it was a joke."

She shrugs. "Well, I guess this was a joke too."

"Ah-ha, so you admit it." I point at her.

"I admit nothing." She tilts her chin up in defiance, her lips pursed. God, she's…she's…fuck, she's cute.

No!

Delete that thought. Delete.

I mean irritating.

Annoying.

Impossible!

Growing frustrated, I say, "If this is how you want to play the game, Storee, I can play it like this."

Max clears his throat and steps in. "I think what he meant to say was, how about we all take a second to breathe and find a more productive way to create some positive chemistry between the two camps instead of continuing to rock the boat?"

"No, I did not mean that," I say. "I *want* to rock her boat."

"Oh, I'm sure you do…pervert," Storee replies.

"I don't want to rock your boat like *that*," I say. "Fuck, you're the furthest thing from what I'd want to rock."

"Says the guy who secretly wants to date me."

"I'd rather date the hoof of one of my reindeer," I snarl.

"Well, if we were honest," Max says, "you did crush on her when she came to visit, back in the day."

Jesus fuck, Max.

"Oh...is that right?" Storee says, sitting up, looking so fucking ridiculous in her blankets, headdress, and feet in a bucket of water...water that I assume is hot. "You had a crush on me?"

Yes.

Terribly.

Embarrassingly so.

"No," I say flatly.

"Well, it seems like your friend thinks differently." She casually points toward Max.

"Max was mistaken. He sometimes thinks Martha and Mae have a crush on him."

"They do and you fucking know it," Max says, outraged.

"So let me get this straight," Storee says. "I come into town, and for some reason unbeknownst to me, you have all this...hatred for me after I thought we were friendly, and now I'm your mortal enemy, and all you want is to beat me at a Christmas competition? Is this because you have a crush on me and don't know how to handle it?" She presses her hand to her chest and tilts her head ever so slightly. "Cole, you could just tell me rather than using negative tactics to get my attention."

I feel my jaw grow tense and my eyes narrow. "I do not have a crush on you—that's the furthest thing from the truth, so get it out of your head."

"I don't believe you," she says.

"And I really don't care," I reply. "What I do care about is you trying to sabotage us, and if that's how you want to play it, then let it be known you started this war."

And with that, I head out of the house, Max following. I don't shut the door behind us. Instead, I reach up to a strand of lights framing the front door and yank on it, sending the string to the welcome mat.

A gasp sounds through the house, followed by a distraught Taran. "My display!" she cries out.

But I keep striding forward. They want to play dirty? Well, they have no idea how low I can go.

CHAPTER FOURTEEN
COLE

It was a quarter past dawn; the lights were all dimmed.
The stockings were hung; the trees were all trimmed.

And along Whistler Lane, past the house lit in green,
sat Cole Black on the corner, a planning machine.

His mission: to ruin her, to make sure she loses,
to play dirty, to embarrass, in any way he chooses.

"FOURTH FUCKING PLACE! AND ON a fucking technicality," I say as I pace the barn, my stupid Kringle sash thrown on the bench next to me. "We got fourth place when we should have easily gotten second."

Max chews on a piece of beef jerky, slowly nodding. "Yup, that was a blow, especially to me. I worked hard on that design."

"And yet you were ready to shake hands with the enemy and act like everything was fine."

"Uh, no," he says. "I was trying to act like we were friends so they'd cool it with their sabotage. We were going to *pretend* to be friendly but then upend them."

"What?" I say, blinking a few times. "That's not what you said before we went over there."

"Because I thought about it when we were walking to their house. I was going to tell you, but then you barged in there, freaking guns blazing, ready to take down the female population in that house, including the decrepit Cindy."

"She was anything but decrepit. She was walking, Max. Fucking walking. And yeah, I went in there ready to throw down because I was pissed. You saw Storee—she was wrapped up in blankets and icing her head. Clearly, she was the one who made the commotion outside and messed with our lights."

"Yes, I think we've established that."

"Which means she's the reason we got fourth place."

"Very true," he says with a nod. "But I'd like to point out, after doing the calculations, we're still in first place with thirty total points, and since they took last place...overall they're in third."

I pause my pacing and turn toward my friend. "Who's in front of them?" I've been too angry to check out how the other competitors have done.

"Ursula," he says with a smile. "She beat out Jimmy and took first last night with her display. Going ugly Christmas sweater on her house was genius. And since she got third in the last two competitions, that puts her in second with twenty-nine points and Storee in third with twenty-eight points."

"That's not much of a difference," I say as I push my hand through my hair. "What's the next competition, and how can we sabotage Storee?"

"It's a tough one." He cringes. "It's the Fruitcake Festivus."

"Fuck," I say as I lean against a support pole. "I don't know how to bake."

"Neither do I," he says. "But I was speaking to my mom about it, and she said she could get us ready for the bake-off this Saturday."

"She would?" I ask. "Does she know how to make fruitcake?"

"She said she has a recipe that could help highlight her jam. A fruity fruitcake with cherry jam, nuts, and some other things."

"That could be cool," I say. "And who's judging this round?"

"Tanya down at Warm Your Spirits," Max answers.

"Hmm," I say, twisting my lips to the side, an idea coming to mind. "I think I'm thirsty, are you?"

He smiles. "As a matter of fact...I am."

———

"You've got to be kidding me," I say as I look through the window of the coffee and bakery shop. "What are they doing in there?"

Max peeks through the window quickly and then plasters himself up against the wall like me, trying not to be seen. "They're copying us."

"See, this is why we can't be nice with them," I say as I glance through the window again, spotting Storee and Taran both at the register chatting it up with Tanya. "They're not going to let up."

"You know, for a second I assumed that we could all act like adults, but clearly that's not an option."

"Finally, you realize that," I huff and then turn to him, a plan forming in my head. "Okay, we need to go in there, and whatever I say or do, for the love of God, don't think I mean it."

"What are you going to say or do?" he asks, looking slightly frightened.

"Just watch and see."

"Dude, hold on," he says, a hand to my chest.

"Trust me, Max," I say as our eyes meet.

And with that, I push away from him and open the door for both Max and me, the sound of a bell jingling above us alerting everyone in the bustling shop of our presence. Taran is the first one to spot us, and when Storee glances in our direction, she's struggling to force a smile. The feeling is mutual.

"Merry Christmas," I say with a raise of my hand and a warm expression.

"Merry Christmas," they all reply as I step up to the counter, Max trailing behind.

I get close to Storee and say, "How are you?"

She leans back, clearly disturbed with how close I am. "I'm…I'm good."

"What did you order?" I keep my voice low, pleasant…seductive.

"Um…." She swallows. "A caramel latte with oat milk, extra caramel."

I nod, and then fully go for it while Tanya's watching us. I tuck a piece of hair behind her ear, letting my hand linger for a second. "Caramel latte with oat milk, extra caramel. Committing that to memory."

"Uh…excuse me, what's going on here?" Tanya asks, a huge grin on her face.

I glance in her direction. "Trying to get this girl to see me." I bring my attention back to Storee. "Are you ever going to take me up on my offer?"

Max, clearly catching on, takes that moment to lean in. "You really should, Storee. He's a good guy."

"What offer is that?" Tanya asks, practically frothing at the mouth.

Here's the thing about Kringle. We love being in each other's business like all other small towns, but because we celebrate Christmas year-round, and because everyone is always cheery, constantly watching Lovemark movies, they have this penchant for love during the holidays. Any *possible* relationship—they want to know about it.

They live for it just like they live to hear Bob Krampus say ho-ho-ho.

A holiday romance is what their hearts desire, and I'm going to deliver. If anything, the pining man always wins the audience's hearts.

I smile at Tanya. "I'd love to take Storee on a date, but she's holding out on me."

"A date?" Tanya coos, her hand clutching her chest. "Oh, Storee, what's the hold up?"

"Now, now, don't blame her," I say. "She is, after all, taking care of our dear Cindy. She has priorities. I'm just being selfish."

I can *feel* the steam coming from Storee. I don't even have to look at her to know that she's not happy with me. Like I said, I know how to work this town. No doubt Tanya will talk to Martha and Mae—she's best friends with them—who will then talk to Sherry Conrad, and all of them are going to be wishing and hoping that Storee, the California girl, gives this small-town boy a chance.

Smart, I know.

"A selfish man who's finally cashing in on the crush he's been harboring for over a decade," Max says, helping a guy out.

"Oh dear, not to put pressure on you, but over a decade?" Tanya asks Storee. "I can't believe it's been over a decade."

I casually shrug, and even as I talk to Tanya, I keep my eyes on Storee the entire time. "I always looked forward to Christmas, knowing that Storee and her family were coming to visit Cindy. I'd watch her from over the fence, hoping she'd give me a chance to talk to her. And she would, but it was never anything romantic. But I loved those moments with her. And instead of holding her hand like I wanted to, I'd just... watch her from afar and wonder if I'd ever get my chance. And I thought I'd lost it when she didn't return for ten years...so now that she's here, I'm making it known."

Now, here's the strange thing. I cannot in all honesty say this is all a lie. The more I've thought about the hurt I felt when Storee left, the more I've realized that *some* of this is true. The only reason her trash talk and subsequent exit could have hurt me so much is if I did have feelings for her. Yes, her departure coincided with the devastating loss of my parents. But since she's been back in town, so many feelings have risen to the surface. Teenage me was smitten with the little redhead sitting on the porch beside me. Adult me...well, not sure I want to delve into that just yet.

"Oh my goodness, my heart can't take this," Tanya says as she drapes a dish towel over her shoulder. "Storee, you realize Cole is the most eligible bachelor in town, right?"

Before Storee can answer, I say, "I don't know. Max is giving me a run for my money."

Max stands taller. "I think ladies like the smell of reindeer on Cole more. It's those pheromones."

What?

Ew. That makes no sense, and it's actually kind of gross.

Tanya's brows pinch together, no doubt trying to work through that comment as I say, "It's fine though—I know Storee isn't here forever. Her stay is only temporary." I sigh. "But hell, it's hard to not at least give it a shot, you know? And Tanya, isn't she doing such a good job as a Kringle-ee? That performance as Judy Garland, it was a tough act to follow. I don't know if you saw, but I had to wipe the tears from my eyes."

Am I laying it on thick? Of course, but just watch...Tanya will eat it up.

"You know," Tanya says, "I actually thought I saw emotion in your eyes while you were thrusting up on the stage. I thought it was the chill of the air whipping around you, but that was from watching Storee?"

I slowly nod. "She was...she was breathtaking up there."

Storee has remained silent this entire time, her eyes locked on me, probably trying to murder me with her pupils. Obviously, she hasn't blown up my head yet, but it hasn't been from a lack of trying.

"She *was* breathtaking. Such a beautiful tribute to your aunt," Tanya says to Storee.

"Thank you," Storee replies. "It was an honor to do something for her that is so meaningful." Oof, look who's laying it on thick now.

Tanya looks between the two of us, hearts forming in her eyes as her hands clasp in front of her chest. "Oh, you two would be so cute together, and we've never had two Kringle-ees fall for each other. Imagine the buzz that would float through the town—two star-crossed lovers, supporting and aiding each other in their attempt to be named the Christmas Kringle. Someone call up Lovemark. I think we have a story in our midst."

Chuckling, I lean one elbow on the counter. "Want to know a secret, Tanya?"

"Always," she replies, leaning in as well.

"I haven't told Storee this yet because, well, I know she'd get upset, but did you hear that one of my strands was out on my light display?"

Tanya winces while Storee shifts on her feet, looking anxious at what I might say. "I did hear that," Tanya says.

"Well, we did that on purpose," I reply.

Tanya straightens up. "You did?"

I nod. "Didn't we, Max?"

"Uh…yeah…" he slowly says, looking to see where I'm going with this.

"You see, I knew Storee was worried about their display and, despite Taran doing a great job with the lines, the most precise lights in town"—I catch Taran nod in appreciation—"I saw that they lacked creativity. I saw how self-conscious Storee was, and well, I wanted her to feel better and not so alone, so I pulled one of the bulbs out of my strand of lights right before Paula and Peach came by."

"You didn't," Tanya gasps.

I nod, my lips pressed together as I stand up taller. "I did. I couldn't stomach her getting last place all alone, so I sabotaged my own light display to make her feel better."

I glance at Storee, who's desperately attempting to suppress her flared nostrils. She tilts her head to the side. "That's so sweet, Cole."

"Sweet?" Tanya says. "That is more than sweet. That's…oh my, that's Cole riding in like a white knight." Tanya fans herself. "Storee, please give him a chance. Please."

"That's okay, Tanya. Don't pressure her, I know she doesn't—"

"I'd love to go on a date," Storee says with a smile on her face.

Uhhh, what?

Did I just hear her correctly?

"Really?" Tanya clasps her hands together. "You would?"

I glance at Storee, my mouth going dry as she nods. "Of course. How could I not go on a date with Cole after that…that valiant display? I'm not making any promises, but I should at least give him a shot."

Umm, okay, I wasn't actually asking her out, so this is awkward.

"You should," Tanya says. "And how about tonight? Tonight would be the perfect night."

"Why would tonight be perfect?" Storee asks as dread starts to fill me.

Shit, I completely forgot about tonight…

"Tonight is our Cupid Christmas celebration."

Yup, this is backfiring, and this is backfiring hard.

"Oh, is this something new?" Storee asks. "I don't think I've heard of it."

"Just a few years ago, the town came up with the idea to have a date night where couples spend the evening, children-free, in the streets of Kringle, enjoying all the magic of the season. Martha and Mae head up all the festivities. Word on the street is they've added at least a dozen more hidden mistletoe leaves throughout town."

Jesus.

I tug on my neck. "I don't want to put any pressure on Storee. It might be best if we—"

"No, tonight is perfect." Storee smiles back at me. "It sounds magical."

Tanya claps her hands while looking between us. "I can't wait to tell the ladies."

Fucking great.

Look what you got yourself into now…

STOREE

"I don't think this is a good idea," Taran says as I touch up my lipstick in my bedroom mirror, Samantha judging me the entire time. At least I'm old enough to wear lipstick, Samantha.

"Why not?" I ask as I smack my lips together. "He knew exactly what he was doing. He knows Tanya is the judge this weekend and he wanted to make it seem like I'm the bad guy, not going out with the much-loved, if generally grumpy, Cole Black. Well, I'm not going to let him get away with it."

"Yeah, but this…this is different. You're going out in public, on a date, during some cupid love fest. Do you really think that's a good idea?"

"I don't really have a choice, Taran." I turn to face her. "This is where we're at in this competition, and after he took credit for the light display, once again looking like the good guy, I have to rise to his level. If that means I have to suffer a night of pretending to be on a date with Cole, then I'll do that." It's for Aunt Cindy. Everything I've freaking endured over the past how many freaking days has been for Aunt Cindy. It's become my mantra since I walked out of Tanya's shop. *All for Aunt Cindy.*

"Don't you think we could win this without attempting to fool everyone?"

"No," I say flatly as I slip on my long brown boots over my jeans. I'm going to freeze to death tonight, but I can't possibly go on a date all bundled up, looking like Randy from *A Christmas Story*. "And if we were playing fair from the beginning, you never would have powdered Aunt Cindy's face to look emaciated the first time."

Taran shrugs. "That was easy. This is you going on a date with the enemy."

"Fake date," I correct her while I finish putting on my other boot.

"But is it?" she asks. I look up at her as I'm adjusting my pants. "Because I know there was some…you know…yearning there."

"Oh my God, Taran," I say. "There was never any yearning."

"You used to say how cute he was when we were younger."

"Uh, yeah, because he's an attractive guy, but that means nothing. He can be handsome and still have an ugly personality."

"Are you sure? Because I was talking to Aunt Cindy this morning and she was worried that we're in third place now, and I know how much this means to her. I don't want you getting distracted."

"First of all, we're in third place because of your light display, and the only reason Cole isn't miles ahead of us at the moment is because I nearly gave myself a concussion sabotaging *his* light display. So we should be thrilled we're in third place. Going on a fake date with Cole is only going to up our merit in this town, and we need that. So why don't you stop worrying about me and start worrying about your light display and how you can improve it before the final judging."

I head out of my room and down the stairs, Taran following closely behind. "I don't think there's much more I can do to enhance the display." I pause on the last step and turn toward her.

"Please tell me you're joking."

She folds her arms across her chest. "If the judges can't appreciate simplicity, then that's on them."

I rub my temples and try to stay calm as I say, "Taran, the reason we're in third place is because of the lights. They're boring. We need more. For the love of God, put more lights on the house. You said it yourself—Aunt Cindy is worried. I'm going on a freaking date with Cole. You can at least pull some weight around here and add more lights."

"Fake date."

"Huh?"

"You just said date. Isn't it a fake date?"

I pinch the bridge of my nose and count to five.

"I want you to remember it's fake," Taran adds.

"Trust me, there will be nothing real about this date. Not a single thing. The sooner I can get it over with, the better. Now, if you'll excuse me, I have to practice my smile in the mirror to make sure I'm not snarling when Cole comes to pick me up."

I move past Taran and head into the powder room.

Remember it's a fake date...as if I could forget.

CHAPTER FIFTEEN
COLE

'Twas the minute before the date,
and all through the house,
not a word was said, not a mention of her blouse.

An eerie calm settled in as she sat ready and waiting
for the man next door she'd never
planned on fake dating.

It was one night, that was it, not a promise for more.
So why did butterflies stir with the knock at the door?

I ADJUST MY JACKET, NERVES shooting through me as I wait for some-one to answer the door.

It took me about half an hour to figure out what to wear, and not because I was nervous, but because I had Max chirping in my ear, attempt-ing to be my stylist for the night, making me change over and over until he thought I was wearing something presentable enough...which happened to be the first fucking outfit I tried on.

He then went into overdrive about my hair.

About my deodorant and whether the scent clashed with my cologne—it doesn't.

And if my jeans should be folded at the top of my brown boots—they are.

Before I left, he gave me a pep talk, told me not to fall in love, to remember the mission, and to look like a charming motherfucker while walking Storee around town. He topped off the pep talk by draping my sash over me and then sending me on my way with a smack on my ass, telling me to take one for the team.

His job while I'm gone? Practice making fruitcake.

Why do I have a feeling I'm pulling more weight than he is?

And sure, this is my fault—I put myself in this mess—but I didn't think Storee would agree to a date. I was going to tease her and let her off the hook, gaining sympathy from Tanya but not putting myself in a situation like right now. Unfortunately for me, Storee was quick on her feet, challenging me to eat my own words.

In all honesty, I'd *rather* be tucked up inside my familiar house with a mug of warm cider. Not only am I preparing for this competition, but the days on the farm are longer because of the season. I'm still keeping up with all the reindeer shows, feedings, and stall cleanings, but my muscles are tired, and I've had to smile far too much while wearing this ridiculous sash.

My face isn't used to smiling.

My personality isn't used to being so cheery.

And my mindset isn't used to having to fake date someone to get ahead in a competition.

The door opens—and *wow*. Storee looks beautiful despite the lack of a smile on her face when her eyes meet mine.

She's wearing a winter hat, but her long red hair is curled underneath it and flowing around her shoulders. She's dressed in a pair of jeans, long brown boots, and a jacket that doesn't seem like it's going to be warm enough for her, but thankfully for her—because I couldn't care less—there will be heaters up and down the streets of Kringle for the night.

"Shit," she says in greeting. "Taran, I need my sash."

"Nice to see you too," I say, sticking my hands in my pockets.

Taran walks up behind her and hands Storee her sash before glancing at me and then back at Storee. "Don't kill each other, and remember what we talked about."

"I know," Storee says in an annoyed tone. "You remember what *we* talked about." She gestures to the house. "Lights, Taran. More lights."

I don't mean to chuckle, but I can't help it because yes, they need more lights. Way more lights.

"Glad you find my torture funny," Storee says as she steps outside of the house. She's about to shut the door when Cindy calls out.

"Storee, are you leaving?"

I see the annoyance drain from her face as her aunt approaches.

"I am," Storee says in a loving tone. "Do you need anything?"

Cindy steps up to the entryway and looks past Storee to me. The smallest smile tugs on the corner of her lips. "Cole, you look very handsome."

That's Cindy for you; despite all the animosity brewing between our two houses, she can still find a way to bridge the gap and be kind like she always is.

"Thank you, Cindy."

She then looks Storee up and down. "Did you pay my niece a compliment?"

I feel my nostrils flare before I glance over at Storee. "You look nice." It's painful to say, because even though I believe it, the last thing I want to do is make Storee think I have any sort of favorable feelings toward her.

Cindy elbows Storee in the side. "Aren't you going to say anything?"

Storee looks my way. "Your jeans are clean."

"*Storee*," Cindy chastises.

"What? They are." Storee points to my jeans. "That's a nice thing to say."

"Let's just get this over with," I say as I step aside, making room for her to join me.

"You know," Cindy says as she grips her walker tightly, "there was a time when you two got along. Perhaps you could revisit those old feelings tonight."

"No," Taran says, stepping in. "They need to remain enemies, Aunt Cindy. This is a competition after all. We'll not be blindsided by him." She looks at Storee. "Keep your guard up."

"No problem there," Storee says.

Cindy sighs but doesn't say anything else, so I head down the barely lit porch, Storee joining me. "Have a good night, Cindy."

"You too, Cole. And if anything, at least try to be kind to my niece."

"Sure," I say, even though I don't mean it.

When they shut the door, Storee and I head down the sidewalk toward town, silence falling between the two of us. Not surprised—what do we really have to say to each other?

Nothing of substance.

Nothing that would create the opening to a long, deep conversation.

Nothing that wouldn't get us to start yapping at each other.

Pushing the competition to the side for a moment, I am sad that we've lost our way with each other, that we shared that one night ten years ago when I was hurt, and she was hurt, and we couldn't quite see past our own heartache to glimpse each other. We did used to be friends. She was my once-a-year breath of fresh air who flew into Kringletown with sunshine and vigor. Yes, she'd complain about the cold, but that was par for the course—and I kind of liked it. She brought brightness and hope to my quiet soul. A friendship I loved. *And yet, we're enemies.* But right now, I can't imagine anything different.

So we continue to stay silent as we move down the sidewalk, straight to Krampus Court where the first store we walk by is Frank 'n' Scents on the right.

"So what's the plan?" Storee finally says. "Because I don't want to be wandering the streets with you with no plan in mind. We need people to see us, and then we can go home."

"So romantic," I say, causing her to look up at me.

"You're the one who got us into this mess, so you're the one who needs to come up with a plan."

"You didn't have to say yes to the date."

"*Fake* date," she says. "And I didn't have a choice. I wasn't about to look like the asshole who is turning down the town's golden boy."

"Aww." I press my hand to my chest. "You think of me as the golden boy?"

"Please, for the love of God, don't test my patience tonight, Cole. I already can't feel my legs."

I glance down at her jeans and then back up at her. "Surprised you didn't wear your snowsuit. It would have added an extra level of defense from me."

"Defense?" she asks with a raised brow. "Are you planning on...disrobing me?"

"Jesus, no," I say. "I didn't mean it like that. I just mean, like...from being close to me...you know what, never mind." We walk past the hardware store and then right to the place I want to be...Prancer's Libations.

"A bar? Really? That's where you're taking me? Do you really need to be drunk for this?"

I stare down at her. "They're serving mulled apple cider to go. It's my favorite, and I thought it might be a good start to keep you warm so we can make it through the night, putting on this farce."

"Oh," she says, not a witty comeback in sight.

I open the door to Prancer's Libations and let her go in first.

Thachary is at the bar, serving a few couples, while the rest of the room is full, visitors and townies milling about, enjoying the Christmas music and free appetizers being passed around.

Even though I've never taken part in Cupid Christmas, I have to admit it's a good idea for anyone in a relationship. Gives the town the opportunity to focus on the older crowd, brings in more business, and creates a memorable moment for the loving couples.

And it gives me the opportunity to win the hearts of the judges.

I walk up to the bar and nod at Thachary when we make eye contact. Storee sidles up next to me and rests her arm on the bar as she turns toward me.

"Wow, it's packed," she says just as another couple arrives and moves in next to Storee, causing her to step into my personal space.

"Getting cozy?" I ask her.

"No," she says, her eyebrows turning down.

"Ah, you might not want to frown when looking up at me," I say. "There are eyes everywhere, watching us." I reach out and pick up a strand of her hair, twirling it with my finger. "Unless you want people to believe I'm the hopeless romantic with no shot at winning the heart of the out-of-towner? If that's the case, by all means continue to frown because I'd love the sympathy."

Smiling now, she says, "You realize how pathetic you are, right?"

"Pathetic...or incredibly intelligent?"

"Pathetic," she replies just as Thachary comes up to us.

"Hey, funny seeing you two together," he says as he wipes his hands on a bar towel.

I place my arm around Storee's shoulders and bring her in close to my chest. "I took a chance and asked her out on a date. Somehow I got her to say yes."

I can practically hear Storee's internal eye roll.

Thachary looks between the two of us and smiles. "You know, I heard some rumblings about a possible romance between the two of you. Frank said he heard something from Tanya, but I didn't believe it. Guess I was wrong. Happy for you two."

"Thanks," I say, "but it's just one date, not sure where it will go after tonight."

"Well, if I know anything about you, man, it's that you don't give up easily." He smirks. "Mulled cider?"

"Two to go," I say, squeezing Storee in close. "Going to take a walk down by the river."

Thachary winks. "Smart choice, man. Frank told me they just finished the lights over there this morning in time for tonight."

He grabs two to-go cups and then moves over toward a large kettle where they make the mulled cider and starts pouring us each a cup.

"Is the riverwalk where you're going to bury my body?" Storee asks in an undertone.

"I thought about it," I say. "But with it being lit up now, I couldn't be discreet while I try to dispose of you."

"Ah, so plan B is in action?"

"Yes, poisoning the mulled cider," I say as Thachary tops our cups and brings them over to us.

"Put them on your tab?" he asks.

"Yup," I say. "Thanks, man."

"Anytime, and good luck." He winks and then offers to help another couple. I hand Storee her cup, but she just eyes it.

"For the love of God, I didn't poison it."

"Can never be too sure," she says.

"Just take it."

After some more careful eyeing, she finally takes the cup from me but doesn't drink.

"You're going to regret not drinking this," I say as I take a sip. The warm, spiced cider runs over my tongue and then down my throat. When she still doesn't take a sip, I switch cups with her. "There, now you know it's not poisoned."

"Do you expect me to drink from this after your lips were on the rim?"

"Do you really think I'm that disgusting?" I ask. When she doesn't answer, I roll my eyes, set both cups on the bar, switch the lids, and then hand her back the "un-poisoned" cup. "There, happy?"

"We shall see. If I keel over, Taran knows it's you." She lifts the cup to her lips, blows, and then sips. I watch as her eyes light up before she glances down at her drink.

"Good, right? You can't even lie. I can see it all over your face."

She takes another sip and nods. "I'm not offering you the compliment because you don't deserve it, but yes, this is very good."

"Glad I could start our date off with a bang."

Her expression falls flat. "Fake date."

"Kind of salty for someone who should be feeling the Christmas spirit. Don't you think?"

"I don't know, you're rather lively for someone who should be acting like the Grinch overlooking Whoville...don't you think?"

"Maybe your presence has made my heart grow two sizes too big?" I say with a smirk.

"Or maybe it's your ego that's motivating you to act like a charming asshole."

"Hmm, we might never know," I say as I head toward the door of the bar. When I glance over my shoulder, I ask, "You coming?"

She huffs and then joins me. Before walking through the door, I turn to her and whisper, "Don't look too excited—we don't want people to think you're actually having fun with me."

"I'm not," she deadpans.

"That's because we haven't gotten to the good part yet."

STOREE

A few things...

Cole Black is handsome.

Let's just get that out in the open, okay? He's a handsome man, there's no debating it, there's no denying it. If you put his face into some sort of facial recognition device that tells you whether he's an attractive human or not, he'd get an exceedingly high score.

Secondly, he smells nice. It of course pains me to say such nice things about him, but it's true. A stranger would sniff him and be pleased with the scent. That's just how he presented himself tonight—unfortunately for me.

Thirdly, he's a cocky asshole. Now, this I was not expecting. He walks around town like the nice guy that everyone loves and can't get enough of because he's the hometown boy that never left and is instead hanging lights for old ladies. But this side of Cole, the competitive side, will do anything, and I mean anything—including tossing his arm over my shoulders and walking down the streets with me secured to this side—to win.

And he seems to not even think twice about it either.

He's comfortable.

In his element.

While I'm over here fumbling, trying to maintain a smile as we pass people in town, offering them a *Merry Christmas* and simultaneously sipping cider.

It's a lot for a girl who came to Kringle to help take care of her great-aunt.

I didn't sign up for this, and yet here I am, in the throes of fake passion with a man I can barely stand, in a town that likes to watch every little move you make.

"Merry Christmas," Cole says to a couple sitting on a bench.

"Merry Christmas," they call back.

"Season's greetings," I say with a nod.

"That sounded stiff to me," he says as we make our way to Ornament

Park.

"When you say, 'Merry Christmas,' it sounds like you have marbles in your mouth when you try to get out the words," I reply.

"Really? And here I thought I was getting better at it." He shifts, but keeps his arm firmly attached to my shoulders.

"You know, you don't have to continue to hold me close to you. I'm not running away."

"It's all for show, but if you'd rather I hold your hand, that works too."

"Uh...no," I say.

"Then an arm drape it is."

"How can you be so...casual about this?" I ask. "Aren't you uncomfortable?"

"Yes, fake dating Satan's mistress has caused me some distress, but I'm able to block out the anxiety and focus on what's important—convincing the town that I'm the one who should be earning Christmas Kringle this season." In a lower tone, he says, "And from the standings in points, looks like I'm headed in that direction."

"Oh my God, you're ahead by two points. Big deal."

"Two more points than you," he says.

"God, you're irritating." I try to shrug him off, but it doesn't work as we head over to the bridge that's lit up by what looks like thousands of twinkle lights. And those lights lead to an archway that has been erected over the riverwalk. If we were a real couple, I'd think this was the cutest, most romantic walk ever, with Christmas music in the background, snow on the ground and mountainside, and the creaking of water under the river's half-frozen ice.

But since I'm with Cole, I find it mundane, lifeless, a boring attempt at trying to gain stardom in the town.

"You know you started all of this, right? If you hadn't used your aunt as a pawn, or tried to sabotage my light display, we wouldn't be here. But you had to take it to the next level. I'm just matching your energy."

"By pretending to crush on me? Oh wait..." I smile. "I mean, resurrecting a crush from years ago."

He scoffs. "You can't believe everything Max says."

"Probably not, but I believe this." I look up at him as we cross the bridge. The lights from above highlight his sharp jawline that's barely hidden under the guise of his beard. "Thinking back to when we were young, you always tagged along to the Myrrh-cantile with me. You *just so happened* to be outside when I was outside, so I believe there was a crush there. Question is, why didn't you ever do anything about it?"

"Because I caught one whiff of you and said, nope, can't suffer with that stench," he quickly replies.

"Hence why you're hanging all over me tonight," I sarcastically reply.

"You know, I'm glad you brought that up, because it's been a gallant effort on my part."

"Are you ever serious?"

"Yes," he says as we make our way under the glowing tunnel arching above us. "With you...no."

"And why is that?"

"Not worth my time," he says. *Ouch.*

I know that *shouldn't* sting, but for some reason, it does. Being told you're not worth someone's time never is something you want to hear. But why? Am I not worth his time because of how I look? How I act? Who I am in general? Too many questions, too many thoughts.

"Aren't you pleasant," I finally say.

"Try to be," he answers and then stops us, pausing under the archway.

"What are you doing?"

"Letting you enjoy the lights."

"Why?" I ask suspiciously.

"Because you barely have any on your house—thought you might like to gather some ideas, get inspired."

My nostrils flare as I step away from him. "Are you going to goad me this entire night?"

He drags his hand over his jaw. "I wasn't thinking I was going to, but hell, I think you just bring it out of me. Can you not handle it? Do you want to ask each other questions, get to know each other better? Although that would fall in the lines of a real date, and I think we established this is fake."

"This is very fake. Everything about this is fake. Trust me when I say never in a million years would going out with you be real."

"Wow," he says while taking a sip from his drink. "Can't hear that enough."

"Don't you even dare act hurt. You've been throwing punches all night."

"I don't agree—"

"Merry Christmas!" The booming voice of Bob Krampus startles both of us.

"M-merry Christmas," I say, turning toward Bob and Sylvia who are walking hand in hand—in their Mr. and Mrs. Claus outfits—toward us.

"Merry Christmas, Santa," Cole says as he takes a step closer to me.

"What are you two doing walking down Lovers' Lane?" Sylvia asks as she holds on to Bob's arm.

"Lovers' Lane?" I question.

"That's what they call it on Cupid Christmas night," Cole says and then turns to Bob and Sylvia. "Well, I sort of asked Storee out, and she said yes." Cole reaches down and takes my hand in his.

The grip of his palm over mine, the feel of his callused hand against my skin...it's...it's...ugh, its annoyingly comforting. It feels right.

It feels like I should always be holding his hand.

And yet I need to block that out of my mind. This is not a feeling I want to explore.

"So I wanted to take her out for a nice evening, starting with cider from Prancer's, then a walk along Lovers' Lane, followed by a stroll through the stalls. Hoping to grab a bratwurst."

Bob pats his stomach. "Got a brat myself, quite delicious tonight."

"Oh, Santa, you're missing the point, they're…they're dating," Sylvia says with stars in her eyes.

"Just on a date," I clarify, not wanting any more rumors to spread. "Just seeing how things go."

Cole smirks down at me. "She's still trying to figure out her feelings, whereas I know exactly what I want." And then to my utter surprise, he lifts our connected hands and places a kiss on my knuckles.

The warm, soft press of his lips sends a chill right up my arm.

"Well, hopefully she can figure them out fast for the sake of your heart," Bob says and then offers me a wink. "Have a nice night, you two."

"Thank you," Cole says.

"Yeah, thanks," I say as they trail away. When they're out of earshot, I say, "What the hell was that, Cole? Now they're going to think I'm some sort of heartbreaking wench."

"Who cares," he says. "Not like you live here and need to save face."

"I still visit."

"Every decade," he mutters and continues to walk down the lit-up archway.

"Uh, why do you sound so bitter about that?"

"I don't," he says as he turns around and walks backward while he continues to talk. "Just surprised you actually came back."

"My great-aunt needed help, so of course I came back."

"You know she was sad, right? Martha told me it was one of the reasons she started entering the Kringle competition, because she wanted to feel the Christmas spirit again. And a lot of it had to do with you and Taran not coming back to visit her."

Guilt consumes me as I think about Aunt Cindy celebrating Christmas on her own. Then again, Cole could just be saying that to get under my skin. But he is right; we all stopped visiting. Taran was busy with school and internships, Mom and Dad had their timeshare that they had to visit during the holiday season, and I...well, after what happened the last time I was here, all that public humiliation, I didn't really want to come back.

And I see how wrong that was.

"Did she actually say that to you, or are you fishing for things to make me upset?"

"As much as we don't get along, I wouldn't invent something just to make you upset. I would hope you would know that."

I shrug. "I honestly wouldn't be able to tell at this point. You're different, Cole, and not in a good way."

"Yeah, well...you're different too," he says and then continues toward the bridge that leads back to Ornament Park.

COLE

"There they are," Tanya coos from where she's seated with both Martha and Mae in Ornament Park on one of the many benches scattered across the Astroturf. "Oh, they look so adorable together, don't they, ladies?"

"They do," Martha says. "I approve of this coupling."

"I don't think they were looking for your approval," Mae says. "But I second that opinion."

"Thank you," Storee says, surprising me as she cuddles into my chest. Given the cold exterior I faced only a few moments ago, this is a complete one-eighty.

Going with the farce, I throw my arm around her again. "Pretty happy over here."

"I can see it all over your face," Martha says. "Oh, our little Cole, finally finding someone. You'd better not break his heart, missy. We're very protective of Cole, especially since he lost his parents."

Fuck. Should have known someone was going to let the cat out of the bag.

And from the announcement, I feel Storee stiffen next to me.

I can see this going south for me very quickly, so to avoid any questions from Storee or more revelations from the hens, I take Storee's hand in mine and say, "Well, we're starving, so we're going to hit up the stalls."

"Oh, how fun. I heard the fresh gingerbread cart is there too," Tanya says. "Would make a fine dessert."

"Unless they have something else planned for dessert," Martha says with a wink.

I muster up a laugh and wish them a good night. Storee does the same, and then we take off toward the stalls.

There was an empty field behind Chadwick's Candy Shop, Poinsettia Pizza, and the Myrrh-cantile that was supposed to be turned into extra parking, but a few years ago the town assessed our parking arrangements and realized that we didn't need more barren lots. Instead, they paved the space and added the candy cane swings that twirl about twenty feet in the air, along with vendor stalls. The only fresh food allowed is brats and gingerbread so that sales aren't taken from the main strip of restaurants. Other than that, the stalls are full of crafts and handmade food items like jam.

"What was that back there?" Storee says as I release her hand and head toward the passage to the stalls between the Caroling Café and Poinsettia Pizza.

"A couple of old ladies gossiping," I say.

"No, about your parents."

"Nothing."

She tugs on my arm, stopping me in my tracks. "Cole, seriously, you lost your parents. Aunt Cindy mentioned this the other day, but I guess...I don't know, I guess in all the Kringle chaos, I forgot. When did this happen?"

I push my hand through my hair. "We're not talking about this."

"But—"

"No buts," I say, my voice growing terse. "We're not friends, so don't try to act like we are by asking about my parents." I glance around. "Let's just…let's just get this night over with."

STOREE

Well, if there is one way to shut Cole down, it's to ask about his parents.

So far, he's been silent. No longer the cocky instigator he was under the archway or in Ornament Park. His taunting is long gone, and it's as if he's almost curled in on himself and forgotten what he's supposed to be doing—acting like we're on a charming date for the town.

"You good with one brat?" he asks.

"I can get my own dinner," I say.

He turns to me. "Do you want a brat or not?"

Sensing the tone, I say, "Yes, please."

He turns back around and orders us two brats and a bottle of water for each of us. Once he pays, he pulls me off to the side where we're supposed to wait.

No longer does he hold my hand or drape his arm over my shoulders. Instead, he sticks his hands in his pockets and keeps a safe distance from me as he stares at the ground.

I don't know how to handle this.

How to go about dealing with a closed-off Cole.

I can handle the grump.

I can tolerate the instigator.

But the morose, shut-down Cole…he's on a whole other level.

I'm not sure how to go about the rest of this night because technically this is all for show, and right now we're not showing off anything. We just look like two people who barely know each other. So I might as well offer to end this.

"If you want," I say, breaking the silence between us, "once the brats come, we can go our separate ways."

Shoulders scrunched, head turned down, his eyes find mine. "Not happening," he replies.

"Not happening? So we're just going to suffer through the rest of the night in silence? At least before it wasn't awkward. We were just...fighting, holding hands—"

"You liked holding my hand, did you?" he asks, that sarcastic energy coming back in full force.

Gone is the man whose shoulders slumped—the cocky man from earlier has returned. It's as if I snapped my fingers and he just reappeared. Talk about whiplash.

I grind my teeth together. "No, I didn't. I found it repulsive."

"Repulsive, huh?" He stands taller now. "Never heard that before."

"Have you even dated before?" I ask.

He glances around. "Do you think a guy who has never dated before would come up with a date like the one you're on? Mulled cider, a walk under the lights, brats...that screams of a guy who knows what he's doing."

"Ah yes, nothing screams *date* like a bratwurst in my mouth."

His brow raises as a smirk tugs on the corner of his lip. "On the first date, even? Wow, Storee, wouldn't have guessed it."

"Ugh, be mature," I say.

"You're the one talking about wieners in your mouth on dates."

I fold my arms over my chest. "I did not say wiener."

"Eh, you alluded to it."

"I will have you know I've never...copulated on the first date."

"Yeah, because you use words like *copulated*," he shoots back.

"You know, I liked you better when you were silent and brooding. Now you're just annoying me."

"Good, now you know how I've felt all night then."

And before I can respond, our order is called, and Cole walks over to the window where he grabs two brats and hands one to me.

I glance down at the bun-encased wiener doused in mustard. "Wow, this is girth-y."

Cole brings his brat up to his mouth, and before he takes a bite, he says, "Eh, I've seen girthy-er." Then he winks and takes a big bite.

Well, guess I know how the rest of this evening is going to go. Poor company with even poorer, sarcastic, insulting dialogue. Yay for me.

"I can pay for my own gingerbread," I say to Cole as he takes out his wallet and pays for the gingerbread cookies I plan on bringing home for myself, despite telling Cole they're for Aunt Cindy and Taran.

"And what kind of date would I be if I let my crush buy her own gingerbread?" he asks in that snarky tone that he's really ramped up since the mention of his parents.

Deflect much?

I see right through him, and he probably knows I see right through him, hence why he's especially annoying now. But despite it all, I have to admit this new part of town and the stalls are a great addition. The twirly swing is super cute, and the lights strung all around the perimeter offer just enough light to see what you're doing but not too much to take away from the ambiance. It reminds me of a German Christmas market but on a much smaller scale, and if that's what they were going for, they nailed it.

Once purchased, Cole hands me the bag and I reluctantly mutter a "thank you."

"Anything for my girl," he says as he drapes his arm over me again.

Yup, we're back to that.

He's had his arm around me for the entire stroll through the stalls, playfully showing me different handmade crafts, ornaments, and even a stall full of jam that apparently is in a rivalry with Atlas's mom's jam. I almost bought a jar out of spite but held off.

"Not your girl," I say as we head toward the exit.

"Yeah, I'm getting the sense there won't be a second date, not from the lack of me trying, though," he says.

And God, I didn't even think about a second date. Because the town will want to know. Martha, Mae... Fruitcake Festivus Tanya. Oh God, even Bob Krampus. They're all going to want to know where this is going, how the date went—and what am I going to say?

I know what Cole will say. That it was the best night of his life and how he wishes I'd say yes to another date. Then he'll say something along the lines of how I'm just not into him like he's into me and once again garner sympathy.

"There will be a second date," I say.

"Oh yeah?" he says, sounding intrigued. "And here I thought I wasn't winning you over. Tell me all about this second date."

"It will be one that we come up with on our own, not out in public so we don't actually have to go on it."

"Sounds romantic," he says.

"But we'll talk about it, get our stories straight. That way the town thinks we're still seeing each other without people actually seeing us together."

"Never knew dating you would feel so much like getting ghosted."

We stop under an archway, and I turn toward him. "Please, Cole, as if you want to go through an evening like this again."

"I don't know." He tugs on a strand of my hair, his ability to be affectionate mind-boggling to me. "I've had fun."

"There is no way—"

"Oh, look at them," a voice coos from the side.

Christ, are these women following us around?

Plastering on a smile, I look to the side where Martha and Mae are watching us, their hands clasped together in front of them, looking like they're watching their very own Lovemark movie come to life right in front of their eyes. If only they knew the truth—this man would never be a hero in one of the movies I edit.

"You're still out and about?" Cole asks in an annoyingly charming voice. "Isn't it past your bedtime?"

They both chuckle and wave at him. "We were hoping to catch you two one more time, and it looks like we caught you in just the right place," Mae says as she points to something above us.

Dread immediately fills me because there could only be one reason why they'd be pointing above us, looking like giddy little schoolgirls.

Together, we both direct our attention toward the sky, and sure enough, there it is, one of many mistletoe bundles I've avoided this entire evening. Unfortunately, this one went undetected.

"Well?" Martha says. "Aren't you going to kiss? It's tradition, after all."

"Oh, I don't think—"

My words are cut short as Cole closes the distance between us. His brawny, overbearing stature moves in as his hand lifts between us and gently grips my chin with his forefinger and thumb.

Uh, excuse me, sir.

Is he serious right now?

Is he really going to do this?

My eyes meet his, and I can see nothing in them, not the slightest hint of humor, irritation...even nerves. He almost looks like he's been planning this...this kiss...all night long.

Looking for a moment just like this as he lowers his head.

Oh my God, this is really happening.

He's doing this.

My body buzzes.

My nerves ramp up.

And as his mouth moves in close to mine, a whisper away, I can feel my legs shake beneath me.

"Tell me no," he whispers only for me to hear.

Tell him no?

I mean…I should.

I should push him away.

I should throw in the towel on this entire farce.

But I don't say anything.

I don't know why.

Maybe because I'm caught off guard that he's actually going for it.

Maybe I'm thrown off by how…intimate this feels, despite the lack of intimacy between us.

Maybe, deep down, I want to see what it's like to kiss him. I'd be lying if I said I didn't think about it when we were younger. That there weren't some romantic thoughts about the boy next door.

But when I don't stop him, he sees the green light and closes the last few inches between us, his soft lips playing against mine.

At first, it's friendly, a light graze of our mouths. And when I think he's going to leave it at that and pull away, he parts his lips and kisses me again.

It's a subtle move, but one that causes my hand to fall to his chest for balance.

For my stomach to tie itself in knots.

And for my mind to beg for another.

But that's it, nothing more, and he pulls away, both of our eyes slowly opening as we catch our breath.

Silence falls between us as he stares at me and I stare back at him.

Confusion laces both of our brows, while my lips feel like they've been stung yet worshipped all in the same moment.

"They're so meant for each other," Mae coos from the side.

"Shhh," Martha says. "Let's give them some space."

From the corner of my eye, I can see them hurry away, but it doesn't distract me as my eyes remain locked on Cole. Looking...searching for answers as to what that kiss was.

And he doesn't seem to have any answers as he tugs on his neck.

"Uh...looks like they're gone," he finally says.

"Yeah, looks like it," I reply.

"So, we should probably take off then."

"Yup, we should," I say, my body still buzzing, my mind reeling.

"And we can, uh, talk about that fake second date on the way back to our houses," he says calmly, rationally.

"Yeah, sounds like a plan."

Sounds like a plan?

What the heck just happened?

And why does a part of me want it to happen again?

CHAPTER SIXTEEN
COLE

Dare I say a not-so-fake romance is in the biting air?
You caught that kiss; you saw that longing stare.

Lips were locked, and they both felt
it all the way to their toes.
Now the question is, will they heat up? Nobody knows.

"THIS TASTES LIKE SHIT," I say to Max as I toss the piece of fruitcake he cut for me into the trash.

"Yeah." He scratches his head. "Wasn't a fan of it either."

"What the fuck are we going to do?" I ask. "We're an hour away from the competition, and we can't seem to bake a decent-tasting fruitcake to save our lives."

"I think it might be the jam," Max says. "Maybe we skip the jam and go for something more simple, more classic. Maybe we don't need a secret ingredient and we should just hope that Tanya likes you enough to bypass this horrible tasting lump of cake. Which, speaking of horrible things, you never told me how the date went—you keep changing the subject."

"I'm not changing the subject. I'm trying to figure out how to win this competition." I stare down at our ingredients. "I know your mom said these candied cherries are what we need to use, but they have a waxy taste that's very unappealing. Maybe we go with real ones."

"Real ones have moisture, and they could make the cake soggy," Max says.

"Given the fact that I nearly choked on the dryness of the cake we just made, we could use some moisture."

"Maybe," Max says, leaning against my kitchen counter. "So, we'll do real cherries…oh, or we can do maraschino cherries."

"There's an idea. Everyone likes those."

"And nothing screams Christmas like a maraschino cherry in a baked good."

"Very true," I say, gripping Max's shoulder. "Okay, let's run to the Myrrh-cantile and grab some cherries. And we'll use the recipe that we found online."

"The one on All-Recipes?" he asks.

"Yeah, seemed legit."

"That's risky, going in with a new recipe we've never tried," Max says.

"Can't be worse than what we just made. No offense to your mom, but that was shit."

Max scratches his chin. "Yeah, it wasn't great. Although…have you ever had a fruitcake that tasted good?"

"Never," I answer.

"Exactly."

"Okay, let's pack up our supplies, grab the cherries, and then head on over to the school for the competition."

Since we need to show our work in front of Tanya and demonstrate how well we can bake, the competition takes place in the K-12 school, in the gymnasium where they have portable convection ovens set up and baking stations ready to go. We provide the ingredients which are quickly looked over, and then we have three and a half hours to mix and bake. Max and I have been timing ourselves and so far we've hit the time limit, but the taste? Well, that's been a miss.

I fill up a tote bag while Max does the same—me focusing on the ingredients, him focusing on the tools we're going to need.

"So...about the date," Max presses.

I roll my eyes. "Dude, there's nothing to talk about," I say. "We went out, we irritated each other, put on a show for the townspeople, and then went our separate ways."

"Is that all that happened?" he asks with a lift of one brow.

Christ.

"Dude, if you know something, just say it."

"You kissed her." It's a statement, not a question. Clearly, he's been participating in the town chatter. And here I thought he might be better than that. But I guess since I've been avoiding the topic, he had to go somewhere else for the information.

"I didn't kiss her because I wanted to," I say. "I kissed her because Martha and Mae spotted us under some mistletoe and made us."

"Uh-huh...and how was it?"

Unexpected.

Soft.

Fucking delicious.

A kiss that I can still feel now. A kiss that I wish I could forget, but for the life of me, every time I think about that night, I think of how her lips felt against mine, how they were tentative, but then forceful when I parted our mouths. I think about how I wish I'd have pulled her in closer, dug my fingers into her hair, and spent so much more time exploring her mouth rather than pulling away.

And of course, all these feelings and thoughts have maddened me because the last thing I want to be doing is thinking about Storee in that way, especially since the hate is still there.

The irritation.

The need to challenge her.

Beat her in this competition.

I don't need thoughts of her mouth on mine weakening my plan of attack.

I shrug casually. "It was barely even a kiss. Our lips touched, and that was it. Seriously, everyone is making a big deal out of nothing."

Max leans in. "I heard your eyes slowly opened after."

"My eyes opened at a reasonable rate."

"I also heard that you two stared at each other for a while once you broke apart."

"Describe *a while*."

"I don't know, like you were looking into each other's souls," Max answers.

I shake my head. "You need to stay out of the gossip—you're starting to get all starry-eyed like the rest of them."

"So are you denying that you looked into her soul?" Max asks, completely ignoring me.

I prop my hand on the counter and glare at my best friend. "I did not stare into her soul. I barely even looked into her eyes. There was mistletoe, people were watching, and we kissed. Lips barely touched. There was nothing magical about it. More clinical if you removed the twinkle lights, music playing in the background, and the cooing onlookers."

"So what you're telling me is that the kiss meant nothing."

"It meant absolutely nothing," I say, keeping my expression still.

"And you're not thinking about the kiss a few days later."

"It was forgettable," I say.

"So the crush you had on her, it didn't ramp up?"

"Jesus Christ, Max. No!" I shout and then grab my tote bag of ingredients. "If I learned one thing from that date, it's that my childhood crush was just that, a childhood crush. There's nothing going on between us, and there isn't a future for anything else. When I say that date was a one and done thing…I mean it."

"Hey, Cole," Storee says in a greeting as I set our bags on the baking station next to hers.

Is her hair different?

It looks different.

Not that I'd notice something like that...although if I did, it's not because I stared into her soul or anything. It just looks...oh, maybe it's because she's not wearing a winter hat. So *that's* her forehead.

Nice.

I mean...no, not nice.

I don't care what her forehead looks like.

It's just a forehead.

There's nothing nice about it. It's bland. Boring.

"I can see your forehead," I say in greeting.

"What do you mean you can see my forehead?" she says as her hand covers it.

Yeah, what do you mean, Cole?

"It's uh, it's there." I point to her forehead.

"Yes, people usually have foreheads."

"Well, good for you on growing it," I say with a nod and then turn to my ingredients, feeling my cheeks flame with embarrassment.

She leans closer to me. "If this is some sort of way to get under my skin, fake me out, and mess with my head, it's not going to work. So you can take your forehead talk somewhere else."

"Whatever you say," I reply, keeping my head down, not wanting her to spot my red cheeks.

She grumbles something under her breath and then goes back to setting up her station. Max is filling out our ingredient form with Tanya, letting her know everything that's involved in our fruitcake while I attempt to settle my racing heart.

And why is it racing, you might ask?

Don't think it's from seeing Storee, because that's not the case at all. I'm nervous about the competition. As a last-minute item, Max grabbed pineapple and said it was a needed addition while we were at the Myrrh-cantile. I told him pineapple wasn't in the recipe, but he's seen it in others, and it was the ingredient we were missing. I think the only thing we're missing is common sense in baking.

So yeah, nice try, but these nerves have nothing to do with Storee.

"And I'll have you know," Storee says, coming out of nowhere and invading my station, "I have an unbeatable fruitcake recipe. Aunt Cindy took first last year, and we're replicating the same recipe."

Great.

Just what I need to hear.

Especially when we just tossed pineapple into the mix.

But not wanting to show an ounce of fear, I turn toward her. "Yeah, well, does your fruitcake have pineapple in it?"

"It does," she replies with a lift of her chin.

Huh, okay.

Maybe this won't be so bad then.

"Dates?"

"If your fruitcake doesn't have dates, then it's not a fruitcake," she counters.

"What about...uh...walnuts?"

"Face it, Cole, we have a good recipe and you know it, so you're trying to throw me off with your forehead talk."

Yup, that's exactly what I was trying to do.

I wasn't fumbling around, thinking about the kiss we shared, or how pretty she looks today, or the fact that the feelings I've tried to repress for a long time are miraculously starting to show up out of the goddamn blue.

It was a kiss, dickhead.

Get the fuck over it!

"It's not going to work. So why don't you worry about yourself and focus on not making Tanya gag rather than coming up with something stupid to distract me?"

"Well, you got me." I shrug. "Guess I should leave your forehead alone."

"Best you do." She taps on my worktable. "Wishing you the worst of luck. I hope you burn the shit out of your fruitcake."

I grip my chest. "The way you flirt, it really cuts me deep, Storee."

"Did I hear flirting over here?" Tanya says as she walks up to us, a huge smile on her face.

"Trying not to," I say, "but when she shows up to the competition looking beautiful, I can't hold back." I let out a sigh and tilt my head toward Tanya. "I think she's trying to distract me, Tanya, so excuse me if my fruitcake is a little off today. I'm going to be fighting an inner war between paying attention to what I'm doing and trying to catch glimpses of her."

Tanya gleefully looks between us. "Oh, after I heard about the kiss, I know what I'm dealing with. Don't worry." She winks in my direction. "I'll take your crush into consideration."

I press my hands together. "Thank you, Tanya. Now, to get my head in the game...shit, one more hug."

I push off my workstation, walk over to an annoyed Storee, and pull her into a tight embrace. And just for added measure, I kiss the top of her head. "Good luck, babe."

"*Babe!*" Tanya squeals. "Oh, I can't take it." She waves her hand in front of her face. "I need to tell Martha and Mae about this." She hurries off, pulling her phone out of her pocket as she moves toward the back corner of the gym.

Storee pushes away from me, a look of disgust on her face. "Babe?"

"Thought it was a nice touch." I smirk.

"If you get anything higher than third place in this Fruitcake Festivus, this entire system is rigged."

"Why do you say that? You haven't even tasted my fruitcake."

"I don't need to taste it to know it's going to be terrible. I smelled burning cake from over the fence when you were apparently practicing."

"That was on Max and him setting the timer wrong, nothing to do with our recipe."

Also, we overfilled the pan, used a pan far too small, and the batter was dripping over the sides when we pushed down the toppings, but she doesn't need to know about that.

"Either way, you have rigged this competition by playing with Tanya's romantic heart. You should be eliminated."

"Says the person whose aunt is being rolled in on a wheelchair right now, looking rather paler than she was the other night."

Storee glances over her shoulder, catching sight of Cindy and Taran approaching. When she turns back around, she whispers, "This could be her last Christmas."

"Bullshit," I say. "Cindy has many more Christmases left in her. So don't be throwing rocks at glass houses, Storee. If you're not playing fair, neither am I. So…good luck, *babe*." I wink, which causes her to huff and push me out of her workspace.

Her workspace that's right next to mine.

"Kind of wishing you had a door to slam to separate us?" I ask.

"No, because with the way you've been working, you would probably hang mistletoe in the doorframe."

"Ah, thinking about that kiss still?" I tsk at her. "I knew you would. I could tell from the hungry look in your eyes when we parted. If you want another one, you can just ask."

Defiantly, she replies, "You know, I really hope you burn your finger."

"Ah, and I hope you use salt instead of sugar."

"Here's to you tripping with your fruitcake in hand."

"And cheers to you sprinkling your hair in your batter."

Her anger spikes as she leans over the table and whispers, "I hate you."

"Feeling is mutual...*babe.*"

STOREE

"You look worried," I say to Cole. He's standing next to me, waiting to be judged by Tanya, who is currently taking a bite out of Jimmy's burnt monstrosity. Just based off what it looks like, I will be shocked if Jimmy doesn't get last place.

"I'm not worried," Cole says as he rocks on his heels next to me. "Confident. You should be worried. Who puts mashed potatoes in their fruitcake?"

"The winner from last year does," I say, still smirking over the look on Cole's face when we pulled out the mashed potatoes.

It was an epic showdown of culinary skills, all five contestants in the kitchen, attempting to make the perfect fruitcake that people actually love to eat. From what I could see, Ursula went with candied everything—dates, walnuts, fruit. I fear she's going to give someone a cavity with her fruitcake, which resembles more of a candy bar than an actual cake. Jimmy, well, we know where he went wrong. Dr. Pedigree went with a more...organic approach with all fresh ingredients, which could lack flavor but help with density. We shall see.

And then there were Cole and Atlas who were running around their kitchen space, sniping at each other, trying to figure out how much pineapple was too much pineapple. If I wasn't so focused on what I was doing, I'd have sat back and enjoyed the show, because from what I could hear, it was hilarious.

I think at one point I heard Cole mutter to Atlas to stop being a little bitch about the pineapple but can't be too sure.

"Storee, please bring your fruitcake to the judging table," Tanya says.

Muttering so only I can hear him, Cole says, "Don't trip." Then he tacks on, "Good luck, babe."

Such an idiot.

For good measure, I walk over to Aunt Cindy in her wheelchair, give her a quick kiss, and then carry the fruitcake to Tanya.

I know it's good. I know we have a pretty solid chance at first place. I don't have the slightest bit of worry inside of me.

I set the plate in front of Tanya and then take a step back. "This is Great-Aunt Cindy's recipe, with mashed potatoes and all."

Tanya smiles. "And maybe a dash of romance? I saw you sneaking peeks at your man."

I hold back the eye roll and nod. "Of course, made with a dash of romance."

"Ooo, I love it."

She cuts a piece for herself and examines the loaf, the slice, the density. She sniffs, she rotates the cake, and when she finally takes a bite, she lets it sit on her tongue for a few seconds before she starts chewing.

The only tell of her enjoying it being a nod and the fact that she went in for seconds. She did not go in for seconds on Jimmy's. I don't think she even wanted to try his.

After a few moments of chewing, then swallowing, she picks up her pen, marks a few things in a folder that she keeps hidden from view, and then smiles up at me.

"Nicely done, Storee."

"Thank you," I say and then take my fruitcake back to my station.

I can feel Cole's eyes on me, but I don't give him the time of day as pride flits through me.

"Cole, I'd love to taste your fruitcake now."

Love to taste it. Wow, favoritism much? I swear if he beats me on this one, I'm going to be livid.

224 | MEGHAN QUINN

Cole brings his fruitcake over to Tanya, and despite my mind telling me to focus on anything but his ass, my eyes take in his tight rear end that's encased in his nicely worn jeans.

"This is my take on the fruitcake. Made with maraschino cherries, not candied, as well as pineapple, dates, and walnuts."

"Looks great," Tanya practically coos. She slices into it. "Wow, what a great cut."

What a great cut? Is this a piece of steak or a cake?

Seriously, Tanya. Sure, he's a handsome man who apparently knows how to work the crowd to his advantage, but she can't see through his tactics?

In disgust, I watch Tanya eat his fruitcake...taking three bites, Cole chatting her up the entire time. What happened to him being the grumpy dick? How is he so friendly all of a sudden? How is it he can be grunting out a response one day, and the next be the chattiest one in town?

After what feels like forever, Tanya thanks him, and he carries his fruit-cake back to the table. I will be taste-testing that thing and comparing it to mine. I will have the final say in all of this, even if I don't get to make the final decision.

Tanya goes through her notebook, tallying up points, assessing who she wants to assign places to while I wait with bated breath to see if we won.

"Whatever happens, I still want to go on that second date," Cole says next to me like the jackass that he is. "Maybe you can make me some fruitcake."

"I'm making you nothing."

I fold my hands in front of me, trying to look like I'm the happiest person in the room despite the irritation pulsing through me.

"And here I thought we could have a cozy evening together."

"I'm invoking the no-talking rule," I say.

"On the date? Well, if we don't talk, then there's only one other thing we can do…"

I turn to him and catch the waggle of his eyebrows. "Are you a child?"

"For the sake of dating you? I sure as hell hope not."

"Oh my God, you're irritating," I whisper, just for him to put his arm around me again and bring me in close to his chest.

"I know."

Tanya takes that moment to look up and catches us close together. Her smile grows even larger as she finishes up her notes.

"I swear if you win this, I'm going to throw a temper tantrum. I very well might toss my mixing bowl at your head."

"At me?" he asks quietly. "But then how could I make you weak in the knees with my kisses if I'm unconscious?"

"You did not make me weak in the knees," I shoot back.

"I felt you waver."

"There was no wavering."

"A little bit. I steadied you."

"Are you freaking delusional?" I hiss as Tanya stands and walks in front of her desk. Bob Krampus joins her, and the room quiets down as Bob takes the results from Tanya.

He clears his throat, looks through his spectacles and then out to the crowd. "It seems as though we have a verdict. Coming in fifth place, we have…Jimmy Short."

No surprise there.

His fruitcake belongs in the compost.

The crowd lightly cheers as Jimmy kicks the ground, clearly disappointed in himself.

"In fourth place we have…" Bob pauses as he attempts to read the card. Confused, he confers with Tanya who nods. "Sorry about that. In fourth place, we have Ursula."

Damn it. I wish Cole was fourth, but what can you do? Ursula gave Tanya a brick of candy.

"And in third place," Bob continues, "ahh, our lover of the week, Cole."

A large grin stretches across my face as I turn toward him and give him a gentle pat on the back, looking like the ever-doting crush. He smiles down at me and then brings his attention back to Bob.

Either he's a particularly good actor, or he agrees with his placement.

Either way, if we can pull ahead with the win on this, it will give us a significant lead.

"And our runner up is…" Bob pauses for dramatic effect. "Dr. Pedigree. Giving the win for the second year in a row to Team Cindy!"

Now…if I wasn't being judged on my Christmas spirit, this is what I'd do with this news: I'd do a set of three cartwheels while yelling *yippee!* I'd finish right in front of Cole and then shimmy so hard that my boobs would pop right out of my bra, but I wouldn't care because I won. I beat him…him and his pineapple debacle and forehead distraction.

But since I'm being watched very carefully, I smile, clap, and offer congratulations to the rest of the group, then walk over to Aunt Cindy and give her a hug because we took this one. I knew we would. It was the mashed potatoes.

"Well done, everyone. We do have some new leadership in the overall competition, though," Bob says. "In first place, our winner for today is Storee with forty-three points."

"I'm so proud of you," Aunt Cindy says, pulling me into a hug again. "And serves them right, trying to mess with us."

I chuckle and lift up from her.

"In second place, we have Cole and his holly jolly sidekick, Atlas, with thirty-seven points."

The boys give each other pats on the back and…are they waving to the crowd? Good lord.

"In third, we have Ursula with thirty-four points, following with a tie at twenty-three points each between Jimmy and Beatrice." Bob removes his spectacles and continues, "Nothing is set in stone, though, and the rankings can change with one single competition. With our coveted candy cane-making competition next, I have a feeling the tides will turn. So good luck to our Kringle-ees and ho-ho-ho! Merry Christmas!"

The crowd offers a "Merry Christmas" as well and then starts dispersing. I take that moment to turn to Cole, a smile on my face. "How's the view from second?"

"Not bad," he says, his teeth pulling over his lip.

"Ew, don't be a pervert," I say, pushing at his shoulder.

"You're the one who asked."

"Yeah, and I wasn't talking about my backside."

"Shame."

"Stop that," I say, getting closer. "The fake flirting."

"Why? You getting confused?"

"No, but you're annoying. I liked you better when you were a grump. This...this act you're putting on is frankly inappropriate."

"Inappropriate?" he asks with a raised brow.

"Yes, you are—"

"Wonderful fruitcakes," Tanya says, coming up to us. "Storee, how could I not pick Cindy's for first? It's easily the best I've ever had, and you executed it so brilliantly."

Switching from irritated to happy within a blink of an eye, I say, "Thank you, Tanya. That means a lot to the both of us. I know how hard Aunt Cindy has worked on that recipe. I'm glad I could bring it to life."

"You did a wonderful job." Tanya then turns to Cole with a warm smile. "Cole, I was shocked with yours. Honestly, I expected a Jimmy-type fruitcake from you two and that's not what I got at all. I think the only thing that lowered you on points was that there was a lot of pineapple, which took it in a more tropical direction instead of Christmas. But

I will say this, if I was served your fruitcake while celebrating Christmas in Hawaii, I would have been absolutely tickled."

"Thank you, Tanya. And thanks for the note—we will have to go back to the drawing board and refine."

She pats him on the shoulder. "Great showing, though, for it being your first time with a change in recipe, and I have to admit I was grateful you didn't make me eat Atlas's mom's recipe. She thinks the jam makes it, but she couldn't be more wrong."

Cole smirks. "I told her the same thing."

"Oh, you naughty boy." Tanya laughs and then waves. "Enjoy the rest of your day."

"You too," I say as Tanya takes off.

Cole turns to Atlas. "I fucking told you it was too much pineapple."

Atlas, with his hands in his pockets, nods. "Yup, you were right, dear."

CHAPTER SEVENTEEN
STOREE

And just like that, the tables have turned.
Thanks to mashed potatoes, first place was earned.

But the winds seem to be changing;
is romance really in the air?
In love and Christmas competitions, is all really fair?

Could his crush blossom to something
that's so much more?
Could true love develop in the
town's candy cane store?

"YOU'RE KIDDING, RIGHT?" I SAY as I look out the window at the snow falling to the ground. "I'm not driving in that."

"You don't have a choice," Taran says. "This is the only class offered before the competition, and you have to take it."

"It's an hour's drive away," I say. "And if you haven't noticed, it's snowing."

"The roads will be clear," Aunt Cindy says. "They always take care of the roads here. No need to worry, dearie."

"Umm, but it's snowing. I don't drive in the snow. I don't know what I'm doing."

"Stay on the road," Taran says, being unhelpful as she maps out more lights on a chart of the house that she created.

"You're seriously okay with me driving your car through a snowstorm an hour away to Clayton to take a candy cane-making lesson from a guy named Theodore Garvey?" I ask.

Taran sighs and brings her attention to me. "Yes, I am. I can't take you because I have to take care of Aunt Cindy, and Aunt Cindy needs to do her physical therapy. So I suggest you put your big girl pants on, get dressed, and start driving."

Irritated with my sister, I retreat to my room and shut the door. This is ridiculous—can't I watch a YouTube video or something? Wouldn't that be safer than driving in the snow? I mean, if you're a seasoned snow driver, then you know the tactics to stay on the road. But this is terrifying. Don't they care about my safety at all?

I glance out the window and catch the white flakes floating from the sky down to the ground. Sure, it's not a heavy snow, but it's enough to worry me. To make me sweat, to create this prickling feeling that goes up the back of my neck, letting me know that this might not be a good idea.

I know Taran won't let me stay home though, so I grab a pair of leggings, a warm sweater, and fuzzy socks along with undergarments and bring them into the bathroom where I take a quick shower, leaving my hair up since I washed it yesterday.

Once out of the shower, I wipe my hand across the fogged-up mirror, revealing my reflection.

You can do this.

You can drive in the snow.

It's for the competition.

Do you really want Cole to win?

"No," I say to myself. "He will not win. You are going to drive to Clayton, you will be fine, and you will learn how to make candy canes. Done and done."

"I'm going to die. I'm going to die," I chant, my hands clutching the steering wheel in a death grip.

I've turned off my music.

My eyes are as wide as can be.

And despite attempting to have X-ray vision, I can't seem to see through this snow that has picked up since I left Aunt Cindy's house.

"Where are the lines in the road?" I shout as my emotions get the best of me and my eyes start to well up with tears.

No, don't cry, that's not going to help you see better.

I swipe at my eyes and slow the car down to five miles per hour, turning on my hazard lights and praying that I don't fall down a ditch.

Maybe...maybe if I pull off to the side for a second and let this heavy snow pass, everything will be okay.

I swipe at my eyes again and very carefully find the shoulder of the road and pull off to the side.

"See, we'll just wait—" The car bumps, and then jolts downward.

I scream bloody murder, terrified that I've fallen into a ditch.

"This is my death," I scream, waiting for the car to keep falling, but when it doesn't, I open my eyes and glance out the window. To the right of me, I see a guardrail. Thank God for that, because at least I know I won't be falling into any sort of mountain death trap. I look up ahead and see a sign that says LOOKOUT POINT. Oh, there must be a bigger parking spot there.

I'll pull forward and rest there.

I press on the gas, but the car doesn't move.

Um...

I nervously chuckle.

Okay, let me just press a little harder.

Nothing.

No...no no no.

I flip my hood over my head, put the car in park, and then open my door, only to be blasted by Father Snow.

"Mother of God," I say as I make my way to the back tires to examine what's going on. I can barely see with the snow pelting me in the face, but when I reach the tires and see that one of them has fallen victim to a decently sized pothole, I realize...I'm fucked.

Quickly, I make my way back to the car and settle into my seat before grabbing my phone.

And would you guess it? Not a bar of reception. Freaking mountains.

I press my head against the steering wheel, tears filling my eyes again.

My worst nightmare has come true.

Deserted, alone, in a winter storm with no cell service. This is exactly why I didn't want to drive, Taran!

Tears stream down my face as I try to figure out what to do. I have no idea where I am in proximity to any town.

I can't see a freaking thing.

And the last thing I want to do is stand outside, waiting for someone to come rescue me, because who in their right mind would drive in this snow?

No one.

No one would drive in this weather.

Only idiots like me from California who are convinced—

Knock. Knock.

I nearly jump out of my skin as I turn to the side and spot a figure standing outside of my car door.

I'm so relieved that there is another human in the area that I don't even consider if they could be a murderer.

I roll down my window, the wind and snow whipping into my car as the stranger lowers their head.

And that's when I see him.

Those memorable eyes.

That carved jawline.

Those lips…

"Cole?" I say, wiping at my eyes, honestly too relieved to even care that it's him.

"Having some car trouble?"

I nod, and I can't help it, more tears stream down my face.

"Yeah," I say right before a sob escapes my lips.

"Shit," he mutters and then opens my car door. "Grab your bag," he says as he helps me out of the car.

I grab my things and stand next to the car as he hops in, rolls up the window, puts the emergency brake on, and then turns off the engine. He then gets out, pockets the keys, and shuts the door. He takes me by the elbow and escorts me toward his truck that's parked in front of my car.

I must have been so upset that I didn't even notice him pull in.

He brings me to the passenger side of his truck and opens the door before helping me in. When I'm in the warm confines of his truck, he shuts the door and that's when I attempt to wipe at my eyes, but it's no use, the tears keep coming.

When he joins me, he turns on the heat to full blast and then reaches in his glove box, handing me some tissues.

"Thank you," I say as I blot at my face, knowing damn well any makeup I put on is probably smeared all over.

"How long were you stuck there?" he asks, his voice terse, almost… angry.

"Not long at all. You were like a minute behind."

"Good. Are you okay?"

I look up and see the concern in his eyes, the worry etched in his brow and it…it casts him in a different light. Makes me remember the boy I used to talk to on his porch while drinking hot cocoa. This isn't the same man I've been sparring with; this is the boy who I used to think about every Christmas. Even when I was far away in a warmer environment, I often wondered about my blue-eyed friend. The girls at school used to be jealous when I came back from the holidays talking about him. And I missed him. Truly missed him.

"Yeah, I'm okay," I say as more tears stream down my cheeks. "Ugh, I'm sorry."

And then to my surprise, he scoots across the bench seat and pulls me close to his chest. I go willingly and rest my head against him as he cups the back of my head.

"You shouldn't be driving in this snow," he says softly as he sifts his fingers through my hair.

"That's what I told Taran," I say. "But…the candy cane class is today so…she made me go." I sniffle. "Is that…is that where you're headed?"

"Yes," he says tersely. "You should have asked for a ride, Storee."

I pull back so I can look him in the eyes. "I should have asked you? After all the fighting we've been doing? Would you have even said yes?"

"I would have," he says. "Competition is one thing, safety is another. I don't want you getting hurt."

"You don't?" I ask.

His hand comes to my cheek. "No, I don't."

"Oh," I reply, not sure what else to say.

After a few seconds of us just staring at each other, he says, "Do you want me to take you back home?"

Yes.

But also…no.

"Umm…you're headed to Clayton?"

"I am," he replies as he strokes my hair, tucking a strand behind my ear. "I know shit about candy canes."

That makes me laugh. I blot my eyes with my tissue. "Same. Would you mind…um, taking me?"

"As long as you don't annoy me."

I smirk. "Can't make any promises."

He chuckles.

Actually chuckles. Then he pulls away just enough to look at me better. "You good?"

"Yeah." I nod. "Thank you."

"You're welcome." And when I think he's going to move back to his side of the truck, he stays where he is, his hand moving into mine. When our eyes connect, he says, "You sure you don't want to go back home? I don't mind driving you."

"No, I need to take that lesson. Can't have you beating me."

"Yeah, can't have that," he says absentmindedly. There he is. There's the nice boy I once knew. No malice. No snark. Just personable and good-natured.

He studies me for a few more moments before he finally retreats to his side of the truck.

"When we get into Clayton, I'll let Max know about your car and have him arrange to have someone take care of it."

"Oh, that's okay. I can, uh, call...someone."

"Yeah, and who would that be?" he asks as he takes off his jacket.

"Uh...someone."

"Nice try," he says and then offers me his jacket. "I know you get cold, so would you like this for your legs?"

I roll my teeth over the corner of my lip. "You don't need it?"

"Nah, I'm good."

"Okay, sure, I'll take it." He hands it to me, and I drape it over my chilled legs, grateful for the extra layer. I glance over at him. "You're being nice to me."

"I'm not really a dick, you know."

"Then why do you act like one?"

He puts his truck into drive. "Defense mechanism."

"From what?" I ask.

He glances in my direction and then focuses back on the road. "Nothing."

"Why don't I believe you?" I say.

"Because you can probably see right through me, and that scares me, hence why I said nothing."

Wow, okay, so he's being really open and honest. This is such a stark contrast from the man I saw the other day at the Fruitcake Festivus. So what's changed?

"That's a heavy statement," I say.

He just shrugs. Clearly, if I push him too far, he might shut down, so I decide to leave it at that.

I like this side of him. This open, warm side, and I don't want to lose that.

So I change the subject. "This snow is pretty heavy," I say. "You're okay driving in it?"

"I grew up here, Storee. What do you think?"

"I would take that as a yes," I say. "But don't you ever get scared?"

"If you allow fear to take over your actions, then you're never going to accomplish anything."

"You say that as if you have experience in the matter."

"Maybe," he says his eyes fixed on the road.

"Perhaps you'll tell me what kind of experience."

"And give you insight into the competition?" he playfully says. "Nah, think I'll pass."

"Doesn't seem very strategic to save your competition from a snowstorm."

"As a matter of fact, it is," he says. "If I left you there to freeze to death, then it wouldn't be a competition at all. I'm not one to win because of a forfeit—I want the challenge."

"Ah, I see, so saving me back there was a selfish move?"

He glances over at me for a split second. "Probably in more ways than one."

COLE

What the fuck are you doing, Cole?

It's a question I keep repeating to myself over and over as I glance toward Storee, checking for the hundredth time that she's okay.

When I saw her car pulled off to the side, I felt my entire being go hot with fear. I knew immediately that it had to be her. I've seen that car parked in the driveway next-door, and it was headed the same direction as me. It had to be her, and when I saw her tear-stained face, well…fuck, it made me drop the animosity, the pent-up anger, and all I wanted to do was help.

Protect.

Make sure that she wasn't scared.

Make sure that she was okay.

I went into helping mode.

And when she continued to cry in my truck, visibly shaking, she broke another wall that I had erected between the two of us, and before I knew it, I was holding her, stroking her hair, wanting to remove all the fear that was taking over her body.

Because I know that fear.

I feel it every time I drive in the snow.

It's the way my parents died…driving in a snowstorm.

Nearly ten years ago. I got that phone call, telling me what happened. Altering my life forever.

And it's times like these that I wish I'd been with my parents and hadn't been left alone.

The fear is so strong, so prevalent during the winter that I make sure to drive in the snow. I make sure to practice. I make sure I don't allow the fear to turn me catatonic, because that's what it would do if I allowed it.

So when I woke up this morning and saw that it was snowing, I didn't even think twice about driving to Clayton. If only I'd checked in on Storee first to see if she was going. Selfishly, I didn't consider her. I was so focused on myself, focused on conquering the fear once again that always pricks at the back of my neck when I travel in the snow.

I should have asked.

"I'm sorry," I say before I can stop myself.

"Sorry for what?" she asks, sounding confused as she blots at her tears.

"For not checking in with you before I left, seeing if you needed a ride today."

"Oh...why would you?"

"It would have been the right thing to do," I say as I look her in the eyes.

She glances away, staring down at her lap. "You don't need to apologize, Cole."

"I do. I really should have checked. That was shitty of me."

"Cole," she says, a note of trepidation in her voice. "You owe me nothing. It's not like we're friends, right?"

Yeah...I guess we're not.

I look out toward the snow pelting my windshield, the wetter flakes dragging streaks of water across the glass and collecting on my wipers.

"Right, Cole?" she says again, almost sounding unsure. "We're not friends."

I bring my attention back to her. "We were...a while back."

Her lips press together as she slowly nods. "We were. I miss that side of us."

I swallow the lump in my throat and nod. "Yeah, me too." And then because the mood seems to be tense, I say, "You know, we do have a good rapport going on in town. Everyone seems to think we get along just fine. Maybe we're friends and we don't know it."

I glance at her and catch the way the corner of her lip tilts up, joining me in lightening the mood. "I mean, it *is* friendly of you to stop by my car on the side of the road and check on me."

"That was awfully kind of me," I reply with a grin.

"So are you trying to tell me that maybe, possibly, we might be friends?"

I shrug. "Isn't that what they say, the enemy of my enemy is my friend?"

"Yes, but there needs to be a third involved for that to be true. So if both of us were enemies with Atlas, then we would be friends."

"I see. Then perhaps the candy canes will be our enemy today, which then would make us friends."

"From what I heard about candy cane making, I have a feeling that might be true," she replies, relaxing into her seat, crossing one leg over the other.

"Are you warm?" I ask.

She nods. "Yeah, you could probably turn down the heat. I'm sure you're hot."

"Yeah, I'm about to sweat out of my flannel," I say as I turn down the dial.

She chuckles. "You know, you can be kind of funny when you allow it. Reminds me of our conversations when we were younger."

"Ah, so you do remember me," I say. "Here I thought I was Connor to you."

"That was a stupid joke that didn't quite hit the way I thought it would. And then of course I saw how irritated it made you, and I just...kept going. Who knows why."

"Because you're the instigator. I recall you driving your sister crazy when we were younger...and me for that matter," I say, thankful the snow is lightening up as we head over the mountain pass. Clayton is not that far away now.

"I still drive her crazy. And apparently you as well."

"Seems to be a theme with you," I say.

"Guess once an instigator, always an instigator." She turns slightly toward me. "Can I ask you a question?"

"Depends," I say as I switch on the radio, letting Christmas instrumentals lightly play in the background. I feel like I'm transported back to ten years ago when conversation flowed easily with her.

"Depends on what?" she asks.

"If I want to answer the question or not. I have the right to veto."

"That's fair." She shifts so she's fully turned toward me now. I can feel her eyes on me, and it takes everything in me not to look in her direction, because I know if I do, I'll want to look for a beat longer. "When I first came into town, why were you so upset with me? Did I do something wrong? Was it because my family hadn't visited in ten years? Was it because you saw how sad Aunt Cindy was?"

"None of that," I say, my throat growing tight. I'm not sure I want to have this conversation.

"Okay, then what was it?"

My grip on the steering wheel grows tighter as the snow breaks, and only flurries now fall over us. The worst of the storm is behind us, its wake evident in the powdered trees and mountainsides that surround us.

"Seriously, Cole, what did I do?"

"You know, I don't think this is the sort of conversation we should be having right now."

"Why not?" she asks.

"Because it's probably something I should tell you when I look you in the eyes."

"Oh," she says. "Well...then pull over."

"Pull over?" I ask. "We don't want to be late."

"We won't. Pull over, Cole."

Knowing she's not going to let this go, I do as she says and put my hazard lights on even though, there's probably no one else driving right now.

When I put the truck in park, she tugs on my hand, forcing me to look at her. "Talk to me, Cole, because I don't like this...this animosity between us. It's tiring. The constant fighting, battling, the fake façade. I'm just...I'm overwhelmed, and I can see that warm side of you come out, that side I used to know."

She presses her palm to mine, and I entwine our fingers before I look her in the eyes.

Crystal clear.

Not a hint of treachery in them like she's waiting to strike when I open up, ready to take me down.

There's genuine care.

Concern.

And it breaks me because it's been...fuck, it's been lonely during this time of the year.

And it's my doing. I've secluded myself. I've neglected to participate in activities with the town. I've been hiding in a hole, only coming out at Christmas to spend a few days with the Maxheimers. I've actually been surprised I haven't received a million side-eyes from the townsfolk. They must be shocked at my abrupt change in personality. Yet they've...welcomed me.

But seeing Storee here again, it's reminding me of all those Christmases when we would build snowmen in our front yards. When we would walk around the town, never holding hands, but enjoying each other's company while looking at the lights. She'd be freezing, and I'd offer her my jacket. She'd ask questions about what it's like to live in such a secluded, kitschy town, and I'd reciprocate by asking her what it's like having access to a beach all the time.

In a weird way, I've associated Storee with Christmas. Whenever I saw her family pull up in the driveway, it felt like the season truly started, and, well…after my parents died and she didn't come to visit anymore, it darkened the season for me, to the point that I didn't celebrate anymore. Couldn't. Because there was no joy left for me to celebrate.

"Please, Cole," she says, squeezing my hand. "Tell me what I did."

I wet my lips and lean my back against my door. "It was the last Christmas that you were here."

"The Christmas where I knocked Mrs. Fiskers into the river?" she asks.

"Yeah, that Christmas."

"That was such a horrible Christmas for me. I was in such a foul mood. If I said anything mean or stupid, I'm sorry. I was embarrassed, I was mad, I was confused about what I wanted to do with my life, and, well, I didn't have the best Christmas that year. I ended up leaving Christmas Day because I was over it. Taran took me to the airport. Why, what did I say?"

I glance out the windshield, feeling all that pain come back. Because I remember looking for her the next day, despite everything she'd said, hoping to find her, talk to her, have her get my mind off the pain I was feeling, but she wasn't there.

She had left.

"Cole," she presses. I try to release her hand, but she doesn't let me. "Please tell me."

I let out a sigh and just go for it. "That Christmas Eve, when you talked to me on the porch, you said that you hated the town."

"Oh." She shakes her head. "I didn't mean that. It was—"

"And that was when my parents went missing."

"Wait…what?" she says, sitting taller.

"I was out on the porch, hoping to run into you because I was scared, nervous. They couldn't find my parents after a big snowstorm. They were supposed to come back that day, but no one had heard from them. When I saw you, I was relieved, but then…"

"Oh my God," she whispers as tears fill her eyes again. "I went off about the town, how it was so stupid and how I didn't understand why anyone would want to spend day in and day out celebrating Christmas."

"Yeah," I say lightly.

"Cole..." Tears fall down her cheeks. "I'm...oh my God, why didn't you say anything?"

"I was numb," I answer. "I didn't want to fight with you. I didn't even want to defend the town that was trying to help find my parents. I just...I slipped into another frame of mind." I wet my lips. "And then the next day when I wanted to tell you what happened, you weren't there. You had left, and I just...I don't know, I took that as your goodbye. You were done with Kringle—you were done with me."

"No." She shakes her head. "No, I'm sorry. Oh my God, I'm so selfish and stupid. I'm so sorry, Cole."

I shrug. "It was ten years ago. When I saw you come back into town, it just brought back all that animosity I was feeling, and then when I heard you were going to try to become the Christmas Kringle, I thought *how dare she*. And, well, the rest is history."

She scoots closer on the bench seat and brings my hand to her chest. "I'm sorry. I should have been there for you. I should have asked what was wrong. I was so caught up in myself, I neglected to think about you. And then...God, not coming back. You must hate me."

"I don't hate you," I say.

Not even close, Storee.

Not even a little.

"Cole, I'm sure you do—"

"I don't," I say with conviction. "I really don't, Storee."

She presses her lips together. "Well, you should." She glances down at her lap and lets out a sigh. "I'm just so deeply sorry. I should have been there for you, and I wasn't. I can't imagine what it's been like. How lonely you must have been. I mean, I don't see my parents much these days—they have their own adventurous life now—but if I want to...well, I can see them." She pauses, and I can see how deeply she's grieving for me. Her presence is somewhat soothing in this moment. But then she looks up. "God, I didn't even know. I'm wrecked that I didn't know what you were going through. I'm—"

"Because I made Cindy promise not to tell you."

Her eyes shoot up to mine. "You did? Why?"

"Because I was angry with you at the time. I didn't want your sympathy. I just wanted to deal with my new reality on my own. Plus, I knew you were headed to college, and I felt like you leaving that Christmas was you starting a new journey. You were done with Kringle, and I needed to accept that."

"I would have come back if I'd known."

"And that's exactly why I made her promise. You weren't into this town, this life, and I didn't want your pity. It...it just was meant to be that way." I drag my hand over my face. "And when you came back, I treated you like shit, and I'm sorry. I was just, hell, I was surprised. I didn't know how to handle my feelings and I acted childishly. I'm sorry, Storee."

She shakes her head. "Don't be. You had every right to act the way that you did."

"Losing my parents doesn't give me the privilege to be an asshole."

"How about this, we're both sorry for separate reasons, and we both accept the apologies?" She squeezes my hand, and it makes me smile. "We can move on from this, Cole. We don't need to live in a past of apologies, because that is not going to do anything but make us go around in circles."

"You're right," I say, clearing my throat.

"So let's accept what we've said, and move forward from here."

"Yeah, I think I can get on board with that."

"Good." She glances out the window and back at me. "Now, that doesn't mean I'm going to take it easy on you. You're still going down... Snow Daddy." My brows shoot up and she chuckles. "Atlas told me about his nickname for you. I was just waiting to use it. Has a nice ring to it, if you ask me."

"Yeah, well, that's a Max nickname only."

"Mm, I don't know about that." She releases my hand. "I'm partial to it."

I shake my head and then put the truck in drive.

"Hey, Cole?"

"Hmm?" I glance over at her.

"Thank you for telling me."

No, thank you, Storee, for coming back, for caring, for helping me smile again.

"Thanks for listening, Storee."

STOREE

"Sooo, this looks just like Chadwick's Candy Shop," I say quietly to Cole.

"Yeah, sore subject."

"I don't get it," I say as we wait for Theodore Garvey to bring out the ingredients from the back of the kitchen. "Why would Mr. Chadwick send us here for lessons when clearly Theodore is stealing all his ideas from Mr. Chadwick?"

"I think it's many things. One, Jefferson doesn't have to deal with us. Two, people can see how Theodore's is a rip-off. And three, if we fail, Jefferson has a reason to hate Theodore more."

"Makes sense, I guess."

Since Cole and I showed up together, they put us as a group. Jimmy and Ursula are in a group as well. Beatrice didn't come—apparently, she knows what she's doing—and there are two other couples who are here that seem to be out-of-towners, based on the number of photos they're excitedly taking.

Just like Chadwick's back in Kringle, the store is white with red accents. Red-and-white striped curtains in the window, a display case of candies that stretches across the back of the store, and even the logo is the same: an oval with red lettering. Whereas Chadwick's advertises that his store was established back in the early 1900s, Theodore's is the early 2020s. What a joke.

But despite all of that, it feels kind of odd, but also nice, being here with Cole. The conversation in his truck was heavy, and I'm sure it's going to weigh on my chest for a very long time, because I wasn't there for him when he needed a friend. And that's not something I think I will ever get over.

But since we accepted each other's apologies, things feel…different.

He's not so uptight.

He's smiling more.

Friendly.

Talkative.

It's as if he was holding on to the past, what happened between us, and it was building and building into a dark cloud that hung over him, and the minute he let it out…it all dissipated.

It's a relief.

"Have you done this before?" I ask him as I take in the copper bowl in front of us.

"Never," he says. "But I heard it's not easy, so good luck to us."

"Great," I say as Theodore reappears. His assistant brings trays with our ingredients and then hands us a recipe.

"There you have it," he says. "I'll be around if you have any questions."

Uhhh…what?

What happened to the lessons? Does he really expect us to do this ourselves?

Jimmy's the first to speak up. "Are you not going to demonstrate?"

"No," Theodore says. "I've heard rumblings that Chadwick is waiting for all of you to fail due to my teachings. Therefore, I will not be teaching, just offering you the opportunity to practice. For those of you who are not part of the Kringle competition, please step in the back with me and I'll be giving you a private lesson."

"But...we paid for this," Jimmy says. "And if you're in the back, how can we ask you questions?"

"Let one of my assistants know, and they'll call me if they think the question is important enough." And then with that, he moves to the back of his kitchen with the non-Kringle-ees.

I turn to Cole. "Well, that's rude."

"Rude, but it feels right. Their feud is pretty heavy, so I'm not surprised this is how we're being treated." He picks up the recipe. "Well, might as well give this a shot. Okay, we need to grab the water, sugar, and cornstarch, dump it in the pan, turn on the burner, and then stir and let it boil until it's 320 degrees Fahrenheit."

"That seems simple enough," I say. As we work, I ask, "Why didn't Atlas come with you? Isn't he your holly jolly sidekick?"

"He is," Cole says as he starts stirring. "But he had some things he needed to do on the farm today. So he told me to take, in his words, 'copious notes.'"

"I don't see a pen and paper," I say.

Cole taps the side of his head. "All up here."

"Oh, I'm sure he's going to love that."

"He'll bitch, but that's nothing new." He hands me the wooden spoon. "Want to stir?"

"Sure," I say. "How do we know the temperature of the mixture?"

Cole lifts up a thermometer. "I think with this thing. The instructions say to set it on the side of the pan but to make sure it doesn't touch the bottom." While I carefully stir, he adjusts the thermometer, and then together, we watch the heat rise. "Huh, this isn't too bad."

"Yeah, I was going to say the same thing. Although I think it's the second part that's the hardest."

"You might be right," he says. "Good thing you have me helping you—you know, since I'm so good at this Kringle stuff."

That makes me dramatically roll my eyes. "Says the guy who made a Hawaiian fruitcake."

"Hey, that was on Max, not me. He was heavy-handed with the pineapple, and I tried to tell him, but he insisted he knew best."

"Maybe you shouldn't let your sidekick take charge."

"Ehh, he's into this maybe more than I am. I have to throw him a bone every once in a while."

"That's very holly jolly of you."

"Hence why I'm the front runner for Christmas Kringle."

"You're in third place," I say. "That is not the front runner."

"That means nothing. We will get back up there, especially after this candy cane competition." He takes the spoon from me and stirs. "Look, I'm winning already."

"You're so stupid," I say with a laugh.

CHAPTER EIGHTEEN
COLE

The sugar is boiling, the snow has stopped falling,
peppermint is in the air, and cupid's arrow is calling.

"He's charming, he's sweet, and I love his sexy smirk,"
she thought to herself. "He's so different
now; he's clearly not a jerk."

"YOU HAVE TO PULL, STOREE," I say from over her shoulder, eyeing our sugar lump on the hook attached to the wall. "The air has to get in there in order for it to turn white."

"I know...that..." she grunts. "Ugh, this is hot and unpleasant."

"Let me help," I say as I come up behind her, wrap my arms around her body, and then together we pull. "Like this."

Immediately I notice how her back fits perfectly against my chest.

How her head comes up to my chin.

And how her hair smells like fresh flowers.

Things I shouldn't be noticing, but for the life of me, I can't stop myself.

"Oh my God, I'm not going to be able to do this on my own," she says as we continue to pull the sugar and wrap it around the hook, watching as the once amber-brown substance turns a bright white. Kind of cool if you ask me.

"Your aunt Cindy did this on her own, which means you have to as well."

"Maybe there's something wrong with our sugar," she says as we continue to pull together, the scent of her hair floating up, distracting me from what we're doing.

"Nothing is wrong with it," I say. "Look, it's turning white. That means we did it right."

"Are we done?" she asks as she stops. "God, my hands and forearms are on fire. Folding the sugar and kneading in color and flavor tired me out."

I chuckle. "How the hell are you going to do this by yourself?"

"With some Christmas magic. Do you know if Bob Krampus or anyone around town sells that?"

I laugh. "Not that I know of, but if I hear of anything, I'll let you know." I tug the sugar off the hook and carry it to the heating station. "Okay, I think we have to divide this up now. We have our red sugar, but we need a base, then we need to make a blanket of stripes according to the diagram, and then stack it all together, pull, twist, and cut."

"Oh, just that simple," she says sarcastically before rubbing the back of her hand over her forehead. "You know, I think it's sort of irresponsible to ask newbies to make candy canes as part of the Kringle competition. Don't you think it's negligent? Boiling sugar, tugging, and pulling? I mean are we making candy canes or are we arousing sugar?"

That makes me let out a wallop of a laugh, prompting Jimmy and Ursula to shoot us annoyed looks.

"I'm never going to tug and pull on sugar the same, thanks for that," I say.

"Just here to help ruin the process for you."

Together, we cut the red-and-white sugar into strips, form a striped blanket of sorts, and then drape that over our white base. Then we take a solid piece of red sugar, place that on the bottom, and tug on one end, drawing the sugar into a long strip. We twist the sugar, creating that iconic twirl of white and red, then snip and make a curve at the top, forming an actual candy cane.

Both of us stand there, a little flabbergasted.

"Did we just make that?" Storee asks.

"I think we did," I say.

"Wow. I'm shocked. It looks like an honest-to-goodness candy cane. Like something Bob Krampus would stick in a stocking."

"When referring to his Christmas duties, he prefers you call him Santa."

"Oops." Storee's cheeks turn pink. "That looks like something *Santa* would stick in a stocking."

"It does," I say as I drape my arm over her shoulders. She snuggles into my chest, a vast difference from her prior reluctance. "I'm proud of us."

"Me too." She glances up at me and offers me that sweet smile of hers. "Thanks for rescuing me and bringing me here."

"Like I said, I want to win because I know I'm better, not because you were stuck in your car."

"Uh-huh, I think that's what you're telling yourself, but I know the real truth."

"And what's that?" I ask her as I begin to shape another candy cane.

"I think you secretly like having me around."

Probably more than you realize...

"So do you think you can handle that on your own?" I ask Storee as we walk toward my truck, carrying a bagful of candy canes and some chocolates because we were both interested in the huckleberry truffles.

"No," she says. We reach my truck and I open the passenger door for her. Her body brushes up against mine and instead of stepping in, she turns toward me. "You know, you don't have to open the door for me."

"Habit," I answer.

"It's a nice habit to have."

The clouds have parted, and the sun is shining, barely peeking past the peaks of the mountains. And despite the chill in the air, the snow isn't quite sticking to the roads, which is a good thing. But given the time of the day and the mountains blocking the sun, it's going to get dark soon.

"Thank you again for today, Cole. I really appreciate it. I appreciate everything."

"Yeah, of course," I say, looking anywhere but into her gorgeous eyes.

"Does this make us friends now?" she asks. "Like actual friends, like we were when we were younger?"

"I don't know," I say as I hang on to the door. "Are you going to call me Connor?"

She chuckles. "No, I thought we established that you're Snow Daddy now."

"If you call me Snow Daddy, we are one hundred percent not friends."

"Oof, someone can't take a joke."

"Someone doesn't want to be referred to as Snow Daddy."

"I don't see why not," she says as she leans against the truck with clearly no intention of getting in. "Snow Daddy makes it seem like you own Christmas, like if Christmas wanted a spanking, you'd be the one that gave it to them."

My brow raises. "If Christmas wanted a spanking?"

She chuckles. "Oh yeah, Christmas can be a real kinky bitch."

"Umm, I'm going to need you to explain."

"Well, first, there's the whole mistletoe thing. Forcing people to kiss on cue? Kinky. Then there's the whole sitting on Santa's lap thing…old man kink. Not to mention the wreathes and candles."

"What about the wreathes and candles?" I ask.

"Oh my God, Cole. It's like vaginas and penises hung all around."

"What the hell are you talking about?" I ask with a laugh.

"The wreath is the vagina, the candle is the penis. Put them together and, well, sex."

I tug on my hair. "Charming as that is, I don't think Christmas is kinky."

"Clearly, you're not looking at it the right way. You're stuck in your head, in your perfect little Christmas town."

"Are you telling me there's more to Christmas outside of Kringle? But I thought we had a choke hold on Christmas."

"Ah-ha!" she says, pointing at me. "See? Choking…kinky. Christmas is kinky."

"Jesus," I mutter in a soft laugh. "Get in the truck. I'm taking your perverted ass home."

She hops up into the truck, and I shut the door when she's settled.

Christmas wants to be spanked—where the hell did she come up with that?

Shaking my head, a smile tugging on my lips, I get into my side of the truck, and I glance over at her. She's smiling brightly, clearly pleased with herself, and I realize for the first time in a really long time, I feel… light.

I don't feel the weight of this holiday on my shoulders, the dread of it all.

I'm actually having…hell, I'm having fun.

"What?" she asks.

"Nothing." I shake my head and start the truck.

"No, tell me."

"No, it's stupid."

"It's probably not," she says, pushing at my shoulder. "Just tell me."

I lean my head back. "Just…you know…just having fun is all."

She gasps and tugs my hand, forcing me to look at her. "You're having fun? With me? Your nemesis? Ring the bells, call the town crier, Cole Black is having fun with me."

"And that's exactly why I didn't want to say anything," I reply as I tug my hand back from her.

"I'm not even sorry. I'm going to shout it out the window when we get to Kringle, letting everyone know that Cole Black finds me fun to be with."

"You do that, and while you're at it, tell them how much you enjoy my kissing."

She scoffs. "Okay, now we're just telling lies, and during the Christmas season? Cole..." She *tsks*. "I think we've deceived the people enough, don't you?"

I pull out onto the road and head toward the highway, thankful it's a straight shot from here. And given that it stopped snowing, and the roads are clear, it might take us less time to get home than it did to get here.

"We wouldn't be deceiving them—we would be telling them the truth. I saw the way you looked at me, felt the way you kissed me back. All passion."

She laughs. "That was not passion."

I reach across and pat her leg. "It's okay, Storee. No need to be embarrassed. I get it. I'm irresistible to you."

"Oh my God."

"Exactly what you thought when our kiss ended," I say with a smirk.

"And now you're back to being incredibly annoying," she says, folding her arms across her chest.

"Then my work here is done."

STOREE

"Taran just texted me that the car was dropped off in the driveway and that Atlas said it was all checked out and everything was good." I turn toward him. "Thank you, Cole."

"Not a problem," he says.

"She also asked how I was doing since I had to be in your presence for more than a few minutes. I told her my skin was melting off."

He chuckles and glances at me. "I don't know, your skin looks pretty normal to me."

"She would absolutely have a conniption if she knew that we were getting along."

"Would she?" he asks. "Why?"

"Oh, you know, the whole 'needing to win this for Aunt Cindy' thing. I don't think she'd appreciate me being friendly with the competition."

"Well, then, I guess we have to go back to sparring."

"I guess so," I say.

"How did she feel about the fake dating?"

"Hesitant at first but then encouraged me, because she knew that it would help me in the long run." I pause and think about it for a second. "Hey, that night when we were talking to Martha and she brought up your parents—that's why you shut down, wasn't it?"

He nods. "Yeah, wasn't in the mood to really talk about it then."

"Then why did you talk about it today?"

"Because..." He trails off, and I wait for him to say more. "Because seeing you in your car, scared and crying, I don't know, it tore down the walls I've kept up. I felt like I needed to protect you in that moment. Not to mention the snowstorm, cars...well, it brought back all these memories, and I felt the need to, for lack of a better word, *save* you."

"Well, I'm glad you did tell me. I wish you would have said something earlier. I might not have allowed you to put that many pineapple chunks in your fruitcake."

"Saboteur," he says, laughing. "You knew it was too many and you didn't say anything."

"It's best when we learn from our mistakes, Cole. Also you never would have believed me. If I'd said something, you would have easily added more out of spite."

"You're right about that." He passes someone on the left and then switches back to the right lane. "So what have you been doing the past ten years? Fill me in."

Finding it completely adorable that he wants to know, I say, "Well, went to college, had a long-time boyfriend who ended up breaking up with me when he got his first directing job. Weirdly, I was okay with it because he was a tool anyway. I've found solace in editing Lovemark movies, taking care of my ficus, Alexander, and never leaving my apartment until Great-Aunt Cindy broke her hip."

"Never leaving?" he asks.

I shake my head. "Yeah, I was a bit of a hermit. I would go on walks, but I really…I don't know, I just didn't bother with the outside world all that much."

"Why?"

"I guess maybe because I didn't need anything other than what I had."

"And how do you feel about that now since you've been here?"

"Silly," I admit. "Even though this has been stressful, and I've had to put myself out there more than I ever wanted to with this competition, I've forgotten what it's like to interact, to know people around you. Living in California, especially in LA, I can be anonymous, and I kind of just stayed in my own bubble. But in Kringle, I'm forced outside of that bubble and required to talk to others even if I don't want to."

"So are you saying that you actually might like Kringle and not hate it?"

"Maybe," I say, feeling very foolish. "Ugh, you know when you said you can't let fear take over your actions…well, I think I let that happen. When I was a kid, I aspired to be something bigger, maybe even the person in front of the screen instead of behind it, but after the incident with Mrs. Fiskers, the embarrassment that followed, I lost all my confidence and, well, it just…trickled into my everyday life."

"I don't know, you look pretty level-headed and confident to me," he says as he pulls off the highway, taking the exit to Kringle. "And I wouldn't bullshit you, Storee. Ever since you've returned, I've noticed just how confident…how radiant you are."

"Radiant?" I ask as I steal a glance at him.

"Yeah," he says, his cheeks flushing adorably.

"Well, thank you. What have you been up to?"

"Taking care of the reindeer over at Evergreen Farm," he answers. "I tried going to college, but I was only eighteen when my parents passed, and I couldn't leave the house. The town rallied around me, the Maxheimers took me in, and I found comfort in being here, the place I grew up. I found comfort in seeing my parents in places all around town. Memories of them walking around Ornament Park, or having dinner at the Caroling Café, or going out for ice cream at the Polar Freeze. There were moments I didn't want to forget, so I dropped out of college, completing only one semester, and the Maxheimers gave me a job working on the farm. Max's dad taught me everything I needed to know about the reindeer, then I did my own research and, well, it just became my thing." He shrugs. "I know it's not much, but I find peace in it."

"Why are you saying it's not much?"

"Because I take care of reindeer."

"So?" I say as he turns down Krampus Court, headed right toward Whistler Lane, our trip soon ending. "I think it makes you more human. Shows the kind of soul you have. I like it."

"Yeah?" he asks.

"Yeah, I do."

We reach our cul-de-sac, and he pulls into his driveway. When he turns off the truck, he doesn't leave the cab but instead tilts his head back against the headrest. "So, what are we going to do?"

"What do you mean?"

He leans his head to the side. "Moving forward, do we still hate each other? Do we find common ground and show everyone that enemies can turn into friends? Do we continue to pretend that we have crushes on each other? Things changed today, and I'm not sure how to handle it all."

"Oh, because we don't hate each other, right?"

"It wasn't hate—it was pent-up anger," he says. "I don't think I ever could really hate you, Storee. You're the girl who drank hot cocoa with me on my porch. Hard to hate her."

And when he says sweet things like that, it's hard not to like him.

Hard not to have feelings.

Hard *not* to harbor that crush from many years ago.

Not wanting to open up that box, I decide to play it safe, stick to the status quo. "Well, I think the town has enjoyed the whole enemies-to-lovers vibe we've been giving off, so maybe we continue with that."

"Yeah." He turns toward me. "So does that mean we need to go on another date?"

"Hmm, I think to feed into what the people of Kringle want, we probably should at least mention that we did."

"Right...mention it," he says, his eyes falling to his lap, not what I was hoping for. After today, I would like nothing more than for him to make a move. Take my hand again, maybe...lean in for more. "We can, uh, we can do that. What about when you're around your aunt and Taran...and Max for that matter? Maybe still spar, argue, all of that?"

"Probably for the best," I say.

"Yeah, probably." His lips crease to the side. "Okay, well, good luck with the candy canes. Hope Taran likes the truffles."

Good luck?

Hope Taran likes the truffles?

That's it?

Nothing else?

When I sense no movement, no temptation to move in closer, I realize, yup, that's it.

"Thank you," I say as I grab the bag of goodies, feeling disappointed. "And thanks for everything, Cole. I really appreciate it."

"Yeah, sure."

And then together, we leave the truck, him going to his house, me going to mine. I just don't know why I feel...as bereft as I do.

CHAPTER NINETEEN
COLE

Peppermint candies, huckleberry truffles,
and chocolate-covered chips.
Boy oh boy, he hoped that maybe, just
maybe, they would lock lips.

But poor Snow Daddy came up short,
sent on his way without a kiss.
Some might say he struck out, fell short
of love, a total and utter miss.

"YOU KNOW, YOU DON'T HAVE *to be a dick about it.*"

Narrator: I'm just telling it like I see it.

"*Yeah, well…there weren't any chocolate-covered chips. Everyone can see right through you and your inability to be clever and find a rhyme for lips.*"

Narrator: Watch yourself, Snow Daddy. I control this story, and if you want any shot at locking lips, then check the attitude.

"*Who says I even want another kiss?*"

Narrator: Oh, Cole, all the readers and listeners can smell the desperation. Cute that you think otherwise. Now on with the story…

Sitting on my porch, the starry night sky above me, I drape a blanket over my lap as I breathe in the wintry night air. Fuck, that conversation did not go the way I wanted it to, but what was I even expecting the outcome to be?

That she wanted to set everything aside and go on another date?

That she wanted to tell everyone that we solved our differences and that we were friends, that maybe there was more to our relationship than some friendly smiles and touches?

Nitwit.

That's what I am. An absolute nitwit.

She's always been better, brighter, bigger than me.

That's how it will always be.

Stupid of me to think otherwise.

My phone buzzes in my hand and I see that it's a text from Max.

Max: How did it go? Going to fill me in? Taran was surprised that I delivered her car. I need all the details. Wait…is Storee still alive, or did you kill her?

Rolling my eyes, I text my idiot of a best friend back.

Cole: It was fine. We made candy canes, and we drove back together. She went to her house, I went to mine.

He texts back immediately.

Max: Okay, why did you mention which way you two went when you returned? Were you hoping she'd come back to your place?
Cole: No.
Max: I can smell you lying from here. If we can't be honest with each other, then who can we really be honest with?

Cole: Jesus, you're annoying.

Max: No, I'm your best friend, and given our conversations since Storee has arrived, I would have assumed you'd have messaged me by now, letting me know what kind of wench she was. But I didn't get the wench text, which means something happened, so spill.

This is why you shouldn't have best friends, because they know too much about you.

Cole: Fine, we talked. I told her about my parents, she apologized, kind of aired everything out, and then we made candy canes together and I liked every second of it. Every goddamn second.

Max: Whoa, okay, was not expecting that. Um, so if I were to say the crush is in full force, would I be right?

Cole: You would be very right, but it doesn't matter because she doesn't feel the same way. We're just friends, so we're going to keep it like that, plus she lives in California and she has a whole other life there. It would be stupid to get attached.

Max: I can feel how sad you are through your text messages. Did you tell her how you feel?

Cole: No, because I don't really know how I feel. I mean, today was a one-eighty. I was driving to Clayton intending to show her up, but then when I found her on the side of the road, that all changed. And all those old feelings came back. Now, fuck, now I don't know what I'm doing.

I stare down at my phone as I hear a crunch in the snow. I glance to the left where I catch Storee walking toward me, thermos in hand. I set my phone down to the side. "What are you doing? You're going to freeze."

"You have a blanket. I'll be fine." She crosses over into my yard, and then walks up the porch steps and takes a seat next to me. "I brought hot cocoa." She hands me the thermos, and I uncap the top and pour us a cup to share while she takes some of my blanket and drapes it over her legs.

"Why are you out here?" I ask her.

"Because I saw you and figured I'd join you. Taran's talking to her boyfriend and doing God knows what in her room while Aunt Cindy is asleep. And, well...I thought things were weird when we left the truck, and I didn't want it to be weird."

"It's not weird."

"Yes, it is," she says. She takes the cup from me and sips the hot liquid before offering it to me. "Sometimes, I feel like I don't know how to act around you because you make me nervous."

"I make you nervous?" I ask, pointing to my chest. "How the hell does that work?"

She chuckles. "You just do. You always have."

"You're going to have to explain yourself, because if anything, you make me nervous."

"Oh please, Cole. You know that's not true."

"It is. Sure, maybe when we were under the age of ten, you were just the girl who came to visit Cindy during Christmastime, but when puberty hit, that changed things. You were the pretty girl I wanted to talk to—who happened to visit Cindy."

She tilts her head to the side, those hypnotizing eyes nearly cutting me in half. She has the prettiest face I've ever seen. Wide eyes, long lashes, freckles that span her nose and cheeks, which she covers up when she's wearing makeup. High cheekbones, full lips, and a slender nose decorated with the smallest of nose rings that, if you weren't looking hard enough, you might miss.

"And you were the handsome guy with the broad shoulders and even broader grin that lived next door to Aunt Cindy, the one I'd try to steal glances at whenever I was in town. And on the best of occasions, you were the one who helped me escape from the insanity of my parents during the holidays by just sitting on this very porch and talking about nothing important."

She hands me the cup and I take another sip. "You were the girl from California who was way out of my league, who is still out of my league," I say, not caring that I'm putting it all out there.

"You were the boy who set the standard, a standard no one else has yet to match."

I glance down at the hot cocoa, not sure where to go from here.

"So, yes, I get nervous around you," she says as her hand lands on my arm. "Why do you think I was rambling on in the Kringle Krampus? I saw you, got nervous, and then I couldn't shut up from there."

I chuckle. "You were extremely talkative."

"And you hated every second of it."

"For other reasons," I say.

"For how I left here," she says, understanding the circumstances.

"Yeah." I blow out a heavy breath. "Thinking about it now, I kind of wish I'd asked Cindy for your information so I could have at least contacted you. Maybe seen if you wanted to be pen pals again or something like that."

"Pen pals," I say. "That would have been really cute in our early twenties. I probably would have been better too."

I turn toward her. "Would you have written me back?"

"Yes," she answers, turning toward me as well so our knees knock. "It probably would have made me feel more connected to something."

"But you were done with the town. Wouldn't you have been done with me too?"

She shakes her head. "You were the one thing I would think about every time Christmas rolled around." I hand her the hot cocoa, but she sets it to the side before taking my hand and turning it up so my palm is exposed. She glides her finger over my calluses. "Hard not to think about you now, Cole."

I swallow the lump in my throat. "Even with the tension and anger?"

She looks up at me through her lashes. "Especially with the tension and anger because I wanted to know where it was coming from. I wanted to fix it. I wanted this."

"I wanted this too," I say.

She smiles lightly and then scoots into my side. I take that opportunity to wrap my arm around her and pull her in even closer. She leans against my chest as I rest my cheek against the top of her head.

"How are you doing now?" she asks.

"What do you mean?"

"With the loss of your parents. I know that's something you will never get over, but how are you doing?"

"Probably not as well as I should be," I answer honestly. "There's so much I could be doing that I'm not. I'm settled into a routine. You being here is the first time I've broken that routine. Honestly, it's been chaotic since you arrived."

"Is that a bad thing?"

"If you told me a few weeks ago that my cherished routine, the routine that has helped me accept the loss of my parents, would be flipped upside down, I'd probably panic, but now I'd say this chaos has been welcome." I chuckle. "Fuck, if Max could hear this conversation, his jaw would probably be on the floor."

She laughs as well. "Is he used to you being set in your ways?"

"Very much so. I think he's still in shock that I entered the Kringle competition."

"And all out of spite," she says.

"Is there really any other way?"

"When you act like a Grinch...no."

"A Grinch, huh? You really think I'm a green crotch that tries to steal Christmas?"

"A green crotch?" She laughs out loud. "Jesus, I hope you're not a green crotch."

I chuckle. "That's a term my mom used to use all the time when describing someone ornery."

"Sheesh, an ornery crotch. Seems like that crotch isn't getting enough proper attention."

"Isn't that what makes people ornery in the first place?"

"I don't know—you tell me," she says.

I smile against her hair. "Are you asking if my crotch has been getting proper attention?"

"First of all, can we stop saying the word *crotch*? It's easily the most unattractive word ever created. Secondly...maybe?"

I laugh. "Interested in my sex life? Here I thought we were just innocently sitting together on the porch."

"This is the *adult* version of us sitting on the porch. We talk about adult things now. So go ahead, answer the question."

I sigh. "Well, let's just say it's been a while."

"How long?"

"This isn't a very Christmassy conversation," I reply.

"Yes, it is. The holiday season is all about bringing joy, and joy can be found everywhere. It can be found while hanging ornaments on a tree, sipping a cup of peppermint mocha while watching ice skating, or getting naked with another person and having them play around with your... candy cane."

"Jesus." I snort, my chest vibrating with humor. "These conversations really have matured."

"Yup, now answer the question."

I rub my eye with the palm of my hand. "I don't know, a few months, maybe more than that. Like I said, it's been a while."

"Who was she? The only reason I ask is because you said you have a very scheduled life, so when would you have time to meet someone? Meaning, is this person still in your life?"

"Definitely not," I say. "I think it was actually Max's birthday. We got drunk—"

She lifts up and stares at me. "Was it Atlas?"

"*No*," I say with force, which causes her to laugh. "He rejected me," I add with a smile, making her laugh even harder as she settles back against my chest.

"So you had to go to the second option."

"Unfortunately, which meant it was an out-of-towner, one-night-stand thing. I went back to her hotel room and, well, yeah."

"Interesting," she says.

"Okay, now you have to tell me your last time."

"Uh, no, thank you. I'm a lady. I don't share details like that."

"Oh fuck that," I say, as her laughter rings through the silent night. "I didn't just open up to have you shut down on me. Now tell me, who was the last person you fucked...and when?"

STOREE

Gird your loins, ladies, because the way Cole says *fucked* is the most gratifying sound ever.

It sends a thrill through me like...like...

Like warm cider on a cold day.

Like a freshly iced cookie melting in my mouth.

Like seeing that bitch Samantha fall flat on her doll face because I shut the door too hard.

I find it so appealing.

So attractive.

So freaking alluring that I lean in closer.

Seeking out his warmth.

Wanting desperately for him to tilt my chin up and press his lips to mine.

"I'm waiting," he says. *Cute.*

I pick at a piece of lint on the blanket. "Well, if you must know, it's been a while for me too."

"You really think you're going to get away with that answer? Try again."

"Fine, you asked for it." I clear my throat. "It has been fourteen months and thirteen days."

I feel him go still underneath me, and I can't hold back my smile as he pulls away to look me in the eyes. "Are you being for real? You know it down to the very day?"

I laugh. "No, but your look of concern is cute. Let's just say it's been over a year. It was with this guy I knew in college. He was in town and, well, we got a little handsy and continued the handsy-ness in his car."

"You did it in a car?" he asks, sounding shocked. "How the hell did you manage that?"

"Have you never done it in a car, Cole?"

"No," he says matter-of-factly. "I can barely fit in a regular car, let alone fuck someone in it."

Oof, the use of *fuck* again.

That one made my nipples hard.

"Well, it did cause some fumbling, some bumping, and it wasn't at the greatest angle, which meant I really had to aid in his pursuit of the big O. But we got the job done, shook hands, and went our separate ways."

"Did you really shake hands?" he asks.

"Metaphorically. He's more of a high five kind of guy, but I feel like a high five after sex degrades the act of copulating."

"There you go with *copulating* again."

"Do you prefer fornication?"

"I prefer fuck," he says, making me smile.

I made him say it that time.

"Well, either way, it's been a while for me and that's okay. I think the next time I let someone pull my leggings down, I want it to be someone blond…"

I bite on my lip, waiting for his response.

Preferably a growly, possessive response.

"Yeah, I agree," he says to my surprise. "I want my next fuck to be a blond as well."

My mouth falls open as I push up to look him in the eyes. His expression is full of mirth as he stares back.

"Or maybe a redhead." He winks.

"Well, good luck finding a willing redhead. I've heard they can be very picky."

"I wouldn't be surprised. I know one who is so picky, she only likes to fuck in cars."

"Sounds like she's real bendy."

Cole clears his throat, his grip on me growing more intense. They're subtle reactions, but I love them.

Wanting to keep the convo going, I say, "Have you ever done it in front of a Christmas tree?"

"No," he says. "Don't have a Christmas tree to do it in front of."

"Wait." I sit up and push away from him so I can really look him in the eyes. "You don't have a Christmas tree?"

He shakes his head. "No, what's the point?"

"Umm…well, for the obvious reason that you can fuck someone in front of it, but also, you know, because it's Christmas."

"There's no one in my life who's important enough to fuck in front of a Christmas tree, and I haven't had one since my parents died. I guess I just didn't feel like putting one up. Or any decorations for that matter."

"Wait, so if I went inside your house right now, there wouldn't be one Christmas decoration? Not one bauble? Not one wreath?"

"Nothing," he says.

"Cole, that...that's not right."

He casually shrugs. "It's not like I have anyone to share the holiday with. Just seems pointless to me."

"But it's Christmas!"

"It's also Christmas year-round here—I see all the decorations I need."

"Still, it makes me sad. Walking into Aunt Cindy's house was always my favorite part of the visit because she decked out the entire place for the holiday season. Every nook and cranny had something. The curtains, the rugs, the bathroom, the kitchen. Every inch of the house was covered, and it just made it feel so warm and cozy. Don't you want that?"

"I never wanted anything to do with the holiday, I guess, until this year..." He swallows and then lets out a heavy breath. "Until you arrived."

I roll my teeth over the corner of my lip.

Our eyes connect, and the electricity that's been building between us bounces and sparks as he drags his fingers over my cheek.

I lean into his touch, my tongue peeking out to wet my lips.

Heat builds inside of me as he slips his hand to the nape of my neck, pulling me in just an inch closer. I press my hand to his chest and lean in, letting him know that I want this.

I want this so much.

I wanted it in the truck.

I wanted it when he was helping me pull the sugar on the hook.

And secretly, when he kissed me under the mistletoe, I wanted so much more.

But he's hesitant, and I don't know why. Is he second-guessing himself?

Is he second-guessing me?

Just one touch, like last time.

One taste.

Please, Cole…

He wets his lips, his eyes bounce down to my mouth and then back up to my eyes, and just when I think he's going to pull away because he hasn't made a move yet, he leans in an inch.

But still no connection, and it drives me nuts.

I can see it in his eyes that he wants this kiss just as much as I do.

I can feel it in his hold on my neck.

I could sense it in the truck before we parted ways, but something is holding him back, and I'll be damned if I'll sit back and miss out on another opportunity to feel his lips against mine.

So I sit up, mentally take a deep breath, and then straddle his lap, the blanket falling away. Immediately his hands fall to my waist as his eyes stare deeply into mine. His fingers dig into my skin, I catch the bob in his Adam's apple as he swallows, and when he doesn't shift away from me or ask me to get off him, I slide my hands up his neck to his cheeks and grip them both right before angling his head and pressing my lips to his.

And I swear on everything in me, the burst of electricity that pops between us when he kisses me back is unlike anything I've ever felt before.

It's intoxicating.

I grip him tighter, angling my mouth down as a low growl flows through his throat, right before his hands slide up my back, bringing me in closer.

This kiss, this connection—it's everything.

His mouth, his hold, his taste.

It's perfect.

This is perfect.

Sitting under the green lights, the dark sky just blanketing us, the silence of the still night around us… It's everything I could ever have asked for as he parts his lips, deepening our kiss. One of my hands slides into his hair while his tongue swipes across my bottom lip.

272 | MEGHAN QUINN

I groan and do the same to him, until our tongues meet, tangling, dancing, creating a heat between us. A friction. A connection so great that I never want this to end.

I wish I weren't wearing a jacket.

I wish I weren't covered in so many layers, because I want to feel his callused hands across my body. I want to feel the strength of his hold. I want—

He pulls away, catching his breath as his eyes meet mine.

Confused.

Turned on.

Greedy.

He runs his tongue over his lips before he says, "You taste fucking amazing."

"Then why did you stop?" I ask as I attempt to go in for more.

"Because if I kiss you more, it might go in a different direction, especially with you being on my lap."

I smirk. "Are you saying you're getting very turned on...Snow Daddy?"

"Jesus," he mutters, and if it were brighter out here, I know I'd be able to see that blush on his cheeks that he wears so well. "Let's just say I might have to test out your bendiness in the truck."

"I'm not opposed. There's plenty of room for me to move around."

"Well, I am. Opposed, that is." He smoothes his hand over my cheek and down my neck. "You deserve more than a quick fuck in my truck, Storee. You deserve so much more."

"If that's the case, show me into your house."

He winces. "Yeah, you don't want to go in my house."

"Why not?"

"It's just not...it's not ready for company."

"Are you messy?" I ask.

"Something like that," he says softly. "Plus, what if Taran comes looking for you? You should probably get back to your house."

Okay, any other time I might find this incredibly insulting. I mean, I'm on the man's lap, making out with him, more than willing to take this so much further, and he's trying to send me on my way. But I know it has nothing to do with me and everything to do with him and his readiness to explore something more.

I can respect that.

"You might be right about Taran. She would have a coronary if she saw us kissing on your porch. That, and I think I'm having a tough time feeling my toes."

"It's not that cold," he says with a laugh, which I'm glad to hear because even though he's shutting this down, at least he's still in good spirits.

"It is to me." And for the hell of it, because he tastes too damn good, I lean in and move my mouth over his one more time, reveling in the way his beard grazes my skin, the softness of his lips, and the way he surrenders his control, letting me kiss him again.

When I pull away, his eyes slowly open this time. He lets out a low, deep "fuck."

Just the reaction to make a girl feel like she has all the power.

I smile to myself and then climb off his lap. I hold my hand out to him. "Walk me to my house?"

He stands, adjusts himself, and then tosses the forgotten cocoa into the snow. Then he places the cup back on the top the thermos and offers it to me before he takes my hand in his.

Together, we walk along the shoveled sidewalk and up the porch to Aunt Cindy's door, Taran's bright lights showing off Cole's handsome face.

"Thanks for coming over," he says quietly.

"Thanks for letting me sit on your lap."

He smiles. "Yeah, you can do that anytime."

"Noted." I stand on my toes and kiss him again, but when I pull away, I poke my finger into his chest. "Don't think this changes anything, though.

You're still my number-one competitor, and I have no problem showing you who should win this competition."

"Storee, I can tell you right now, Snow Daddy is going to take this one."

I chuckle. "We shall see. Good night, Cole."

"Good night," he says softly.

And then with one more final kiss, I pat him on the chest and head back into Aunt Cindy's house, a smile on my face, that empty feeling in the pit of my stomach no longer there.

CHAPTER TWENTY
COLE

Cole stumbled around, chest puffed,
with a smile so pleasant.
For Christmas came early, her lips a tasty present.

He was floating around, his feet
never touching the ground,
as he smiled, shook hands, and
waved to the Kringles in town.

Then he tended to the reindeer, his
expression laced with glee.
"And now"—Snow Daddy grinned—"I
must decorate a tree."

"WHAT ARE YOU DOING OUT here?" Max asks as he shoulders the axe he uses for chopping.

"I need a tree," I say.

"You what?"

"I need a tree," I repeat.

He tugs on his ear and laughs. "Shit, I thought you just said you need a tree."

"That's exactly what I said."

He doesn't move, doesn't blink. "Umm…what?"

"Max, don't make this a thing, okay? I need a tree, so if you can just help me—"

"For what?" he asks.

"For my house."

He shifts, looking very confused. I don't blame him. He used to urge me to get a tree for the holidays, but after a few years, he knew he was fighting a losing battle. My mom and I used to decorate a tree every year together—even when I thought it was uncool. "Are you saying you're in the market for a Christmas tree?"

"I am, and if you're going to make a big deal about it, then I'm going to go somewhere else."

"No, no," he says quickly. "You've come to the right place. Just let me get my bearings first." He takes a deep breath and then shakes his head. "A tree." He makes eye contact. "Does this have anything to do with her? You never really finished telling me what happened last night."

"Nothing to talk about," I say.

"Cole, if you're coming to me for a Christmas tree, there's a lot to talk about. So why don't we hike out to the field, find you a nice pine, and you tell me what the hell is going on."

Normally, I'd just keep something like this to myself, but I want a tree and he has the axe. Therefore, I guess it's time to have that conversation.

But where to start?

Thankfully, Max starts. "So last you told me, things had changed and you were looking at her differently. Care to fill in the blanks?"

I lead the way, and Max falls in line. The trail to the trees is shoveled as much as it can be—the team is constantly laying dirt down to help with slipping, but it just turns into mud. It's why we always suggest wearing boots or shoes you don't mind getting dirty while visiting. And thanks to the fresh flurries from yesterday, the untouched pines that surround the farm are covered in snow, the wind blowing up puffs of it every so often.

"It was sort of a mature conversation that I wasn't expecting," I say. "We talked about how we felt when we were younger, how we feel now, and, well…" I pause, knowing Max is going to freak out. "We made out on the porch."

Just as expected, a stunned Max turns, slaps his hand to my chest in shock, and grips my shirt.

"You made out?" he yells, drawing attention from other groups traipsing across the farm.

We casually smile and wave to the visitors, thankful no one from Kringle is around.

"Dude, can you keep it down?" I hiss. "Fuck."

"I'm sorry—I'm just surprised. I wasn't expecting you to say you made out with Storee, the girl who, a few weeks ago, you were hell-bent on putting in her place."

"I wasn't expecting it either," I say honestly as we continue out toward the grove. "But I was out on the porch, staring up at the sky, texting you, and she came over with hot cocoa. We talked and…she moved onto my lap and started kissing me."

"Moved onto your lap? Nice. So she made the first move?"

"I think so. I mean, it wasn't like I was being shy about what I wanted."

"Look at you, Snow Daddy taking what he wants."

We stroll around the bend that takes us toward the front of the pine grove where many trees have already been cut down for the holiday season. But there are still a lot left.

"I didn't take what I wanted, I just…fuck, I broke, man. Seeing her tears, airing my grievances, and then spending some time with her, it kind of felt like if I didn't kiss her, I was going to lose my mind."

"Which is different for you."

"Very different," I agree.

"So what does this mean? Are we still trying to win the Christmas Kringle? Are we still enemies? Are we trying to show her who the king of this town is?"

"I mean...she playfully said at the end of the night that she was still going to beat me, but I also think we don't have to worry about her tampering with our lights again."

"Ah, so a solid competition but a fair one."

"That's what I'm assuming," I say. "And we have to keep arguing in front of her sister, because apparently Taran would get mad if she knew Storee and I were friendly. But then there's the town who thinks we're possibly dating, so we get to be open about our feelings in front of the town—but not in front of Taran. I don't know...feels complicated."

"Feels like reverse fake dating if you ask me," Max says. "And I'm interested to see how this plays out."

"Glad you're invested." I chuckle but then grow serious. "This whole thing makes me nervous."

"What? The reverse fake dating? Dude, just pretend you hate her in front of her sister—"

"No, not that," I say. "Letting myself feel anything for her."

"Why? Do you think she's playing you?"

I pause for a moment, letting that question sink in. Playing me, as in being friendly to throw me off and win the competition? I mean...I don't think so. Not after the conversation we had last night. Not after that kiss.

She wouldn't play me.

"No," I answer. "But...she doesn't live here, and I know she apologized for saying she hates this town and that she didn't mean it, but it still worries me. What happens when Cindy is better? Does she go back to California to be with her ficus?"

"She has a ficus? Nice. Do you know if it's a fiddle leaf?"

"Really, Max?"

He bashfully smiles. "Sorry. I just love all trees and plants."

"Right, so what happens when she leaves?"

"Well, you could follow her."

I shake my head. "No, I couldn't." I pause as we stand in front of a tree that's about an inch taller than me. "I can't leave Kringle."

"If you're worried about me," Max says with a smile, "I can handle being on my own. I might cry into my pillow every night knowing my best friend left me for his lady friend, but I'll survive."

"Don't be an idiot," I say and sigh. "I can't leave here because this is where I feel my parents the most. I feel their presence. And I can't leave the house. That's...that's all I have left of them."

"Is it, though?" Max asks. "You have sheets covering the furniture so it doesn't collect dust. You still live in the finished attic because it was your teenage bedroom. You don't even open the door to your parents' room, and you haven't unboxed the Christmas decorations in ten years, not since my mom and I put them away for you. I love you, man, but you haven't been really living. You've been shuffling through the day-to-day."

"I know," I say while tugging on my hair. "And I'm trying... Doing this competition, seeing her again, I don't know, it's making me feel like I don't have to hide all the time. That I don't need to avoid the holiday. But what if...what if I put myself out there and she leaves?"

"Valid concern," Max says. "And if she does, then we look at it as maybe she was brought here to get you out of your funk. Maybe you needed that blast from the past to shake you free of the weight you've been carrying, the weight of your parents' death."

"Maybe," I say.

"Hey." Max grabs my attention away from the tree that I'm pretending to study. "Cole, I haven't done you any favors as a best friend when it comes to making sure you move on, and that's why when you wanted to do this Kringle thing, I was all in. Do you really think I wanted to pant like a dog while you pranced around in lederhosen?" I chuckle. "I didn't. But I saw a spark in you that I haven't seen in a really long time, and I know credit goes to her. So don't let this opportunity slip by. If you like her, go for it, and see where it takes you. Living situations can be reworked. What can't be reworked is the way you feel about someone."

I let out a heavy sigh and look my friend in the eyes. "When did you become so wise?"

"I always have been," he says with a puff of his chest. "You're just finally opening your eyes."

I pull into my driveway with a Christmas tree in the bed of my truck as I spot Taran and Storee in their driveway, packing up the car.

Suitcases.

Pillows.

Dread immediately fills me.

Is she fucking leaving?

After one kiss, she's leaving?

Trying to keep calm, I hop out of my truck and remember the position I need to take—reverse fake dating.

I move around my truck, lean against it, and fold my arms as I stare over at them. "Leaving so soon? What a shame." The sarcasm in my voice is heavy, but the pounding of my heart is nearly making me want to walk up to Storee and pull her into my chest so she can't leave.

Not yet.

Not when things have just started.

Storee looks up as she's putting a suitcase in the car. She's about to say something when Taran steps in. "I'm taking Aunt Cindy into Golden for a doctor's appointment. Not that you need to know that, but don't go thinking we're out of this competition." She shuts the trunk of her car and turns toward me. "We are totally in it, and Storee has been coming up with a candy cane idea that's going to blow your lederhosen right off."

She crosses her arms, and Storee steps up next to her, looking cute as shit as she adds, "Yeah, blow your lederhosen right off."

I hold back my smile as I lift off the truck. "Doubt it. I saw your candy cane-making abilities. Good luck stretching the sugar—you're going to need it."

"Don't listen to him," Taran says to Storee. "You're going to kill it. And don't let him mess with your mind when we're gone. Stay strong."

"Ha, as if he could mess with me. Remember who's in first," Storee says.

"Girls," Cindy calls from the car. I didn't even notice her in there, I was so fixated on the suitcases. "If we're going to make it to Idaho Springs for a driving break and dinner, we must go. You know I'm going to need breaks."

"Hold down the fort," Taran says to Storee before moving toward the front of the car.

I watch Storee say goodbye to her aunt and sister, and then she stands in the driveway, bundled up in her jacket, waving to them as Taran pulls out and drives away.

Once they're down Whistler Lane and headed onto Krampus Court, Storee turns to me with an evil smile.

"What a shame?" she asks, walking up to me. "You would have been happy to see me go?"

"Would have been easier to be named Christmas Kringle, that's for damn sure."

"Aw, so you really do see me as a threat."

"Have you seen our competition?" I say as she stands right in front of me now. It takes everything in me not to pull her into my chest.

"I have. I'm specifically waiting to see if Jimmy Short can pull an upset."

"You might have to keep waiting."

She tugs on my flannel. "Why is there a tree in your truck?"

I glance back at the bed of my truck. "Uh, thought I would put it up in my house."

Her brows quirk up. "You got a Christmas tree?"

"I did," I answer as I tentatively place my hand on her hip. Her smile grows.

"Do you need help bringing it into your house?"

"Umm." I bite down on the corner of my lips. "I could probably handle it."

"Okay, but do you need help decorating it?"

My skin prickles as I realize I didn't think this all the way through.

Max wasn't lying when he said that I haven't really been living in the house. There are white sheets draped over most of the furniture, I eat meals up in my room, nothing has been moved or touched since my parents passed—it's a house frozen in time. And if she came into my house, she'd see that.

The question is, do I want her to see that?

"Your face has gone a little white," she says, her hand smoothing up my chest now.

"Sorry." I swallow the lump in my throat. "I'm, uh, just thinking."

"Okay, do you want to talk it out?"

I sift my hand through my hair and think about what Max said to me out in the field. *Don't let this opportunity slip by. If you like her, go for it, and see where it takes you.* I could do just that. Go all in and see where it takes me.

"I would like your help," I say hesitantly. "But, uh, I need to warn you about my house."

She rubs her hand over my heart. "Cole, you don't need to warn me about anything."

"I do," I say. "It's, um…it's preserved."

Her expression softens. "I get it, Cole. If I'd gone through what you did, I would have probably done the same thing. There's nothing to be ashamed of, if that's what you're feeling."

"A little, yeah."

"People deal with grief in their own way. If you're really that uncomfortable, I don't have to help, but I'd love to hang out, so if you want to come over to Aunt Cindy's, we can hang out there."

The option is tempting. To not give her a view of the life I've been living for ten years, to just fall in the comfort of continuing to hide.

But that's not what I want to do.

I want more.

I can feel it deep within me. This change. The certainty I have surrounding me, telling me that I'm ready. That I can do this, and I don't want to lose that courage.

So I clear my throat. "I'd actually like it if you came over."

"Are you sure?"

"Positive," I reply.

"Okay." She smiles up at me, her expression like a warm summer's day, pulling me into a tight embrace. "Do you want me to help you with the tree first?"

"Think you can manage?" I ask. "I watched you trying to stretch sugar and saw what an embarrassment that was."

She playfully pokes me. "I can handle a tree."

"We shall see." Before I move away, I pull her into a hug. Her arms wrap around me tightly, and I love the feel of it. I love the contact with another human. I can't remember the last time I actually hugged someone like this.

Probably when my parents were still alive.

"You okay?" she asks as she looks up at me, her chin resting on my chest.

"Yeah," I answer. "I am."

"Okay." She squeezes me one more time and then moves to the back of my truck. She takes in the tree, feeling the needles on the branches. "This is so soft."

"It's the Evergreen Farm way," I say as I lower the tailgate. "Full, lush pines with soft needles. They've perfected the Christmas tree, which is why people come from many miles away to grab a tree from them."

"I can see why," she says as I tug on the trunk. "I'm surprised you didn't wrap it up. Weren't you afraid you were going to lose needles?"

I shake my head. "Short drive, and we tend to not wrap trees up when we can avoid it. The Maxheimers are all about sustainability and the netting has been found to be dumped in the ocean. Max went on a rampage one day about it, tearing through the farm and telling every single person, including his parents and siblings, that there would be no more netting usage. Then he flashed a picture of a seal being strangled by netting and that was that."

"Oh God, that's sad."

"It was. So now when people buy their tickets to come to the farm, there's an email sent with a barcode for their tickets, and then a large warning in red that says 'If you plan on buying a tree, bring old sheets or blankets and we'll properly wrap your tree up for you.'"

"That's a good idea, actually."

"Max was proud of it for sure." I tug on the tree until it slides out of the bed of my truck and stand it up by its trunk.

"Wow, that's pretty tall," she says, staring up at it. "You don't get a Christmas tree for ten years and then you just…go for the biggest one."

"This wasn't the biggest one," I say. "But it's up there."

"Daring," she says with a smirk. "Now, how do you want to do this?"

I could really handle the tree on my own, but knowing she wants to help, I tip the tree down so it's on its side and say, "You can take the top, I'll grab the base. Let's bring it up on the porch and then leave it there while I get everything else ready."

"That works," she says.

Together, we lift the tree and haul it down the walkway to my house and up the steps to the porch. We slide the tree to the side and then brush off our hands.

"Any sap on your hands?" I ask her.

She flashes me her gloves. "Wouldn't know."

"Oh, right." I shake my head. "You really put on gloves to pack the car?"

"Uh, yeah. It's freezing here. I will never get over it and will always bundle up because I don't want frostbite."

"Ridiculous," I say as I move to my front door, nerves starting to inch up my spine.

She must notice because she places her hand on my back. "I won't judge you, Cole."

I look over my shoulder and softly smile at her.

"Thank you," I reply and then open the door, letting her into the first floor that has gone completely untouched.

And unseen by anyone besides Max and myself.

To the left is the dining room and the long table that's covered in white linen. A place where we used to have "fancy meals," as Mom used to call them, but has been vacant for quite some time. I can't remember what it's like to hear silverware clatter against fine bone china or my father's boisterous laugh as he sipped on his bourbon after a three-course meal.

To the right is the living room, with a fireplace, couch, and two wing-back chairs where I used to sit and chat with my dad about the upcoming Foghorns season.

The chairs are covered in sheets, but the couch is not.

Because the couch is where I sit and stare at the fireplace.

"I, uh...I covered everything up so it wouldn't get dusty or sun-damaged since the rays are stronger here."

"You don't need to explain yourself," Storee says softly as she takes in my home.

She's never been in here before. She's only ever been on my porch.

She walks over to the fireplace and runs her finger over the mantel and across the nails where we used to hang stockings. She takes in the pictures one by one, a smile playing on her lips when she sees the one of Dad and me when I was twelve. We found a lake on a hike and decided to fish bare-handed. Somehow, I grabbed one, and I'm holding it up in the photo. Storee then walks in front of the most recent picture of Mom, Dad, and me, when they dropped me off at college. My first and only semester at UC Boulder.

"That was the last picture we took together," I say, stepping in closer to her.

"I remember this boy," she whispers. "I remember all these versions of you, Cole." She picks up the picture of Bob Krampus and me when I was fourteen. "I remember this haircut. God, I thought you were so cute."

"Thought?" I ask, loving that she can make this hard moment feel so...easy.

She looks over her shoulder. "You're still cute, but now you have this rugged handsomeness about you that's actually really unfair to possess."

"Rugged handsomeness?" I smooth my hand over my jaw. "Think it's the beard?"

She motions over my body. "It's the whole package."

That makes me smirk.

She puts the picture back and moves over to another. It's of Max and me, our arms around each other, standing in front of the Ornament Park Christmas tree.

"You two really haven't changed, have you?"

"If you look inside the frame, you'll see that we have."

"What do you mean?"

"My mom took a picture of us in front of the Ornament Park tree every year. This is the one from when we were seventeen because she never got the chance to print the one from when we were eighteen. But she kept all the past pictures one on top of the other in the frame."

"That's so sweet," she says and then turns to me. "Do you look at these pictures often?"

"Not so much anymore. When I first lost my parents, yeah. I'd mindlessly sit on this couch for hours just staring. It's why it's the only piece of furniture not draped in a cloth. I would numbingly sit here and do nothing. It wasn't until Max offered me the job at the farm that I started to leave the house. For a while there, all I had were the people in town coming in and out and offering me support. Since I was eighteen, I was technically an adult. My parents had a hefty life insurance policy, so I didn't need to work if I didn't want to, and, well…at the time, I couldn't fathom leaving. But the Maxheimers couldn't take me being alone all the time, so they took me in as one of their own."

"Makes me love Atlas even more."

I raise a brow at her. "You love him?"

She rolls her eyes. "Not like that. But I'm glad he was there for you. Was Aunt Cindy ever helpful?"

"Yes," I reply. "She had me over for dinner once a month. It was only once a month because it's all I would allow. I think if she'd had it her way, she would have done once a week. But those dinners fizzled out once the feeling inside of me started to return again. It's why I always helped her with her lights, why I shovel for her—"

"You shovel for her?"

I nod. "Yeah. I want to make sure she's safe. I know it's not easy for her to shovel, so I just do it when I do mine. It's not a big deal."

"I thought she'd hired a service. She never said that it was you," Storee says, looking confused.

"Probably because I was adamant about her not talking to you about me."

"Yeah, I guess she kept that promise," she says, her lips twisted to the side. "I wish she hadn't, though."

"It's fine," I say.

She takes my hand in hers and entwines our fingers. She then presses a soft kiss to my knuckles.

"What do you want me to help you with, Cole? I'm here to help you with anything you need. Anything you want."

I glance around the room, taking in the emptiness of it all. My mom would hate it looking like this, especially now. She would be upset with me, with how I've blocked out the season, how I've set it aside when, as a family, it was the time of year that brought us that much closer.

The joy.

The traditions.

The togetherness.

On a whim, I ask, "Will you help me decorate for Christmas?"

CHAPTER TWENTY-ONE
STOREE

For someone who hated Christmas,
and hated Christmas a lot,
his strict position on the holiday
he conveniently forgot.

Stockings, baubles, bright garlands, and cheer.
Wreaths, bells, and even cranberry beer.

And they're hanging it all, while
their pulses are thrumming.
Because surely tonight, without
doubt, they'll be coming...

COLE'S QUIETLY UNWRAPPING SOME DISHES by the tree while I open a plastic bin marked CHRISTMAS LINENS. We've spent the evening bringing up Christmas decorations from the basement, starting with the tree stand, then setting up the tree. Afterwards, Cole wrapped his arm around me and stared at it for a few minutes.

I asked him if it was okay to turn on some music, and he of course said it was fine. I set the tone with one of my favorite Spotify Christmas playlists. We then wrapped garland around the tree, decorating it while he told me about the different ornaments. How there are misfit ornaments—broken pieces, missing elements—that his dad always hated but that his mom loved, so they would spend the whole season moving them around on the tree, from the front to the back. They divided them up and put half in the front, half in the back for each of them, even though Cole was always on his mom's side.

The look on his face when he was hanging them nearly made me cry. I could see the love but also the heartache at the same time.

Then I helped him with the star on the top, and when we plugged everything in, well, it was a beautiful sight. After that, we ordered pizza and ate it while staring up at the tree. Now, we're trying to decorate the rest of the living room. Cole didn't want to go overboard—he said the living room was fine—but I did tell him he should pull out some of his mom's holiday dishes so he could enjoy eating off them leading up to Christmas. He thought that was a good idea, kissed me on the forehead, and then went to the basement to find the bin.

When Taran told me earlier today that she needed to take Aunt Cindy to Golden and that it was going to be an overnight trip, my immediate thought was *how can I spend the time that they're gone with Cole?*

Even though Taran asked me to hang some lights.

Even though she told me I should be working on my sewing skills for when I have to make a stocking—I pushed that all to the side, because yes, it's important I represent Aunt Cindy, but helping Cole, being there for him, I think that's so much more important.

And after last night, when he opened up, I felt like spending more time with him was essential…so he wouldn't be alone. My heart was still breaking for the eighteen-year-old boy who lost his parents on the cusp of becoming a man. He never deserved to be considered grumpy.

And I had some selfish motivations too. I was with him because *I* wanted to be with him.

"Do you want me to set out any of these linens?" I ask as I sift through doilies and table runners.

"There's one in particular that my mom would put on the coffee table," he says as he unwraps a green candy dish and smiles down at it.

This coming from the man who wasn't into anything Christmas…a candy dish is making him smile.

"What does it look like?"

He walks over to me and helps look through the linens. "It was red and had reindeer along the border, sort of looks like—ah, here it is." He hands me the candy dish, and I hold it as he pulls out the runner. "Looks like a Christmas sweater."

"Oh, yeah."

I take in the red-and-white runner that is the perfect size for a coffee table. With cross-stitched images of holly leaves, trees, and reindeer, it really does look like it belongs on a Christmas sweater.

"I love it," I say as he closes up the linens bin and then carefully sets the runner on the coffee table. "Wait, wasn't the tree skirt in there as well?"

"Shit, you're right." He checks through the bin again, and I set the candy dish on the coffee table.

"You need some peppermints for your candy dish, those puffy pastel ones."

"Those are so good—they'd be gone in a day."

He pulls out a quilted tree skirt made of vintage fabric in shades of red, green, and white. Tiny candy canes, toy trains, presents, and Santas are strewn across the fabric, and it's truly the sweetest thing I've ever seen.

It reminds me of something Aunt Cindy would have.

All of his Christmas decorations do, which just makes me feel more at home, more in the spirit.

"I'm so stupid," I say, surprising him.

He turns to eye me. "Uh, care to explain that comment? Because I don't agree."

"I should have come back way sooner, not just because of you but because of the joy I get during this time. I was so bitter, so upset with what happened with Mrs. Fiskers and how I was treated after, that I shut down and I spent my Christmases away from the one true thing that brought me joy during this season. And going through these decorations with you, helping with the tree, it's just a reminder of everything I've been missing out on."

His expression softens as he comes up to me and pulls me into his chest. I wrap my arms around his waist and press my cheek against the soft fabric of his shirt.

"I know what you mean. Going through all of this, I thought it would hurt more. I thought that it would be far too painful, but I don't know, it just makes me feel closer to them. Like I'm honoring them by putting out these decorations and letting my memories fly."

"You are honoring them for sure," I say, giving him a squeeze before letting go. "Okay, is this all you wanted to do?"

"It is," he says. "I'll stack this box with the rest of the ones by the stairs, and I can take them down tomorrow."

"Are you sure?" I ask. "I can help you."

He shakes his head. "No, that's okay, I'd rather spend time with you. Plus...I have dessert."

"You have dessert?" I ask, surprised.

"Yup. I got it earlier today in the hopes of luring you outside to sit on the porch with me, but since you're already here, we can have it in front of the fireplace."

"You wouldn't have to lure me here with dessert," I say as he carries the last bin over to the stairs.

"Are you saying that I'm prize enough?"

I chuckle. "I don't want to, because I think it might go to your head, but yes...you are prize enough, Cole."

He offers me the sweetest grin before taking my hand and bringing me back to the kitchen. He takes two of the crystal-cut mugs that we unpacked, rinses them in the sink, and then dries them off with a towel.

"How can I help?"

"Stand there and look pretty."

"Not sure how productive that is," I say. "But if I must." I sigh and bat my eyelashes at him dramatically.

He chuckles. "Not sure I like how good you are at that."

"You're the one who wanted this."

He goes to the fridge where he pulls out a beer bottle and holds it up. "Uh, I have cranberry beer or eggnog."

"Eggnog," I answer.

"Eggnog it is," he replies as he grabs the carton and pours some into two cups.

"Is this your Eggnog Wars recipe?" I ask.

He shakes his head. "No, just regular. Sorry."

"That's fine, regular works."

"I still think I should have won that competition. The only reason you won was because you used decrepit old Cindy to your advantage."

"Oooo, I'm going to tell her you called her that," I tease.

"Go ahead. While you're at it, tell her you made out with me last night as well and that our tongues touched."

I don't know why that makes me snort, but it does. "Oh my God, I would never say that to her."

"Because you're ashamed of me?" he asks playfully.

"No," I drag out. "Because I don't say things to her like 'my tongue touched a man's tongue.' I don't even think she knows I've had sex. Fairly sure she still believes in her heart of hearts that I'm a buttoned-up virgin."

"Even after not seeing you for ten years, I could tell you weren't a buttoned-up virgin."

"Are you saying I'm giving off ho-ho-hoe vibes?"

"I mean...you did make out with the enemy under the mistletoe."

I point my finger at him. "That was a peck, and I didn't have a choice."

"Eh, I think it was more than a peck."

"Because you made it more than a peck. You were the one who opened your mouth."

"I see it differently," he replies as he moves to the pantry and pulls out a cookie tin. Not just any cookie tin, but *the* cookie tin. The cookie tin that Baubles and Wrappings is known for carrying. The cookie tin that I used to secretly buy for myself and hide under my pillow, swearing to Taran that I had no clue what she was talking about when she saw crumbs all over my bed.

"Umm, we're getting back to the kiss in a second. Please tell me there are cookies in that tin and it's not some secret stash of sewing materials."

He chuckles. "I wouldn't trick you like that." Then he pops open the tin, revealing the most delicious cookies, shortbread filled with jam and topped with sugar crystals.

I press my hand to my chest. "You amazing, amazing man."

He winks at me and shuts the lid. "That's the kind of praise I like to hear. Now, tell me about this kiss again and how you think I was the one who made it more than a peck."

I pick up the cups of eggnog and follow him out to the living room. He sets the cookies on the coffee table and then spreads a blanket on the floor. I join him and hand him one of the cups as we sit on the floor in front of the fireplace.

"You made it more of a peck because you opened your mouth, which is classified as *deepening* the kiss."

"According to whom?" he asks.

"Uh, everyone."

"Great defense." He laughs. "Well, I opened my mouth because you moaned."

"Oh my God, I did not moan!" I scoot my legs underneath me and lean on one hand as I stare at the flames bouncing off his carved face.

"You did. People were talking about it the next day. The moan heard around the town."

"Stop," I say on a laugh. "That did not happen."

"No, it didn't. Maybe I imagined it and that's why I opened my mouth."

"Ah-ha, so you admit that you opened your mouth."

"I mean…yeah, but you were the one who climbed on my lap last night. What I did was for show, what you did was for…well…your satisfaction."

"Please, that kiss under the mistletoe was not just for show or else you wouldn't have opened your mouth. And I climbed on your lap last night because you didn't kiss me in the truck after we came home from Clayton."

He opens the tin of cookies and sets them between us. We both reach for a cookie at the same time, and he playfully swats my hand away.

"Hey!"

He chuckles and hands me one.

After he takes a bite, he says, "In all honesty, I was nervous in the truck, sort of reeling after what happened, and stunned that, well…we were getting along. I was also hoping you wanted me to kiss you, but it felt like you blew me off, so…yeah."

"That was self-preservation," I say. "I was nervous about my feelings and was waiting for any indication from you that maybe you wanted more. I didn't get one, so I just kind of brushed everything off as casual."

"I see," he says, sticking the rest of the cookie in his mouth. Honestly, I'm surprised he took a bite of it in the first place. I would have expected him to just pop the whole thing in his mouth. Maybe he likes to savor them like I do. "And what kind of sign were you looking for?"

I shrug. "You know, some body language. Some leaning in, anything to let me know that you weren't disgusted by me."

"Jesus," he mutters. "I did not give off disgusted vibes."

I smirk at him. "You didn't, but still there wasn't much of a *come-hither* vibe either."

"You weren't giving off that vibe either, not until last night when you sat on my lap."

"Well, someone had to take action around here," I reply.

"What about me opening my mouth under the mistletoe?"

"Oh, so now you want to take credit for moving things along for us?"

He chuckles. "When the timing is right, yeah, I do."

"Absurd."

COLE

The mood is right; the fire is blazing.
Will he take her lips like he's been
desperately craving?

Cole, Connor, Snow Daddy, which man will he be?
Guess we should sit back and just wait and see.

"*That was an unnecessary addition in the middle of this scene.*"

Narrator: Not sure you should be critiquing me when I've set the mood for you. I have no problem giving you a wonky willy and sending you on your way.

"*I'm just saying the 'Cole, Connor, Snow Daddy' thing makes no sense. I don't see how they differ.*"

Narrator: Cole is just regular you. Connor is the forgotten man. And Snow Daddy is the one with the pelvic thrust that made her "wetter and wetter." Do you not remember chapter twelve?

"*I'm still trying to figure out where the hell you're coming from.*"

Narrator: It will be to your benefit to mind your own business. Now, I believe I was setting the mood…

The logs on the fire have turned to embers, the lights from the Christmas tree are just dim enough to cast a hazy glow across the living room, and the scent of freshly chopped pine fills the air.

Storee has leaned into me as we stare at the embers, and I feel a sense of immense comfort. If you would have said a couple of weeks ago that I'd find comfort in decorating for Christmas, I would have said you were insane. But now that I've put some things out, I feel…at home.

Funny to say, since this *is* my home, but it finally all feels right. And yes, I only decorated the living room, and minimally at that, because baby steps are important, but it has created a sense of joy, of peace, like this weight I've been carrying around has finally been lifted and I can see the light at the end of the tunnel. It really comes down to the fact that Storee is here. Once one of my childhood friends, back at just the right time. And perhaps only for a season. Literally.

"So, what's your favorite Lovemark movie?" I ask her.

"Tough question." She shifts, and I wrap my arm around her, resting my palm on her hip. "Hmm, there are so many good ones, *and* some really terrible ones." I chuckle. "And some okay ones, but if I have to pick, there's a series of movies that was filmed in this town called Port Snow, up in Maine. They revolved around some of the real-life love stories in town. The casting was great, and the storylines were wonderful. And because I was editing the series, I was lucky enough to fly out there at one point when they were filming the third movie in the series and got to experience the town itself. I went to this fudge shop called the Lobster Landing and, well…it was really nice."

"Nicer than here?" I ask.

"Different vibe," she replies. "Port Snow is a coastal town, whereas this is a mountain town that spends every day living in Santa's underpants."

"Santa's underpants?" I laugh out loud. "Well, fuck, if we were living in Bob Krampus's tighty-whities, you can bet your pretty face I would not still be living here."

"You wouldn't?" she asks. "You wouldn't want to jingle his bells?"

"Jesus, no!" I shout, making her laugh. "I honestly feel sick to my stomach even thinking about it."

"Poor Bob Krampus."

I lift away from her and look her in the eye. "Poor Bob Krampus? No, poor us. Who knows what kind of sweating, chafing, and moisture collecting happens down there."

"Ew, don't say 'moisture collecting.'"

"You're the one who brought it up. You didn't have to say 'Santa's underpants.'"

"It was the only thing I could think of."

"Disturbing," I say as I decide to rest on the carpet and give my back a rest. To my surprise, she leans across my stomach and stares down at me. "What do you think you're doing?" I ask her.

"Getting comfortable," she replies and then smoothes her hand up my chest.

"Seems like you enjoy getting comfortable and using my body for that."

"Trust me, Cole, if I were using your body, you would know."

I chuckle and tuck a strand of hair behind her ear. I stare up at her and smile. "Why didn't we cross this line before?"

"What line?"

"This intimate one. I feel like whenever you'd visit, we'd just have a conversation here and there, one night out on the porch. It wasn't ever anything more than that."

"I don't know," she says. "Maybe because at the time that's all it could ever be."

"And what do you think it is now?" I ask as her hand floats up to the buttons on my flannel shirt. She runs circles around them as she meets my eyes.

"I'm not sure, but I'm not scared to find out."

"No?" I ask as she starts to unbutton my shirt.

She shakes her head. "No."

And then, just like the night before, she straddles my lap as she finishes unbuttoning my shirt, revealing my white undershirt. She pouts in disappointment, so I sit up and remove the flannel, and then pull the shirt up and over my head.

Her eyes feast.

They wander, trailing over my pecs and my short, trimmed chest hair, across my ribs and down to my abs.

Her teeth pull over her bottom lip as she brings her hands to my stomach and slides them up to my chest while she lowers her body onto mine. She presses light kisses along my collarbone, up my neck, across my jaw, and when she reaches my mouth, she hovers.

Not sure if she's waiting for a sign—hell, my shirt is already off—but not wanting her to second-guess anything, I slide my hand to the back of her head and close that last inch between us, letting her mouth press against mine.

And it's fucking heaven.

It was heaven under the mistletoe.

It was heaven out on the porch.

And it's heaven now.

I love her lips, her mouth...her tongue.

I love the way she tastes. The way she holds me. The way she lightly gasps whenever our tongues touch.

It's addicting and everything I ever envisioned about kissing her.

She wiggles against me, groaning as she attempts to get even closer. So I smooth a hand down her back and over the curve of her ass, letting the feel of her round rear imprint itself on my palm.

Full.

Thick.

Something I can get very used to gripping.

When I squeeze her, she gasps into my mouth and then lifts up. Her hungry eyes meet mine as she brings both of her hands to the hem of her long-sleeved shirt and then pulls it up and over her body, leaving her in a red bra, her round breasts nearly on full display.

My mouth waters, and before I can even take my time soaking her in, she lies back down on my chest, her mouth covering mine. Immediately, her hands find my hair, where they sift and pull while her hips grind against mine, creating a delicious friction.

Taking the lead, she presses our tongues together, and I get lost in the feel of her, in the way she's controlling my mouth. I'm lost in her grasp, in her moans.

In the roll of her hips.

In the warmth of the fire next to us, elevating the heat that's building between us.

And as her hands start to roam over my pecs, her fingernails dragging across my nipples and then down my stomach, a hot ache grows within me, an ache I haven't felt in a really long time.

Aware.

Hard.

Wanting desperately for so much more, I reach behind her and let my hand wander over the clasp of her bra. I hover for a moment, giving her a second to stop me, and when she doesn't, I snap the clasp open and the fabric loosens, the straps falling down her arms.

Her mouth parts from mine for a moment, and then she slowly lifts up and lets her bra fall down her arms completely, revealing her breasts.

Fuck.

Me.

I wet my lips as I take her in.

Round globes with dusty-pink nipples, pert and hard, ready for my fingers. Jesus Christ.

"You're fucking beautiful, Storee," I say as I guide her onto her back and lie on top of her, wanting to take charge now.

Needing to.

Keeping my weight off her but rather letting myself hover over her as I lower my head to her neck, I press light kisses along her sensitive skin, focusing just below her ear where I feel goose bumps spread across her skin, then to her shoulder, across her collarbone and then lower until I reach her breast. I nip at the supple flesh, dragging my beard across her nipple and loving the way her back arches when I do.

"Yes, Cole," she says quietly while I drag my tongue over her breast and around her nipple, never directly on the nub. "Please," she says as her hips seek friction.

But I don't give her what she wants, not yet. Instead, I move down her stomach with my lips, my tongue...my teeth, nipping and kissing until I reach her pants. I glance up at her and when she wets her lips with the tip of her tongue, I know she's giving me the okay. So I pull on her leggings, dragging them all the way off her, along with her socks, leaving her in only her thong.

I run my hands back up her legs, across her thighs and under the thin strap around her waistline, letting my thumbs drag over her pubic bone, while I bring my mouth back to her stomach. She writhes beneath me, equally loving and hating the torture and letting me know with the push and pull of her hands. Keeping her at bay, I play with her skin, running my tongue around her belly button, close to the waistline of her thong, and then back around her belly button.

Her legs try to spread beneath me, but I hold her in place.

She tries to encourage me to move farther south, but I remain where I am, never pushing her thong all the way down her legs—just teasing.

Bringing her to the point of begging as her chest heaves and her hands tug on my hair.

I fucking love it.

I continue to run circles over her skin with my tongue, and when I feel like she's primed and ready, I bring my mouth back up to her breasts where I start to suck.

But not for long because her hands fall to the waistband of my pants, unbuttoning them and using her feet to push them down my legs. I take a second to remove them along with my socks and then kneel in front of her. Her eyes immediately fall to the bulge in my briefs. Her tongue peeks out, her legs spread, giving me the go-ahead.

Fuck.

I lower back down to her, but this time, I press the ridge of my cock right between her legs.

"Yes," she cries out, and then to my surprise, she pushes at my chest to flip me to my back. I allow her to take charge for a moment as she glides her center right over my bulge. "Fuck, you're huge."

Stupid pride surges through me as I grip her breasts in my palms, lightly squeezing as she moves over me, using me to seek out her own pleasure.

And she does.

She rolls her hips.

She undulates on top of me.

She grinds against my cock for her personal need, and I can't get enough of it.

Of how her hands explore her own body, running over her chest, through her hair.

How her mouth opens in shock with every pass of her hips.

And how her beautiful tits bounce along with her movements.

"Mm, this feels too good," she says as her head bows and her hips move faster.

So fucking good.

Like a goddamn dream.

I swipe my thumbs over her nipples, and I'm gifted a pure, unadulterated reaction as she tilts her head back, her mouth parting as she continues to ride me from above.

"You're so fucking hot," I say as the friction builds between us.

Her teeth pull on her lip.

Her fingers dig into my skin.

Her hips rock uncontrollably over my length.

"I...fuck...Cole. This...this..." The muscles in her neck strain, her mouth falls open, silence capturing her before a long rumble of a groan falls past her lips. "Oh fuck, oh God, Cole...I..."

Her head falls forward, her fingers dig into my skin, and she cries out my name as she reaches her apex, her hips flying over my ridge as she comes.

And it's so goddamn sexy.

It's perfect.

Her tits bouncing.

Her hips building up my own orgasm.

Her groans of pleasure. It's more than I can bear.

So much so that when she's falling back down to earth, I flip her to her back again and hover above her. I pull down my briefs, straddle her chest and then release myself, pumping my cock as I stare at her.

Cheeks flushed.

Eyes heady.

Skin red and sweaty.

Jesus fuck, she's so hot.

And this tension between us, this buildup, it's all coming to a crashing head as I grip my cock, sliding my hand over my precum and using it to lube my palm.

I tug and pull, keeping my eyes on her the entire time, pleasure racing up my spine.

A white-hot numbness erupts down my legs.

I'm right fucking there.

It's never been this fast before.

Ever.

"Shit," I mutter as my stomach starts to clench, my balls tightening. "Storee, open your mouth." She looks up at me seductively as she opens her mouth, and I lower my cock just as I start to bust all over her tongue. "Fuck," I groan as I watch beads of cum decorate her mouth, and when I'm done...she swallows, and I fall to the floor at her side.

I drape my arm over my face and breathe heavily as I try to bring my body back down from the high. That was...fuck, that was incredible, and I wasn't even inside of her.

I feel her hand trail up and down my stomach before she presses soft kisses to my shoulder. When I finally look up at her, I'm met with her gorgeous smile.

"Okay, Cole...that was hot and unexpected."

I chuckle and then rub my eyes. "No, it was fucking amazing." I lift up on my elbow and reach around the back of her neck, pulling her close. I lightly kiss her on the lips and then ask, "Will you spend the night?"

"I thought you'd never ask."

CHAPTER TWENTY-TWO
STOREE

They pat themselves down and
they gather their clothes.
They turn off the lights, and up the stairs they rose.

For orgasms were upon them.
With a grunt and a groan,
they'd fuck and they'd screw and
they'd moan, moan, moan.

"THANK YOU FOR THE TOOTHBRUSH," I say as I sit cross-legged on his bathroom counter, brushing my teeth. I'm in his flannel shirt that he let me use to cover myself as we cleaned up the living room. He stayed in his briefs, and it took everything in me to stop leering at him.

But now that we're in the bathroom and his hand is on my thigh, I'm okay with taking in an eyeful with zero shame...because he's been doing the same.

When we were bringing our cups and the cookies into the kitchen, he casually slipped his arm around my waist, his hand slipping into my barely buttoned-up shirt where he proceeded to kiss my neck and lightly caress my breast.

And when we were folding the blanket in the living room that we "copulated" on, I kept catching his eyes wandering over my body.

And when we walked up the stairs together, he trailed behind me, and I know he was checking out my ass because when we reached the top, he whispered in my ear how sexy I was.

So yeah, I'm going to get my fair share of staring in.

From his broad shoulders to his thick pecs to his trim body, which seems to have sinew popping out in every curve and contour. The V in his hips, the trimmed chest hair, the…bulge.

God, if only I'd been brave when I was younger, if only I'd come back earlier. If only I had reached out and acted upon those lustful feelings I had whenever he was around, maybe I wouldn't have been with so many duds.

And I know they're duds now. One hundred percent, no doubt in my mind they were duds, because what I just experienced was so different from anything I've ever done with a man.

And the best part of it all? It was just a good dry hump.

That dry hump was better than any other sexual experience I've had.

Sure, the fire was nice, and the lights were dimmed, and it was romantic, but that all played a small part. The big part…that's tucked just beyond Cole's black briefs.

We both spit our toothpaste into the sink, rinse our mouths, and then he helps me off the counter. Holding my hand, he brings me to a doorway that leads to another flight of stairs. When he turns to me, a look of insecurity pulls at his features.

"What's wrong?" I ask.

"It's just…this is my bedroom from when I was a teenager and, well, I haven't changed anything."

I smile. "Ooo, so I finally get to see your bedroom in the same state it was when I started wondering what it was like?"

"You wondered what my bedroom was like?"

"Uh, yeah, Cole. All the time."

"Well, not one thing has changed, and now that I'm much older, it feels kind of stupid bringing you up here. I just want you to be prepared."

"Cole," I say seriously as I cup his cheek, "you never need to worry about me judging you, okay? People move at their own pace when faced with grief, and if keeping everything in your house the way it was before your parents passed was what you needed to do, well, that's your way of dealing with your pain. There is nothing to judge. I promise."

He lets out a heavy sigh and then tilts my chin up. "You're amazing, Storee. You know that?"

"I do." I grin at him right before he places a kiss on my lips.

"Thank you for being so understanding and supportive."

"Of course," I say. "Now show me this room. I'm dying to explore."

He starts up the stairs, and I follow. "Why do I feel like I'm going to regret this?" he mutters as I stare at his taut ass.

"Do you do a lot of squats?"

"Huh?" he asks, looking over his shoulder as we reach the top of the stairs.

"You have a really nice ass, and I'm just wondering if you do a lot of squats."

He tugs on his hair, his embarrassment adorable. "Uh, no. But I lift a lot of things at the farm."

"Well, keep it up. It's nice and round."

"Thanks," he says with a laugh and then pulls me through the door to his bedroom.

The first thing I notice is the slanted ceiling that falls to just above his head. In height alone, he's clearly outgrown the space.

The next thing I notice is the smaller bed. Not a twin, not a queen, it has to be a double. Not a problem—I don't mind clinging onto him tonight.

And then from there, my eyes traverse the room, taking in the shelf that's stacked with books, a few trophies, and some knickknacks. There's a desk with an out-of-date laptop perched on it, some notebooks, and a cup for his pencils. Not sure why, but the thought of him using a pencil over a pen makes my heart warm.

A braided rug spans the floor, and since there's no closet, he has a clothes rack in the corner full of flannels and a dresser right next to it.

But the item that is really getting my attention is the poster on the wall right across from his bed.

He must sense it because he says, "Don't say anything."

"I promised I wouldn't judge."

"I can feel you judging."

"No," I say with a shake of my head. "Just...fascinated with your choice."

"It's not what you think," he says. "It was a gag gift from Max, and when I left for college, he hung it up there, and I just never took it down."

Turning toward him, I say, "But can I ask you a question about it?"

"Sure," he says, probably regretting that answer immediately.

"Have you ever gotten off to it?"

"A picture of Miss Piggy from *The Muppets* sitting on the beach—do you really think I've gotten off to that?"

"I don't know," I say with a laugh. "It's just...I mean, she's in a bit of a provocative position."

"The answer is no," he says, his face as serious as can be.

"Okay, fair, just making sure." I pause and stare at the poster. "Another question, what are your thoughts on taking it down? You know, since I plan on sleeping over tonight and I don't quite feel right about bouncing up and down on your penis with Miss Piggy watching."

He chuckles and then moves toward the poster. "I can take it down."

"Only if you want to, no pressure. We can drape a blanket over her."

"No, we can take it down, and I can take it to work tomorrow and hang it up in Max's office area where he sharpens his axes. Give him something to yearn for."

That makes me laugh as I watch him take the poster down, revealing a fist-sized hole in the wall.

"Oh shit, I forgot that was there," he says.

"Uh, what was that from?"

He rolls up the poster and then sets it to the side. "It was after I fight I had with an ex from high school."

"You punched the wall?" I look him up and down. "I'm sorry, but I don't see you as that kind of guy."

"I'm not that kind of guy," he replies. "It was stupid. She broke up with me because she wanted freedom for the summer. Anyway, she left, I got pissed, and that happened. Last time I punched a wall though—it hurt like a motherfucker and did nothing other than prove that punching a wall is a stupid thing to do."

"Well, lesson learned," I say as I take a seat on his bed. Instead of a comforter, he has a fluffy blanket and a quilt covering his mattress. And the bed is made, the sheets carefully folded over. "I'm impressed that you make your bed."

"Jesus, your standard for men must be low."

"Before you, it was," I say. "But you've raised the bar."

"Have I?" he asks as he steps up to me. I place my hands on his hips and nod.

"You have."

"Good to know." He tilts his chin toward the bed. "Get in."

Excited, I scoot back and slip under his flannel sheets, loving how warm they are, and then I lift up the covers for him, letting him slip in as well. We each take a pillow to rest our heads and then turn to each other.

"So, you were in college for how long?" I ask him.

"One semester," he answers. "Dropped out after my parents passed."

"What were you going to major in?"

"Wasn't sure yet. I was thinking about business, possibly engineering, but neither sounded at all interesting. I was trying to feel it out."

"So you weren't into animal sciences at all?"

"Not even a little," he answers as his hand pushes aside his flannel shirt I'm wearing and lands on my bare hip. "Everything I know about reindeer is from what I've read over time and talking with the Maxheimers. Honestly, it was a pity job, and then I got good at it and it became a permanent thing."

"Well, maybe you can introduce me to your reindeer one day."

"Yeah?" he asks.

"Yeah," I answer.

"Okay, then maybe after, you can show me one of the Lovemark movies you edited."

"Would you even like watching one?" I ask. "They don't seem like your cup of tea."

"If you had a hand in it, I'd like to watch it. Plus, I used to watch them with my mom all the time. They're predictable, but isn't that what's so great about them? There's no anxiety over what's going to happen—they're just feel-good movies."

"Yes," I say excitedly. "Thank you. That's what I try to tell people who scoff at them. Is it so wrong for us to just be happy while watching something? Do we always have to be thinking? Do we always have to be depressed? Do we always have to participate in entertainment that highlights drugs, abuse…sexual assault? Life is hard enough as it is. Why can't we just escape that and enjoy something that doesn't sprinkle us with a heavy dose of depression afterward?"

"I agree," he says. "There's nothing wrong with escaping reality. Fuck knows I've done it for the past decade."

I bring my hand to his face, running it over his beard. "What did you do to escape?" I ask.

"Hung out with the reindeer. Did a lot of reading…history stuff, mostly. Did a lot of hiking and mountain biking. Snowboarding with Max. Anything that got me out of the house during the day, leaving the nights as the only time I had to face my reality."

That makes me really sad.

"Have you had a hard time sleeping?"

"At first, yes," he answers. "I'd spend a lot of nights at Max's place, but then I started to realize that if I kept hiding away from the house, I was setting myself up for failure in the long run, so I'd come back at night and force myself to try to be normal. And over time, it became more and more...accepted in my brain. I don't think I'd ever call it normal, but I've come to terms with it. Well, mostly. Probably should have taken down Miss Piggy a while ago."

I chuckle. "Probably, but I won't hold it against you."

"Thanks," he murmurs.

Still stroking his beard, I ask, "Are you proud of yourself for today? Because you should be. You got a tree, Cole. You decorated it, you decorated your house...you took down that poster. Those are big steps."

"I know," he says and sighs. "I just felt...confident. Like I could do it because, well, because you were here."

That pulls on my heart as I sit up and bring my mouth to his. I kiss him for a few seconds as his grip on me grows tighter, but I pull away and stare down at his handsome face. "I'm glad I could be a part of it, Cole. And I'm glad Taran and Aunt Cindy are gone so I could be here."

His hand slides over my backside. "You don't think they would appreciate you being here with me?"

"No, I don't," I say as I slide my hand down his neck and across his chest, the short stubble prickling my palm.

"Why not?"

"The whole competition thing. I don't think they'd want me to get wrapped up in feelings when there's a crown to claim."

"I get that," he says. "And I hope you know this isn't about the competition for me. You and me—it's separate. I'm not trying to distract you."

"Oh, I know," I say quickly as I caress his chest. "I know you wouldn't do that."

"Okay, I just want to make sure," he says, insecurity in his voice. "What's happening between us, it's on a different level for me. Kringle competition aside, having you here feeds me in a way I wasn't expecting."

"Really?"

He nods and brings his wandering hand to my stomach and then up between my breasts. I lower onto my back, and it's his turn to lift up on his elbow. He undoes the one button I have holding the flannel together and then he parts the shirt, baring my front.

Lightly, he trails his fingers up my stomach and around my breasts, teasing. "You've brought some life back into my mundane days," he says softly. "I knew I was living in the dark, going week by week, month by month, but I didn't realize how far I'd sunk until you came back."

His finger moves inward, twirling around my nipple now, creating a tingling sensation throughout my body.

"You made me feel things again, Storee. Anger. Annoyance. Determination…lust. Whereas before, I'm not sure there was much that I felt at all."

I shift my legs, spreading them ever so slightly, letting him know exactly where I want him. But he doesn't give in, he keeps circling my nipple, turning me on, making me wet, bringing me to a point that I'm going to beg soon.

"I feel the same way," I say in a breathy voice. "I've felt more alive here then I have in a while."

"Because of the competition?"

I shake my head. "A little maybe, but also because of the town. Because of you. This feels right, being here, and I hate that I stayed away for so long."

"Yeah, that was pretty stupid," he jokes as his fingers trail down my stomach and circle around my belly button.

"Very stupid," I say as I make more of a show of spreading my legs.

He glances down my body and then back up. "You telling me something, Storee?"

"Yes," I answer.

"Say it." He drags his fingers right above my pubic bone and then back up my stomach, making me groan in frustration.

"I'm wet, Cole. I'm turned on. I want you to make me come again."

He smirks and then circles my nipple again. "How wet?"

"Very wet," I answer.

"Show me," he says.

I hesitate for a second, unsure of what he wants me to do, but when his fingers pinch around my nipple and my back arches, my hand falls between my legs where I rub my fingers over my arousal. Then I bring them up to his mouth and without even thinking about it, he sucks them, cleaning them off. When he's done, he pops my fingers out of his mouth and growls.

"Fucking delicious," he says and then lowers his head to my breasts, gripping one and lapping at the other with his tongue.

His beard rubs against my skin.

The weight of his body blankets me in warmth.

And his mouth does naughty things to my breast, building a warm sensation in the pit of my stomach, driving me to need more. So much more.

He lifts up and switches sides, and it makes me crazy with need.

His tongue flicking over my nipple. His teeth nibbling. His lips sucking.

It's an onslaught of sensations all at the same time, creating a dull throb between my legs.

"Cole," I say as I sift my hands through his hair. "Please."

But he doesn't listen, he continues to suck, to play, to pinch.

My pelvis starts to move, seeking out any type of friction, but all I'm met with is air, so I twist my lower half just enough to find his leg. I hook my heel around his calf and start rubbing myself over him.

"Fuck," he says against my breast. "Storee, you're so wet."

"I told you," I say as I continue to try seeking relief from the way he's turned me on.

And then to my surprise, he grips my hip and pins me to the mattress, freeing me of any sort of relief.

I groan in frustration while he continues to play with my breasts.

"Cole, please," I groan. "I don't...I don't want to come like this."

"How do you want to come?" he asks.

"By your mouth." He lifts up and grins at me before pressing a kiss to each breast, and then works his way down my stomach, kissing a path until he reaches my pubic bone.

My breath is heavy.

My stomach is hollow.

And I lift up on my elbows to watch him spread my legs, making room for his large body. He settles in, parts me with two fingers, and then to my utter satisfaction presses his tongue right against my clit.

I sigh in relief, letting my body drop back down to the mattress and allowing myself to get lost in the feel of his mouth.

"Yes," I moan, my hips shifting, my hands finding my breasts. "You're so good, Cole. Fuck...ahhh, yes, you're so good."

He smoothes one hand up my stomach and moves my grip off my breasts, playing with them instead. He takes a nipple between his fingers and starts rolling it while his tongue makes long, languid strokes across my clit.

Heat builds deep within me.

My legs tremble.

And I can feel my orgasm start to climb.

"Cole, I'm...I'm close," I say, which makes him pick up his pace.

His tongue makes short, concise flicks over my clit, driving my need to the point that I can barely breathe.

He pinches.

He flicks.

And then he sucks my clit between his lips, and my back arches off the mattress as a feral cry falls out of my mouth. My orgasm races through me, numbing my limbs, and spiraling through my stomach. He allows me to move my hips, to seek out every second of the intense pleasure until I'm completely sated.

"Oh…my…God," I say, breathless and barely able to comprehend what he just did to me in mere seconds. "Cole." I look down at him and he's licking his lips. Jesus. "That was…God." I dip my head back to the pillow and I hear him shuffle around. When I glance in his direction again, he's completely naked and gripping the base of his cock, tugging on it as he stares down at me. Wanting to return the favor, I hold out my hand to him and he takes it.

I pull him down on the bed and lay him flat on his back. With his flannel shirt still on, I move over his legs and bring my mouth to the tip of his cock.

He places one hand behind his head and brings the other to my face, gently running his thumb over my cheek. I smile up at him right before I run my tongue along the underside of his cock.

He hisses in pleasure, his eyes squeezing shut, and I wonder how long it's been since he last had someone do this to him. I know it's been months since he's had sex, but this level of intimacy…when was the last time?

I bring my hand to his balls, cup them gently, and then start to roll them in my palm while I continue to let my tongue do the work, running up and down his length, playing with the sensitive part under the head, swirling around.

"Jesus," he groans as his legs fall open more. "I want your mouth, Storee."

I debate if I should torture him like he tortured me, but when I see precum on his tip, I decide otherwise and bring my mouth to his head. I look up at him and watch his eyes turn heavy as I take him all the way to the back of my throat.

"Fuuuuuck," he draws out, squeezing his eyes shut. "Shit, Storee, you're...you're going to make me come early."

I pop my mouth off him. "Want me to stop?"

"No," he groans and runs his fingers through my hair, lightly encouraging me to keep going. "Just...just stop when I tell you because I want your cunt."

A thrill shoots up my spine from the gravel in his voice and the dirtiness in his words.

I take him back into my mouth, and as I guide my lips and tongue around the head, I work the root of his cock with my hand, pumping and squeezing, attempting to edge him to the point that he needs to take control because I want him. I want him inside of me.

I want to feel his girth stretching me. I want to see his eyes when he enters me.

The thought of it makes me so excited, so turned on that I work his cock harder, faster.

He breathes heavily.

He writhes.

He grips my hair tightly.

And then...

"Fuck, okay, stop. Fucking stop."

I remove my mouth and stare down at him.

At his twitching cock.

At his hollowed stomach.

At his hard nipples and heady eyes.

I move up his legs and right over his length.

"Protection," he says.

"I'm on birth control and clean," I say as I lift his cock and position it at my entrance. "You good with that?"

"Fucking great with that," he says as I tease my clit with his head. "Wet again," he says. "Fucking perfect." He reaches up and takes my breasts in his hands as I slowly start to lower down on him. The pressure is too strong, and my eyes flutter closed as I take my time, attempting to relax.

"Eyes on me," I hear him say.

"What?" I ask as I open my eyes.

"I said eyes on me. I want to see your expression when I fill you up."

Those words, those simple words, they amp up my need.

My desire for this man.

And as I lower down on him, letting him stretch me out in the best way possible, I keep my eyes connected to him even though when I get halfway, I want to shut them.

"Breathe," he says softly, still playing with my breasts. "Relax. Show me how you love my cock."

I take a deep breath and then sink down another inch.

"That's it, Storee," he says softly. "All the way down."

I let out another deep breath, keep my eyes on him, and then sink down until I bottom out. The flannel falls off my shoulder, and I don't bother fixing it as my hand falls to my stomach and my mouth drops open.

"Oh my God, Cole."

"Shit," he says nearly at the same time. "Fuck, you feel amazing." His hands go to my hips, and he shifts, causing a wave of friction to shoot up my spine.

The fullness, the way I fit so perfectly around him, how my clit is moving against him at just the right angle—it creates a storm of desire racing through me so intensely that I start to rock my hips.

"That's it, Storee. Fucking use my cock."

My head falls forward, my hands now on his chest as I frantically start to pump over him, rubbing my clit over him, allowing myself to get lost in how large he is, how he's hitting me in a spot I've never felt before, creating an addiction that I foresee never being satisfied.

"I'm close," I say as I continue to rock my hips. And then to my surprise, Cole sits up and brings us both closer to the headboard. He leans against it and the angle offers me a completely different feel, one that spikes adrenaline through me as he hits that one spot inside of me repeatedly.

He wraps his hand around the back of my neck and brings his mouth to mine, kissing me senseless.

His lips captivating mine.

His tongue dancing, tantalizing.

His groans are so incredibly sexy that I can feel my orgasm start to ripple through me.

At first it's slow, a numbing sensation at the tips of my toes, and then it climbs higher and higher until it pools between my legs. Pulling back from his mouth, my head tilts back and his name flies off my tongue. "Cole, oh fuck," I cry, my body starting to seize, my inner walls convulsing around his cock.

"Oh fuck," he yells, his hips moving now. "Shit, Storee. You're...you're making me fucking come."

He roars out another grunt and then he stills, the sexiest sounds coming from him as we both ride out our orgasms.

"Fucking hell," he breathes as his eyes open and connect with mine.

"What happened to eyes on me?" I tease him as I lean forward and press a soft kiss to his lips.

"You made me black out."

I chuckle and rest my head against his shoulder as his bulky arms wrap around me. "I can assume that our friendship has effectively changed."

He laughs and kisses my bare shoulder. "It changed the minute you sat on my lap on the porch."

I lift up and look him in the eyes. "No, it changed when you parted your mouth under the mistletoe."

"I thought we were still enemies then, not friends."

"We were always friends," I say. "Just had a dispute."

He lifts an eyebrow. "Ten years apart is quite the dispute."

"Let's just call it a miscommunication and move on."

"What the hell are you talking about?"

I sigh and rest my head back down. "Never mind."

CHAPTER TWENTY-THREE

Where did they do it? That question is fair.
In the bed, against the wall, and
in the living room chair.

He thrust and thrust, and thrust some more.
He thrust until they wore a hole in the floor.

And now with Aunt Cindy back,
they can only send texts,
but that didn't stop Cole from sending sext after sext.

Cole: Taran didn't see the hickey I left on your collarbone, did she?

Storee: No, I borrowed a turtleneck from Aunt Cindy. It's green with mini candy canes. I played it off as a way to show more Kringle spirit when I walked down to Warm Your Spirits for drinks.

Cole: Where's my picture? I want to see what this turtleneck looks like.

Storee: [Picture]

Cole: That is…something.

Storee: I thought about pairing it with a Christmas vest but didn't want to make you fully erect with the picture I sent.

Cole: The only way I would have been fully erect is if there were bells hanging from your nipples and you bounced to make them jingle.

Storee: You know, I'm seeing a new side of you I didn't know existed. I just assumed you were a grump who didn't really talk all that much. Lo and behold, you're texting about jingling nipple bells.

Cole: Maybe if you hadn't stayed away for so long, you would have found out more about me.

Storee: Maybe if you hadn't acted so shy on the porch all the time, I would have been able to dig deeper into your true personality.

Cole: I wasn't shy.

Storee: You were, but so was I.

Cole: Not shy anymore.

Storee: I think shyness is out the window after you spanked me.

Cole: You said you liked that.

Storee: More than I expected.

Cole: I did not like it when you said, "Do it again, Snow Daddy."

Storee: LOL! I thought it was a nice touch.

Cole: It wasn't.

Storee: Sheesh, and here I thought I could have some fun with you.

Cole: You can have fun with me, just don't call me Snow Daddy.

Storee: What do you prefer?

Cole: Big Daddy Dick Dong.

Storee: LOLOLOL no, you don't!

Cole: Ha ha. You're right, I don't. Cole works. When you moan it in that raspy tone of yours, that works even better.

Storee: I think that's something I can arrange.

Cole: I'm assuming tonight is a no-go?

Storee: Yeah, I don't think I can make it over. Taran has been a beast today about the light display. And I have no excuse to leave the house.

Cole: I understand. But fuck do I wish you were here right now.

Storee: Yeah? What are you doing?

Cole: Just lying in bed. My pillow smells like you.

Storee: Is that your subtle way of saying you miss me?

Cole: I don't think it's subtle at all. I was really hoping you'd be able to come over tonight.

Storee: I know. Me too. Are you wearing anything?

Cole: [Picture] Just briefs.

Storee: *CRIES* That was not a nice picture to send.

Cole: Why? I thought I look good.

Storee: That's the problem. You look too good.

Cole: Yeah? Tell me more.

Storee: Are you really digging for compliments?

Cole: I don't think it would hurt to elaborate on what pleases your eyes when you look at me.

Storee: A weird way to say that, but okay. How about this, I give you a compliment, you give me one.

Cole: Easy. I fucking love your lips. From the moment you first kissed me under the mistletoe, to making out on the porch, to last night, I'm addicted. I need more.

Storee: Um *rolls teeth over lips* that was sweet.

Cole: It's the truth. Your turn.

Storee: Okay. I really like your hands. I love how large they are, the length of your fingers, the calluses on your palms. I love their grip and how they like to dig into my skin when you're holding on to me.

Cole: Your eyes captivate me, Storee. And I don't mean that in a cheesy way. It's so true—whenever you look at me, I have this really hard time looking away. And when I'm inside of you, and you keep your eyes on me, it sends me reeling.

Storee: Your voice. It commands me in a way I've never experienced, especially when you're deep, pulsing, taking every last ounce of my pleasure.

Cole: Fuck...Storee.

Storee: And your chest. God, I love it so much. It's thick, sturdy, and the perfect place to land when I'm seeking warmth and comfort. I want nothing more than to curl into your chest right now.

Cole: Then come over.

Storee: And your abs...they're not human. No one should have a stomach like you, such perfectly individualized sets of muscle. I love running my tongue over them.

Cole: Storee, seriously...

Storee: And then there's your cock. I'm getting wet just thinking about it. You fill me up, Cole. I've never felt anything like it before. The only comparison to what gives me the same pleasure is your tongue...

Cole: Jesus. Come over here. Now. Come sit on my goddamn face. I want to eat that cunt.

Storee: God, I wish. I'd ride your tongue until I'm coming all over your mouth.

Cole: Do it then. Stop teasing me. Come over here.

Storee: You know I can't. But now I'm so turned on.

Cole: So then touch yourself.

Storee: Are you touching yourself?

Cole: [Picture] What does it look like?

Storee: Oh my God, Cole. Your dick is so huge. I want it in my mouth.

Cole: I'd fuck the smile right off your face. I'd listen to the way you gag as you take me all the way to your throat. And I'd watch those beautiful eyes widen as I pull out, only to slam to the back of your throat again.

Storee: I'm so wet.

Cole: Are you touching yourself?

Storee: Yes.

Cole: Are you thinking about me?

Storee: Yes.

Cole: Picture me sucking on your tits, tugging on your nipples, nipping my teeth around them.

Storee: I love your mouth. I can practically feel you playing with them. It makes me wetter. How hard are you?

Cole: Stretched up my stomach. Precum. Balls tightening.

Storee: You're close. Me too. Fuck, I'm moving my hand faster.

Cole: Rub your clit, Storee. I want to know you're getting everything I'd give you.

Storee: Cole...I'm so close.

Cole: Me too. Fuck.

Storee: God...Cole, I came. I so wish it were you instead of my hand.

Cole: Trust me, I wish the same thing.

Cole: Good morning, beautiful.

Storee: [Picture] Good morning.

Cole: Shit...did you really have to send me a picture of you all rumpled in bed without me?

Storee: Just pretend I'm right there next to you, curled into your chest.

Cole: I don't want to pretend. Come over today.

Storee: I'll see what I can do, but I have a feeling Taran is going to commandeer my time again.

Cole: Does the light display really need that much attention from you?

Storee: You saw it. She's determined. What are you up to? I don't see your truck in the driveway.

Cole: I'm at the farm right now. Just finished feeding the reindeer. Now taking a break before I start putting their bridles and reins on. We have three reindeer walks today. We add more during the season.

Storee: What does a reindeer walk entail?

Cole: Come visit me and I'll show you.

Storee: I would, but Taran has me going over a song list today and possible dance routines for the Christmas caroling competition. I am dreading it more than anything. Why does Bob Krampus think people need to sing in order to win?

Cole: It's part of the joy of Christmas.

Storee: Aren't you nervous about singing at the Caroling Café?

Cole: Not really.

Storee: If you come barreling in with a voice like an angel, I'm going to be mad at you.

Cole: LOL. Nothing to worry about. I think after I thrust at the crowd while decked out in green paint and lederhosen, nothing really fazes me at this point.

Storee: That is very true. I can still remember how the ground rumbled after that air humping.

Cole: I got some powerful hips, something you know a lot about.

Storee: I wouldn't say a lot…we had one night.

Cole: One night where we got no sleep. Must I remind you about how we fucked in my bed twice? In the shower, against the wall…in the living room chair the next morning, and then when I bent you over the stairs on the way up to the shower?

Storee: To name a few. Sheesh. You make me sound like a loose woman.

Cole: Loose? No. Desired? Without question.

Storee: You sure know how to make a girl blush.

Cole: Hopefully it propels you to come see me.

Storee: I'll try. When I say Taran is being psychotic, I'm not kidding. It's like she came back from Golden a different person. I think she must have been talking to Aunt Cindy about the competition because she's in full panic mode with Christmas Eve being twelve days away.

Cole: Is she worried about the candy cane competition?

Storee: No, but she's been asking me what my plans are and if I need to practice. I told her I was good and that I'll be fine, even though I feel like maybe I should practice. But what am I going to do with all those candy canes?

Cole: I can think of a few things you can do with them.

Storee: Are you always this horny? Tell me now so I can prepare myself for when we see each other again.

Cole: Who's to say that was a horny comment?

Storee: Oh my God, Cole, I could taste the horniness from here.

Cole: Taste, huh? *waggles eyebrows*

Storee: Dear God.

Storee: I told Taran I was going for a walk, aka walk straight into your house, and she now has me practicing my sewing skills instead.

Cole: Noooooooooo. Seriously? I got some ingredients for a hot cocoa bar that I was hoping to use on your body. Like chocolate syrup, whipped cream, and cherries.

Storee: Stop, did you really?

Cole: Yes. I had to get them when Max was with me, and he was giving me the side-eye the entire time.

Storee: Maybe use them on yourself?

Cole: Oh, should I paint my nipples with chocolate syrup and try to lick it off?

Storee: I'd be really impressed if your spine lets you bend like that.

Cole: Hell, I'd be impressed too. Seriously, you can't come over?

Storee: Not looking like it. Do you hate me?

Cole: No, but I'm going to sulk.

Storee: You won't be the only one sulking. I was looking forward to spending some time with you.

Cole: You were?

Storee: Yeah, not just because of…the copulating…but because I have things I want to talk about.

Cole: Don't say copulating, and what kind of things do you want to talk about?

Storee: Like…what is your favorite kind of Christmas cookie?

Cole: Ah, the hard-hitting kind of questions. All right, well, I'm up for some questions if you are. But be warned, I'm not going to hold back. I have every intention of getting to know you even better.

Storee: That's fair. So…favorite Christmas cookie?

Cole: That would have to be my mom's butter cookies. She'd cut them in circles, cover them in green icing, and then put a small red heart on the side. She called them Grinch Cookies.

Storee: I love that.

Cole: Haven't had them in a while, but they'll always be my favorite. Okay, my turn...what's your favorite Christmas decoration?

Storee: Aunt Cindy's Happy Days nativity scene. I can't get over the Fonz as baby Jesus.

Cole: What? Happy Days nativity? How come I've never seen this?

Storee: Have you spent much time in Aunt Cindy's house?

Cole: Uh...not enough to notice a Happy Days nativity set. I'm missing out.

Storee: You are. Okay, first girl you ever kissed, like a real make-out kiss? And was it good?

Cole: Well, it was good for me. Not sure if it was good for her. Her name was Harriet. Her dad got a job out in Aspen so they moved away, but we made out behind the Polar Freeze after sharing a banana sundae. It was the first time I felt a real boob. I got hard as shit.

Storee: Behind the Polar Freeze, ahh, good times. LOL!

Cole: It was. Who was the first person you made out with?

Storee: His name was Renny Bottom—legit that was his name—and it was at prom. We made out under a table so we wouldn't get caught. He touched my breast and got scared that he touched it too hard.

Cole: Did he?

Storee: I wish he'd touched it harder.

Cole: LOL!

Storee: Okay, favorite Christmas movie?

Cole: "Home Alone." Kevin is a badass. I thought I'd booby-trap our house once, ended up gluing my pillow's stuffing to my dad's bare chest. Mom had to shave him to get it off. He complained about his nips being cold all winter.

Storee: LOLOL! Oh my God. That's amazing.

Cole: What's your favorite Christmas movie?

Storee: Ugh, tough pick. Hmm, I think I'm going to go with "The Year Without a Santa Claus."

Cole: What's that?

Storee: Seriously? It's one of those puppet stop-motion movies. It's about a year when the world stopped caring about Santa, so he went to a small town to see if people believed in him. It's where we get the wonderful characters of Snow Miser and Heat Miser and their beautiful mother, Mother Nature.

Cole: You know what, sounds familiar.

Storee: So good. Music is on point, the puppets are weird, and Santa is skinny the whole movie until Christmas Eve when he eats something and fills out. My mom will still give my dad his dinner and say, "Eat, Papa, eat."

Cole: Oh shit, I do know what you're talking about. It's been a long time since I've seen that movie.

Storee: Well, that needs to be fixed.

Cole: Only can be fixed if you come over here.

Storee: Working on it. Don't worry. It will happen.

Cole: I'll believe it when I see it.

CHAPTER TWENTY-FOUR
COLE

Despite the grim distance, the happy
humpers made it work.
Through texts, randy photos, and
passing by with a smirk.

We are sad, they are sad, everyone's
sad the thrusting has ended,
but now it's competition time, and
everyone has attended.

"ARE YOU READY FOR THIS?" Max asks as he rubs my shoulders as we stand at our workstation.

I swat him away. "Can you not do that?"

"You look tense. I thought you needed it."

I'm tense because it's been two days since I've been able to kiss or even see Storee, and now that I'm waiting for her to arrive at the Candy Cane Showdown, I'm anxious.

It hasn't stopped us from talking though.

We've been texting, communicating. She's been sending suggestive pictures, and I've been dying inside that she's just a house away and we can't do anything about it.

Ever since Taran came home and saw that Storee didn't do anything that she'd asked—because Storee was doing me—Taran has been on her case about the lights and about practicing for the caroling portion of the competition. Hence, she hasn't been able to sneak away.

But something has to change because, yeah, I'm tense and I don't want to lose the momentum we have. I don't want to lose her as Christmas approaches.

"I'm not tense," I lie to Max. "Just focused."

"Uh-huh, focused, is that what they're calling it these days?"

"What are you talking about?" I ask as I turn to look at him.

"You think I don't see what's been happening?" he whispers. "You're abandoning me for her."

Jesus.

Christ.

"Please tell me you're not serious," I deadpan.

"And this is exactly why I didn't want to bring it up," he says, crossing his arms. "I knew you were just going to brush me off and act like it's nothing. Well, it's something to me." He points to his chest. "You didn't even practice with me on this candy cane-making stuff. How can I be a good holly jolly sidekick if I don't know what I'm doing? Fortunately for you, even though you abandoned me, I won't treat you the same way. I had a private lesson with Jefferson Chadwick myself after calling in a favor."

"You...what? You did?"

"Yes." He crosses his arms again. "I did. And I learned everything we need to know to win this competition—something I feel like you've forgotten about."

"Hold on," I say, holding up my hand. "When did you become so invested in winning?"

"I'm invested because you're invested."

I shake my head. "Not buying it. What's going on?"

"Nothing," Max says defiantly.

"Tell me."

"There's nothing going on," he repeats.

"Atlas," I say, using his real name, which I very rarely do. "Tell me."

The real name does it. He sighs and then leans against the wall behind him. "I ran into Dwight Yokel on the farm, and he was making fun of us for being in third, and I didn't appreciate the criticism."

"Dwight Yokel?" I say, unimpressed. "Max, that guy has been trying to get under your skin since high school, and you're letting him."

"Yeah, I am, so get your head out of Storee's cleavage and let's win this thing."

"First of all, don't degrade her like that, and second of all, just because we're actually seeing each other, that doesn't take away from me trying to still win this—"

I pause just as I catch Storee walking through the door, with Taran pushing Cindy in her wheelchair. Storee is wearing a red cropped jacket that shows off a pair of high-waisted jeans. Her hair is pulled back into two braids, and she has matching red lips which are calling out to me.

I want to see that color rubbed all across my dick.

I wet my lips when she makes eye contact with me, her eyes traveling over my green-and-black flannel and then back up to my face. She offers me a wink and I swear I can feel my heartbeat in my throat.

"Uh...you were saying something about not getting distracted," Max says while leaning in close to me.

"Yes," I say as I turn away from Storee and focus on Max. "We're still going to win this."

"Uh-huh, and when we're making candy canes, are you going to be able to keep your eyes off her? Because sorry to say but that shirt she's wearing is pretty low-cut."

I look over my shoulder and my mouth waters at the sight of said shirt. Fuck me. She's unzipped her jacket to reveal a square neckline that cuts low to her breasts, the green color looking beautiful against her skin. And with the way she has it tucked in, showing off her curvy frame…yup, I'd have no problem asking her out after this. Maybe I should, as a fake date for the town but a real date between the two of us.

"Not going to be a problem," I say to Max. "Excuse me for a second."

"Sure," I hear him huff behind me.

I walk over to her station where she's setting her things up, and because Taran is near, I put on a smile but say, "I hope you burn your sugar."

Her eyes flash up to mine, and they glint as she smirks. "And here I thought that maybe you might be nice to me today."

"What gave you that impression?" I ask, sticking my hands in my pockets so I don't touch her.

"The holiday spirit?"

I shake my head. "Nope, I plan on making the best candy cane Old Man Chadwick has ever seen."

"Do you call him that to his face?" she asks as she sets down a vial of liquid I assume is her flavoring. We haven't spoken much about our plans for the competition, and that's probably for the best since Max seems to be having some sort of crisis about winning now.

"I don't. That's a special pet name I gave him for myself and myself only."

I watch as she tries to hold back her smile. She fails miserably so she tilts her head down and pretends to adjust her bowl.

"Ah, there they are, my new favorite couple," Martha says as she walks up to us, Mae trailing behind. "You know, if you connect your candy canes together, they'll make a heart."

Just the two people I need.

With them around, I can touch Storee as much as I fucking want.

I move over to Storee, pull her into my chest, and try not to lean in too hard to get a better smell of her hair. "That's what I've been telling her, Martha. But she's kept her recipe a secret. We haven't connected candy canes in days."

"I do enjoy a competitive spirit in a girl." Martha winks at her. "Are there plans for any other dates? I feel like we haven't seen you two out and about much."

"Busy with candy cane making," I say. "But I was planning on taking her to the farm tonight."

"You were?" Storee asks.

"You were?" Taran repeats, leaning in to the conversation as well.

I glance around at all the expectant faces and nod. "Yup. Want to introduce her to the reindeer."

"That will be so sweet," Martha says.

"And romantic," Mae chimes in.

"And smelly," Taran mumbles as she walks away.

Martha gives Taran the stink eye and then whispers to us, "Looks like someone is missing the Christmas spirit."

"She's just upset about our light display. Don't worry about her," Storee says, defending her sister.

"Ah, I see, well, you're still in the lead, so no need to worry. If anyone should be worrying, it's this guy," Martha says, thumbing toward me.

"Not worried," I say. "Max and I have this one in the stocking." I wink and Martha chuckles.

"Well, good luck to both of you," Martha coos and then she and her sister move toward a pair of chairs in the front.

We're once again in the school gymnasium with our own stations set up. But unlike last time when I was next to Storee, this time Jimmy Short is between us. Probably best so I won't get as distracted.

"So, the farm tonight?" she whispers.

"Only if you want to," I whisper back.

Her eyes meet mine. "I want to."

"Okay, you good to go after this?"

"Yup." She grins, and just to put on a show for the town, I tilt her chin up and press a very soft kiss to her lips, eliciting a round of *ahhs* through the gym. When I pull away, I catch the glare in Taran's eyes, so I offer her a wink and then take off toward my station where I find Max looking over a recipe in his hand.

"What's that?" I ask.

"A recipe I found online." He pulls a vial from his pocket. "It's pineapple flavoring. I think we go with the same theme as the fruitcake."

"No," I say, moving past him. "Have you lost your fucking mind? We're not bringing back pineapple. That was a mistake, and we're not making it again. We're making a traditional candy cane, and we're going to impress with our technique, not our flavoring."

"Fine," he grumbles and pockets the vial. "But can we at least make it a triple-striped candy cane with red, green, and white?"

"That I think we can do," I say as I move toward our station. "Okay, let's make a quick plan."

STOREE

"Is something going on between the two of you?" Taran hisses in my ear while I watch the thermometer on my sugar.

"What?" I ask, not looking at her because I don't think I could look her in the eye. "No, why would you think that?"

"Uh, because of the way you keep glancing over at him, the way he keeps glancing over at you, and the kiss right before this competition started."

"Ugh," I groan. "That's all part of his plan to make the town think we're together. I have to match his energy or else I come off looking like the asshole who won't date the hometown hero. It's annoying. Come on, Taran, you know what I've been dealing with."

I can feel Taran's eyes on me. Studying, seeing if I'll break.

But I don't.

"Yeah, I guess that is kind of annoying," she replies.

"And now I have to go to his freaking farm tonight because he told Martha I would. Probably just going to sit in the barn and stare at the hay until an appropriate amount of time has passed." I inject annoyance into my voice despite being filled with glee.

I've been so busy with Taran and Aunt Cindy the last two days that I haven't been able to focus on finding time to be with Cole, and it's been driving me crazy. Sure, the texts are nice, and the pictures he's sent me of himself lying in bed shirtless and sad that I wasn't with him have been great to stare at, but they haven't been enough.

I want to be able to touch him, have him hold me…kiss me.

"That is annoying because I could have used your help looking at some new lights I've been thinking about purchasing."

"You know, maybe we can talk about this a little bit later," I say as the temperature of the sugar reaches 320 degrees.

"Maybe tomorrow at breakfast—I'm going to get to bed early tonight."

"Sure," I say as I lift the pot off the heat and bring it over to the marble slab where I pour it out. I glance past Jimmy, who's adding air into his sugar, and spot Cole and Max whispering to each other. It looks like a disagreement because Cole shakes his head and Max seems adamant.

Those two…they're ridiculous.

I set the pot on a trivet and then pick up one of the spatulas to start flipping the sugar over, adding air to it and letting it cool down. After a few minutes, I divide the sugar up. I put red food coloring in one portion, knead it and set it to the side. And then I put the peppermint in the other and move that around, the fragrance strong as my hands start to grow tired from all the kneading. This is where Cole came in handy as he did most of the grunt work with the sugar.

Ugh. Hand aching, I bring my sugar lump over to the hook behind my station, loop it around and start to pull, but my hands are tired, and the sugar still feels hot despite wearing gloves. Panic sets in as I realize that if I don't start really pulling, I could mess up this whole thing.

I tug and loop...tug and loop, but after the third round, I'm exhausted, and the sugar hasn't fully changed into white yet. I'm about to step back when I feel a warm body come up behind me.

"Let me help," I hear Cole say as he brings my hands back up, and together we pull on the sugar, looping it back around the hook over and over until it's pure white and ready to go. I remove the sugar from the hook and turn toward Cole. He smiles at me and then kisses the tip of my nose, causing the crowd to let out another round of *ahhh*s.

He sure knows how to work them.

Thankfully, I know whatever he's handing out is real, even though it's supposed to be fake in my family's eyes.

"Thank you," I say to him. I glance over my shoulder to where Taran is writing in her notebook while simultaneously showing something to Aunt Cindy on her notepad. So I whisper to him, "I'll pay you back later tonight."

"Looking forward to it." And then he jogs back to his station where Max is lining up their colors and making a striped blanket like we learned. Kind of wish Taran would jump in and help, but she doesn't want Aunt Cindy to need anything and we're both distracted. So I'm doing this on my own.

I spend the next twenty minutes putting my base together, stretching it out, which again is hard and tiring, and my forearms are on fire, but once I start cutting and shaping, I can see my product come to life and I love it.

They look like real candy canes.

Even if they're simple and not original, I still love what I was able to do, with a little help from Cole, of course.

To the right, there's a giant clock that's counting down our time, and I finish up my last candy cane just as the clock runs out. We were supposed to make two dozen identical candy canes, and honestly, I feel really good about what I did.

I look down the line and observe everyone's different take on the classic sugary confection.

Jimmy did a green-and-yellow candy cane.

Cole and Max went with red, green, and white. Wow, okay. Theirs look pretty cool.

Ursula made…are those hearts? Uh-oh, not sure that was a smart move given how cranky and exacting Jefferson Chadwick seems when it comes to tradition.

And then at the very end, Beatrice Pedigree seems to have created pink-and-red candy canes. I wonder if those are strawberry-flavored. Possibly cherry. Or could be peppermint as well.

Who knows?

All I know is that Jefferson Chadwick is stepping up to the tables, not bothering with the fanfare that Bob Krampus usually puts on when it comes to these competitions. He adjusts his glasses on his nose, holds a clipboard close to his chest, and starts with Beatrice.

I watch as he picks up one of her candy canes, examines it, taps it on the counter, and then lines up each candy cane she made and goes down the line, comparing all of them.

I glance at my batch and feel inferior as I pick out all the flaws that I didn't notice when I was making them. The curves aren't all the same. The heights aren't matching up. And did I twist the colors enough?

I gnaw on the corner of my lip as I look up and catch him moving down the line, clearly disgusted with Ursula's heart candy canes. That was a very bold choice that I knew wasn't going to pay off, from just one look at Jefferson Chadwick.

Now standing in front of Cole and Atlas who…are they linking arms? I hold back my smile as Atlas bounces in place, looking far too excited, while Cole sticks his hands in his pockets, his expression neutral. While Chadwick studies their candy canes, I find myself studying Cole.

His sleeves are rolled up to his elbows, showing off his impressive forearms that bounce and bulge as he moves. His shoulders are broad, but not too bulky like a weightlifter, longer and leaner. His jaw is covered in the thick scruff that I've felt scrape deliciously over my body. His lips are perfect, the bottom one being a touch fuller than the top—I know this because I've pulled on it with my teeth. And those eyes, they're hooded by thick brows and highlighted by long, dark lashes. Growing up, I always thought he was cute, but seeing him as a man now, he's practically irresistible.

He glances over in my direction, pulling his attention from Old Man Chadwick, and when he catches me checking him out, the sexiest grin tugs on the corners of his mouth. I feel my cheeks heat up as I glance back down at my candy canes, unable to maintain eye contact because I fear what Taran might notice.

The situation is difficult to navigate. We have to act like we hate each other while pretending to date, even though we are actually sort of seeing each other. It's complicated and hard to process, especially when Taran and Aunt Cindy are around, because I don't want them to think that I'm giving up on the competition. I still very much want to win.

Jefferson Chadwick moves over to Jimmy's table where Jimmy stands with pride, hands clasped behind his back, looking extremely confident. His candy canes look rather good from where I stand, very thick, about the diameter of a quarter, but the color is an odd choice, and when I catch Chadwick take a taste, his eyebrows shoot up and then bunch together as he makes a note on his clipboard.

Oof, that doesn't seem like it will bode well for Jimmy.

Chadwick makes a few more notes and then steps up to me. I feel my legs tremble with nerves as he examines each candy cane, picking them up and looking at the way the sugar has hardened. He brings the end of one of the candy canes to his mouth and takes a taste, before setting it back down. He jots down some things and then without a word walks over to Bob Krampus and hands him the clipboard.

Sheesh.

For someone who owns a candy shop, you'd think he would be—no pun intended—sweeter, but he's just a big grump with no hair, apart from bushy eyebrows that seem to curl and stand out of their own volition.

Bob Krampus in all his Santa glory takes a microphone from Mrs. Claus and then holds it up to his mouth as he roars out a hearty ho-ho-ho.

You have to give the man credit for his dedication to the character—never breaking, never showing anyone an ounce of identity besides Santa.

"Mr. Chadwick has spoken, and we have a winner for the best candy cane this Kringle season." He looks at the paper and then smiles. "In fifth place, we have Ursula Kronk—with a note from Mr. Chadwick saying he didn't like the heart shape."

Yup, called that one.

The crowd politely applauds and Ursula leans against her table, looking none too pleased.

"In fourth place…" *Please not me, please not me.* "…we have Beatrice Pedigree."

Thank Jesus.

"Mr. Chadwick liked your shapes but was not a fan of the strawberry flavoring."

Strawberry, I was right. Yeah, I wouldn't have ventured out with a new flavor.

"In third place…" I cross my fingers behind my back, really hoping I can get top two. "We have Storee Taylor with her classic candy cane." Damn it. I smile and nod at Jefferson. "Mr. Chadwick enjoyed your traditional rendition but marked you down for not being able to pull your own sugar."

Well, sorry for not having forearms of steel.

"In second place, we have…" He pauses like he always does, leaving the town on edge, and then into the mic he says, "Cole Black and his holly jolly sidekick, putting Jimmy Short in first!" The crowd cheers, and Jimmy fist-pumps the air as we all move toward the front of our tables and line up together. I happen to move in next to Cole, where his arm brushes against mine, sending warmth through me.

When the crowd has died down, Bob Krampus continues, "Mr. Chadwick was very impressed with Cole's three-striped candy cane, but what won him over was the pineapple flavoring that Jimmy was able to incorporate."

I hear a stunned gasp, and when I glance to the side, an angry-looking Atlas is staring Cole down. "I fucking *told* you we should have done pineapple," Atlas mutters.

And to his credit, Cole mutters back, "You were right, dear."

CHAPTER TWENTY-FIVE
COLE

Every Kringle in Kringletown, the old and the young,
Didn't expect Chadwick to like
pineapple on his tongue.

And yet Jimmy took first; he won the whole thing!
While Cole thought of ways to
remove Storee's G-string.

With his teeth? With his hands? With
the hook of a candy cane?
He can't wait, for the bulge in his
pants continues to strain.

"ARE YOU COLD?" I ASK Storee as I rest my hand over her thigh while I drive us toward Evergreen Farm. It's only a few minutes' drive, but I want to make sure she's as comfortable as possible.

"No," she says.

"But you shivered," I reply.

"Because you dragged your hand over my upper thigh."

I glance over at her and smirk. "Did I arouse you?"

"Remove that smirk from your face."

"Why?" I ask as I drag my thumb over her denim-clad legs.

"Because I don't think a man with the kind of sex appeal that you have should be in any way encouraged or have his ego inflated. It's bad enough you make me shiver with one touch of your hand, even worse that you're what I've thought about for the last two days—I don't need you knowing it."

"Then why did you just tell me?" I ask as I smirk again at her.

She points in front of us and gruffly says, "Just drive."

I let out a deep rumble of a laugh as I do as I'm told.

After we'd cleaned up our stations, handed out candy canes to the crowd, and then said our goodbyes, I pulled Storee to the side and told her she was coming with me.

She rolled her eyes in front of her sister, whispered something to her, then gave her a hug—followed by a hug for Cindy—and joined me. When we reached my truck and slid into the cab, I pulled her across the bench seat and devoured her mouth for a solid minute before I let us both grab some air.

The only reason I pulled away was because I was worried Taran might see us, as she wasn't too far behind in packing up Cindy into the car.

But now that we're alone and headed to the farm, I have several ideas of what I plan on doing.

Since the drive isn't far, we pull onto the road that leads to Evergreen Farm as I ask, "Are you going to say anything about the competition results?"

"Yes…why didn't you use pineapple like Atlas told you to?"

I roll my eyes. Should have known that was coming.

"I think you know why. From what happened with the pineapple last time, I was playing it safe."

"Safe didn't secure you the win."

"Secured second, which was better than what you got," I counter, but with a smile so she knows I'm only teasing.

344 | MEGHAN QUINN

"If I'd had an assistant like you did, I probably would have secured second."

"You did have an assistant." I squeeze her thigh. "You were just knocked points for it. Which, by the way, I recall you saying something about paying me back later. Well, now is later..."

She chuckles. "Are you really this persistent?"

"Where you're concerned, yes." I drive the truck down the newly paved path that leads right behind the barn, and then I put it in park.

She glances out the window at the green two-tier barn that is outlined in white molding. "This is where you go every day?"

"My second home," I say. "Wait." I hop out of the truck and round the front, then I open her door. When her eyes meet mine and I hold my hand out, I say, "Trying to be a gentleman here."

"After the texts you sent me, you are *now* trying to be a gentleman?"

"A gentleman can hold the door open for you...and slap your fine ass when you beg for it."

STOREE

I pause and watch the glint form in his eyes. "Cole Black...I think you're trouble."

"You would be right about that," he says as he helps me out of his truck. He connects our palms and holds me close as we walk straight up to the barn to a side door.

"Please tell me it's heated in there," I say with a shiver.

He chuckles. "Jesus, you need to grow thicker blood. But yes, it's heated." He holds the door open for me, and I slip in past him just as he smacks me right on the rear end. I gasp and turn to look at him. He smirks. "See, I can be a gentleman and still smack your ass." He places his arm over my shoulders and walks me farther into the barn—the very clean, neat, surprisingly modern barn.

The floor is cement, there doesn't seem to be an ounce of dirt anywhere, and there are structural wooden beams that look like they're from the 1800s holding up the entire building. It's warm, it smells like…hay, and there is the sound of light huffs and snorts coming from some pens in the back.

"This is not what I expected," I say, still taking it all in as I enter the space.

Off to the right is a room with a sign hanging over the door that says OFFICE. Inside is a desk and a simple chair. On top of the desk is a laptop, some neatly stacked paperwork, and a printer.

"Is that where you work?" I ask, pointing to it.

"Yeah, funnily enough, I'm not just brushing reindeer coats all day. There's a lot more that goes into the job. Some admin work that I really hate. Scheduling. Ordering. Things like that."

"Oh, I had no idea. Your hands screamed farm hand, not keyboard master."

He chuckles. "Well, I tend to spend more time out of the office than in, but it's necessary to stop in at least once a day or else I'll fall behind. The Maxheimers have made it simple with the business and all the facets that go into it. We're all in charge of our own little sections, which are small enough that we can handle them on our own and don't get overwhelmed. So for me, I know what I need for the reindeer and I don't have to depend on other people to get it done. Supplies, vet visits, all of that I get to control. And I just report in every Friday to let them know that everything has been handled and any events coming up have been scheduled. Max is the same with the tree farm."

"That makes so much sense—nothing gets left behind."

"Exactly," he says. "But yeah, this is where I hang out every day. I like to keep it clean. Max thinks it's funny how neat I am. I get pissed at him

346 | MEGHAN QUINN

when he traipses into the barn in his muddy farm boots leaving dirt and gunk everywhere. I always have to power wash the floors after."

"Who knew you were so persistent in needing a clean space."

"Well, I have school trips come visit the barn, and I just think it's important to make sure we present ourselves in a professional way at all times."

"I can see that." I walk down the hall, toward the stalls. "Are they back here?"

"They are," he says, following me. "We bring them in at night so they can calm down from the day's events, get comfortable, and find some peace before the next day starts."

"Seems like you care about them a lot."

"We do," he says as he walks up to one of the pens and makes a clicking noise. I hear a grumble and then antlers appear, followed by a large head and wet nose. "This is Colleen, aka Comet. By day, she is one of Santa's favorites. By night, she's Colleen, a rowdy girl who tends to find joy in shoving her snout in my armpit until I scratch behind her ear. Isn't that right, Colleen?" He reaches into the pen and scratches her ear, and by God, it's the cutest thing I think I've ever seen.

A hot man loving on an animal, knowing the animal's personality... I need to fan myself.

"She's beautiful." I reach in and stroke her cheek, fascinated by her wiry coat.

"She is. And this over here, her frenemy, is David, aka Dasher. David is the eater of the group and, if not separated, will eat everyone's food." I glance over into David's pen and notice a rather large reindeer, broad in size though not tubby in the slightest. Just a beefy fella that I would not want to mess with.

"David looks like he gives off a *don't-mess-with-me* vibe."

"He does," Cole says with a chuckle.

He brings me on down the line, introducing me to every reindeer and telling me different stories about them. Petunia once ate his sleeve right off his flannel shirt. Tore it off and had zero regrets. Vincent is the oldest of the group with his white face and goatee. He's the most docile and was here when Cole's parents passed. They spent a lot of time together. Randy is the rowdiest. Beetle—one of the kids named him—doesn't like anything to do with bells, Christmas, or chilly weather, which I think is funny. And so on. But my favorite is Rutabaga. One, for her name, and two, because every time she's let out of her stall, she takes off cantering, does three circles around the corral, and then bows. They don't know why or where she learned it, but she does it and I think that is fun.

"I can tell you love what you do, Cole."

He nods as he leans against one of the poles in the barn. "I do. Sometimes the reindeer can be a pain in my ass, especially when Petunia thinks she can strip me out of my clothes, but I'm grateful for the job and the freedom."

"Petunia needs to know there's a new girl in town," I say as I walk up to him and place my hand on his chest.

He rests his hands on my hips and pulls me in closer. "I'm not sure she's going to like that. She really likes eating my clothes off."

I chuckle and slip my hand up to his neck. "You know, it's kind of disturbing when you say it like that."

He grins and then tilts my chin up only to bring his lips to mine. He pauses, not closing the distance all the way, making me wait, but after a few beats, his mouth descends the rest of the way and I feel myself melting into him.

He lightly moans into my mouth, our tongues matching up, our desire sparking.

His hands grow tight on my hips while I start unbuttoning his flannel shirt, one button at a time, all the way down until I can flap it open, revealing his thick, strong chest.

He groans as I drag my nails across his pecs, feeling slightly unhinged at the possibility of having this man in the reindeer barn. His mouth continues to work mine as he untucks my shirt from my pants and then drags it up my body and over my head. Thank God it's warm in here.

Then to my surprise, he spins me around and pushes me up against the wooden pole, my back against the firm wood. He takes a step back for a moment and runs his hand over his jaw as he takes me all in. It has to be one of the hottest perusals I've ever been witness to.

His eyes wander, looking me up and down, taking in the way my breath is heavy in my chest, the way my breasts rise and fall to my heartbeat. It's intoxicating. And when he grins, I feel a dull throb start to erupt between my legs.

Cole Black knows exactly what he's doing with those dangerous eyes, and I can't get enough of it.

He walks past me, his hand grazing my stomach, and tells me to stay in place as he reaches a hook just a few feet away. I hear the clang of metal and then feel the smooth texture of leather glide down my arm.

Cole's mouth is right next to my ear as he whispers, "I want to tie you up. You okay with that?"

I feel my nipples go hard as he drags the leather over my palms. "Y-yes," I say quietly.

"Does the wood bother your back?" he asks. "Because I plan on fucking you hard, but I don't want you to get hurt."

"It's smooth," I say as he gathers my wrists and brings them around the pole and behind me. The wooden pole, although old and worn, has been covered in a clear coat of varnish, preserving the wood and creating a smooth surface rather than one that could leave splinters.

"Good," he growls as he loops the leather reins around my wrists, keeping me in place.

When he comes back around, he once again slowly takes me in, and I do the same. I'm drawn to the way his opened shirt gives me a glimpse of his abs, his chest, and his impeccable torso. And the strong set of his legs, the V in his hips…the bulge in his pants. The sprinkling of trimmed hair, the sinew clawing under his skin when he moves, and the dark, devilish stare in his eyes as he reaches into his back pocket and pulls out a thick green-and-yellow candy cane. When did he snag that from Jimmy?

He drags the thick candy cane against his tongue and then steps up to me and tests it on my lips before I open my mouth and he moves it over my tongue. A subtle but nice pineapple flavor floods my taste buds before he sticks it back in his mouth. As the candy cane hangs out of his mouth, he reaches for my bra and undoes the front clasp, releasing my breasts. His hands immediately find them. I groan as he squeezes, tweaks, massages in just the right way, driving me to a point where the undeniable need for friction erupts through me.

He releases me with one hand, pops the candy cane out of his mouth, and then drags it over the tip of my nipple right before he bends forward and sucks the pointed nub into his mouth. A hiss escapes me as I surrender to his mouth, his tongue…his teeth.

Yes. This. I want all of this.

He nibbles his way around my breast, marking his territory and teasing me while he brings the candy cane back to my mouth. This time, I suck it past my teeth, hard. His eyes glance up at me as he leans to take in my other nipple. But he pauses to watch me suck on the thick candy cane. He bites the corner of his lip as I continue to suck on it, over and over, until he starts moving it in and out past my lips.

"Do you want to suck my cock like this, Storee?" he asks in a deep, commanding voice.

"Yes," I say.

He removes the candy cane from my mouth, puts it in his, and then undoes his pants and pushes them down to his ankles along with his briefs, letting his length stretch up his stomach as he takes it in his hand and starts slowly, lazily pumping.

"Then suck me off," he says.

I glance down and then back up at him, wondering how this is going to work with my hands still bound behind the pole. Knowing I have one option, I squat down so my ass is touching my heels, and he steps forward, bringing him right up to my mouth.

"Swirl the candy cane around your head," I say.

He pops it out of his mouth and brings it down to his dick, running the sugary substance over his length, around the ridge, and over the tip, coating himself.

"Lick me clean," he mumbles before placing his hand on the back of my head and encouraging me forward.

I bring my tongue to the base of his cock, flatten it, and then slowly drag it upward as I watch for his reaction. The muscles in his neck strain as he shifts his pelvis forward, clearly wanting more, so I continue the sweet torture, licking in the same spot over and over again until he groans out of frustration. That's when I form a point with my tongue and make circles along the tip, loving the taste of pineapple as I do so.

I maintain control despite wanting to take him into the back of my throat. I continue to clean him up, lick every surface, not once, not twice, but three times until the veins in his cock are straining and precum rests at the tip. That's when I open my mouth wide and suck him all the way into the back of my throat, and I swallow.

"Fuck," he says as his hand slaps against the pole behind me. "Shit, Storee."

I do it again, bringing him all the way back, but this time I gag in the best way.

"Fuck, yes. Again," he says as he rubs his thumb over my cheek. "All the way to the back, Storee. Swallow my cock."

I bring him to the back, swallow twice, and then pop him out of my mouth, only to lick him again…and again…and again.

When he grows frustrated, I kiss down his cock to his balls, where

I run my tongue along his seam, causing his cock to twitch. When he doesn't tell me to stop, I open my mouth and suck him past my lips.

"Fuuuuuck," he draws out, his head falling forward as he braces himself against the pole. "Your goddamn mouth, Storee." I can't help but smile as I drag out my return to his cock and take him past my lips. Sucking him hard, squeezing him to the point that he's panting.

"Shit," he mutters. "You have to stop."

But I don't.

That's exactly what I wanted him to say. I open wide and take him all the way back in my throat again, allowing him to gag me, which causes him to slam his fist against the pole before pulling away from me, releasing himself from my mouth.

He stands there, muscles firing off, staring down at me, his cock fucking beautiful as it stretches out in front of him, ready to burst.

And I want him to.

On my tongue.

On my face.

On my chest.

I want him marking me, claiming me.

"Come on me," I say as he slips the candy cane over his lips.

"The only way I want to come is in that sweet pussy of yours," he says as he brings his hand to my chin and guides me back up the pole until I'm fully standing again.

As he steps in closer, I feel his length press against me and I'm inwardly cursing as I want so desperately to grip him.

But before I can ask him to untie me, he brings the candy cane to his mouth, and then undoes my pants, pushing them and my G-string down to my ankles. Rather than leaving them on, he helps me step out of them, along with my shoes.

He then kicks my feet apart so I'm spread for him, and he fingers between my legs, testing me.

He lets out a feral groan as he finds just how wet I am.

"You want this cock, don't you?" he asks while he strokes himself with his other hand.

I nod. "I do."

"You'll get it, but first…" He brings the candy cane down between us and parts me before dragging it along my clit. Everything—the warmth of his mouth from sucking the sugar to the smooth surface—is a new sensation I wasn't expecting.

"Oh God," I say as he passes over my clit a few times before bringing it back up to his mouth and he sucks my taste off the candy cane, keeping eye contact with me the entire time.

"Fucking delicious," he says before bringing the candy cane back to my clit, rubbing it up and down.

Up and down.

And then back to his mouth, letting his tongue roll over the candy cane before bringing it back to my clit one more time.

It's erotic.

It has me reeling.

It has me panting, wanting so much more.

"Stop teasing me," I say.

"Teasing?" he growls as he pops the candy cane in his mouth and then brings his fingers to my clit where he makes small circles, massaging me in just the right spot that my body starts to climb higher in pleasure. "I'm not fucking teasing." He offers me the candy cane and I suck on the tip. "I'm edging you like you fucking edged me."

I let go of the candy cane. "That was *pleasuring.*"

He grins and then brings the candy cane back to my clit, rubs the smooth surface over me a few more times before he sucks on it, a groan falling past his lips.

"You taste so fucking good," he says right before he gets on his knees in front of me, lifts one of my legs over his shoulder, and parts me for his tongue.

My head falls back against the pole as he goes down on me, his tongue running along my sensitive clit, his lips kissing, sucking, his fingers sliding inside of me. He knows exactly how to work me, how to get me to where I need to be. And he's relentless about it, pushing me and pushing me, edging me to the point that I'm about to tip over, but then pulls away and presses small kisses all around where I need him the most.

"Please, Cole," I beg as he starts to slide his fingers inside of me again. "I need...more."

He sucks my clit between his lips in response.

"Oh my God," I shout as my hands tug on the reins. "Oh my God, Cole...oh...oh fuck."

He sucks harder, sending pleasure shooting through me, collecting like a burning flame in the pit of my stomach, churning and ready to explode.

"Yes...yes," I say, my body tensing. "Right there. Oh my God, you're so good."

I bite my lip, wishing I could force him to stay where he is, to get me off.

And just as the burning pleasure deep within me starts to erupt, he pulls away from my clit, stands, and then positions his rock-hard cock at my entrance. I have no time to protest the absence of his mouth because he fills me, looping my leg around his waist and thrusting into me with such force that I swear I can feel him all the way against my kidney.

"Can't get enough," he says, his hips forcefully rocking against me. "Squeeze my cock, Storee."

Unable to hold on to him, I use my leg as an anchor and when he thrusts inside of me, I clench around him.

The first time, he groans so loudly that I fear the entire farm might hear him.

The second time, he bites down on the base of my neck.

The third time turns him into a frenzied man as his hands fall to my ass, propping me up more and driving frantically into me.

Pounding into me.

Rocking.

Twisting.

Fucking with so much force that it creates an unbelievable friction against my clit.

And then he starts moving me up and down as well, and that's when he hits me in a spot I've only ever felt with him.

"Oh fuck," I yell as pleasure sparks through me.

He does it again, making my entire body break out into chills.

One more time and I'm seeing stars.

Then he bites down on my shoulder with one more thrust, sending me right over the edge, and together we come, my pussy contracting around his cock, his body stiffening as he groans against me, filling me with his cum.

"Jesus fuck," he mutters against my shoulder and then pulls away just enough to look at me. When our eyes meet, he offers me a smirk before pressing a kiss to my lips.

Then he gently pulls out and sets my feet back on the ground. He places his cock back in his briefs and pulls his jeans up before buttoning them back up. And then to my surprise, he squats in front of me and with the candy cane—how on earth did he hold on to that the whole time?—he scoops up his cum from near my pussy and brings the candy cane up to my mouth.

I look him in the eyes, then down at the candy cane, and when I part my lips, his eyes go feral as I lick him off the candy cane.

When he pulls the candy cane out of my mouth, he drops it to the ground, scoops his hand behind my head, and kisses me so hard that I feel it all the way down to my toes.

COLE

I'm overwhelmed.

Really fucking overwhelmed because I like her.

I like her a lot.

And because I like her so much, fear is pulsing through me. What's going to happen when she decides to leave? I don't want to lose this, lose her, when I'm feeling this way, like...like she's brought the life back into me after so many years of listlessness.

Like she's brought me back home.

Like I can enjoy the things around me without the heavy cloud of grief engulfing me.

Like I can *enjoy* the Christmas season.

Like I have new air to breathe.

And it's terrifying.

"You've gone quiet," Storee says as she presses her cheek against my bare chest.

"Just thinking."

After I released her from the pole, we got into my truck and drove back to town. I parked around the corner behind Prancer's Libations, but instead of going to the bar, we snuck through the alleyway, through some trees, and straight to my backyard where we entered through the kitchen door, ensuring neither Taran nor Cindy would be the wiser. I would have stayed in the barn, but I wanted something more peaceful and soft with her after what we did against that pole—a pole I'll never look at in the same way anymore.

So we made some peanut butter and jelly sandwiches, ate them while sitting on the kitchen counter, and then went up to my room where I slowly peeled off her clothes and moved her over to my bed, running my lips and tongue over every inch of her body until she was panting, begging for me. I languidly fucked her, taking it slow, feeling every second of pleasure roll through the both of us.

"What are you thinking about?" Storee asks, bringing me back to the moment as she draws small circles over my skin.

"You," I answer as I kiss her forehead.

"Good things or bad things?"

"Good things." It's a bit of a lie, but the last thing I need to do is have a needy conversation about where this is all going.

"Oh yeah?" she asks as I caress her ass, loving how goddamn round it is, how it's more than just a handful. "Tell me more."

I smirk and kiss the top of her head. "I don't think I need to inflate your ego any more than it already is. Hell, you already know that you can make me black out with one squeeze of that tight cunt."

She chuckles. "Oh, the power I have."

"Yeah." I blow out a heavy breath. "Some real strong power, that's for damn sure."

She chuckles and kisses the underside of my jaw. "Do you think we should have made more of an appearance out in town so people could see us?"

"Nah," I say as my hand glides over her hip and then back to her ass. "I think they could tell we were headed out tonight. Not to mention I probably would have been all over you if we were in public, which I'm not sure screams Christmas spirit."

"Feeling someone up in public sure as hell gives me the holly jollies."

I let out a low laugh. "Yes, but it's also a G-rated town. We'd be docked points in our Kringle endeavor."

"Ooo, we can't have that, especially since we're so close in the competition standings. A three-point difference. I double-checked with Bob Krampus before we left for the barn."

"How does Taran feel about that?" I ask.

"Well, this is the first time I've been allowed out of the house except for coffee runs in two days, so you tell me how she feels about the competition."

I chuckle some more. "Who knew she was going to be so involved?"

"I didn't. I think she and Aunt Cindy had some sort of secret meeting when they went to Golden, because ever since they've come back, it's like they've kicked it into overdrive. Or at least Taran has. I'm sure if I checked my phone, there'd be a ton of text messages from her asking where I am."

"What are you going to tell her when you get back to the house?"

"I was thinking about this," she says as she lifts up on her elbow to stare down at me. The smirk on her lips is fucking sexy, and the way her unkempt hair is tossed to the side reminds me just how much I ran my hands through it only a few moments ago. "How about...you got a flat back at the farm, and because you're stupid and an idiot, you didn't have a spare tire. So then we had to wait for someone to help us, but because the only mechanic that could come was returning from helping someone out in the mountains, it was going to take some time."

"Stupid and an idiot?" I ask, raising one brow.

She chuckles. "Playing the game here. I have to convince her that I want nothing to do with you. Stupid and an idiot would be terms I use."

"Okay, but just so we're on the same page, I don't think the man who just made you come so hard that you shattered beneath him is stupid or an idiot."

Her fingers dance over my chest hair. "No, that man is magic."

"Magic, huh?" I say as I drag her on top of me.

"Mm-hmm," she says as she moves her fingers over my beard. "God, who knew this was where my trip to Kringle was going to take me. I thought I'd be freezing and helping clean an elderly woman's crevices."

"Uh, okay. Don't use that term again."

She lets out a boisterous laugh.

"Seriously though, I love that we reconnected. Don't you?"

I shift her and say, "My dick gets hard whenever you're around, so *you tell me.*"

She chuckles and moves to the side, gripping my once-again hardening cock in her hand. "God, it's as if you haven't had sex in a long time and you're trying to reach your quota for the year."

I shake my head. "No, I haven't had good sex with the right person, and now that I have, I don't want that to change."

Her smile turns sultry as she slowly runs her hand over my length. "I don't want it to change either," she says. "I've had so much fun with you, Cole."

"I've had fun with you too," I say as she continues to stroke me.

"And we're going to have to continue to be creative about seeing each other."

"We will," I say as I feel my body melt into the mattress from the feel of her hand. When she lifts up and straddles my legs, I take in her whole body—from her full breasts to her curvy hips and her pointed nipples—and I know without a doubt that no one will ever be better than her. "Or," I say as she sits up on her knees and poises my cock at her entrance, "we tell Taran the truth."

Storee pauses, her eyes meeting mine.

"Tell her the truth?" she says, not letting me enter her as she looks to me for answers. "I don't think that's a good idea."

I want inside of her.

I fucking need to feel her warmth, but it doesn't stop me from asking, "Why not?"

"Because...I just think we should wait."

"Wait until when?"

"Until the competition is over," she says.

"Why? What does it matter?"

She glides the tip of my cock over her wet clit, and I nearly choke on my own saliva.

"Because I don't want Taran ruining this, and I don't want anything to distract us from what we have. One thing at a time," she says as she slowly lowers so I enter her.

Hell, what did she say?

I can't process.

Not when she's letting me inside her...bare.

Since she's on birth control, we're both comfortable with not using condoms, and this is easily the best fucking feeling I've ever experienced. I swear her pussy was made for me.

"You're so goddamn perfect," I say, forgetting the conversation and focusing on what she's doing. "Jesus Christ, nothing feels better."

"I love how you fill me up, Cole," she says as she lowers herself all the way down and then pauses, taking a few deep breaths. "Your cock is amazing." She starts shifting her hips, taking charge as I lie there and stare up at her face and the way she pulls on the corner of her lip. The awe in her eyes. The desperation in her breathing as her pace picks up. "It shouldn't be this good."

"It fucking should," I say as she moves faster, and my eyes narrow on her breasts that are bouncing, begging me to touch, but I don't. I lace my hands together behind my head and let her use me.

Her hands fall to my pecs, her fingers clawing at my skin, her head falling forward, and her stomach hollowing as she seeks out her own pleasure.

It's fucking sexy.

Hot.

Delicious.

Watching her rock over me, feel the friction she needs to come all from my cock, from my body. I love it. I fucking love it so much.

"Fuck my cock, Storee," I say, my hands itching to touch her.

"God," she moans, her body propped up now as she repositions herself, her hands falling behind her, her back arching.

And what a fucking view.

"Jesus," I mutter, my eyes fixed on our connection. I can see her wetness glisten. I can practically taste her arousal on my tongue. Her pretty pink clit is on full display as she rocks her hips forward.

"Oh God…oh fuck," she says as she lifts and slams back down, causing my eyes to roll in the back of my head.

"Mother…fucker," I grind out, because I know when she slammed back down, she clenched. There's not a doubt in my—"Fuck!" I yell when she does it again, making me feel like she's slamming my cock through the tightest fucking hole. "Jesus, Storee."

She does it again.

And again.

And again, until I'm fucking heaving, my balls tightening, my legs numb…

"I'm there, Storee. Fuck, I'm right…ahhhh, Jesus *fuck*!" I yell as she lets out a feral moan, her pussy contracting around me, her body convulsing, sending me right over the edge as I come hard inside her.

Her body falls forward, her head to my chest, and I wrap my arms around her, holding her in place.

A few moments later, she lifts her head just enough so I can see those heady eyes. She grins and whispers, "I love your cock so much."

I chuckle. "I could tell."

And then I carry her to the bathroom where I help her clean up and then clean up myself. After a few seconds of silence, she finds her clothes and starts putting them on.

"Don't like what you're doing," I say as I slip on my briefs and then lean against the wall, watching her snap the front clasp of her bra together.

"I know," she answers. "But Taran's going to start freaking out."

I let out a disgruntled sigh. "What are you doing tomorrow?"

"Probably practicing choreography."

"Choreography?" I ask with a raised brow.

"For the Christmas caroling portion of the competition," she answers as she finishes putting on her shirt.

"I know, but you're going to have choreography?"

"And you're not?" she asks. "That seems like a mistake. Does Max know you're not going to have choreography?"

"Yeah," I answer. "He's planned out this entire performance."

"And there's no choreography?"

I shake my head. "No, we're going to kind of wing it like we did for the Upcycle Christmas."

"That seems dangerous, although probably better for me if you're not prepared." She smirks and walks up to me, pressing a kiss on my cheek before heading down the stairs away from my bedroom. I follow her.

"I don't think they're going to be looking for a whole choreographed routine. I think it's more about the caroling."

"Well, I can't sing to save my life, so it's going to have to be about the choreography."

"Are you nervous?" I ask as we make it down another flight of stairs to the main level. "You know, after everything that happened last time you were in Kringle?"

"Yes," she says. "Terrified, actually. I've been dreading this section. At least with the others, I could hide behind the task, produce something to be judged. But this…this is sort of all on me. I'm being judged, and I don't like that. Makes me extremely uncomfortable."

"I can understand that." I pull her hips toward me and kiss the top of her head. "What song are you singing?"

"Not going to tell you," she playfully answers. "I might be obsessed with your penis, but I'm not about to give you the secrets of my plans to win the Town Kringle."

"I don't need insight to win," I respond. "I'm going to win either way, with intel or without. My merit alone will take the crown."

"Oh my God," she mutters as she moves away from me and heads to the back of the kitchen. "Could you sound any more ridiculous?"

"I could," I say. "Want me to try?"

"No." She slips her boots on and then her jacket and turns toward me. I pull her in close. "Thank you for coming out with me tonight."

"Thank *you* for showing me a different way to enjoy a candy cane." I let out a low laugh. "Any time."

I lift her chin and press a kiss to her lips, keeping it light or else I'll want more from her.

"I would walk you to your house, but I'm pretty sure Taran wouldn't appreciate seeing me in my briefs and boots."

"I mean, I wouldn't mind it," she replies. "But yeah, Taran might find issue with the getup." She kisses me one more time. "I'll text you, okay?"

"Okay," I say and then reluctantly let her leave. I close the door behind her and then lean against the counter for a few seconds contemplating what the hell is going on with my life.

I push off the counter and find my phone, only to see a few texts from Max.

Max: Dude, what the hell did you do in that barn? I had to grab something from the shed and heard extreme moaning. And yes, I mean extreme!

Max: Can you please let me know you're at least alive?

Chuckling, I call him. He answers on the first ring.

"Cole, is that you?"

"Don't be a fucking idiot," I say as I move into the living room where my Christmas tree is lit up.

"Excuse me for caring about your well-being. From the noises I heard, I was genuinely concerned someone was dying. Oh shit, wait. Did you kill her?"

"No," I groan. "No one died."

"Are you sure?"

"Positive. I just said bye to her, actually. She's headed back to her house from mine."

"You went from the barn to your house? What kind of stamina do you have?"

I laugh. "With her...a lot."

"Clearly."

I drag my hand over my face and say what's been on my mind. "I feel like this is what we should have been doing this entire time."

"Scaring people into thinking you're one thrust away from croaking?"

"No," I say in exasperation. "Being with her. It feels so right, Max. Like she was supposed to be mine all along. All those times we sat on the porch together and talked about mindless things, it's all led to this point, and I just wish back then I'd had the balls to tell her I liked her."

"Have you told her now?"

"Yes," I say. "I tell her all the time because I want her to know that if she's willing, I want to keep this going, to let it be more than a Christmas fling."

"Is that what she thinks it is?"

"I don't know," I say. "I mean, it doesn't seem like it."

"Yeah..."

He's silent, which is concerning. "What are you not saying, Max?"

"Nothing, don't worry about me."

"I am fucking worried, so just say it."

He sighs. "Dude, what if this is something else?" I can hear the trepidation in his voice.

"What do you mean?"

"Okay, hear me out. I'm not saying this is what she's doing, but what if, hell, I don't know, what if she's using you, getting in your head so she can win this competition?"

"No," I say with a firm shake of my head even though he can't see me. "She wouldn't do that."

"Are you sure? And I don't like being that guy, so don't fucking hate me, but didn't all this just happen overnight? What if this is part of the plan?"

"Do you really think that little of her? Think that she'd be someone who played with another human's feelings in order to win a stupid town competition?"

"I know, dude. I hate even thinking it, but I'm just...well, I'm protective of you, and I want to make sure that you're okay, you know? I don't want anyone fucking with you."

"I get it, man, and I appreciate it. But trust me when I say she's not doing that. That she wouldn't do that."

"Okay. Good. And I'm sorry."

"Don't apologize—I appreciate you looking out for me."

"It's my duty. You're my little Snow Daddy nugget. I have to make sure you're always taken care of."

"Don't fucking call me that," I snap.

"It's cute that you think I'll stop. Now"—he pauses and then adds—"let's talk about the candy cane and how we should have done pineapple."

"I'm hanging up."

"Hold on." He pauses again. "Just for the record, since I don't think it's sunk in...I told you so."

"Goodbye," I shout and then hang up the phone.

I then shoot a text over to Storee.

Cole: Get home okay?

Thankfully she texts back right away.

Storee: Yes, and the entire walk back, I swear I could still feel you inside of me.

Jesus Christ.

I drag my hand over my mouth, my smile impossible to hide.

Yup, she has captured me, mind, body—and dick.

CHAPTER TWENTY-SIX
COLE

And now it was time for what
Storee dreaded most of all,
to perform on the stage in front
of the small and the tall.

With eyes staring at her, the Christmas bells will ring,
and she will have to sing and sing and sing, sing, sing.

The more she thought about it,
the more she grew sick.
"I must stop this at once, and I must do it quick."

"SHOULD WE PRACTICE ONE MORE time?" Max asks, staring up at me from the couch.

"No," I answer. "I think we're ready. Plus, I don't want to wear out my voice."

"Smart." Max taps the side of his head and packs up his guitar. "Before we head to the Caroling Café, I want to run something by you."

"What?"

When he finishes packing up his guitar, he sets it to the side, scoops up his duffel bag and looks at me. "I got us outfits."

"Jesus," I mutter. "Dude, I'm not going up there in fucking lederhosen again."

"It's not lederhosen." He reaches into the bag and pulls out two buffalo plaid shirts. One is red and green. The other is red, green, and white.

"What's the catch?" I ask, staring at the normal shirts.

"No catch. I think it would be nice if we matched up there. But there's one more thing."

"What is it?"

He lets out a deep sigh, reaches into his bag, and pulls out a picture frame. He doesn't show me what's inside. Instead, he says, "Before you say no, I don't want you to think this is for anything or anyone but you."

He turns the frame around. It's displaying a picture of my parents and me in front of Evergreen Farm when I was maybe ten. We're all wearing matching flannel shirts like the ones Max purchased.

"Shit," I mutter as I grab the picture and take it all in. Mom's holding my hand, and Dad has one hand on my shoulder while his other arm is around Mom. Mom's wearing a Santa hat while Dad sports a silly white beard. I have a jingle bell around my neck and am wearing a huge smile.

"I think it would be a nice tribute," he says, pulling out a Santa hat, white beard...and jingle bell necklace. "I'll wear the beard, man. You can wear the hat and the necklace."

My eyes never leave the photo. "Mom was so sick the night before we took this picture. She had food poisoning, and Dad was trying to convince her that we could push getting a tree to another day, but she wouldn't allow it. She knew how excited I was, so she put on a smile and made it through the day. I didn't know until years later that she wasn't feeling good."

"She was a really good mom." Max places his hand on my shoulder. "She wore that Santa hat almost year-round."

I chuckle. "The only reason she could was because we lived here. I think people would have thought she was crazy anywhere else."

"Probably." He squeezes my shoulder. "So, what do you say? You up for it? If not, then we can stick to what we're wearing right now—"

"No, I want to do it." I want to do this for them. I've pushed away these memories, my Christmas traditions, for so long that this...this feels right. This feels like something I *need* to do in order to preserve their memory, to have them with me on this new chapter in my life. I turn to my friend. "Thank you for this. I didn't even consider a tribute, but...but I think I'm ready for this."

"I think you are too. Look how far you've come." He gestures to the living room. "I never thought you'd get to this point, but here you are celebrating Christmas, involved in the town, and opening yourself up to another person. I'm proud of you."

"Thanks, man," I say as we both stand, and I take the red, green, and white plaid from him and strip out of my current shirt.

"Holy shit," he says, his eyes falling to my chest. "Dude, what the hell happened—" He pauses, and his expression changes from shocked to knowing in a matter of seconds. "Are those hickeys and scratches from Storee?"

I push my arms through the sleeves and start buttoning up the shirt. "Yeah."

"Yeah? You're just going to answer that so casually? Dude, you look like a leopard under there."

I roll my eyes. "It's not that extreme."

"Cole, that is a lot of marks."

Smirking, I make eye contact with my friend. "You should see her."

"I don't even want to know," he says as he changes into his shirt as well. "I'm starting to get jealous, and I don't need to feel jealous about your sex life."

"Why not?" I finish buttoning the top of my shirt and then put on the jingle bell necklace.

"Because I have enough going on with this Kringle competition. I don't need to be wishing I had a sex life to go with it. Someone has to be the backbone of this operation, and clearly that person is not you since your head has been in the clouds."

"Can you blame me?" I ask.

He shakes his head. "I actually can't. I'm more than willing to be the backbone because I can see my friend returning, and that's what matters to me most."

"Max, you getting emotional on me?"

"I mean, I'm not crying if that's what you're leading to."

"I don't know. I think I can see a tear."

"There are no tears, and even if there were, I'd embrace it. Hell, want me to squeeze one out right now? Give me a second." He comically attempts to bulge his eye out of its socket and force himself to cry.

"Can you not do that? It's creepy as fuck."

"You're the one who wants to see tears." He gets in a squatting position now, hands on his legs, his ass jutted out, his face straining. "I'm going to give you tears."

"Jesus Christ." I swat at him. "Stop that. You're going to burst something."

"Yeah, burst into tears," he says, still straining.

"Stop it." I push at his face and force him back on the couch. "I don't need you tearing up. Lord knows you'll cry enough when we're performing later."

"Can you blame me?" he says. "What we have planned is going to knock the apron and hairnet right off crotchety old Karen back on the grill. And the town votes on these performances. The town knows you, so this is in the bag." I shrug, and I can tell he's not happy with that response because he says, "What the hell happened to you? Where's the competitive spirit? When you started this competition, you were ready to wield a candy cane like a sword and stab anyone who came near you. Now you're...you're soft."

"I still want to win, but, yeah, maybe I've softened. Maybe it isn't about the competition as much as doing something I would never have thought to do a few months ago. Maybe it's about growth. Maybe it's about coming out of my shell and letting myself live again. Enjoy the season…and honor my parents."

Max slowly nods. "I couldn't agree more." He pauses and places his hand on my shoulder again. "But we should win while accomplishing all those other things."

I chuckle and place the Santa hat on my head while Max straps on his beard. "Yes…we should win while accomplishing all those things."

"Atta boy." Max slaps me on the back. "Now let's go blow this competition wide open."

STOREE

"I'm going to puke," I say to Taran as I clasp my shaky hands together. "I can't do this."

"Stop that," Taran whispers in my ear. "It's all in your head. Nothing will happen other than you rocking this competition, and doing it with pizzazz."

"I don't feel very pizzazz-y right now," I mutter back as I glance up at the Caroling Café stage where Beatrice Pedigree is currently singing "Little Drummer Boy" like Angela from *The Office*. I don't think she planned on doing a spoof from the popular Christmas episode—I just think this was the approach she took with her performance. It's stiff, people are bored, and I worry she might get booed.

"Do you need me to show you the video of the routine again?" she asks, pulling out her phone.

"For the love of God, no. That makes it worse," I say. "We need to find a way out of this. Like...pull a fire alarm, shout 'rat,' or even faint. Maybe I should faint. How do we feel about fainting?"

"You're not going to faint. You're not pulling a fire alarm. And you're not shouting 'rat.' You will get up on that stage and perform the routine like we practiced."

"But, Taran—"

"What's going on, dears?" Aunt Cindy says from her seat beside us. For public appearances, she's moved from a wheelchair to a walker, which we put green-and-red tennis balls on and then decked out the rest to show her Christmas spirit.

"Storee is feeling nervous and pukey," Taran says. "And she's trying to sabotage the whole competition by fainting or screaming 'rat.' I'm trying to reassure her that she's fine."

"You're not the one who embarrassed herself ten years ago and knocked an ornery woman into the river."

"That was ten years ago," Taran says. "And she was fine, just wet."

"Not to mention," Aunt Cindy says, "you did the Judy Garland rendition so well."

"That was different," I say. "I was still nervous, but I just had to sit there and look out a window while mouthing lyrics. This routine has me moving all around...and singing."

"Yes, but we practiced," Taran says. "Now just watch on my phone one more time, and everything should be—"

"Ready to lose?" Cole says as he comes up behind us.

I turn around to catch a smirk cross his lips.

"Get out of here, you pariah," Taran says. "We don't need you over here messing with Storee. She's already flustered."

"You're flustered?" he asks, and I can see the concern in his eyes.

"No," I say, crossing my arms, trying to play the part. "Taran is just saying that so you think you can win this when in reality you don't have a routine half as good as mine."

"That's the spirit." Taran fist-pumps the air. "You tell him."

Okay, Taran, bring it down a notch.

"I'm sure it will be great," Cole says in a sarcastic tone that I know he doesn't mean. "But I need to pull you to the side for a moment. Tanya wants to say hi to the new couple. We must give the people what they want."

Taran rolls her eyes. "This whole farce you have going is completely ridiculous, and there's no merit to it."

"The reason you're in first right now is because I put you girls on the map with this idea."

"Oh, please," Taran says. "We're in first because we're the better team." She shoos at him with her hand. "Now hurry along. I need to get my Kringle-ee mentally prepared."

Cole grabs my hand and brings me to a secluded corner of the café, away from the ruckus and near the bathrooms. I glance around. "Where's Tanya?"

I can barely get the sentence out before his lips are on mine. My hand floats up the soft flannel of his shirt as he pulls me in tighter, his mouth opening just barely.

This is exactly what I needed. This kiss. This moment of ease.

Him.

His comfort and reassurance.

When I pull away, I glance up at his beautiful eyes. "Thank you."

"Feeling better?"

"A little," I say.

"Don't be flustered or nervous, okay? It can't get worse than Beatrice up there."

I chuckle and nod. "I think she's scaring the children."

"I saw a mom block her child's eyes."

I laugh a little more and lean into him so he can wrap his arms around me and pull me into a hug. His hand soothingly rubs over my back for a few seconds before I pull away again out of fear that Taran might come searching for me.

"You going to be okay?" he asks.

"I think so." I let out a deep breath. "I just want this to be over."

"It will be soon." He tugs on my coat. "What do you have hiding under there?"

"Nothing." I hold my coat tighter together.

"You're hiding something. What are you hiding?" He tries to unzip my parka, but I don't let him.

"You'll see."

His brows raise. "Uh…what do you plan on doing, Storee? If it's flashing everyone, I do not approve."

I chuckle. "I'm not going to flash people."

"Storee!" Taran calls. "We're up."

"Got to go." I quickly offer him one more kiss, then take off, that moment with him giving me the slightest bit of confidence as I head up toward the stage.

I try to focus on the decorations of the Caroling Café and not the people. Just like a Broadway diner, booths fill the restaurant, offering people an unobstructed view of the stage. The walls are decorated with a hunter-green plaid wallpaper while wreath chandeliers hang from the ceiling. Each booth has a gold table with green leather seats, Christmas tree salt and pepper shakers, and Christmas-themed tableware, from reindeer mugs to Christmas china and gold silverware. It resembles Christmas Eve dinner at the grandparents' but with a selection of classic diner food tailored to the season.

"You ready?" Taran asks as she joins me onstage, along with Aunt Cindy who is clutching her walker and looking more excited than I've ever seen her.

"Ready," I say, and together we all remove our jackets, revealing our Santa Claus outfits…well…naughty-ish Santa Claus outfits—and yes, that includes Aunt Cindy. The rules state we can have backup dancers, but I must be the one singing, so…we took full advantage.

I spot Cole in the crowd and see the lift of his brows as he takes in my high black boots, red skirt trimmed with fur, and long-sleeved red bodysuit. Taran tosses me a Santa hat. I secure it on, adjust the black belt around my waist, and then grab the mic, my heart racing.

Taran and Aunt Cindy come up next to me, wearing versions of my outfit. Aunt Cindy is in red silk loungewear, and Taran wears a red romper with white fur trim.

The music thrums through the speakers. I swallow hard and start singing "Jingle Bell Rock" while performing the same dance from *Mean Girls*.

My voice is shaky at first, my moves a little stiff, but once the café starts to realize what we're doing, the cheers erupt, clapping occurs, and I start relaxing as I continue to dance and sing, hitting my every mark.

I catch Cole in the crowd a few times. His enthusiastic smile spurs me on. I flow with the music. I swing my hips. I add some facial expressions. I even add a little hip pop here and there, and all the while, Taran and Aunt Cindy are my backup dancers—Aunt Cindy with her walker bopping around and Taran with her comedic timing of "messing up" the moves just like Gretchen in the movie.

On the last note, we all pose, and the café erupts with cheers, filling me with so much joy that I could actually cry.

I put the mic back on its stand, and then together we help Aunt Cindy off the stage and toward the back, where Jimmy is waiting to go on next.

"Oh my God, you nailed it," Taran says, pulling me into a hug, something completely out of the ordinary for her. We don't hug. We barely high-five. We're not that kind of touchy-feely sisters, but look at her hugging me…actually hugging me. Mom and Dad would probably faint in shock. "I'm so proud of you."

She's…she's proud of me?

Huh, that's also new.

"Thanks, Taran," I say, feeling my cheeks go red.

"Well done, girls," Aunt Cindy says as she takes a seat in one of the chairs to the right of the stage, her bedecked walker in front of her. "If that doesn't take first place, I don't know what will."

Jimmy is introduced onstage, and instead of grabbing the mic, he plugs his electric guitar into an amp and places one foot on top. With just a few strokes, he starts to fill the room with "Carol of the Bells."

Huh, who knew Jimmy had it in him?

"I see you pulled out all the stops," Cole says as he comes up next to us. To my surprise, he tips my chin up and places a chaste kiss on my lips. When we pull away, I can feel Taran's eyes like lasers on me. "Not going to be good enough, though."

"Can you not touch her, please?" Taran says. "We don't need you tarnishing the talent."

"Yeah, we don't need you tarnishing the talent," I say with a hair flip.

"The town expects me to congratulate my girl on a job well done, so I'm just playing the part for the fans. Should we kiss again?"

"Spare me," I say with an eye roll, trying to hold back my smirk from the slight shock in his eyes.

"Please spare us all," Taran adds. "Also, you're ruining our vibe over here. We were celebrating, and now you're suffocating us."

"It's all about keeping up appearances, Taran. Although I guess you don't know what that means, given your light display."

Oh.

Shit.

I glance over at Taran, and her once-jovial expression has morphed into that of a woman ready to split a man's skull in two with her bare hands. I understand what he's doing, especially since he's attempting to keep our secret…well, a secret, but disparaging Taran's light display? *No, Cole…no.*

"How…dare…you," Taran seethes as the music in the background starts to build, the crescendo of the song blasting through the speakers. "I will have you know I like to take my time, not just throw up some generic decor I saw in a magazine."

"You might want to throw *something* up. Christmas afternoon is when the Christmas Kringle is announced, and you have until midnight on Christmas Eve to get it all together. In case you forgot."

"Why don't you just worry about yourself and stop creeping on my sister?"

"Okay, why don't we just move ourselves to the side?" I say as Jimmy finishes and the crowd cheers. It seems pretty loud, so maybe they were impressed. I honestly couldn't tell you if he was good or not because I was a bit distracted.

Atlas approaches us. "Okay, I got a projector for us." He takes in the group's tension and places his hands on his hips. "Did I miss something?"

"Nothing at all." Cole turns to me. "Aren't you going to tell me to break a leg, babe? Maybe a good luck kiss?"

"See?" Taran points at him. "Pariah."

"Okay, Taran," I mutter. Turning toward Cole, I say, "Break a leg."

"Uh...the kiss?"

I make a dramatic sigh for Taran, then inwardly squeal as I stand on my toes and press a chaste kiss to his lips.

He smiles back at me and goes up onstage with Atlas, who's wearing a Santa beard for God knows what reason.

They're the last act to go since Ursula went first. She performed a rendition of "The Twelve Days of Christmas" which wasn't too bad. It would have been better if she hadn't messed up the lyrics, saying "four French hens" and "three turtle doves." But hey, we all get messed up with that song every once in a while. It would have been even better if she hadn't done it while performing as a ventriloquist.

Or if her puppet's arm hadn't fallen off at the end...

I think it will be a battle for last between Ursula and her armless puppet...and the stiff-as-a-charcuterie-board-lacking-in-cheese Beatrice.

The café crowd turns quiet while both Atlas and Cole take a seat on stools brought out onto the stage. The lights dim down, not too dark but just dark enough to see the projection on the screen behind them, and when it focuses, my heart swells in my chest. Because I remember that boy on the screen. Cole in matching plaid flannels with his parents. His mom wearing a Santa hat, and his dad in a Santa beard. Atlas and Cole are wearing the same thing, bringing the picture to life, but in a different way.

Then Atlas strums the guitar, Cole brings the mic up to his mouth, and in a deep, rich timbre, he starts singing "Blue Christmas."

My hand immediately goes to my chest as his eyes shut, the lyrics conveying the pain of missing his parents during Christmas. Atlas plays the guitar subtly in the background, and Cole's voice takes the lead as the café is enamored by the performance.

"Oh my God," I say softly, staring up at them. Cole's past, matched with his present. Atlas filling in the role of his family, matching the traditions Cole once shared with his family.

Tears well in my eyes, and I attempt to tell myself not to get too emotional, not to get caught up in the beautiful moment onstage because I can feel Taran watching me, but I can't help it.

His voice is beautiful.

The gesture is heartwarming.

The meaning behind it all, a son singing to his late parents, has me in a bucket of emotions.

And when the song ends, Atlas finishing on a soft strum, Cole looks up and wipes his eye as Atlas pulls him into a hug and they share a moment up on the stage, the café crowd cheering for the both of them.

"That was...beautiful," Aunt Cindy says as she wipes her eyes. "Just beautiful."

Thank God she's crying, because that gives me the right to do the same.

I wipe at my eyes as they walk offstage, and when Cole meets my gaze, I can see the water in his eyes—the need for comfort—but I fear if I run up and hug him, it will send Taran into a tailspin, so I keep my distance as they walk up to us. Though Aunt Cindy grabs him by the hand.

"That was so touching, Cole."

He smiles down at Aunt Cindy. "Thank you." He sniffs and then walks off to the side with Atlas where they hug each other one more time. Dammit, I want to be the person who's hugging him. Who's celebrating him. Who's sharing this moment with him. Mourning with him.

"Damn, that was good," Taran says and then looks me in the eyes. "Are you crying?"

"Just a little," I say and wipe at my eyes. "We knew his parents and him back then. It just…I don't know, it made me sad for him."

"Don't feel sad for him. He's going to take first."

"You think?"

Taran nods. "Yes, I do. We'll be lucky if we get second."

"Lucky?" I ask. "I thought we would for sure get second at least. This is a caroling competition. Jimmy didn't even sing."

"Playing an instrument is allowed. I saw women throw their napkins up on the stage when he was playing. Remember, the people vote, and he showed chest hair, so he'll take second. Now I just need to do the calculations."

Taran disappears while Bob Krampus goes up on the stage, taking the mic in one hand.

"What a wonderful set of performances, some of the best I've seen since being the emcee of the Kringle competition. I hope you've been taking notes, because now it's time to enter your vote into the system. Please pull out your phones and scan the QR code on the table to place your vote. Please note you're accepting all terms and conditions when voting and will need a valid email address that will be shared with Kringletown tourism when entered."

I chuckle because, man, do they have it down with this whole Kringle competition and maximizing every facet of it to grow the town.

"We'll give you about a minute to enter your votes. Meanwhile, can we please get our Kringle-ees up on the stage?"

I feel a hand grab mine, and just as I look up, Cole pulls me toward the stage so we're the first ones on. A bunch of hooting and hollering is coming from the back where Tanya, Martha, and Mae are sitting. Bob Krampus gives us a gentle nod, and Cole wraps his arm around my shoulders as we stand side by side, Jimmy, Ursula, and Beatrice falling in behind.

I whisper, "Your performance was beautiful, Cole."

"Thank you," he whispers back just as Bob Krampus clears his throat.

"Okay, I believe the results are in. Karen, could you please bring them up to me?"

Karen, in her hairnet and apron, walks up onto the stage and hands Bob a piece of paper. I don't know what system they used to tally the votes, but I'm impressed with how fast it worked.

Bob scans over the results like he always does and then looks out to the crowd. "Well, what a close competition, but we have a clear winner. Starting with fifth place, we have Ursula Kronk with 'The Twelve Days of Christmas.'" The crowd claps, and Ursula takes a bow with her puppet.

I'm not surprised about her last-place position. The arm falling off was a real nightmare. Pair that with the look on her face as she tried to keep her mouth as still as possible...and, well, it was a fail all around.

"Coming in fourth, we have Dr. Beatrice Pedigree with her interpretation of 'Little Drummer Boy.'"

Cole squeezes my shoulder, and I know he's happy for me, given how worried I was.

"And our third-place winner..." Bob looks surprised. "Was not expecting this, but Storee Taylor with 'Jingle Bell Rock.'"

Dammit.

I thought I was a guaranteed second after the way the crowd reacted, but it seems like I was overlooked for Jimmy Short's guitar.

"Good job," Cole whispers before Bob continues.

"And in second, we have...Jimmy Short! Making our very own Cole Black our first-place winner with his beautiful tribute to his late parents."

Everyone cheers.

I clap.

Cole stands there with pride, his hands in his pockets, smiling to the crowd and looking quite...shy. I can't stop clapping and cheering as loudly as I can. This man is absolutely incredible. That took true bravery.

"And we have a new leader," Bob says into the mic. "Taking over first place with sixty-two points is Cole Black. Trailing five points behind is Storee Taylor. Coming in third is Jimmy Short with forty-eight points. Fourth we have Ursula with forty, and in last is Beatrice with thirty-three points. We have one competition left, the Super Santa Speed Round, which will take place Christmas Eve eve, followed by the check-up on the light displays on Christmas Eve. And then the announcement of the Kringle winner will be on Christmas Day out at Ornament Park. I hope to see you all there."

He turns off the mic and heads off the stage where he walks around the café, taking pictures with people.

"Did you hear that?" Cole whispers in my ear. "We have a new leader."

Normally, I'd be irritated by his prodding, but I don't mind, not when he took the lead with that performance. He broke out of the shell he was living in and brought his parents back to life through a beautiful memory.

"I did hear. I think it was well-deserved."

"Storee Taylor, are you...are you in favor of me being in the lead?"

We step off the stage, and I turn to him. "I'm in favor of you stepping out of your comfort zone and finding ways to celebrate the season you used to shy away from."

He smiles down at me, and I can tell he wants to pull me into his chest, kiss me, love on me like he does when we're in private. But for the sake of Taran and Aunt Cindy, he holds back and places his hands in his pockets once again.

"Come over tonight."

"I'll see what I can do," I say. "Making no promises."

"Storee, let's go," Taran calls out. "We have some strategizing to do."

I wince. "God, can't wait."

"Text me."

"I will."

And with that, I take off, following Taran and Aunt Cindy out to the car, my mind on one thing and one thing alone.

It's not the competition.

Or the fact that I'm in second.

Nope, it's the man who has no problem looking straight into my soul with those mesmerizing eyes.

CHAPTER TWENTY-SEVEN
STOREE

The houses were dark; fluffy snow filled the air.
Cindy and Taran dreamed sweet dreams without care.

"I must be quiet, and I must be quick," Storee hissed.
Tonight, she was resolved to have her pussy kissed.

I BOUNCE ON MY FEET, the cold seeping through my pajamas since I didn't wear a jacket out of fear of it being too loud as I escaped.

I waited until Taran and Aunt Cindy both retired to their rooms, then texted Cole for a good hour and a half. When I heard nothing coming from Taran's room, I snuck down the stairs, sliding on the banister because the stairs were too creaky, and then slipped out the front door, leaving it unlocked. I sent up a prayer for it to still be unlocked when I returned.

"What the hell is he doing?" I mutter as I shiver all the way down to my bones.

Just then the door unlocks and opens. I don't give him a second to say a thing. I'm in the house and in front of the fire before he can even welcome me inside.

"Jesus, man, it's freezing out there."

He chuckles and shuts the door. "Sorry, I was making you some hot chocolate." He lifts a cup from the coffee table and hands it to me. I quickly wrap my hands around the warm ceramic, letting it heat me.

"Thank you, this smells amazing."

He guides me back to the couch, and before I can protest at being pulled away from the fire, he places a blanket over my lap and then slides in next to me, where he drapes his arm over my shoulders and pulls my back up against his chest, offering me some body heat.

"This okay?" he asks. "Are you comfortable?"

"Very," I say as I snuggle into him. "Thank you." I take a sip of the hot chocolate after blowing on it a few times and let the warm liquid flow down my throat, warming me from the inside out.

When I lower the mug, he nudges my head to turn toward him, and when I do, he lightly presses his lips to mine, sweetly taking the kiss he so rightfully deserved when I snuck into his house a few seconds ago.

When he releases, he sighs with a goofy grin. "That will never get old."

I lean into him again and take another sip of my drink. "It won't."

He loops his free arm around my waist, his hand resting on my stomach as we stare at the tree we decorated together.

"I know I said it a million times in text messages, but your tribute to your parents was so heartwarming, Cole. I get emotional every time I think about it. How did you hold it together?"

"Barely," he says. "Any time we practiced, I was fine, but something about what we wore and having my parents projected behind us got to me. Originally, it was supposed to be just a picture frame, but at the last minute Max remembered they had a projector and made it happen. We went last because he was trying to figure it all out with the café."

"I think the projected picture made it that much better. Seriously, it was amazing. How do you feel afterward?"

"Good. Relieved that it's over. But also proud. My mom always loved listening to me sing when we were in the car together. She would turn the music down subtly so she could hear me better."

"I don't blame her. You have such a rich voice. Very sexy."

"Sexy, huh?" he asks, his hand splaying across my stomach. "Should I sing for you some more?"

"You know, I wouldn't be opposed to it. Do you know who you sound like?"

"Who?"

"Hayes Farrow. The same rich voice, deep and sultry. I swear you two could do a duet and sound like the same person."

"Are you a Hayes Farrow fan?"

"Yes," I gush. "I love him so much. And he just came out with a Christmas album this year. I've been listening to it a lot."

"Yeah?" he asks. "Let me pull it up."

He leans forward, shifting us as he reaches for his phone, then settles us back on the couch. He connects his phone to the Bluetooth speaker in the living room and searches for Hayes Farrow's Christmas album. He stares at the cover art for a second and then leans forward to look at me.

"You know, I never knew what he looked like. Is this why you like him?"

"I mean, I like him for his music, but his face doesn't hurt to look at."

Cole chuckles and presses play on the first song, a slow, melodic rendition of "Let it Snow."

"The entire album is acoustic, so it's a very chill sort of Christmas, none of the bells and whistles that go into a big production of Christmas albums. Probably why I think you sound so much like him."

"Yeah, I can hear it," he says as we listen to the song together. "He has a much better voice than me, though. More controlled."

"I bet if you practiced as much as he does, you wouldn't think that."

"Are you saying you want me to get into the music business?" he asks, his lips briefly finding my neck.

"No," I say, chills racing down my arm from his mouth. "I like you the way you are. The grump who takes care of the reindeer and plays with candy canes during sex."

He chuckles. "Would you still classify me as a grump? I don't think I've had very grumpy tendencies as of late."

"That's because I've blown joy back into you...through your penis."

He nearly chokes on his hot chocolate, sputtering and coughing as he leans forward, a chuckle in his throat.

"Jesus," he says after a few seconds. "Warn a guy, Storee."

"Where's the fun in that?" I smile over the rim of my mug before taking another sip of my hot chocolate.

"Clearly none. And since you brought it up, yes, you've blown me a lot, and I've liked every second of it. Best blowing of my goddamn life."

"I'm oddly proud of myself." I laugh.

"I'm proud of you too, especially the use of your hands while said blowing is being done."

"You know, that's a new addition to my process. Particularly the massaging of the balls. There was something about your balls that really made me want to try. I'm glad it was enthusiastically accepted."

"Very," he says, mirth in his voice. "Like, *very* well received."

"Well, I'm glad to hear it. It's always nice to get positive feedback about your work."

"It is...which leads me to see if there is any sort of feedback you want to give me."

I turn just enough to see the smile tugging on his lips. "From the way I came on your face last time we were together, I don't think you need any feedback. I think you know you're doing well."

He chuckles. "Yeah, I know, just fishing for compliments."

"You're better than that, Cole."

"I'm really not." He kisses the top of my head. "So, change of subject because if we keep talking about this, I'm going to want to test out the theory of how good I am, and I'm trying not to maul you first thing."

"I wouldn't mind if you did, but I get it. What's your change of subject?"

"What are your family's Christmas traditions?"

"Umm, I mean, we always came here to Kringle. We would make gingerbread with Aunt Cindy. We'd sing 'Happy Birthday' to Baby Jesus Fonz on Christmas Day."

"Really?" Cole laughs.

"Yeah, that was Aunt Cindy's doing." I sip from my mug and stare at the lights of the tree as I continue. "Aunt Cindy brought out her scrapbooking supplies every year, and we'd have a day where we'd make pages for the pictures we took the year before. There were pictures of us on Christmas and everything that we did that holiday season, but there would also be pictures of what Aunt Cindy did before we arrived. A good mixture. I enjoyed the scrapbooking. That was fun. And then on Christmas, Taran and I would have to wait in our rooms until we were called down. Mom, Dad, and Aunt Cindy would stand at the bottom of the stairs, recording us as we came down the stairs and saw all the gifts. I don't know how Mom and Dad did it, but we always had the best Christmases with the best presents. What about you?"

"Same," he says softly. "Well, about the presents, not about the scrap-booking or singing 'Happy Birthday' to the Fonz masquerading as baby Jesus." We both laugh. "They were thoughtful with their gifts. Some of my favorites were things I never thought about wanting."

"Like what?" I ask.

"Well, there was this marble baseball game my dad got me one year. It's a piece of wood that has been lasered into, turned into a baseball field, with a scoreboard, and a little chart spelling out different rolls of dice up top and what they meant. So if I rolled two ones, that would be a home run. Or a two and a three, that would be a strikeout. It was all luck, but oh my God, we had so much fun playing. And we would play every Christmas Eve eve."

"Christmas Eve eve? Why then?"

"Because Christmas Eve was about the town, but Christmas Eve eve was about us as a family. For the past ten years, I've taken the game over to Max's place, and we usually play until very late at night. We'll do a whole playoff bracket. We name the teams and work through the bracket until we get to the World Series. The last three years, Max has won, but I'm thinking this year I can claim the title."

"I love that," I say. "Is that the one thing you kept doing every year?"

I feel him nod. "Yeah. But it wasn't my idea. It was Max's. He brought me over to his house one Christmas Eve eve, and he'd got his own board because he wasn't sure I wanted to play on mine. But yeah, we always play, eat junk food, drink, and then pass out in his living room."

"Right on the floor?" I ask.

"Nah, Mrs. Maxheimer has blow-up mattresses for us that she insists we use after the one year we slept on the floor and woke up with bad backs, despite being in our mid-twenties. She said never again, so yeah, now it's blow-up mattresses. The last two years, Max has purchased us matching pajamas, and of course Mrs. Maxheimer has eaten up that opportunity to take pictures."

"That's so sweet. I love your relationship with Atlas. You guys seem so much closer than Taran and me, and she's my actual sister. We've just always been sort of different. Ever since we were little. We aren't that far apart in age, but she's more rigid, more serious, and I've kind of just gone with the flow. I think it's hard for us to relate. That doesn't mean I don't love her, though. Just kind of wish I was as close with her as you are with Atlas."

"Maybe you can be. Have you tried to get closer with her since you've been here?"

"I mean, there have been moments, but as soon as Taran's fixated on something, she won't let it go, so it's hard to actually hang out. So now that she's all in on this competition, nothing else matters. Of course, Aunt Cindy gets the treatment she needs, so Taran's priorities right now are Aunt Cindy and the Kringle competition. I don't think there's any bonding with her sister on that list."

"Well, maybe after the competition is over," he suggests.

"Possibly. I actually got her a few puzzles for Christmas since we used to love doing them together. Maybe we can do one Christmas Day and chat."

"That's a good idea. Ease her in with a puzzle. Is she seeing anyone?"

"Yes, she has a boyfriend back in Denver. His name is Guy. He's nice, from what I've seen. She doesn't talk about him much, but I think that's because she's also pretty private. I don't know, she's just different. Or maybe it's me. Maybe I'm the hard one to talk to."

"No, that's not the case. I've had no problem talking to you over the years."

"You are the one person I seemed to always be able to talk to," I say. "I'm a bit of a homebody. I talk to my ficus, Alexander. But he's not much of a conversationalist."

He chuckles, his chest rumbling against my back. "Maybe he's just a good listener."

"The best kind."

We're silent for a moment as Hayes Farrow starts singing "White Christmas" in the background.

"What about your parents? Are they going to come here for Christmas?" he asks.

"No," I answer. "They have a timeshare in Cancun that they visit during the holidays. They've become accustomed to Christmas on the beach, decorating a palm tree with ornaments, and being able to get a nice holiday tan."

"Wonder what that's like," Cole says. "I don't think that's something I'd want to experience. I've just always seen Christmas as a time when you cozy up in front of the fireplace, under a blanket, with some hot chocolate."

"Same," I reply. "Like this right here, this moment with you, it's ideal, and I truly hate that I stayed away for so long. I love everything about this, about being here, about feeling the spirit of the season." I curl in closer to him, and he kisses the top of my head. "I never want to leave."

COLE

I never want to leave…

That sentence has been on repeat in my head all night.

Because I don't want her to leave either. I want her to want to stay here in this year-round Christmas town. I want her to love it here like I do. And I want…hell, I want to be with her.

And the unknown of whether or not that's an option is scary. Terrifying, actually.

"Where do you plan on spending Christmas?" she asks, now resting her head on my lap while I play with her hair.

"With the Maxheimers. They've taken me in, and we're family at this point. When I spent my first Christmas with them, they showered me with gifts. I told them it wasn't necessary, but Mrs. Maxheimer doesn't really listen all that well when it comes to gift-giving. As Max and I got older, she began lessening the gifts, and now it's usually some homemade cookies, a new flannel shirt, and then a special gift she saw sometime during the year that she thought I would like. She really enjoys getting Max and me matching flannel shirts."

She chuckles. "God, I love that so much. I wish you'd both wear them together."

"We've accidentally done it before, and of course Max then goes around town asking who wore it better. Let me tell you, it's always me."

"Oh, you would get my vote." Her beautiful eyes stare up at me.

"I'd better."

My other hand rests on her stomach while I casually run my fingers through her hair, which she seems to enjoy.

"Did you get your aunt Cindy anything for Christmas?"

"No, actually." She tugs on her lip. "I probably should. Hmm, maybe I should go to Baubles and Wrappings and find something for her. It's like a Christmas emporium there."

"That's what the Dankworths were going for."

"They're odd people, yeah?" Storee asks.

"The fucking weirdest," I say, and we both laugh.

"And they live across the street, right?"

"Yup," I confirm. "During the summer, they will march out into the yard like the Von Trapp family in their matching outfits and practice their caroling."

"Are their outfits made of old curtains?"

"You know, sometimes I wonder."

She chuckles. "So they just sing out front? Weird."

"Yup, at oh-six-hundred hours."

Her mouth drops open. "Six in the morning?"

"Oh yeah. Martha and Mae lose their shit about it. They never say anything because it wouldn't be very Christmas Kringle-ly of them, but they bitch to the entire neighborhood. Between me, your aunt, Frank, and Thachary, they are ready to start buying T-shirt cannons and blasting them from behind. Their words, not mine."

Storee snorts. "Oh, that's not very Christmas Kringle-ly of them at all."

"Nope. But I don't blame them. There have been many weekends when I wake up to their singing, and it makes me want to crack my skull. I don't even know why it's during the summer. They're home-schooled, so it's not like they can't do it any other time of the year. But it's torturous."

"How many kids do they have?"

"Seven," I answer.

"Seven?" Storee's eyes widen. "My God, what are they doing with seven children?"

I chuckle. "You make it sound like they collected them."

"Didn't they? Seven children, my goodness. That's their own choir. A basketball team with two extra players. A full-on tug-of-war team."

"Tug-of-war?"

"I don't know. That's just a lot of kids. What do they do with all of them?"

"Have them sing Christmas carols in the front yard at six in the morning during the summer."

"A travesty."

"Yeah, well, they also put on part of the Christmas festivities at Ornament Park. They sing a few songs, and Bob Krampus loves it. He sits on his Santa throne, drinks hot chocolate, and delights in their melodies. Not to mention, the Dankworths also are judges in the Super Santa Speed Round."

"They are?" she asks.

"Yup, well, just the parents—not the whole basketball team. Along with Bob himself and Martha and Mae."

"Is that why you've been buddying up to Martha and Mae and feeding their hearts with this romantic farce between us?"

"I would hardly say the way we've been fucking has been a romantic farce." I slip my hand under her shirt, letting my palm press against her warm skin.

"You know what I mean. The whole situation is so convoluted. It started as a farce, became a reality, but is still a farce to some, a reality to others. I don't know what the heck is going on."

I slide my hand up her stomach, loving how warm she is. "It has been confusing, but I think I've been doing a good job playing the role of the enemy in front of your sister."

"Uh, have you not witnessed my incessant eye rolling whenever you're around Taran and me? I'm surprised my eyes are still attached."

"You've done a good job, but I think I've been winning for the both of us with my quick barbs and then out-of-the-blue kisses. They always seem to catch you off guard."

"They do...but I love them."

"You do, do you?" I ask as I slide my hand below her breast. Since she's not wearing a bra, I run my thumb over the underside, reveling in her soft skin.

"I do," she says as she wiggles against me, trying to get my hand to go up farther.

"What do you think it's going to be like when we tell everyone the truth?"

"You know, I haven't really thought about it," she says as I glide my thumb a little higher, right below her nipple. Her teeth pull on her lip.

"I have. I've thought about how people from all over, including your aunt and sister, will cheer for us and tell us what a marvelous couple we make."

"*Marvelous?*" She lifts a brow.

I take that moment to graze her hard nipple with my thumb. She exhales loudly.

"Am I not allowed to use the word *marvelous*?"

"I mean, it doesn't fit the lumberjack aesthetic you have going on."

"Oh, sorry." I pause, letting my thumb graze over her nipple again. "Uh, how about a growl with an added *People will like us*."

She laughs. "Much better."

I then return my hand to her stomach and love the disappointment in her eyes. But she's not disappointed for long as I play with the waistline of her pants. My fingers drag over the fabric, occasionally dipping under.

"Are you trying to turn me on?" she asks.

"Is it working?"

"Yes."

"Good," I say, then just rest my hand on her stomach, not moving north or south.

"Cole."

"What?"

"What are you doing?"

"Thinking about the cheering and how Taran will shake my hand for a job well done with our faking—but then tell me how happy she is that I'm with her sister."

"Wow, you're living in a dream world. Taran would never."

"Never say never. I can see the way she looks at me. She wants to welcome me into the family."

She chuckles. "You've lost your—oh God," she moans as I slide my hand down, stopping just above her pussy, toying with her. Her legs spread, and she presses her hand on top of mine, trying to make me go further, but I don't.

"Cole...please."

But I don't listen. I take the hem of her long-sleeved shirt and drag it up. Thankfully, she allows me to take it off and drop it to the floor. I stare down at her bare chest and feel myself go hard.

"You're so goddamn beautiful," I say as I gently dance my fingers across her breasts, loving just how fucking hard her nipples are. "I love seeing you like this, surrendering to me, letting me play with you."

"I love it," she says with a sigh as she brings her hand between her legs.

"No," I say. "Don't touch yourself."

"But Cole..."

"No, that's my pussy. You don't come until I tell you."

I continue to draw gentle circles around her breasts as she groans, then starts moving around her bottom half. When she pushes the blanket down, that's when I realize she was taking her pants and underwear off, leaving herself completely bare to me.

"That's my girl," I say as I drag my fingers down her stomach and to her pubic bone. Her legs spread even wider, and her pelvis thrusts up, seeking friction, but I don't give it to her.

"I want your cunt squeezing my cock tonight, Storee. And I want you to spend the night."

"I…I can't," she pants as my fingers find her breasts again, but this time I circle around her nipple, her chest heaving now, her pelvis wiggling.

"You can. I want you in my bed."

"But—"

"But nothing," I say as I pinch her nipple. She groans loudly, her chest pushing into my hand.

"Yessss," she drags out.

I pluck at her nipples, playing with them, watching her writhe beneath me, looking for so much more.

"Yes, you will stay?"

"I…oh God…Cole."

"Answer me," I say, driving up her pleasure by bringing my free hand to her pussy and cupping her. She tries to wiggle against me, attempting to create some heat.

"You know…I…can't."

"Not what I want to hear," I say as I move one finger along her seam.

"Oh God. Please, Cole, I'm throbbing."

"Then you'd better answer me," I say while playing with her nipples.

"They…they'll find out."

"We'll wake up early and get you back to the house before they wake up," I reply as I swipe at her slit again. She doesn't answer, so I swipe again…and again, already feeling how aroused she is. I bring my finger up to my mouth and suck on it. Her eyes go wild. "Say it, say you'll stay."

"Pr-promise we'll get me home?"

"Promise," I say as I return my hand to her pussy and slip my finger all the way against her clit.

"Fuuuuck," she draws out. "Yes. I'll stay."

"Good girl," I say as I move two of my fingers inside her. I play with her clit, massaging and circling it, applying just enough pressure with my thumb to make her pleasure climb.

"You're so good," she says as her hands go to her breasts.

"Don't touch yourself. That's my job."

Frustrated, she lowers her hands as I take over with my free hand, playing with her breasts. Cupping them, squeezing them gently, then running my fingers around her nipples.

"This pussy is so greedy. I can feel you squeezing already, wanting more."

"Because I'm close," she whispers as her chest arches and her legs wiggle.

"Do you usually come this fast?"

"Never," she says. "It's you, Cole…all you."

And that does something to my possessive soul as I move my fingers faster, playing with this woman's body, wanting her to come so goddamn bad that it feels like my next breath depends on it.

"Yes, Cole…oh my God, right there. Right…there…" She groans, her hips thrusting into my hand, her lips parting. Just as I feel her starting to tighten around my fingers, I pull away.

"No!" she yells. But I lift her, strip my pants down, and let my cock spring up.

"Fuck me, Storee. Fuck me hard."

She straddles my lap, places me at her entrance, then slams down, making my eyes roll in the back of my head from her sweet, tight warmth.

"Fucking hell," I whisper as her grip falls to my shoulders, and she starts bouncing up and down on me. The sound of her ass hitting my thighs fills the air, mixed with her beautiful moans. "That's it, Storee, ride me."

She moves her pelvis back and forth, up and down, in circles, seeking out every angle she can. All the while, her breathing grows heavier and heavier.

Her need goes wild.

Her pussy tightens with every thrust.

"Fuck, I'm close," I breathe out as I grip her hips and help her move. "Jesus, so close. Take my cock, Storee. Fucking take it."

She lifts off me, and it's my turn to protest, but then she turns around and sits back down on me. The angle must be hitting her in a different spot with her back to my chest because her thrusting has become feral.

I help her, shooting my cock up into her, meeting her pace. My hands find her breasts, and I play with them while she rubs her clit.

"Fuck yes, fuck yes," she says as her pussy clenches around me. "Oh my God, Cole. I'm...I'm coming."

She tightens.

She contracts.

She arches and grips the back of my neck as she shatters on top of me, pulling and tugging on my dick in such a delicious way that my balls tighten, my cock swells, and I'm coming inside her with such force that I bite down on her shoulder.

"Fuck," I yell when I release her and let my head fall back to the couch as she leans into me. "Jesus Christ," I mutter, coming down from the best high in the world.

"Cole," she whispers, her hand falling to her chest. "Oh my God."

"I know," I say, my breathing ragged.

"You...are amazing." Still on my lap, she turns around and leans her forehead against mine. "No one has ever made me feel the way you do."

"Same," I say, stroking her hair.

"You are ruining me."

"That's the plan," I say, then I notice the bite mark on her shoulder. "Shit, Storee. I'm sorry." I smooth my hand over where my teeth imprinted her skin.

"Don't be... I hope you do it again."

Our eyes meet, and I smile right before I bring her lips to mine.

CHAPTER TWENTY-EIGHT
STOREE

All was very quiet, not even a squeak of a mouse,
while Storee tiptoed over the snow back to her house.

The plan was simple: to sneak in without detection
and go upstairs to hide her hickey-
covered complexion.

SLOWLY AND QUIETLY I CLOSE the front door, my shoulders tense, my body sore, and my mind still wishing I was in Cole's warm bed rather than in Aunt Cindy's house. It was risky, spending the night with him, but even though I protested at first, deep down I wanted to stay. I wanted to have the night we had. I wanted to fall asleep in his arms only for him to wake me up with kisses.

And when his alarm went off this morning, I was entirely too reluctant to get out of bed, but Cole helped me, encouraged me, and then watched me hop through the snow to get back to Aunt Cindy's house. And now that I was able to make it undetected—

"What are you doing?"

I freeze, my back stiffening from the sound of my sister's voice.

Shit.

Apparently not undetected.

400 | MEGHAN QUINN

Think of something and think quick.

I turn toward my sister, who is on the base of the stairs looking stiff with her pajamas askew and her ponytail barely tied together. "Checking to see what kind of snow we got last night. Does this shit ever stop?"

I see her glance out the window, then back at me. Arms crossed, she studies me for a moment, causing sweat to form at the nape of my neck. Then she says, "It's winter in the mountains. You can expect this every day."

Some of the tension eases.

"I just thought that maybe we would catch a break," I say as I flip my hair over my shoulder.

"Oh my God, what happened to you?" Taran points at my shoulder where Cole bit me last night.

Crap!

"Is it a bruise?" I ask, deciding not to play dumb and just own up to the mark.

"Yes."

I nod as I casually let the lies flow. "This is embarrassing, but I was really excited that I nailed the routine yesterday. I tried to have a quiet celebration to myself in my room last night and ended up jumping, hitting the mirror on the dresser, and it crashed down on my shoulder." Holy crap, I can lie fast. "I'm surprised you didn't hear it. I groaned."

"Oh, I was on the phone with Guy, and we were...well...anyway." She studies me. "Did you ice it?"

"Too embarrassed. Looks like I have to suffer now."

She nods...still studying me. A stretch of silence falls between us before she says, "You seem happy."

Because I spent the night with Cole, and neither of us wanted to sleep. Instead, we'd sleep for an hour, wake up and play around, then sleep, then fuck...and before I left, he fucked me up against the door. I can still feel him all over my body.

"Relieved is more like it." I lean against the front door as Taran stays on the bottom stair. "I was really worried about that performance and making a fool of myself, so I'm glad it's over and we can focus on the last contest."

Her lips purse, but she nods—thankfully. "Yeah, I'm glad it's over too. You were looking a bit green there for a second right before you started singing," she says, lightening up. She heads toward the kitchen, and I follow her just as I receive a text. I glance at it and see it's from Cole.

Cole: Screw them…come back to me.

I can't hold back my smile as I reply.

Storee: OMG Taran caught me sneaking back in, but I played it off as checking on the snow. She bought it.
Cole: Shit. Really? I'm sorry.
Storee: It's fine. She seems clueless.
Cole: Good. Maybe we shouldn't have fucked against the door.
Storee: What a silly comment. Of course we should have.

"Want some coffee?" Taran asks, tearing my attention away from my phone.

I take a seat at the countertop and say, "Yeah, sure."

My phone buzzes again, and I glance at the text.

Cole: Want to go to Baubles and Wrappings with me today? We can pass it off as the town needing to see us together, but really I want to get lost in the store with you.
Storee: Tell me what time. I'll be there.

I set my phone down and watch Taran make us coffee. "So how was your phone call with Guy?"

"Fine," she says and keeps it at that.

O-kaaay. Just trying to have a sisterly conversation.

"What's he doing for Christmas?"

"Going to his parents' house."

"Oh," I reply. "Not coming up to Kringle?"

She shakes her head and turns toward me. "No, he has nieces and nephews, and they do this big Christmas thing at his parents' house. I told him not to bother coming here since we'd be leaving soon."

"Oh…we are?" I ask, dread filling me immediately.

"I mean…you saw Aunt Cindy up on the stage. Not sure how much care she's going to need after Christmas. And I already spoke with Martha and Mae about helping her out with meals."

"Huh…" I run my finger over the pink marble countertop. "I guess I just assumed we'd stay longer, maybe through the new year at least."

"Well, I have a job to get back to, don't you?"

"I mean, I brought my computer with me, so I could work from anywhere. I just fear if we leave too early, and she tries to do something, she might reinjure herself."

"I think she'll be fine," Taran says without a worry in her voice. "Why do you want to stay longer? I thought you didn't care for being here."

I didn't.

And then I realized it was everything that I was missing in my life.

"I don't know." I shrug. "It's grown on me."

"It has?" she asks, brows lifting. "That's surprising."

"Why is that surprising?"

"Maybe because the entire drive up here, you were bitching about having to live in Kringle for weeks."

"Well, I guess my mind was changed."

She crosses her arms over her chest, and her eyes laser in on me.

Oh, shit.

The death scan is coming.

She doesn't use it often, but when she does, I swear she can see right through me.

"What are you not telling me?" she asks.

"Nothing," I squeak.

"You're hiding something."

Cue the sweat.

"Taran." I feign laughter. "I'm not hiding anything from you. Can't a girl change her mind because she's full of the holiday spirit? I guess I just forgot how magical it is here."

She studies me some more. Those X-ray eyes cut through me, and after what feels like a full minute, she says, "You're seeing him, aren't you?"

"What?" I ask, my eyes wide, my heart pounding.

"Cole. You're seeing him."

"Uh...what? Ha, no," I say.

"Yes, you are."

"No, I'm not." I stab my finger against the counter, trying to make a point.

"Then why do you want to stay? Why...why are you crying when he sings? Why are you allowing him to kiss you?"

Shit. She's too smart, too clever.

I consider telling her the truth, but I really don't want this to blow up before the competition is over, right before Christmas. From the way she's reacting now, I know it won't go over well.

"Because...because I've been feeling low," I say, which isn't a lie. I have been. I didn't know how low I was feeling until I showed up here and started to hang out with Cole more. "And Kringle just reminded me that I don't have to be living this dull, cooped-up life in my apartment. That there is community all around. And things to do. I just...I like it here. And the thing with Cole, that's...that's..."

So real.

So wonderful.

404 | MEGHAN QUINN

So life-altering.

"That's for the competition."

The coffee brews behind her, the fresh, comforting smell filling the kitchen. She tilts her head to the side, and I try to remain as cool and calm as I can while I wait for her response. After a moment she says, "You've been feeling...lost?"

I let out my pent-up breath and nod. "Yeah, didn't really realize it until I got here."

"Why?" she asks, looking concerned.

"I don't know." I think about it for a second. "I guess I've felt lonely. Hard to have a job in a place where you don't know many people and you don't have to report to an office. I have a few friends, but it feels different being here. Everything happens on a deeper level. You know?"

She nods and then grabs two reindeer mugs for us.

"I know what you mean. I don't have the connection to this place like you do, but I do love Aunt Cindy, and I've been feeling nostalgic since being here." Jesus, she's talking to me. I try not to make sudden movements because I don't want to scare her away. "It's why I've really wanted to help her win this thing. I know how much it means to her. I know that she's okay, but she was talking about how she's not sure how many more healthy years she has left to compete in the competition. So this means a lot to her."

For some reason, guilt consumes me.

Don't know why.

I haven't been doing anything wrong.

I've been putting in my best effort.

I've been trying to win, and up until this last competition, I was carrying the team in first.

And I'm not that far behind.

But I still feel guilty.

Maybe because you're lying to your sister.

She hands me my cup of coffee and then grabs the cream from the fridge. "I wish Mom and Dad were here," she continues. "I know Aunt Cindy would have liked it."

"Yeah, I wish they were here too. Once they got the timeshare, though...everything kind of changed, and then we were both in college. I don't know, I feel like all of us have been letting Aunt Cindy down every Christmas. She must have been sad without us."

"She was," Taran says softly, ratcheting up that guilt that's consuming me.

"Maybe we make more of an effort then. I could talk to Mom and Dad. I mean, imagine if they were here this year. They could have joined in on the *Mean Girls* dance. It would have been so much fun."

She smirks. "Imagine Dad in that getup?"

"You know he would rock it."

Taran chuckles. "He would."

"What are we laughing about in here?" Aunt Cindy comes into the kitchen, leaning on her cane. She's been using that more around the house rather than the walker since it's clunky.

"Dad in our routine outfits," I say.

Aunt Cindy looks between us and laughs. "Now that is a sight I would not want to see."

"I don't know," Taran says. "Could be good fodder to use if we ever needed blackmail material."

Aunt Cindy gestures to Taran. "Very good point."

COLE

Max: Sewing tonight at my house. My mom has everything you need to learn.

Cole: Okay, need me to bring anything? I can grab sandwiches or pizza.

Max: Bring pizza and stop at Prancer's Libations for some cans of cider. I think we might need it.

Cole: That doesn't sound promising.

Max: If one thing takes you down…it's going to be the sewing.

I pocket my phone just as I see Storee walk up to me on the corner, wearing one of her lighter jackets but decked out in a scarf, winter hat, and boots.

"Hey," I say as I take in her cute red nose from the cold.

"Inside," she says, motioning to the store.

I chuckle and hold the door open for her. She walks right past me and then lets out a deep breath.

"How are you just in a flannel shirt? You don't even have gloves on. Are you insane?"

"No, you are. It's thirty degrees out today."

"Yes, and I fear my nipples fell off during the five-minute walk from Aunt Cindy's house."

"Hell, I hope not," I say as I pull her into me and press a kiss to her lips, loving that we can be open about this.

When I pull away, I try to take her hand, but she shoos me away. "What do you think you're doing with those icicles you call fingers?"

"Trying to hold your hand."

"Uh, no, thank you. Defrost first and then I'll consider it."

"They're not that cold," I protest.

"Cold enough to make me shiver." She rubs her hands together and then blows on them.

"If this is going to work between us, then you're going to need to grow some thicker skin."

"Not sure how to do that," she says. "Don't think I care to do the research."

I chuckle and wrap my arm around her shoulders as we walk farther into the store.

Baubles and Wrappings combines two buildings, with an added second-floor loft area that overlooks the signature tree in the center of the store and offers a kids' section of unique and vastly overpriced toys.

The rest of the store has rows and sections of specialized gifts tailored to Colorado, trimmings and decor for every Christmas lover, packaged baking mixes, wrapping paper, and even some Christmas dinnerware that has grown in popularity. And the Dankworths, well, they're always walking up and down the rickety wooden floors, offering help and making sure no one is doing anything illegal since there are a lot of small things that could be stolen.

But Baubles and Wrappings is one of those small-town stores that people talk about because you're able to find a unique gift, something that isn't so run-of-the-mill.

"So where do you want to start?" I ask Storee.

"Well, I should really get presents for Aunt Cindy and Taran."

"Anyone else?"

"No…I don't think so."

"Are you sure there's no one else you want to get a present for?"

She glances in my direction. "If you're referring to yourself, I already have something for you."

"Wait, really?" I ask, surprised.

"Yup." She guides us over to the kitchenware. "I've had it planned for a while now."

"Is it you wrapped in a bow?"

"No, but glad to see where your head's at."

"Storee, where you're concerned, my head is always thinking about that."

She chuckles. "That makes you incredibly easy."

"Yeah, it does, and I'm not even sorry."

"I bet you're not." She picks up a pair of salt and pepper shakers that have been made into Mr. and Mrs. Claus. "These are adorable."

"Bob Krampus has a pair in his kitchen."

"Do you think he looks at them and thinks…boy, am I salty?"

I snort and pull away so I can look her in the eyes. "Is that a dad joke?"

"Possibly. Think I should submit it to the Dad Joke Emporium?"

"Is that a thing?"

"I don't know. Sounds like it could be a thing."

"Maybe you should."

She sets the salt and pepper shakers down. "Maybe I will. Ooo, look at these tea towels. I love the vintage print on them."

"That's a recurring print," I say. "You'll find it on place mats and tablecloths and then on some knickknacks. I think it's the print Mrs. Dankworth chose for the season. There's always a new one every year."

"Well, good on her. But I don't think Aunt Cindy needs another tea towel or tablecloth. She has so many. Taran has been in charge of changing them every week, so they all get equal time in the light. Aunt Cindy's words, not mine."

"My mom would do something similar. She has a lot of mugs and dishware, and she would be sure to rotate them so they all had a chance to celebrate Christmas."

"Isn't it weird that we can believe that inanimate objects have feelings?" she asks.

"Yes. But my mom was a huge believer."

We move over to the candles, and Storee picks up a balsam-scented one, takes off the top, and gives it a sniff. "Wow, that smells amazing."

She leans the candle in my direction, and I take a sniff as well. "Smells like Max's office."

"Ooo, we should have had sex in there. I would have loved to do it surrounded by the smell of trees."

I laugh. "That can be arranged."

She picks up an apple pie-scented candle and sniffs it. "Would you really have sex in your friend's office?"

"I would have sex on top of my friend if it meant being able to be with you."

She pauses and gives me a sideways look. "Did you hear how that sounded?"

I shrug, not caring. "I said what I said."

She nods and picks up a candle labeled *Christmas Sweater.* "Now would that be considered a threesome if we had sex on top of Atlas?"

I sniff the candle when she offers it, not too impressed. "Uh, I don't think so. I think he would be considered an object in this scenario, like a bed or a desk."

"Hmm, and like all other inanimate objects, would he have feelings too?"

"If we were fucking on top of him, I'm pretty sure he'd have feelings about it. And knowing him, it would probably be idiotic feelings."

"What do you mean by that?" She picks up the balsam candle again and tucks it into the crook of her arm as we move toward the ornaments.

"Meaning he probably wouldn't be annoyed. He'd be more proud, like he needed to encourage us and offer pointers. That's the kind of guy Max is."

She chuckles. "Oh my God, I could so see him doing that. Like...'Hey, Cole, try fingering her with three fingers.'"

"Shhh," I say on a laugh. "Christ, I don't want to get kicked out of the store because you're talking about fingering. Remember, the Dankworths patrol the aisles. And you're on their watch list ever since you knocked over the signature tree."

She pauses and turns toward me. "Wait, am I?"

I nod. "Oh yeah, there's a picture of you behind the register and everything."

"Seriously? That was an accident. I should go ask them to take it down." She heads toward the front, but I tug on her arm, laughing.

"Storee, I'm kidding."

Her brow pulls together in a frown as she pops her hand on her hip. "That is not funny. That was a very traumatic moment for me."

I tilt her chin up. "It's okay to laugh about it now. It's been over a decade."

"Yeah...but still. There may be whisperings of what happened."

I shake my head. "Trust me, the things they whisper about now are how Jimmy Short accidentally peed himself by the make-your-own-wreath display."

"Wait, really? He peed himself?"

I nod, and we move through the ornament aisle pretty quickly, soon heading into the clothing section. "He peed himself. He said he had a burst water bottle in his pants, but no one believed him, especially after the security footage was passed around."

"What did he do in the security footage?"

"He was talking to his now ex-wife, looking at the display. He was shifting side to side, looking like a three-year-old trying to hold his pee, and when they got spooked by one of those motion-detecting decorations, the pee was scared right out of him. His wife was humiliated, and shortly after the season, they divorced."

"Because of what happened in the store?"

I shake my head. "No, I think they were headed in that direction to begin with, but I don't think the incident helped. He's been trying to recover ever since. Hence why he keeps trying to win the Kringle competition. I think he sees it as the ultimate way to get back at his ex and show her what she's missing out on since it's such a huge honor in this town. I don't know if you've seen her in the crowd watching, but she's the one in the bright green jacket and large peppermint candy earrings."

"Oh my God, I know who you're talking about. That's his ex-wife?"

"Yup. At the Caroling Café, Max told me she was licking her lips a lot while watching Jimmy."

"Licking her lips?"

I nod. "Yup, like she was enticed. Word on the street is people saw them talking outside the café. Who knows, maybe they'll find love all over again."

"Aw, a second-chance romance. Well, if he wants that, I hope it happens for him. What about Ursula Kronk? What's her story?"

"She's one of our first responders," I say as Storee picks up a scarf. She wraps it over her own scarf and smiles up at me, looking adorable. I unwrap it and shake my head. "Ursula wanted to represent her team, so she decided to join in. She does some side hustling with donations, and then at the end of the year she announces how much she raised for the town's first responders. Last year, she raised enough to make repairs to the firehouse that were desperately needed. Also new beds for the living quarters and updated computers. And she also won last year, so I'm sure she entered looking for a repeat."

"Oh, that's pretty cool. I kind of feel bad that she's struggling this year. What place is she in again?"

"Fourth. It's a weird showing for her. I've heard—and when I say heard, I mean Max telling me the gossip—that she liked competing against your aunt and that it hasn't been the same this year."

"Well, she could compete against me."

"Not the same, apparently." I pick up a pink crewneck sweatshirt with red lettering that says THERE ARE HOS IN THIS HOUSE and hold it up to Storee. "This feels fitting for you."

She glances down at it and then laughs. "Oh my God, I love that. Grab me a medium."

"Seriously?"

"Oh yeah, I'm going to need that in my wardrobe. Thank you." She moves to a green one and holds it up to me. It has a picture of Santa on the front, and around it the words *Big Nick Energy.* "I think this one was made for you."

A rumble of a laugh comes out of me. "Damn right."

"What size? Because you're getting it. Maybe you can wear something other than a flannel shirt."

"I happen to like my shirts, but an extra-large will do."

"Ooo, beefy man." She pulls out an extra-large and drapes it over her arm.

"What do you think you're doing?" I ask.

"Getting you this sweatshirt."

"I can get them." I reach for it, but she shies away from me.

"No, I'm getting this—you get me my pink ho shirt."

"Or I can get both."

"Or you can listen to me and just get the pink one." She stares me down, and I decide to listen to her.

"Fine. But if you see something else you like in here, you tell me so I can get it for you."

"I do see something." She looks down at my crotch. "But I don't think it's for sale."

I smirk at her. "Don't worry, I'll tie a bow on it for later and give it to you."

"Oh yeah? You're going to…give it to me?" She waggles her brows.

"And here I thought I could be the cheesy one."

"Afraid to tell you, but there's some cheese in all of us."

"That…that's a weird comment," I say, causing her to laugh and then lean into me. I take her hand—she lets me this time—and we move over to the knickknacks.

"Okay, what about Beatrice? She's in last place, right? I feel like there has to be a story behind why she's doing so badly."

"I don't think there's a story there. I just think she doesn't get it. She kind of follows her own taste, and people might not like her…eccentricity."

Not to mention she totally messed up her scene from *Die Hard*. I think that was embarrassing for everyone to watch."

"Yeah, you're right about that. And her caroling performance was from a horror film. I swear I can still hear her monotone voice."

"It wasn't her greatest moment. She's a hell of a veterinarian, though. Bob Krampus swears by her wart removal."

"Wait, hold on, you said she's a vet."

I slowly nod. "Yup."

A cute wrinkle forms on her nose as she tries to comprehend. "So why is she removing warts off Bob Krampus?"

"From what I heard, the first wart was an emergency visit, and no one was around to help but her, so she treated his 'dangler,' as he calls it—"

"Oh God, no details, please." She shivers. "How do you even know that?"

"Well, he's left multiple Google reviews and has told people around town. He always talks about it during the summer when he's wearing his Hawaiian shirts. He shows off his elbows and tells us the tale of how she helped him."

"That's...that's TMI. But also...Bob wears Hawaiian shirts during the summer?"

"Yup, because Santa is on vacation."

"Oh my God." She laughs. "You can't be serious."

"Very serious. He goes all in."

"What's going to happen when he's...you know...too old?"

"His son has been in training for decades."

"They have a son?"

"Yup." I pick up an angel tree topper and flash it to her as a suggestion for a present. She shakes her head, so we keep moving through the store, toward the ceramic villages. "His name is Bob Krampus Jr., and he works one of the stalls."

"Really? Which one?"

"The wooden toy stall. He's carved every single one of them. Calls himself an elf."

"Oh goodness." She chuckles. "That whole family went all in, didn't they?"

"They did." I nod. "They really did. But that's why they are so well-loved in this town. They're the glue, the ones keeping this all together. So yeah, BKJ will be taking over when it's time, and we've already been assured that he'll be able to fill Bob's boots."

"You call him BKJ?"

"Everyone in town does. Even Bob and Sylvia."

"Look at me learning all the different townie things. And here I thought you were a bit of a recluse and wouldn't know much." We head over into the vintage section of the store where the Dankworths resell antique Christmas items they've found at estate sales or have purchased for cheap off eBay.

"The only reason I know half the shit I do is because of Max. The guy never stops talking. He always comes into the barn in the morning when I'm feeding the reindeer and informs me of what he heard the day before."

She presses her hand to her chest. "Is...is Atlas a town gossip?"

"One of the biggest," I say as I pick up a doll. "This thing is creepy."

"Oh my God." She snags the doll from me and looks it over. "This is Felicity in her original blue holiday gown and pink stomacher. Holy shit."

"Uh...what?"

Storee hands me the sweatshirt and candle she was holding and looks over the doll. "Pearl necklace, dainty shoes, and blue satin ribbon and pinner cap. This is it, Cole. This is really it."

I swallow nervously. "Uh, what the hell are you talking about?"

She shows me the doll. "It's Felicity in her holiday outfit."

"I can somewhat see that, but who the hell is Felicity?"

"Are you really that dense?" she scoffs. Apparently I am. "She's an American Girl, Cole. One of the originals, and Aunt Cindy doesn't have this doll. She has all of the rest, Addy in her plaid tartan, Molly in her velvet dress, even that bitch Samantha in her plaid taffeta. But this, this would complete her collection."

I scratch the back of my neck. "Your aunt collects dolls?"

"Oh yeah, she collects them, has a whole room of them, and guess who's been sleeping in that room?"

"You?"

She slowly nods. "Yup, I've been sleeping with them all staring at me."

"But...you've gotten off in front of them," I say, thinking about all the dirty things we've done over the phone.

"And I'll be honest, Cole, I wasn't proud of it."

STOREE

"You need to be more precise with your cutting," Taran says. "They'll pay attention to that."

"To how I hold my scissors?" I ask. "Come on, Taran."

"She's right," Aunt Cindy says. "They judge everything during the Super Santa Speed Round. Not only does this include your gift wrapping, your ability to create a joyous Christmas card, and your stocking-making capabilities, but they also look into how clean your workspace is, even the way you hold your scissors and smile while creating these masterpieces. They have eagle eyes and watch every little thing. Especially the Dankworths."

"But this is paper cutting," I protest.

"And it needs to be precise." Taran hands me another roll of wrapping paper. "Do it again."

I can't believe I left Cole to come back here and be berated. I should have gone with him to the farm to check on the reindeer, but nooooo, I was trying to be a good sister and niece and practice.

The minute I stepped through the door, Taran took my bags, plopped them on the floor with a clunk, and dragged me into the dining room, where she had a practice station set up for the Super Santa Speed Round.

I was having so much fun walking around with Cole. After Baubles and Wrappings, we went back to the stalls since I didn't find anything for Taran, and I wound up grabbing a wind chime I know she will love. It's made of wood and makes a subtle sound when the pieces knock together rather than a high-pitched tone. And it's easy to untangle when the high-speed Colorado winds come flying in.

After that, we shared a brat, grabbed a cookie from Warm Your Spirits, and found a couple of chairs where we talked some more. Tanya gushed over us the entire time, especially since Cole wouldn't let go of my hand—not that I wanted him to. He asked me if I wanted to slip through the back door of his house, and I was tempted, but after the conversation I had with Taran this morning, I knew I was on thin ice, so I opted to go back to the house.

And now...now I'm being told how to cut wrapping paper.

"The guidelines are there for a reason. You need to follow them," Taran says.

"Yes, follow the guidelines," Aunt Cindy parrots.

I slide the scissors along the preprinted guidelines. "But what if the wrapping paper they provide doesn't have guidelines?"

"It does," Aunt Cindy says. "It's one of the things they watch for."

"Okay," I drag out. "Now, are we sure it's going to be a regular box that I have to wrap and not some weird shape?"

"Depends," Aunt Cindy says. "The first few years, it was a simple box, and they judged who decorated it the best, but last year they gave every-one a hexagonal package, and we had to figure out the angles. It was very hard."

"That doesn't seem like fun."

"It wasn't." Aunt Cindy plops a hexagon-shaped box on the table. "We're going to practice both."

Oh joy.

I sigh and take a seat in my chair, working on wrapping the box. I can feel Taran's eyes on me the entire time. When I finally look up at her, I ask, "What?"

"You seem reluctant to practice."

"I'm not."

I am. I want to be over at Cole's. How great would it be if we could practice together? Like we did with the candy canes. That was so much fun. But sitting here with my aunt and sister hovering over me...not so much fun.

"Then why aren't you cheerful?" Taran asks.

"You're not cheerful either. You're more into regiment mode at the moment."

"Well, someone needs to be. Honestly, you spent hours out in town today and the last contest is coming up soon. We need to be prepared. We're five points behind. We have to take first in this next one, and Cole needs to come in last if we have any chance at winning this."

"That seems a little dramatic," I say. "We also have the lights contest and the overall Christmas joy scoring from the spies around town, and Cole hasn't really improved on his display at all, *and* we have added some things to the house. The candy cane lollipops along the porch were a nice touch."

Taran perks up. "Thank you. It took a while to make sure they were straight, but once I started using the level, I thought they added some pizzazz."

"And changing the bulbs in the porch lights...also a nice touch."

"That was my idea," Aunt Cindy says.

"It was a good one."

I tape the paper together at the top, using the double-sided tape so it doesn't show. I even fold the raw edge over.

"And listen," I continue, "the card making will be a breeze. I've been scrapbooking with Aunt Cindy for years. I know what goes into a good Christmas card. We only need to worry about the stocking, but I have an idea."

"Oh?" Aunt Cindy says with piqued interest.

"Yes. We'll need some felt, an upholstery needle, and some yarn."

CHAPTER TWENTY-NINE
STOREE

Up Whistler Lane, on the left side of the street,
the two happy humpers kept things very discreet.

They'd text, they'd call, they'd send naughty pics,
all the while growing a bond through
this season of sticks.

And now that the last Kringle contest is finally here,
I'm not so sure it will end with a happy new year.

For someone is lurking, ready for
the truth to come clean,
through the cheery Christmas decor,
the bright red, white, and green.

"HOW DO MY EARRINGS LOOK?" I ask Taran, showing off the Christmas tree earrings that I bought at the stalls when I was with Cole. Well...that he bought for me.

"Festive," she says as she glances around the gymnasium, taking in the setup.

Like every other competition—at least the non-performance

ones—stations have been set up for each contestant. We are allowed to bring in judge-approved supplies, and then like in the show *Chopped*, there's a "pantry" full of supplies like wrapping paper, string, tape, fabric, baubles, and trinkets. There are sewing machines and a Cricut machine, and irons and ironing boards. Everything we might need to get crafty.

And since this is the last competition of the Kringle contest, the gymnasium is decorated in a winter wonderland theme, dripping with lights, banners, fake trees, and wreaths. It looks breathtaking in here.

"Can you take note of the rugs they have spread throughout the floor? Those are tripping hazards, and we don't need you to fall flat on your face," Taran says.

"I saw them," I tell her.

"And remember what we practiced with the wrapping paper. Hide the seams as best you can."

"Yes, of course," I say.

"And the stocking, don't sew too close to the edge or you're going to fray the edge and lose the proper stitching."

"I know, Taran," I say, annoyed because this is how she's been for the entire freaking day leading up to the competition.

"Don't get snippy. I'm trying to help," she says.

"Yes, but you've said the same thing over and over all day. At this point, I can stitch the damn stocking with my eyes closed."

"Please don't do that."

"I wouldn't," I reply just as I see Cole walk through the door with Atlas.

They're decked out in ugly Christmas sweaters, jeans, and boots. They have their sleeves rolled up, and even though the sweaters are ridiculous, they make them look so good.

Especially Cole, since his has a giant reindeer with a red ball for a nose. How fitting. When he spots me over by Taran, he grins, and then I catch his eyes wandering over my outfit. A red velvet dress with green stockings and black booties. I tied my hair back into a tight bun on the top of my head so it's out of my face while I work, and I stuck some holly into the bun for added flair.

When his eyes meet mine, he wets his lips, and I feel my entire body heat.

The competition is almost over. It's Christmas Eve eve, so tomorrow the lights will be judged, and on Christmas Day, the winner will be announced. After that, Cole and I are coming clean to my family, and then we're going to figure out where to go from there. I know Taran's itching to get back home, but I am more than willing to stay longer. I don't have to start work back up until after the new year, which means I could spend the whole holiday week with Cole, and I could even stay in his house at night and help out Aunt Cindy during the day. It will be perfect.

Just a few more days.

A few more days to see how long-term this thing between us could possibly be, because yeah, that's where my head is at, but I can't know exactly how long until I get a better read on Cole after the holidays.

"What are you looking at?" Taran says, startling me right out of my reverie.

"The, uh, the flocked trees," I say. "Not sure why anyone would want to deal with that mess. Sure, they're pretty, but just think about that white stuff all over the house."

She glances over at said trees and then back at me. "A nightmare if you ask me."

"Total nightmare," I say just as Cole walks up to us with Atlas.

"Darling, how not lovely to see you," he says in a sarcastic tone as he leans in and presses a kiss to my cheek.

I cross my arms over my chest. "The feeling is mutual."

He nods at Taran. "How's the evil sister doing?"

"It would behoove you not to address me in such a way," she says. She looks both Cole and Atlas up and down. "I see that you chose to wear your tight pants today. I hope they split while you're running around."

"So do I," Cole says with a grin. "Martha and Mae are judging, and I know they have a penchant for men popping out of their clothes."

I hold back the snort that wants to come out of my mouth and instead cover it with a smirk while I pretend to scratch the bottom of my nose.

"I will have you know we've been practicing night and day, and no one is more prepared to take this win than Storee."

"Night and day? Huh, I thought I saw Storee around town. Couldn't possibly be all day...and night."

Oh my God, Cole.

"You know what I mean," Taran says, hands on her hips. "Just be prepared because she's bringing her A game."

"I'm shaking," Cole says and then comes up to me again. This time, he kisses me on the other cheek, his face blocked by mine as he whispers, "You look beautiful."

I feel my cheeks blush as he pulls away. "Don't trip over the rugs," he says as he moves away from us and over to the station with his name on it. He and Atlas look over the setup and move a few things around.

"He's so arrogant. I can't believe you've even allowed him near you these past few weeks."

It's been a real travesty.

All those orgasms, how dare he!

"It's almost over," I say as Aunt Cindy makes her way toward us.

Taran spent some time curling her hair this morning at the dining room table while I speed-wrapped. I was able to get the perfect wrap job done in a minute and ten seconds. We are going to be judged by how fast and how accurate our wrapping is, so I think I have that covered. Most importantly, though, Aunt Cindy said she wanted to look her best today. Therefore, we found her best red turtleneck and paired it with a white-and-green Christmas vest and green slacks. She looks like Aunt Cindy in all her holiday glory again.

"I think we can win this, girls."

"I think so too," Taran says. "We just need Storee to focus."

"I'm focused," I say. "Okay? I'm plenty focused, but I'm going to be less focused if you keep bothering me about being focused."

"All right, girls, all right. Maybe we should go around and say something nice about each other," Aunt Cindy says. "Because I can feel the tensions are high, and we need to rely on each other, not battle."

God, she sounds just like Mom...when Mom isn't sipping margaritas down in Cancun.

"I'll start," Aunt Cindy says, taking both of our hands in hers. "These past few weeks have been some of the best I've had in a long time." Her eyes tear up, and I can feel a wave of guilt pass through me for all the bad weeks that came before. "I've thoroughly enjoyed being around you again, seeing your smiling faces in the morning, seeing you work together, enjoying the holiday season like we used to. It's meant so much to me. And Taran, you've been so wonderful taking care of me, helping me with my rehab. Not to mention, your precision with hanging the lights has been a sight to behold." Taran smiles brightly, something I haven't seen in a while. Then Aunt Cindy turns to me. "My dear Storeebook, you are who I've worried about the most."

"Me?" I ask, confused. "Why me?"

"Because I saw you shut down after what you went through with this town all those years ago. I saw that beautiful heart of yours shrink a size or two, and to me, that was a huge tragedy. You have always been the girl who loved Christmas, who'd spend every waking moment with me participating in the holiday season. So when I didn't see you come around anymore, I thought that maybe you'd lost your precious, infectious spirit."

"I was only...I think I was just trying to find myself."

She pats my hand. "I understand that, but seeing you here, seeing you smile, seeing you participate in the Town Kringle competition has been so beautiful to witness. I'm just overjoyed that you'd compete in my honor. It means the world to me."

"Of…of course," I say. "I want nothing more than to win this for you, Aunt Cindy."

"Thank you," she says sweetly and then glances at Taran. "Okay, your turn."

Taran lets out a heavy breath. "Aunt Cindy, ever since I can remember, you have always made the holiday season fun. And this year is no exception. But what I liked the most were our conversations where you shared your wisdom with me. I will always cherish those talks."

What talks?

Taran looks at me. "Storee, I don't say this enough, but I'm proud of you." Uhh, what? And why…why am I getting choked up? "You have overcome some big fears by participating in this competition, and you've done it with grace, with excellence, and with a dedication that I know means so much to Aunt Cindy."

I nod, my throat growing tight.

"Umm, wow, okay. I wasn't ready to get emotional." Aunt Cindy squeezes my hand. "But yeah, thank you for everything you guys said. That means a lot. Uh, Aunt Cindy, you make Christmas what it is—what it always should be. I forgot that. I forgot how much I need this holiday in my life, how much I need you to be a part of it, and I can't believe I've stayed away for so long. I promise that won't be the case moving forward because you are why I have the magical memories I do."

A tear rolls down Aunt Cindy's cheek as she brings my hand up and presses a kiss to my knuckles.

Now I turn to Taran and take a deep breath. "Taran, I know we don't get along all the time, and there are moments when I think we don't quite understand each other, but that doesn't mean that I don't appreciate you and love you, because I do. I appreciate your warm heart and the way you take care of anyone who needs help without question, the big and the small. I appreciate how you set aside your life to come visit me in California, even if all we do is sit around and watch the Lovemark movies

I edit. I appreciate you pushing me to be a part of this competition and being by my side during the process. I wouldn't have made it this far without you."

Taran softly smiles. "You would have, but you wouldn't have had such a great light display."

I laugh and shake my head. "A light display that isn't fully done yet."

"Just need to make a few tweaks." She pinches her fingers together.

"Can we have all the Kringle-ees please approach their stations?" Bob Krampus booms through the gymnasium.

Time to compete.

"Good luck," Aunt Cindy says.

"Don't forget to give yourself room with the thick needle," Taran says.

"Oh my God, Taran."

She holds her hands up in defense. "Just a subtle reminder."

COLE

He can't keep his eyes off her. She's much too pretty.
And everyone can see it, even the judging committee.

Will it make him lose? Will he forget how to sew?
Will he only think about how well she
grips his penis and can blow—

"Come on, can you not, right now? I'm trying to focus."

Narrator: Says the man who keeps looking over at Storee with hearts in his eyes.

"That's because this is a romance. Am I supposed to look at her like she's a piece of trash hanging out of a dumpster?"

Narrator: Don't you get mouthy with me! I have control over your pants, and I have no problem splitting them so your dilly dong falls right out because, oops, I forgot to put underwear on you.

"Jesus...Christ."

Narrator: Luckily for you, I'm allowing you to wear a thong today, so when you bend over, everyone sees your choice of underwear.

"Uh, fuck no."

Narrator: Too late. On with the story.

"Dude, are you wearing a thong?" Max asks as I straighten from picking up a piece of construction paper I accidentally dropped on the floor.

"What?" I say, pulling my sweater down and covering my ass.

Max lifts my sweater and then tugs on the strap of my thong, snapping it against my skin. "What the hell is this?"

"Uh...Storee dared me. While we were shopping the other day, she found it and dared me to wear it today."

Max studies me for a second, shifts on his feet, then leans forward. "Is it comfortable?"

"Surprisingly more comfortable than I expected."

"Nice." He nods. "I've thought about trying a thong before but never found someone to wear it for. Looks like you found someone who can appreciate a no-panty-line in your strut. Let me ask you this, does it look like Santa's pants, buckle and all?"

"You know, I'd rather not talk about this right now."

"Talk about what?" Storee says as she approaches our station. The competition's ready to begin.

Max leans in and whispers, "The thong you dared him to wear."

Her eyes widen. "You're actually wearing it?"

"Now is not the time, you guys. We have a good portion of the town watching us." I look upon the crowd all decked out in their Christmas gear while soft holiday music filters through the gym.

"He's right. We can discuss thongs after we take the win in this competition," Max says.

"You really think you're going to win this one?" Storee asks, looking so damn adorable that I wish I could just skip the contest and take her back to my place.

"We know we are. We had a secret weapon prepping us."

"Oh?" she asks. "And who might that be?"

"My mom," Max says with pride. "She's a sewing queen, and we're going to make the best stocking ever seen."

"You realize it's not just stockings, right?" Storee says.

"Well aware," Max says. "Cole and I have been wrapping fake presents for years while working at the farm. We could do it in our sleep at this point."

"Really?"

I nod. "Yeah, we're pretty good at it."

"And card making…well, let's just say we've sold some at the farm before."

"Wait, seriously?"

I shrug. "There was a time in our lives when we needed to make some side cash, and Christmas cards were the way to do that. We had a cart near the gift shop and made enough to buy a PlayStation one year."

"Why didn't you tell me?" she asks.

"Busy doing other things," I say with a waggle of my eyebrows.

Max leans in. "He's referring to the sex."

Storee's lips thin. "I know what he meant, Atlas."

"Okay, just making sure," he says with a wave of his hand.

"Storee, please get to your station," Bob Krampus says as he takes center stage.

Storee's station is right next to mine again, which is a blessing and a curse. I want to be able to sneak peeks at her, but I also don't want to get too caught up in watching her. It's a fine line, and I'm sure Max will be on the lookout for me getting distracted.

As Bob Krampus speaks to the crowd, laying out the rules of the competition today, I glance around the gym, noticing people from all over town.

The Dankworth kids sit in the very front, lined up from tallest to smallest, all wearing matching red polo shirts and khaki pants. Their hands are in their laps while their parents sit at the judging table.

To the left is Tanya along with Jefferson Chadwick—surprised he's here—and neither of them is talking to the other, but that's not uncommon. Jefferson talks to no one.

Frank and Thachary are in the middle, surrounded by friends, and... yup, I believe that's a thermos in Thachary's hand. I can only imagine what's inside it.

Sherry Conrad, the antiques store owner, sports a very large hat blocking the view of the irritated people behind her.

Peach and Paula make their way up the bleachers toward Frank and Thachary, both of them carrying a thermos as well. The middle section is going to get rowdy.

And then there's Mr. and Mrs. Maxheimer along with Felix and Ansel, Max's siblings. When I make eye contact with them, Ida—Mrs. Maxheimer—waves at me with a huge smile and then holds out her phone to take a picture. I wave back and then grab Max by the shoulders so she can photograph us together. When she's done, she offers me a thumbs-up.

Losing my parents was the hardest thing I've ever had to endure in my life, but I will say this: Ida and Otto Maxheimer helped me immeasurably during that time, and they still do. Ida treats me like one of her sons, always giving me hugs and kisses, treating Max and me like we're the same. And Otto, well, he gave me a chance, a job, a place to heal when I was hurting the most. I'm so grateful for both of them.

"You ready for this?" Max says.

I nod, ready to win this for my family. "Yeah, I'm ready."

And so the contest began, the
Kringle-ees running around,
Jimmy with the wrapping paper, Ursula with a frown.

They cut and they taped, and they taped and they cut,
Cole stealing glances at Storee's round butt.

Beatrice sneezed, and Jimmy said bless you,
while Ursula haphazardly stuck her hair with the glue.

There were ribbons and holly and Christmas-y junk
While the crowd in the middle got very, very drunk.

Bob Krampus called out the time was halfway done,
and now for the dreaded stocking-y fun.

The fabric was thrown; the thread
tumbled to the floor.
They pasted, they sewed, they ironed
some more, more, more.

Clock's a-ticking, but did that stop
them? No. They simply said,
"We don't have time to sew;
we'll simply just glue it instead."

Ursula and the doctor used glue like they were pros.
Jimmy stood bewildered, just scratching his nose.

Storee and Cole, they stuck with the thread,
even though Storee's stocking began to shred.

"Hands up," Bob said, his voice
booming through the air.
They threw up their hands and hoped with a prayer.

The stocking was lacking, the cards were askew.
Beatrice skipped red and green, and opted for blue.

Who did it? Who won? Who proved to be the best?
Cindy bounced for results in her Christmassy vest.

STOREE

I have never in my life felt so much adrenaline as I did in that last hour and a half.

Holy.

Crap.

I stand next to Cole, our items placed on the judging tables, perusing gazes taking in every last detail and every last flaw.

My wrapping was good but looked to be on par with everyone else's.

My card was a beautiful depiction of a winter day in the country, and I even used some fabric to add texture.

And my stocking... well, it was looking really good until I sewed it too close to the edge and the felt tore.

I could hear Taran's groan from across the gym when it happened.

And sure, I might have glanced toward Cole right before it happened because I was impressed by the way he was sewing like a fiend, so perhaps I was a touch distracted. I attempted to cover it up with a patch, but I'm not sure how the judges will take it.

Beatrice struggled. And her theme of blue and silver, although nice, doesn't really speak to Bob Krampus, a traditional red, green, and white man through and through. I mean, I even know that at this point.

Ursula excelled in her wrapping. She did some weird technique that I've only ever seen done on Instagram. Those people who record themselves wrapping presents for a living? Well, she channeled them and did some double-fold technique that came out beautifully. Her card though? Average. And her stocking was a glued disaster—and I won't even mention the glue in her hair.

Then there's Jimmy, the threat I never saw coming. He grunted and groaned and was the most vocal of the group, but looking at what he put out on the table, I'm both worried and impressed.

He and Cole both seem to be the dark horses in today's competition.

And the intricate, embroidered stocking…the fact that he sewed that in the time that we had. How, is the question…just how?

"Well," Bob says as he speaks into the mic. "Can we please give our Kringle-ees a round of applause?" The crowd erupts, and I feel chills spread down my arms. Even though it was hard and there were times when I wanted to just stop what I was doing and cry, I have to admit I'm proud of myself, because I did it.

Bob gives a speech about everything we've gone through the last few weeks, and after what feels like several minutes, he clears his throat, ready to report the results. I want to grab Cole's hand badly. I want to tell him that no matter what, I'm proud of us. But I keep still as I stare out at the crowd.

"In fifth place, with her blue theme, is Beatrice Pedigree."

Yup, we all saw that coming.

"Coming in fourth…" Bob looks up at us, making eye contact with me, and I feel my heart sink. Then he says, "Ursula Kronk."

Wow, okay, that was mean—not very Santa-y if you ask me.

"And this is where the judges struggled," Bob continues. "We went back and forth because there were aspects of everyone's entries that we enjoyed, so we had to turn to the flaws."

Shit.

"Coming in third...Storee Taylor."

Fuck!

That's not good. How many points is that? I glance over at Taran, and she's scribbling away in her notebook, probably calculating even as Bob continues.

"Coming in second, we have...Cole Black and his holly jolly sidekick, which means Jimmy Short is our first-place winner!"

Jimmy steps forward and raises his fists in the air as he pumps them up and down, his victory puffing his chest as he points at the woman in the front row who I now know is his ex-wife. She blows him a kiss, and he catches it while the crowd erupts.

I glance over at Cole, my disappointment making me emotional because I don't even know if I'm in the running for first anymore.

"Now remember," Bob says. "This competition isn't over. We still have the town vote on who has been the most spirited of them all, and the finals of the Christmas light display. Nothing is set in stone, so the next two days matter the most. Congrats to our Kringle-ees and merry Christmas!"

Together, we all say, "Merry Christmas," and then we start dispersing.

I turn to Cole and give him a sad look, which causes his frown to deepen.

He walks up to me. "What's wrong?"

"I just..." I see Taran headed my way, so I say, "Meet me by the large tree over in the corner."

He nods and takes off just as Taran closes the space between us.

"You pushed the needle too close to the edge."

I sigh. "I know, Taran."

"I told you not to."

"I know," I repeat. "But it's way more stressful than you think."

"You kept looking over at Cole," she says.

"Because he was using a sewing machine. It was loud and distracting," I say. "Who knew he could sew."

Taran folds her arms. "Yes, that was annoying."

"But how did Jimmy win?"

She glances over at Jimmy, who's talking to his ex-wife. "I'm going to go inspect those entries."

"Okay," I say. "I'm, uh, I'm going to go to the bathroom."

While Taran walks up to the table to do her inspection, I walk to the back corner where Cole is waiting for me. When I reach the tree, he pulls me behind it and lifts my chin so I can meet his gaze.

"What's wrong?"

Lip quivering, I say, "I messed up my stocking and I know that's why I came in third. Taran's not happy, and I have no idea what the points are adding up to, but I've gotten third for the last three competitions and that can't be good."

"You're eight points behind," Cole says, clearly able to calculate fast. "There's still points you can earn."

"With our light display? Have you seen Aunt Cindy's house? We're not taking first with what Taran has put together."

"It's about improvement," he says. "Not overall. So you might get lots of points for improving what you started with. Who knows."

"Did you make any improvements?"

He smirks at me. "Well, we fixed the lights that were oddly out when Paula and Peach came by." That brings a small smile to my lips. "And tomorrow morning after our Christmas Eve eve celebration, Max and I plan on putting some lights on the lawn, but nothing too fancy. If anyone has a chance for improvements, it's you and Taran. If I were you, I'd talk to her tonight and see what you guys can do to spruce it up and work on it all day tomorrow."

"Yeah, that's a good idea." I heave a sigh and then lean in to him as he wraps his strong arms around me. "God, I was so distracted by you."

He chuckles. "Was it the sewing?"

"It was." I look up at him, resting my chin on his chest. "The sinew in your forearms was popping as you pushed the fabric through. It was really hot."

"Is that right? Should I sew naked for you later?"

"I would say yes, but aren't you going to Atlas's tonight?"

"Oh right...well, when this is all over, I'll sew naked for you ...in this thong you made me wear."

I laugh, feeling lighter already. I slip my hand down the back of his pants, my hand passing over the thong. "I can't believe you wore it."

"Anything for you, Storee. Anything."

CHAPTER THIRTY
COLE

What a shame Storee's stocking was a shredded fail.
Surely, this can't be the end of her holiday tale.

It's not, because there's something you did not see.
Something tricky, something sneaky,
something not so jolly...

"WHAT IF," I SAY AS I shift on my air mattress and look at Max as he snuggles into his pillow on his air mattress, which is lined up beside mine. "What if we don't make any improvements to the light display tomorrow?"

He pauses and stares at me.

The family is asleep after a fun night of games, cookies, and eggnog, the fire in the fireplace has now died down to embers, and the Christmas lights on the house are sparkling through the curtains.

"Why on earth would you not want to make..." He leans up on one elbow. "Is this because of Storee?"

I groan. "Dude, you should have seen her today. She was devastated."

"Then maybe she should have performed better." I quirk a brow at him, and he continues, "And I mean that with respect. But it's not our fault that you've become a master with the sewing machine. Or that your card-making skills are unmatched, or that you're able to wrap a present perfectly in under a minute. We can't hide ourselves from the light to make someone else burn brighter."

"Really, Max? You sound like an ass."

"Because I want to win? Because you dragged me into this out of your own spite, and now that I'm invested, I'm just supposed to turn down the heat? Dude, I sat like a dog in shorts too small for me in front of the whole town. I didn't just do that for my own enjoyment."

"I know. I know." I press my hand to my head, frustrated as I lie on my pillow. "I just, fuck, I hated seeing her like that, and her sister was all upset. I wanted to help her."

Max is silent, and I can almost see the wheels turning in his head. "What if...what if this is all a ploy, and she's pretending to be upset so you will drop out or something so she can win?"

"Atlas," I say in a stern voice. "That's not what she's doing."

"I know you want to think that. I'm just, hell, man, I'm just watching out for you, okay?"

"I appreciate that, but Storee wouldn't hurt me like that, betray me like that. I know her. I've felt the way she is around me. I can tell when someone's using me and when someone's actually in—well, when some-one likes me."

"Were you going to say *in love*?" he asks.

"I don't know, maybe." I drag my hands over my face. "Just trust me on this, okay? Storee is not using me. She's just upset that she's been struggling the last few competitions, and she's under a lot of pressure from her aunt and sister."

"Okay," Max says skeptically. "But you know Cindy. I think she'd do whatever it takes to win. She's been desperate for the title. She could be pulling the strings."

"She's not going to mess with me—or mess with someone's heart."

"Well, if that's the case, then I say we proceed with lighting up the lawn tomorrow. We want to win this, right?"

"Sort of. The need to win isn't as strong as it was. I think I'd rather see Storee win."

"Nooooo," Max groans. "Cole, please…for the love of God, do not give up now. We are eight points ahead. That's hard to catch up to. Even if Storee wins first place with the light display, all we have to do is stay above the bottom two and we're solid. This is a win for us. Just see this through. If anything…do it for me. We've been through a lot, and now that I'm invested, I want to win this for us."

Hell, when he puts it like that…

He has done a lot for me, and I want nothing more than to show Max how much I appreciate him.

"You're right," I say. "You're so right. Fuck, man. I'm sorry. Let's…let's try to win this thing."

His smile lights up as he holds out his hand. "Yeah, let's win it."

I stare down at his hand and then back up at him. "Am I supposed to hold your hand?"

"You're supposed to shake in celebration."

"That seems weird," I say.

He curls his hand into a fist. "Then fist bump?"

"Ehhh…"

He picks up his pillow and whacks me right in the face. "How about that?"

I blink a few times and then turn toward him. "You're dead."

He squeals as he rolls away and whisper-shouts, "Don't wake my dad. He'll kill us, and if you wake him, I'm telling him about your thong."

I stand from my air mattress, and we face off with the coffee table between us. "I'll tell him I borrowed it from you."

"Wearing another man's thong? Cole, where are your standards?"

I lunge at him, and he sidesteps, causing me to crash into the end table.

"What's going on down there?" Mr. Maxheimer calls from upstairs.

Max whispers, "Now you've done it, you fuck."

I sigh as we hear heavy footsteps come down the stairs. In a conciliatory tone, I say, "You were right, dear."

TARAN

I stare up at the ceiling, my mind racing, my heart pounding, the thought of betrayal passing through me.

How could she?

Is this why she's been slacking? Getting third in the last few competitions? Because of him?

To say I was surprised when I saw her being pulled behind a tree in the gym was an understatement, but when I saw who it was, anger reached its tipping point.

It was supposed to be a farce. They were supposed to be faking it, but from what I saw, Storee was fully immersed—*and happy*—in his arms.

And I should have known because all the signs were there. The way she watched him up on that stage when he thrust his pelvis at the audience? She practically drooled.

When she went on that date with him, she wasn't as reluctant as she should have been.

Not to mention, after the candy-cane making she was gone for a very long time. She claimed a pothole, but...was that the truth?

And then...oh my God! When I caught her coming back into the house, was she really coming back in from checking on the snow? Or was she coming back in after spending the night next door?

I sit up in bed, remembering the footprints in the snow leading from Aunt Cindy's house to his.

And the bruise on her neck. That was...that was a hickey.

I pound my fist into the pillow. All those strolls into town, all that wasted time...she must have been spending it with him.

Of course that's what she was doing. How could I have been so dumb? So naïve?

They've been seeing each other and...

I pause, my mind racing some more.

Hold on.

He's...he's in first place. Contest after contest, he's been getting better and better, running away with the points and making it pretty damn hard for anyone to catch up to him. And how convenient that his biggest competition has slowly been taking the fall when she started out in first.

I reach for my notebook on the nightstand and flip through the notes I've been taking. It was right after the Fruitcake Festivus that things started to go downhill. The next competition was candy cane making, and that's when she fell to third. He "helped" her in that competition. Why would he do that if he wasn't trying to prove something? Trying to...trying to sabotage her!

He knew she'd lose points for getting help from another competitor, and she did. But she looked grateful. Happy that he was there to help her. From there, she never edged past third, and that's when she started to disappear more. That's when they were spending more time together.

I throw my legs over the side of the bed as I grip my forehead.

How could I have been so dumb?

How could I have let this happen?

He took advantage of her.

He must have known she crushed on him back when we were young and used that to his advantage. And he wasn't even shy about the way he used her. He said their fake relationship was for the town, would help both of them in the competition, but somewhere along the way, he kept it fake, and she...she fell for him.

I stand from the bed now and go to my window, where I open the curtain and stare at his house, covered in those garish green lights.

How dare he!
How dare he mess with her!
How dare he mess with Aunt Cindy's chance at the title!
I can't allow that to happen.
Something needs to be done.
And I know exactly what to do.

———————

So she strapped on her boots and her coat colored tan,
with one thing in mind: I will destroy this man.

Then she loaded up her pockets
with a hammer and pliers,
and took to his house, ready to mess with his wires.

She stalked through the snow, empty bags in her fist.
"He'll regret ever messing with her," she hissed.

Then she propped up a ladder, alone and in the dark.
In the distance, a rowdy dog let
out an ear-splitting bark.

She froze and waited, and when the coast was clear,
she ascended the house to remove
all the Christmas cheer.

She snaked and she snuck with a
smirk quite unpleasant
around the whole roof and took
every twinkle light present.

With a pop and a flop, the wires
tumbled to the ground.
Payback was served and joy she quickly found.

Then she slunk to the porch. She took
every bulb and every light.
She took every Christmas decoration
purely out of spite.

She laughed. "Oh how stupid is he going to feel
when he sees what I took, what I was able to steal."

She took every decoration, and she took it in a flash,
and then walked up to the garage
and threw it in the trash.

"In the morning when they wake, I
know just what they'll do.
The bro-hards on Whistler Lane
will both cry boo-hoo."

She dusted off her hands and
headed back into the house,
while every Kringle in Kringletown
slept, even the street mouse.

CHAPTER THIRTY-ONE
COLE

With boxes full of lights, the boys
drive home feeling bold,
ready to hang more lights despite the frigid cold.

But then they arrive, at a scene they
weren't expecting in the least.
It seems as though all the Christmas
decorations have been fleeced.

"DO YOU THINK WE SHOULD have gone with the red?" I ask Max as we drive toward my house with a plan to update the light display. "Do you think it's going to be too much green?"

Max shakes his head. "No, I think it will be cohesive, and then we'll add the red to the porch to break it up. I think it's genius."

After we got in trouble with Mr. Maxheimer for being "nimrods," we turned on the flashlight on Max's phone, connected our blow-up mattresses so we could whisper, and we devised a plan on how to win the entire competition. Then this morning after a plentiful breakfast from Mrs. Maxheimer, we headed to the hardware store, grabbed some extra things we needed, and are now headed to the house.

"Genius. Okay, yeah."

"Also, the light-up presents we got to line the front of the yard are a great addition."

"I can't believe your dad had those out in the barn and never said anything to us," I say.

"Maybe he knew we had to make improvements, so he held out…" Max trails off as we turn onto Whistler Lane. "What…the…fuck?"

"What?" I ask, looking over at Max as he slows down his truck.

"Cole, your house." He points.

"What about it?" I say as I look out the windshield only to find my house completely dark, stripped of its lights.

Every last one of them.

Not a single light left, just some wires and nails hanging in plain sight. It's…it's bare.

"Holy…fuck," I say as Max parks on the side of the street. We bolt out of the truck and examine what has occurred.

All the lights are gone.

Nothing on the roof. Nothing on the porch, not even a bare strand hanging from the door. It was all removed, every single bulb.

Every decoration.

"Who…how…" I stutter, unsure of what to say. "I…I don't get it."

Hands on his hips, Max surveys my yard, the porch, the roof, and as he makes his way around to the side, he pauses and then slowly turns toward me.

"A ladder and footprints."

"Where?" I say, jogging up to him.

Max points at a ladder that stretches up to the short pitch of the roof and then to footprints that lead from the ladder all the way to Cindy's house.

"No fucking way," I say as my eyes land on the pink house. "There's no way." I shake my head, not willing to believe it.

"Cole," Max says softly. "It has to be."

444 | MEGHAN QUINN

"But...but why?" I ask, pushing my hands through my hair. "There's no reason."

"Except that this will guarantee you last place in the light display, and they know how close you are to winning the whole thing."

I shake my head and search the yard for more tracks, for any indication that this could have been someone else, but when I come up short, when I don't see one single thing, my heart starts to seize and panic ensues.

"It can't be. She wouldn't. I...I don't think she'd do that."

"I know this is hard for you to accept, Cole, but I think she would."

I turn toward my best friend. "You really think she would be that heartless? That she'd fuck with my head? Pretend to like me and just screw me over in the end?"

"You were the first one to take the shot. What would stop her from taking it further?"

I look over at the house again, a darkness starting to creep over me as my mind drifts to a place I didn't think it would ever go, not with her, but I can't stop it.

The idea of her taking advantage, of her pretending the entire time, I can't write it off.

"But maybe," I say, my throat growing tight, "maybe it was someone else."

"Who?" Max asks, throwing his arms up.

"Jimmy?" I say, hoping that's an option.

Max shakes his head. "He was out all last night at Prancer's getting toasted. My mom heard it from Frank this morning. There's no way he could climb the ladder intoxicated. Not to mention, look at the footprints, man. That's all the evidence you need, and there isn't a footprint leading from the sidewalk to Cindy's house either, in case someone was trying to frame them. This was Storee. Remember what she did with the lights last time? This...this was all Storee."

"Fuck," I say as I grip my forehead, my stomach turning queasy immediately. "I thought...hell, I thought she liked me. But this?" I gesture to the house. "Fuck, I guess I was completely wrong. I guess she was just pretending, just using me this entire time." I swallow back my emotion, trying to find a place within me where I don't care. Where I don't mind that she just about ripped my heart out in one night.

But it's hard.

And I don't handle my emotions well.

My anger.

The grief in my life.

And before I can stop myself, I storm up to the pink house, Max trailing behind me. I pound on the front door with my fist and wait.

It takes a few minutes, but when the door opens and Storee's face comes into view, I feel a wave of emotion hit me all at once.

I...I like her.

Hell, I more than like her.

I think I love her.

Yet to her, I was just a chess piece to be moved for her benefit.

She was using me.

Abusing my heart.

And then she just took everything she wanted and needed, leaving me feeling...fucking shattered.

"Cole...what are you doing here?"

I feel my body go still.

My throat clamps down on me.

Thankfully, Max presses his hand to my shoulder. "Cole's been through a lot, Storee. More than any person should ever have to go through, and for you to just use him like that, to play with his emotions, and then when you think the time is right, strike, well...it's all kinds of fucked up."

Her brow creases, and she looks toward me. "What is he talking about?"

I swallow the lump in my throat. "The house, Storee."

"What about it?"

"The fucking lights!" I shout, startling her backward. "Don't play dumb with me. You took them down last night because you were so fucking scared you weren't going to win. You snuck out and stole them. You fucking used me this whole time, faked it, made me believe that there was something between us, only to sabotage me in the end." I shake my head. "Who the fuck does that? What kind of heartless human are you?"

"What? I don't know what you're talking about."

"Sure," I say with a sarcastic laugh. "Play dumb, Storee. You've been so good at it so far, acting like you have no idea what you're doing in this competition, in this town, all to gain sympathy from me. Well, it worked." I slow clap in front of her. "It fucking worked, and now you can revel in your accomplishment because I'm done."

I turn away from her and start walking off the porch when I feel her tug on my arm.

"Hold on," she says. "Cole, I have no idea what you're talking about."

"Stop," I yell, my voice echoing through the quiet cul-de-sac. I tear my arm away from her and stomp toward the steps. "Just fucking stop. I can't...I can't be near you."

Max throws his arm over my shoulders, and together we head down the steps, across the snow, and right into my house, shutting her out.

Shutting out everything.

STOREE

I stand there, stunned.

Confused.

Hurt.

I look over at Cole's house and gasp. Not a single light strand is on display. Not on the roof, not on the porch, not even around the windows. It's all gone.

And he thinks I did it.

He thinks I used him.

That I tricked him.

That these strong, intense feelings I have for him were all made up and that I was playing him the whole time.

He couldn't be more wrong.

"What's going on?" I hear Aunt Cindy say as she walks up to the front door. "I heard yelling."

I sniff, my emotions getting the best of me as I turn on my heel and head back into the house, away from the cold.

When I move past Aunt Cindy, she says in a worried tone, "Storeebook, what's happening?"

I take a seat on the stairs and bury my head in my hands as tears sting my eyes.

"Storee," Aunt Cindy repeats as she stands in front of me, tapping her cane. "Why was there yelling?"

"There was yelling?" Taran says from the top of the stairs.

"Yes, I think it was Cole and Atlas," Aunt Cindy says. "But I don't know why they would be yelling at Storee. Did you two have a lovers' quarrel?"

"Aunt Cindy, they weren't *really* lovers. You know that, right?" Taran heads down the stairs and stops in front of me. "Wait, are you crying?"

I shudder, a sob coming out of me before I can stop it.

"You are." Taran sits next to me on the stairs, removes my hands, and forces me to look at her. "Why are you crying?"

"Because," I say, the lump in my throat making it incredibly hard to speak, "I...I think...I think I love him."

"*What?*" Taran nearly shouts and shakes her head. "Storee, I know he was playing you, but you can't possibly—"

"Playing me?" I ask as I wipe my hand over my cheek. "What are you talking about?"

She sighs, then takes my hand in hers. "I know this is going to be hard to understand given the state that you're in, but he didn't really like you. This whole relationship thing, it was a distraction so he could take the lead in the Kringle competition. And I don't blame—"

"This isn't about the stupid Kringle competition," I say. "This is about me and Cole. We...we've been seeing each other."

"Yes, I know," Taran says.

"Wait, I'm confused," Aunt Cindy joins in.

"It's simple," Taran explains. "Cole was worried that he was going to lose the competition against us, so he made Storee fall for him, and apparently she did, but it wasn't because he liked her—"

"Yes, it was," I insist.

Taran gives me one of those smiles that says she feels bad for me. "Storee, it was all pretend for him."

"It wasn't," I say as I wipe my eyes. "It was real. Everything about it was real."

"No, Storee, he took advantage of the crush you've had on him for years."

"No, Taran," I shout. "He didn't. I know what I experienced with him these past weeks, and I saw the pain in his eyes when he came over here, blaming me for what happened to his house."

"What happened to his house?" Aunt Cindy asks.

I'm about to answer when Taran says, "I took down his lights."

"You did it?" I ask, turning to her. "You were the one who took down his lights?"

"Yes, I was. I did it for you."

"Why on earth would you do that?" I shout.

"Because he was using you."

"No, he wasn't!" I shout again as tears stream down my face. "He wasn't,

Taran. God, I can't believe you did this. That you would stoop so low as to hurt someone like that. This…this is the first Christmas he's actually celebrated since his parents passed, and you…you went and ruined that. You took that away from him. Took away the joy, made him believe that the person who was falling for him betrayed him in the worst way possible." Taran leans back, stunned. "He by no means was using me. He by no means was trying to take advantage of me. He helped me at points, he was my rock through these past few competitions, and he made me realize that I *could* step past my fears and tackle big things. And you…and you went and ruined that." I wipe away my tears. "I have to talk to him."

I slip on my boots and head out of the house just as Atlas and Cole get into Atlas's truck.

"Hold on," I call, holding my hand up and hurrying toward them. They both look at me, and I can see Atlas say something to him. Cole shakes his head, and then without another word, Atlas starts the truck and pulls into the road.

No.

I look over at his house. His plain, unlit house.

How…

How could she have done this?

"Storee," Aunt Cindy calls. "Come back inside."

"No," I say as the chill creeps over me. "Taran, where did you put them?" I'm loud enough that I have no doubt the entire neighborhood will be outside in seconds.

Taran steps into the doorframe. "Storee, it's freezing—"

"Where did you put them?" I repeat, feeling crazed. "Tell me now, Taran."

She sighs. "The trash."

I march away from Aunt Cindy's house and toward Cole's side yard, where I spot his trash cans. I pop the lid off one of them, and lo and behold, it's full of lights.

450 | MEGHAN QUINN

I'm still in my pajamas, but I don't care. Adrenaline fuels me as I start pulling out the strands and untangling them in the process.

"Storee, what are you going to do?" Taran says hurrying up behind me.

"Put them back on his house."

"You can't possibly do that all by yourself."

"You're right," I say as I swipe at my nose, the cold air making my nose run. "I'm going to need help."

I bypass my sister and walk across the street, straight to Martha and Mae's house. I head up their porch and press on their doorbell.

Not once.

Not twice.

But three times.

And when they don't answer after five seconds, I do it again.

Over and over until the door unlocks and opens, Martha standing in her robe and bonnet on the other side.

"My goodness," she says as she adjusts her glasses on her nose. "What on earth are you doing, Storee?"

"I need your help," I say.

"With what?"

"With Cole's house. It's a long story, but I need help putting his lights back up, and we need to do it before Paula and Peach come around for the final judging tonight."

"Why are his lights down?"

"Please, Martha," I beg. "Please don't ask questions. Please just help me. I need you to round up everyone you can. We need to put the lights back up." A tear rolls down my cheek. "*Please*, Martha."

"Okay, dear. Okay." She takes my hand in hers. "We will get the lights back up. You can count on me."

I stand in the bathroom, staring at my reflection in the mirror. My bloodshot eyes are evidence of the tears I've been shedding since this morning.

The downturn of my lips a reminder of the dread I feel in the pit of my stomach that I can't seem to shake.

And the slouch in my shoulders signals a white flag of defeat.

Because how on earth will he forgive me?

Not that I did anything wrong. Quite the opposite, actually. I've been trying to figure out how to grow what we have, not tear it down.

But that look on his face.

The anger in his eyes.

Even with the idea I've formed, I'm not sure it will be enough.

I wet a washcloth and wipe down my face, trying to rid it of the tear stains.

From the bathroom, I can hear the sounds outside, putting my plan into action. The muffled nailing, the commands from Martha and Mae, it's all there, but will it be enough?

Does it matter?

Even if this doesn't work, if he doesn't believe me, if he doesn't want anything to do with me, this is about making it right.

The end goal? To make sure Cole knows I would never hurt him. But even if he doesn't trust me anymore, I at least need to make my sister's wrongdoing right.

Knock. Knock.

I glance toward the door and ask, "Who is it?"

"Me, Storeebook," Aunt Cindy says in a worried voice. "I wanted to check on you."

"I'm fine," I say, the lie flying out before I can even think about it.

"Are you sure? You seemed very upset, and rightfully so."

I am upset.

He's hurt.

The man that I'm…oh God, the man that I'm falling for is hurt, and that hurts me.

That upsets me.

That makes me want to sink to the floor and cry some more.

Because…he just started loving Christmas again, and then this had to happen?

"It's fine, Aunt Cindy."

There's silence on the other side and then the doorknob twists. "I'm coming in. Cover up."

"Aunt Cindy, I said it's fine," I say as she opens the door, her hand covering her eyes.

She leans against the doorframe. "Are you decent?"

"Yes," I reply, exasperated, as I turn toward her, arms crossed, trying to put on a good front.

She doesn't say anything at first but instead uncovers her eyes and looks me up and down, studying me, clearly waiting for me to burst into tears.

I want to.

I want to break.

I want to show her how sad I am.

But that will do nothing.

It won't solve the problem, so I hold strong.

"You don't look like everything is fine."

I feel a sting in my eyes.

"Well, it is." I lean against the counter and look down at the floor, not wanting to see the sadness in her eyes.

"Storee, talk to me."

"I said it's fine," I repeat, slightly more aggressively as tears sting my eyes now.

"Storee—"

"Aunt Cindy," I say, looking up at her through watery eyes. A tear slides down my cheek. "We have a plan. It will be okay."

"Storee, come here."

I hold up my hand, not wanting her to come closer. I then swipe at my tears and blow out a heavy breath. "Please, I need to get changed so I can help out. I don't want to talk about this, not right now. I just need to...I need to fix it, okay?"

She slowly nods, understanding washing over her face. "I understand. But I would like to say, for what it's worth, what you're doing...it will work, Storee. I know this boy and I know his heart well enough from observing him over the years. This will work."

My lips tremble as I look away from her and say, "I can only hope so."

CHAPTER THIRTY-TWO
COLE

It was a sad day in Kringle, a sad day indeed.
How could she take those lights down
at such lightning speed?

Cole's heart was shattered, shattered and crushed,
and now where Storee is concerned
he has lost all trust.

"I SHOULD HAVE STAYED IN here," I say to Colleen, one of the reindeer, as I brush her wiry coat. "Then none of this would have happened."

When I walked back into my house after confronting Storee, I immediately regretted it because I could smell her, I could hear her, I could see her.

I saw her in front of the fireplace with me.

I saw her on the couch, riding me.

In the kitchen, on top of the counter.

On the stairs...

I needed fucking out, and luckily, Max was there to help. He guided me out of the house and into his truck. That's when we saw her pop out of Cindy's house, trying to wave us down. Max asked if I wanted to hear what she had to say, and I shook my head.

There was nothing she could say.

I told him to just take me to the barn.

When we arrived, he wasn't going to leave me at first, but I practically pushed him away, begging for my own space, and thankfully he gave it.

He's given me so much space that now the sun is starting to set and I have no intention of leaving this barn.

None.

I will pull up a cot, grab a blanket, and this is where I'll live.

Where I'll stay.

Because I can't go back to my house.

I just fucking can't.

It's been tainted.

Tarnished.

A place where I don't want to be because it's too painful for so many reasons. It had almost become…*home* again. A place with joy and hope. And now that's gone. *Again.*

"I'm such an idiot." I sigh as I sit on a stool next to Colleen. She nudges me with her nose, but I don't budge as I stare at the ground.

Storee never showed romantic interest in me before, back when we were teens, so why would she be into me out of the blue? Max was right all along—she was in it to distract me, to use me, and when she couldn't stop me from excelling in the competition, she tried another way.

And it worked.

It worked so well because I want nothing to do with the competition now. I'm out.

Done.

Over it.

Wasn't worth my time in the first place.

None of this was.

Who the fuck did I think I was, coming into this Christmas season thinking I could rekindle the same sense of joy I used to feel back when my parents were alive?

It was stupid and naïve and a mistake I won't make again.

Nope.

My house will remain dark now because I'm retreating to what I know best.

Becoming that recluse, ignoring the holiday season, and enveloping myself in rage-filled anger.

STOREE

"Can we talk?" Taran asks as I move through Aunt Cindy's house, looking for the keys to the car.

After I banged on her door, Martha ushered me into her house out of the cold, and I told her what happened. The entire thing. From the fake relationship to the not-so-fake relationship, to what Taran did...to how I feel about Cole.

There was a lot of gasping, a lot of heart clutching, a touch of anger, and then at the end of it all she pulled me into a hug, letting me cry on her shoulder for a solid five minutes.

After that, she told me to pull myself together because we had some lights to hang.

I started with putting some real clothes on, dressing for warmth, and then going outside to Cole's porch where I started untangling his lights in earnest.

And then slowly, Martha showed up, then Mae, then Frank and Thachary...some of the Dankworth children. Then Jimmy and Ursula... and even Beatrice.

Together, we worked hard, and we hung up his lights. We twisted them around his porch and strung them around his yard on top of the snow. Jimmy went up on the roof and did a zig-zag pattern. We hung them all.

And to my surprise, Taran brought out hot chocolate for everyone.

It was a group effort, and now that we're done, there's just one person I have to see.

"Please, Storee, we need to talk."

"I have nothing to say to you," I reply as I find the keys and then move toward the front of the house.

"I want to say I'm sorry."

"Too late," I say as I move to the front door, only to be stopped by Aunt Cindy who is now standing tall without her walker or her cane.

"Girls...we need to have a conversation."

"I'm sorry, Aunt Cindy, but I don't have time."

"You will make time for this." She points toward the living room, and I know there's no way I can say no, so I let Aunt Cindy lead the way. And lead the way she does, not a hitch in her step, not an ounce of pain in her posture.

"Why are you walking so well?" I ask her.

"That's what I need to talk to you about. Please...sit down."

Confused, I take a seat on the couch, and Taran does as well. Aunt Cindy remains standing as she clasps her hands together in front of her.

"I'm afraid I haven't been as truthful as I should have been. You see, back in the summer of this year, I had a conversation with your mother. She was concerned."

"Concerned about what?" I ask.

"About you two. She sensed that you were drifting further apart with each passing year and worried that if we didn't intervene, you might lose touch just like I did with my sister. Like your mom and her own mother. So we devised a plan."

"Please don't tell me your hip was never broken," Taran says.

"Unfortunately, that is the case."

Taran bows her head and presses her fingers to her brow as I try to comprehend what she's saying.

"We thought that if I faked an injury and you two were forced to come take care of me, we could possibly mend the fissures in your relationship."

"There were no fissures," Taran says. "We were fine."

I glance over at her. "Were we, though?"

"What are you talking about?" Taran replies, looking confused. "Of course we were fine."

"Then how come I really know nothing about Guy? Why don't I know about what's going on in your life? Why didn't I feel comfortable telling you how lonely I was in California and how I didn't know what to do with that feeling?"

"You were feeling alone?" she asks.

"Yes. And sure, at first I didn't want to be here, but then...then I realized how much this town means to me. How much I need this town. How much I need you, Taran. How much I need...Cole."

"I...I had no clue," Taran says, completely bewildered.

"Because you don't talk to me. You're so fixated on your job, which I'm proud of you for, it takes a lot to do what you do, but you zero in on it and nothing else. I'll text you, and it will take you three days to text back. I understand you're busy and your job is demanding, but not even a text back at night?"

"I...I didn't know that bothered you."

"Of course it bothers me," I say. "You're my sister. Up until your abhorrent decision to take down Cole's decorations to protect me, I honestly wasn't sure if you even cared about me."

"Of course I care about you," Taran says, turning toward me now. "I love you, Storee, and...I'm sorry if I haven't been as invested in your life as I should be. There's no excuse for it, and all I can really say is that I need to do better."

I feel my lip quiver as more tears spring to my eyes.

She takes my hand in hers and scoots closer. Softly, she repeats, "I'm sorry. I love you, and I...I think I just got so caught up in the competition that I missed the point of all of this, working together as a family."

I nod. "And I'm sorry for not telling you the truth about Cole. I thought that if you knew, you'd get mad at me and think that I wasn't invested in the competition. I was. I wanted to win it for Aunt Cindy..." My voice trails off as I slowly face Aunt Cindy. "Hold on, did you even care if I won the Town Kringle?"

She winces. "Well, not so much."

"What?" Taran says. "But you made it seem like you were desperate to win it this year."

"And my acting coach who has been helping me through our summer community theater productions would be very proud of me."

"I can't believe this," Taran says. "What about the doctor's appointment I took you to?"

"That was a friend of mine, actually," Aunt Cindy says. "I noticed that Storee was starting to care for Cole, so I thought that if I took you away for a night and gave them some time, we could let their little relationship grow."

"Wait, you knew about me and Cole?"

"Storee, everyone did."

"I didn't," Taran says, pointing at her chest.

"And I think we've established why," Aunt Cindy replies, her lips thinning into a disapproving line.

"Right." Taran exhales and leans back on the couch, her hands crossed over her stomach. "So let me get this straight, you never hurt your hip, you never cared about the Christmas Kringle competition, and I was so worked up about winning the damn thing for this family that I stupidly took the lights off an innocent man's house?"

"I believe that's correct," Aunt Cindy says.

Taran rubs both of her eyes with her palms. "I can't believe you lied to us. Hell, I can't believe I didn't realize."

"More like fibbed to bring you together, to bring us all together." She grows serious. "I also felt like I was losing you two. You hadn't visited in quite some time and, well, I'm an old lady now, and sure, I'm active in the community and have a lot going on, but that doesn't compare to the memories of when you girls would visit me during this time. I missed you. I missed this, and I felt like getting you to come again called for drastic measures. So I went for it, and I'm sorry I deceived you. I'm also not sorry." She takes a deep breath. "I got to spend the holiday season with my girls. I got to relive some of my best memories and witness how you both have grown into your personalities. I got to watch you work together, and Storee, from a distance I got to see you reconnect with a boy I always thought belonged with you."

I feel my cheeks warm.

"So I guess...I'm really not sorry, and if I could, I would do it again."

"You would force me to wash your crevices again?" Taran asks, breaking the tension.

"I would." Aunt Cindy sits between us and takes our hands. "I love you two very much, and I want you to remember, you might have your own paths in life, but that should never derail you from the path we all take as a family. If you get lost along the way, we are always here to help you find your way back."

Taran glances at me. "She's right. I'm sorry, Storee."

"I'm sorry too," I say.

With a shaky smile, she asks, "Do you really like him?"

I nod. "I do. I like him so much, and I know he feels the same way."

I more than like him. I love him.

I think I've loved him for a long time and have never noticed it.

But yes, this consuming, heart-wrenching, exhilarating feeling that's pulsing through me? It's love.

I love him.

"Well, if that's the case, we need to fix things," Taran says.

"I'm glad you think that because I have an idea," I say, "but I'll need some help."

"Tell us what you need," Taran says. "We're here for you."

COLE

"Cole," Max calls out. "You still back here?"

"Yeah," I say as I lie flat on the concrete floor, staring up at the barn ceiling. I hear Max approach but don't bother moving.

"Uh, what are you doing?" he asks.

"Breathing," I answer.

"Well, that's a good thing." He comes into view and pulls on the back of his neck. "I hate to do this to you, but my mom said she's not going to allow you to stay in the barn, especially on Christmas Eve."

"Does she know that I have no other choice?"

"You do. You'll stay the night at my parents' place, like every year. Come on, man." He holds out his hand to help me up, but I don't take it. Instead, I keep looking up at the ceiling as I feel a sting of tears in my eyes.

"I don't want to celebrate Christmas, Atlas. I can't...I can't do it."

"I know," he says solemnly. "And I get it. I told my mom, and she actually set up the guest room for you, so you don't have to worry about the family bothering you."

"I don't want to bring down your Christmas mood."

"You won't, I promise. Come on. If you don't come with me, then my dad will have to come get you, and I know he won't take kindly to that when he's supposed to be watching A Christmas Story right now."

He's right. Mr. Maxheimer never wants to miss his Christmas Eve viewing of *A Christmas Story*. So I take Max's hand in mine, and he helps me to my feet. I brush off my ass, and let Max lead me outside to his truck.

"We're driving to your parents' house?" I ask, confused since their house is on the farm.

"I had my truck here because I had to pick some things up from town, so I figured we would just drive over. Plus, I didn't know if I would have to strap you to the bed of my truck to transport you. My mom said to 'bring him over by any means necessary.'"

A small smile tugs on my lips. "Would have loved to see you try."

"Given your state, I would have won."

"Probably right."

We both get in and buckle up. The truck roars to life and we pull away from the barn.

"How're you feeling?" Max asks.

"Like shit," I reply.

"Yeah, I can see that. I'm really sorry, man."

I look out the window at the dark forest of the farm. "Nothing for you to be sorry about."

"Still, this can't be easy."

"You know, I think it will be best if we just sit in silence."

"Sure," he says.

I let out a sigh and continue to stare out the window. That heavy feeling in my chest that lifted weeks ago when Storee kissed me on the porch…has returned.

And that dreaded loneliness I feel every Christmas season has returned.

And that incessant pang in my heart that I have when I watch Max's family gather around the tree on Christmas morning has already started to hurt.

But the Maxheimers have been so kind to me that even though I'm hurting, I wouldn't disrespect them by not showing up.

I rest my head against the headrest, and when Max turns out of the farm instead of toward the private residence, I ask, "Where are you going?"

"Have to grab something from the Myrrh-cantile for my mom. You can stay in the truck."

"Okay," I say, continuing to stare out the window, my mind flashing through every little moment with Storee.

Fuck, it felt so real.

It felt like she cared about me.

Like she wanted me.

Needed me.

Loved me... How was I so wrong? How did she grow up to be so devious and insensitive? And somehow I was so gullible that I believed it.

I swallow another lump in my throat, hating that I'm getting so god-damn emotional, just as Max passes right by the Myrrh-cantile.

"Dude, what are you doing?"

He doesn't answer me. Instead, he drives down Krampus Court toward my house.

"Max."

He starts to slow down and then rolls down the windows.

"What the hell, man?"

"Shhh," he says as I hear something in the distance...

What he heard, it wasn't sad. No,
this noise was quite merry.
It sounded like people, lots of
people, making him wary.

He stared down Whistler Lane, and
Cole widened his eyes.
Then he blinked, for what he saw
was a stunning surprise.

Up ahead on the right was his house lit in green,
the brightest house of all houses he ever had seen.

And one by one, along the cul-de-
sac, they stood hand in hand,
the loving people of Kringle, next
to a large marching band.

And they sang and they cheered and
they stood in Christmas glory,
and right in the middle of it all, the girl
of his heart, his very own Storee.

And he puzzled and thought, and
he puzzled some more.
Then Cole thought of something he
hadn't thought of before.

"Storee," he thought, "maybe I judged her all wrong."
"Maybe she is the one with whom I truly belong."

Max pulls his truck up to the curb and glances at me. "Go get her, man."

"But…"

"But I was wrong. And this?" He gestures to my lit house, to the town caroling together…the marching band. "This was all her. This was her doing. She loves you, man, and I'll be damned if I let you miss out on being with someone who cares this much and tries so hard to make things right. Now go get her."

I look out through the windshield. Storee shivers in front of me, wearing her parka, winter hat, and mittens. Taran and Cindy are behind her while the rest of the town patiently waits.

"But the lights—"

"It was Taran."

"*Taran?*"

Max nods. "Let her explain, hear her out. I promise she won't hurt you."

I look Max in the eyes. "Promise?"

"Promise."

If I'm going to trust anyone, it's going to be my best friend.

With a curt nod, I open the truck door and shut it once I'm out. I tug on my shirt, adjusting it as I approach Storee. In the light from the houses and the streetlamps in the distance, I can see the red of her nose and the water in her eyes.

When I step up to her, she whispers, "Hi."

"Hi," I say, unsure of where this is going.

"Um, I'm not very good at this kind of grand gesture, but after editing so many Lovemark movies, I think I might have an idea." She clears her throat and holds out her hand to mine. I take it, and she brings me over to her lawn. The town continues to sing while she speaks softly.

"Taran was the one who took the lights down. I had no idea she did it until she confessed. It was stupid, and she did it because she thought you were using me. That, uh…that you didn't have real feelings for me, and I tried to convince her that wasn't the case. But then after the argument this morning, I thought maybe, maybe it was the truth—"

"It's not."

"It's not?" she asks, hope springing in her eyes.

I shake my head. "It's not."

The smallest of smiles passes over her lips. "Okay, um, well, that's good to know because, well, I have this thing I have to tell you, and I'm nervous, but I need to tell you." She looks me in the eyes. "I didn't realize just how lonely I was, Cole, until I came here. Until I saw you. Until there was that level of connection, of comfort I always seemed to feel when our eyes met. When I was younger, I didn't understand what that feeling was, but now that I'm older, now that I'd thought I'd lost it, I can tell you exactly what it is." She brings my knuckles up to her lips and she kisses them softly. "I love you, Cole. These feelings I have for you are unmistakable. It's as if whenever I see you, the air in my lungs is refreshed, my pulse is revived, and my soul feels at peace. I don't want to lose that…ever."

And then what happened in Kringle, they would say,
was that Cole's black heart grew three sizes that day.

And the moment Cole's heart
didn't pulse quite so tight,
he grabbed Storee by the waist and
kissed her under the green light.

I look her in the eyes, those smiling, relieved, beautiful eyes, and I say, "I love you too, Storee. And you being here, it's felt like coming home. You've reminded me about the good memories I buried so deep in my heart, and you've carried me through the dark." I pinch her chin and lean in for another kiss. "Thank you."

She smiles and wraps her arms around my neck. "Merry Christmas, Cole."

"Merry Christmas, Storee."

And they decided that night they
didn't care in the least
about the competition, but rather
enjoyed a chicken parm feast.

EPILOGUE
COLE

NARRATOR: DID YOU NOTICE HOW *I came full circle with the chicken parm? Clever, right?*

"Are you really trying to get me to boost your ego?"

Narrator: You've been a complaining ass the whole time. It wouldn't hurt you to throw me a little love.

"I am what you made me."

Narrator: Uh-huh, okay, want to play it that way? I can go back and make it so Storee has a hard time finding your erection.

"Are you really going to act like a child? You just finished the book."

Narrator: I did, and it wouldn't kill you to congratulate me.

"Congratulations. Thank you for letting me end up with Storee."

Narrator: That's more like it.

"Now, how about a little recap for the readers so they know how well Storee and I are doing?"

Narrator: I can arrange that. How about we start it with a year later?

"Sure, but what about who won the competition and what the present was that Storee got me?"

Narrator: You act as if I've never done this before. *Cracks knuckles* Watch and learn.

"Careful, you have to unwrap Baby Jesus Fonz carefully," Storee says from where she's sitting on the couch, nursing our baby girl Florence, or Flo for short.

"Hold on...baby girl?"

Narrator: *Do you really think you could get away with not getting that girl pregnant from the way you humped her through the story? Just be glad she didn't give birth to a pineapple-flavored candy cane. Now, back to my epilogue.*

"I'm being careful," I say as the bubble wrap nearly flies out of my hand along with Baby Jesus Fonz.

Holy fuck, that was a close one.

"So did you see who entered this year's Kringle competition?" Storee asks as Aunt Cindy comes into the living room carrying a tray of eggnog and Grinch cookies—my mom's recipe. Last year for Christmas, Storee surprised me with a tin full of them. She found the recipe in my kitchen and made them for me. They taste exactly how my mom made them, and it was easily the best present I've ever received...well, that and being able to call Storee mine.

"Ursula, of course," Aunt Cindy says with a roll of her eyes. "The minute that woman heard my name was in the ring, she filled out the form."

Storee laughs. "She did. Also, she RSVP'd to the wedding but made a note that she thought it was rude that we were getting married on Christmas Eve."

"Because the woman can only complain. It's her only form of communication." She sits down next to Storee and the baby. "Cole, careful with the Fonz."

"I'm being careful," I reassure her even though my hands feel a touch shaky.

"Anyway, I wasn't talking about Ursula. Someone else entered." Storee smirks.

"Can't be Jimmy," I say. "After he won last year, he hung up his sash. Said he'd never compete again because he wanted to go out on a high note."

"And because he's so busy with his lady, traveling around the Rocky Mountains," Aunt Cindy adds just as there's a knock on the door. "Come in," Aunt Cindy shouts.

I glance over my shoulder to see Taran and her boyfriend, Guy, walk through the door. When I met Guy earlier this year, I was a little skeptical. He was not who I expected Taran to date. Very reserved, very calm, very relaxed. But then I understood. It's as if he sucks all of the uptightness right out of Taran and makes her normal.

"Are you setting up the nativity?" Taran asks.

"We are," Aunt Cindy says.

Taran and Guy live on Christmas Tree Way. Once they found out Storee was pregnant, Taran applied for a nursing job here in Kringle, and she was immediately hired. She said she didn't want to miss a moment of her niece's life. Guy joined her shortly after.

Of course, after Christmas last year I asked Storee what she planned on doing. She asked me what I meant, and I said I wanted to know when she planned on moving in with me.

The smile on her face was infectious.

She answered yes immediately and, well, we've made my house a home again, and I know it never would have happened without her.

"Okay, so who entered the competition?" I ask.

Storee smiles at me as she lifts Florence and starts burping her. "Atlas."

"Atlas!" My eyes nearly fall out of my head. "You mean Max, my best friend? He entered?"

"Yup." She slowly nods. "So did Dwight Yokel. And from what Atlas told me…it's going to be a real sausage show between them, so I can't wait."

"Well, well, well," Aunt Cindy says while cracking her knuckles. "Looks like I have my work cut out for me."

"Good luck," I say. "Because if I know anything about Max, it's that he has no problem showing up onstage wearing shorts two sizes too small."

ABOUT THE AUTHOR

#1 Amazon and *USA Today* bestselling author, wife, adoptive mother, and peanut butter lover. Author of romantic comedies and contemporary romance, Meghan Quinn brings readers the perfect combination of heart, humor, and heat in every book.

Website: authormeghanquinn.com
Facebook: meghanquinnauthor
Instagram: @meghanquinnbooks